LOST HEIR

Also by Richard Coxson
Orphan's Test: The Core Empire Book I

LOST HEIR

The Core Empire Book II

Richard Coxson

Heliosphere®
BOOKS

San Diego

LOST HEIR
The Core Empire Book II

Heliosphere Books®

Copyright © 2022 by Richard Coxson

Published by arrangement with the author.

Library of Congress Cataloging-in-Publication Data

Names: Coxson, Richard, 1952- author.
Title: Lost heir / Richard Coxson.
Description: San Diego : Heliosphere Books, [2022] | Series: The Core empire; book 2
Identifiers: LCCN 2022044453 (print) | LCCN 2022044454 (ebook) | ISBN 9781937868925 (trade paperback) | ISBN 9781937868949 (kindle edition) | ISBN 9781937868932 (epub)
Subjects: LCSH: Science fiction novel. | GSAFD: Science fiction.
Classification: LCC PS3603.O9285 L67 2022 (print) | LCC PS3603.O9285 (ebook) | DDC 813/.6--dc23
LC record available at https://lccn.loc.gov/2022044453
LC ebook record available at https://lccn.loc.gov/2022044454

Cover design by Alina Rakhmanova (Alina_rali), via 99designs.com. | Gun illustration by roman3d and warrior woman 3d by hutangach, via Adobe Stock. | Text effect from freepik. | Star cruiser image by Hansuan_Fabregas; steampunk space ship by Stevebidmead; spaceship image by Yuri_B, via Pixabay.

To those anonymous individuals who fell in the battles of the American Revolution in order to promote a liberty they never knew.

"The prudent heir takes careful inventory of his legacies and gives a faithful accounting to those whom he owes an obligation of trust."

—John F. Kennedy

Galactifacts for Kids 3500

Butterfly Effect. A famous adage that appears to be over two thousand years old explains in this poem why small things are often significant in making large changes happen.

> For want of a nail, the shoe was lost.
> For want of a shoe, the horse was lost.
> And for want of a horse, the rider was lost.
> For want of a rider, the message was lost.
> For want of a message, the battle was lost.
> For want of a battle, the kingdom was lost.
> All for want of care about a horseshoe nail.
>
> —Anonymous

1

Unmoored

Fleet City, Beacon

0900 Beacon Base Meridian Time (BBMT) 30 May 3468

MAEVE UCH ROBERT FIDGETED WITH her brush. She wondered, as she stared at the gangly thirteen-year-old girl looking back at her from the hallway mirror, if she would ever be as beautiful as her mother had been.

Over her shoulder, in the reflection through the half-open door of her father's study, she could see a full-length portrait of her mother. Appraising it in the glass, Maeve remembered her mother as being more than striking, more than merely pretty, but truly galactic-class gorgeous. Her father and mother had circulated at the highest levels of the imperial court, giving Maeve years of personal experience to judge from. She felt confident in that judgment, knowing it to be more than just the aching loss of a girl for her mother taken from her too early. Unfortunately, it made her worry about her own appearance even more.

Captured in the old-fashioned oil painting, Maude Jackson stood laughing, green eyes dancing merrily, wearing a white, silk dress at some court function. Her eyes and hair she had given to her daughter, for which Maeve felt profoundly grateful. Her mother stood in the painting as if in a dream, raven hair set off against the dress and mauve background, a vision that only a true master could have captured.

Even more impressive, the painter had used a photograph after she'd died, gunned down by men sent by Maeve's oldest sister, Morgain. Maeve hurt every time she saw the painting, which might explain why Lieutenant Commander Robert ap Morgan kept it hidden away in the study.

Giving the hem of her cadet-gray blouse a last tug, she raised her chin and headed out to the car. Lieutenant Priscilla Jenks, tall, lithe, blonde, blue-eyed, and pretty, smiled warmly from the back seat as she approached. Although officially her father's naval aide, over the last five years she had seemed to Maeve more like an aunt or governess.

"How's my sweet pea?" she asked with a grin.

"I'm not a little girl, Lieutenant!" Maeve answered with some fire. Priscilla had become Dad's aide soon after the coup and her mother's death, and she still seemed to think of Maeve as a little girl. When she had first arrived, Maeve had wanted to hate her, afraid Lieutenant Jenks wanted to take her mother's place. Instead, she had found in her a friend and confidante she didn't even realize she'd needed. More, she knew Priscilla loved her very much and felt the same way about her. She would trade any of her actual sisters to have Priscilla be hers. "We're headed to the Naval Academy for my entry interview. You should be treating me like an adult!"

Priscilla just kept her smile, tinged with a little sadness, firmly in place. "You keep telling yourself that, sweet pea. We should be signing you up for junior high classes with your friends, not the Academy. The Academy shouldn't take thirteen-year-olds," she stated with a hint of steel.

Maeve gave her a hard smile. "Dad can still pull a few strings. Besides, I earned it through the competitive exams."

Priscilla's face became still, eyes focused on Maeve. "And because there are so few applicants, so don't get a swelled head, young lady."

Maeve flounced into the seat, arms tightly folded across her chest, determined to maintain a stony silence in response. A tiny worry mouse nibbled at the edge of her consciousness. Why were there so few applicants? Dad had always drilled into her that duty to the empire came above all else, even family. She knew that he'd given up so much for the empire and partly blamed himself for her sisters' "failures in character," as he described it. She knew that many considered joining the military to be a sucker's bet, but she'd never understood that.

Entering the Academy, she would never see her friends, especially Kai, Mary, Nikki, and Adia. Or do all the things they liked to do together. Would she fit in? Everyone would be so much older! When she reached that point, she slammed the door on her concerns. Being two years ahead in school, her friends had also been older. She'd be fine, she told herself firmly.

The car's back door remained open next to her, the petty officer driver standing by it as if she hadn't already gotten in. *What's his problem?* she demanded in silent petulance. *Let's get there already!* But just to make her day perfect, Commander Robert ap Morgan hustled up, his enlisted aide, Chief Petty Officer Drago, heading for the front passenger seat. In his dress whites, standing just over six feet tall, with the trim build of an officer who hadn't let time behind a desk put weight on him, short, brown hair turning gray at the temples, and a confidence Maeve could only hope she'd inherited, the commander cut a dashing figure . . . until one spotted the bulging briefcase he carried. *Oh no! If the other students see him with his old-fashioned paper fetish, I'll never live it down. Why can't he just stay home?*

"Pretty exciting, isn't it, Princess?" Robert, brown eyes twinkling, asked, as if he couldn't feel the daggers Maeve stared at him.

After a moment of silence, Priscilla answered with humor evident in her voice and eyes, "The fairy queen is not speaking to mere mortals today, sir. We have displeased the royal person, and she is giving us the silent treatment as a result."

Robert shook his head. "At least I can get some work done on the way. I have a meeting at Fleet Central for a conference call with the other sectors after we drop off Her Highness. I still have tons to do to get ready."

This is too much! Maeve fumed inwardly, already horribly embarrassed by him dropping her off. And he didn't even have the decency to be wounded by her refusal to talk to him! They wouldn't see each other for three months. Although almost inseparable since the day Mom died, he treated her impending entry into the Academy as if he were dropping her at the zoo or a day care! She felt so angry, she didn't know if she should scream or cry.

Two vehicles led them as they pulled out of the secure housing area and merged with the high-speed traffic headed for the Academy. Another pair fell in behind, before one of them moved up to cover their right side and one from ahead dropped back to cover the left, a perfect bubble. Suddenly, Drago pressed his earbud tightly. Turning, eyes wide with alarm, he hissed, "Incoming fighters, no identification. Sixty seconds out."

Robert's head barely lifted from his paperwork as he ordered, "Send our air cover to take them down." Maeve hadn't been aware of any attacks on him recently, but apparently they were so common he didn't show any concern. She felt a flutter of alarm, as well as hurt, as she glanced apprehensively into the innocent blue sky. Someone had attacked him and he hadn't told her about it? The idea rattled her. She couldn't lose him, too.

Drago raised an eyebrow at him. "You sure, sir? SOP is they stay with us no matter what and let the general duty birds take out potential threats."

Robert broke his concentration from the mass of papers covering his lap. "I am not accustomed to repeating myself, Chief."

Drago, with a disapproving frown, gave him an "Aye, aye," and turned back to his com panel. Maeve happened to agree with Drago. After all, what good were standard procedures if they were never followed? She feared for him and couldn't stand the thought of losing her father. For years, she had suffered from nightmares after Mom died, and now this.

Maeve heard Drago speak into his com, feeling a rising panic begin to paralyze her, "Roger. Rear car and right-side cover, drop back and slow or stop oncoming trucks."

She didn't know if she could or should ask, but Dad did it for her.

"Problem, Chief?"

"Two large trucks approaching at high speed from behind,

both came onto the expressway at the last entry point. I detailed two cars to slow the pursuit."

Robert appeared thoughtful for a moment before nodding a silent thank you. He began stuffing his paperwork back into the case. Sighing sadly, he looked at Priscilla. "Looks like Morgain is making a move. Too bad, but she always displays such terrible timing. I wanted to place Maeve safely under the protection of Ward's group at the Academy before she tried again."

Priscilla pulled open a panel revealing an assortment of firearms. Selecting a small-caliber, semiautomatic weapon, she handed it to Maeve. "We'll be there in another minute or so, sir. We may get lucky."

The reality of the situation hit her suddenly, hard. Although familiar from practicing with Dad, Maeve simply put the gun carefully down beside her, not wanting to touch it for what it represented: danger to her father. Staring at the gun, her stomach gave a nervous flip at a second idea. She'd never shot at a real person and today she might have to. The very thought horrified her. Trying to take her mind off that possibility, she stared out the window, examining the buildings and cars they passed.

"This is my oldest daughter we're talking about, Lieutenant," condescension evident in his tone. "She helped start this mess, so I expect we haven't even begun to see the fun she has in mind for today." He pulled a huge, old-fashioned, .45-caliber military pistol from his case before snapping it closed.

Priscilla nodded, returning her full attention to the side window, scanning for threats. "True. All we can do is pray and wait to see what nasty surprises she has in store." In the background, Maeve heard Drago calling for backup.

As for Priscilla's suggestion, Maeve didn't want to wait. She hated waiting. As they sped along, tension mounted, but nothing more happened. Maeve relaxed slightly as they passed through the security gate to the Academy.

Drago spoke an acknowledgment into his com, "Trucks were empty and the bogies turned back when challenged. Top cover should be back by the time we clear the gate toward Fleet."

Maeve expected her father to say *thank you* and settle back to work. He didn't. "Make sure the other vehicles are ready for anything; this whole thing smells. I don't know what's wrong, but it feels like a trap."

"On the Academy campus, Dad?" Maeve asked apprehensively, abandoning her decision to punish him by not speaking to him.

"Maeve, it's the perfect place for an ambush. Safe, surrounded by high security, but with lovely wide-open fields of fire. And security breaches could have happened anytime over the last month. As I said, perfect. The hit team sets up in a place where the target relaxes his guard."

Maeve hoped her dad's fears were just paranoia. Swinging smoothly into the drive leading to the admin building, they slowed to the posted speed, a sedate twenty miles per hour. Outside, everything seemed peaceful as far as she could see. Then the trail car exploded, the shockwave rocking them despite their own heavily armored frame.

Priscilla screamed, "Bandits to the left! Missile headed our way." The driver slammed on the brakes to avoid the lead car suddenly blocking the road in front of them, its security team jumping out to face them, before firing full bore at their car. In a remote corner of her mind Maeve realized that the missile fired at their car had missed.

Her father shouted out, "Looks like a classic L ambush with that car ahead blocking us from accelerating to escape from the kill zone. Out my side, watch for snipers and mines on this side as we do. Bring the heavy stuff, Chief." He slammed open his door, hit the pavement on his stomach and began slithering for cover. Maeve grabbed her pistol before following in a crouch as a huge weapon fired beside her, almost deafening her. Out of the corner of her eye, she saw Drago taking up the slack for a second shot on his monster gun. The second shot completely froze her. Suddenly, her nightmares returned and she saw her mother falling over her again, riddled with bullets. From behind, she felt a sudden shove, pushing her to the pavement, gravel biting into her hands and face, breaking through her paralysis.

Dropping beside her, Priscilla jabbed her with the barrel of her gun before pointing in the direction Robert ap Morgan now took toward the trail vehicle. Nodding, Maeve wriggled away, crawling for her life. Five seconds later, a yellow ball of heat erupted from their car, prickling the skin on the back of her hands and neck. She crawled faster, tears streaming unnoticed down her face. Bullets ricocheted around them as they headed toward the burning trail vehicle. Moving even faster, Maeve scuttled to the limited shelter it provided as the four men from the lead car began to head their way. Looking back, she watched as Drago fired from what seemed a suicidal position nearly under the remains of their car. Their driver seemed to be in action too, because three of the four traitors were down, and she only remembered hearing Drago's elephant gun fire twice. The fourth man continued running straight at them. Maeve felt sure he'd be dead in a second, when, from the side, raking fire cut up Drago. A dozen men broke from the tree line, running toward the drive, all firing on full automatic. Dad and Priscilla returned fire, mowing them down, all of them dropping. At least, any not cut down by their disciplined three-shot bursts gave a good imitation of being dead. Maeve thought with bitter satisfaction, *Good! Stay there and die!*

Focused on the attacking line, a voice from behind froze her, cold and hateful, "Morgain sends her love," followed by a shot. Her head jerked left in time to watch in horror as a flow of red spurted from her father and quickly became a trickle as he fell. The man she adored more than anyone alive crumpled into a blood-stained heap. Turning toward the gunman, her vision focused on the face of the man she recognized as the fourth man from the lead car, the man they had lost track of in the firefight.

As his gun swung toward her, visions of the past overwhelmed her: her mother's lifeless body on the pavement, her wounded father dripping blood as he stood guard over Maeve, and today, the horrifying sight of her father cut down.

The pistol in her hand began bucking repeatedly, as if with a mind of its own. Although never having shot at another person in her life, her first shot stopped the heart of her father's murderer. Her second shot hit him squarely between the eyes, the other rounds flying off somewhere. Then, her pistol stopped firing, empty of all twelve rounds.

Stunned, she stood frozen. What had she done? That bloody mess lying not ten feet away had been a living, breathing human not seconds ago, and now he lay dead, just like her mother and father. Her mind shied away from rational thought, rejecting any justification about him trying to kill *her*, that he *had* killed her father just moments before. She had killed *him*! Her stomach heaved and, losing all control, she threw up, head reeling with dizziness. Tears flowed freely, feeling revulsion at herself, illogically fighting the guilt that she hadn't killed the murderer soon enough to save her father, while ashamed of having ended the man's life. She wanted to curl up and die, anything to get away from this pain!

A warm arm surrounded her, drawing her in, as the sound of sirens and running boots told her help had come. Priscilla's voice soothed her, "It'll be all right, sweet pea, I'll take care of you."

Maeve sobbed brokenly into her shoulder. Bubbling up out of the depths of her misery, she whispered, "I didn't even get a chance to tell him I love him."

Most histories of the Jacksons and their empire focus legitimately on their brilliance as military leaders or the extraordinary strength of the governmental structures they devised. However, without a dedicated corps of spies and counterspies, the empire would undoubtedly have fallen to the forces arrayed against it within a few years of its founding.

Initially, this is the story of one man, David Jones, or as he preferred to call himself, Daffyd ap John. The records show him to be a man of unusual insight, courage, and cunning, beginning with the raid on Cradle with Dave Jackson that delayed the Final Battle of Earth, providing Constantine Jackson crucial breathing space to establish a citadel on Beacon. Rumor and legend make Daffyd ap John an even more impressive figure.

We will try to unravel the mystery of not only him, but his family and the other men and women who fought and died in secret for the ideals they believed in.[1]

1. St. Denis, Peter, *Inside the Imperial Secret Intelligence Services*, Regis, Sector Six, Blauberg City Press Publishers

2

Adrift

Academy Grounds, Beacon
1035 BBMT 30 May, 3468

TEARS FLOWED HOTLY DOWN HER cheeks and wouldn't stop. Inside swirled a strange mixture of guilt, terrible loneliness, and fear. Mom and now Dad were gone. She remembered stories where women terribly wronged would set out to blot out their misery by punishing the ones who caused it, but she had already killed her father's murderer. Even though Morgain uch Robert had caused this, the very core of her being rejected any thought of exacting vengeance on her sister.

Lost. She did not know what to do, where to go, what she *should* do. She grabbed Priscilla's hand, squeezing it as she leaned against her father's aide, wishing she could hide in her arms forever.

Thank goodness Lieutenant Priscilla Jenks had promised she would take care of her, because who else did she have? Morgain, no. Vivian, the next oldest, totally selfish and vain, likely would never take the responsibility. As for the sister just older than her, Nimue, if Maeve uch Robert ever came across her again before the heat death of the universe it would be too soon. Grandmother? Mom had refused to send her to visit, blaming her own mother for what the older three girls had become. If for no other reason than to honor her mother's wishes, she wouldn't go. On the other side of the family, Dad's parents had died in the coup, as well as most of his cousins.

That left Priscilla as her only remaining anchor. But would she stay? Could she? Priscilla had been Dad's aide, so the military would likely reassign her soon. She felt certain of it.

The question loomed ever larger: What now, what could she do?

She felt Priscilla stroking her hair, hugging her just as fiercely, whispering nothing really, just soothing sounds. Mentally, she shook herself, forcing herself to think. Dad would have told her that she must plan, the first priority being to find someplace safe. That's what she would do now. With an effort, she slowed her tears. Reluctantly letting go of Priscilla, she took a deep breath, releasing it slowly. She felt her mental turmoil go with it, at least a little. Anguish still churned inside, growing again as she began to truly comprehend life without Dad, but anguish and confusion were not the same thing.

She forced herself to examine the scene, just as Dad had taught her. From every direction Academy police were descending on the scene, in both regular work uniforms and combat gear. A perimeter now surrounded her, creating an island of purposeful activity in the midst of the chaos. *I could go to the Academy as Dad wanted. It's as safe as any place.*

Looking around, she realized that, quite oddly, none of the responders approached them to ask what had happened. Fleetingly, she wondered why? Her attention focused on two men, one in combat uniform and the other a campus police officer, arguing over responsibility for the area. Most of their team members were glowering at each other. *How odd.* She stood considering, trying to understand why they were acting that way, losing consciousness of the scene around her.

"Come on," Priscilla whispered softly, yanking her hand, disrupting her thoughts. Maeve realized that, while attempting to concentrate on giving her surroundings a thorough review, she had become temporarily oblivious to the immediate area. That wouldn't do. Dad hadn't raised her that way. She must get her act together.

Survival first, plan for the future second. Nodding to herself, she followed Priscilla toward a helicopter that had just landed, rotor still spinning just short of a liftoff hover. Ducking her head, she trotted toward the passenger compartment of the combat bird designed to carry ten people. For an instant, terror jumped back out at her. The crew chief's helmet made him seem to be no more than a robot, mirrored face shield hiding all personality. Panic stabbed at her as she identified him as a threat. Subconsciously, she reached for her pistol but didn't have it. Then she remembered. Priscilla had taken it from her right after the shooting and she had barely noticed. She should have reloaded like Dad taught her to do.

Overhead, the noise of the rotor blanked out all other sound. Squaring her shoulders, she headed through the turbulence caused by the rotors. Priscilla had boarded the copter despite the potential threats, so she could, too. Maeve stepped into the cabin as the crew chief finished strapping Priscilla in.

"Let's get you strapped in," the crew chief yelled over the bird's noise. "We need to get off the ground quickly. The pilot is picking up threat signatures in the area."

Maeve nodded reflexively as the crew chief brusquely pulled the straps tightly around her. Thankfully, she could sit next to Priscilla instead of across from her. Feeling Priscilla's body beside her comforted her. Almost roughly, the crew chief gave her belts a final check before giving thumbs up to the pilot.

Because he had made sure of her straps without fitting her with a headset for the com system, Maeve felt like a package. But headsets dangled from the overhead. Well, she knew how to hook into the com system of a bird like this, so she did. Dad had taught her that, too, over the last five years since the coup. Irritation at being treated like a child helped shake her out of the black thoughts threatening to drown her with questions she had no answers for.

She pulled on the headset, feeling relief as it muffled the roar created by the bird's turbo engines. Brushing her mid-length hair behind the earphones with her left hand she settled them as tightly on her ears as possible.

Priscilla switched the com to a passenger channel. "You okay?" Her eyes were tense, worried, as she asked the question through the comm.

Maeve tried to smile, but her lower lip quivered. Nodding as tears welled up again. "I'm fine," she answered, voice cracking as she almost she lost control again.

Priscilla leaned over as much as she could in the five-point straps, reaching her left arm partially around Maeve, and patting her back while squeezing a hand with her right. Priscilla changed her com to *off*, then removed one of Maeve's headphones before coming as close to Maeve's ear as possible, yelling to be heard over the engine noise that ensured only the two of them were part of the conversation, "You go ahead and cry; being brave is about more than fighting tears. We're headed for Prime Sector Fleet HQ to figure out what to do next."

Maeve merely nodded, squeezing Priscilla's hand as tears began trickling down her cheeks. She slipped her right headphone back over her ear. A vision of her father, lifeless on the road behind them, dominated her thoughts. He would never call her *princess* again, never laugh with her or tell her those impossible stories of their ancestors and some wizard named Merlin, a king named Arthur, a spy named Ian Fleming or James Bond or something, who had accomplished impossible missions. She'd never gotten all of those ancient people straight. Then came the other ancestors up through those who had helped Emperor Constantine, who Dad insisted on calling Jack, create the empire, and the things that had happened since then. She felt so alone knowing she would never see him again.

Did he still exist somewhere else? Whenever he talked about Mom, he had always been sure they'd be together again someday. But Maeve didn't know, her loneliness causing a shiver to run down her back.

"It'll be okay," came Priscilla's voice in her ear from the com.

"Is Dad okay?" she asked bitterly.

"He's fine now. I'm sure he's in a place where no one can hurt him anymore."

In her darkness, Maeve doubted. "How do you know?"

Priscilla's arms tightened. "I just know. It starts with faith; if you don't believe, you'll never know. That's just the way it works."

"It's not fair," she whispered.

The belts kept them apart far enough that she could see Priscilla's tender concern. "No, it's really not fair, or at least it seems that way. It is true, though. We'll be seeing Admiral Davies soon and then we'll know what we can do to keep you safe.

"One more thing, Admiral Davies is something of a stickler for protocol, so when we're with him or in public, it may be better for you and me both if you call me Lieutenant Jenks. In private, you can still call me Priscilla."

Maeve nodded, suddenly feeling all wrung out, and it wasn't even noon yet. Although holding onto her protector made her feel safe, relaxing her, a sudden wave of exhaustion washed over her. Letting go, she eased back into her seat and began to drift off. From under drooping lids, she could see the planet speed by below. The Academy behind them existed as an oasis of calm green . . . or had been before the firefight. In contrast, the area surrounding the fleet base they were approaching looked like a moonscape, even five years after the coup when kinetic weapons had rained down on the capitol city and main military installations. Idly, Maeve thought that it should stay barren forever after such a cataclysmic event, but even here, green had begun to creep back with saplings, weeds, grass, and brambles sprouting across the landscape.

Suddenly, the helicopter jinked down and to the side. Knuckles white and heart beating wildly, she grabbed a handhold. Were they going to die? The pilot's voice came over the intercom, calm and professional as he spoke with flight control. "Admin Center Control, Apache Three One. We are being lased, taking evasive measures now."

"Roger, Three One. Try alternate approach vector Delta 7."

"Roger, Control. Dropping to three zero feet NOE." She knew this meant *nap of the earth* or thirty feet off the ground. "Shifting approach to vector two two zero. I say again, going NOE, over."

"Roger, Three One. We are running a back trace to ID lase location. Are you still under surveillance?"

"Negative, Control."

Maeve suddenly realized that she had been holding her breath. On the ground she could try to hide, do something to protect herself, but not up here. She hated feeling helpless. She forced herself to breathe.

"Three One, pop up for three seconds so we can see if you can still be lased."

"Roger, Control. Popping up now."

Maeve found herself holding her breath again, expecting to hear at any moment the incoming scream of a missile or see a stream of large-caliber bullets that would destroy them in an instant. The thought of having her grief blotted out called to her, while repelling her at the same time. Unbearable sadness filled her, but she wanted to live, too, if for no other reason than to spite Morgain for her parents' sake. She couldn't believe how matter-of-fact the pilot's voice sounded as he reported.

"Control, lasing from one seven zero. Dropping back to NOE. No incoming, over."

"Roger, Three One. Hostile triangulated, over."

"Roger, Control. Many thanks. Over."

Maeve wished she could sound like that in the face of danger. She had been terrified. Priscilla squeezed her hand wordlessly. Suddenly, another oasis of green and calm that seemed out of place in the midst of all this chaos rose ahead. Maeve watched as they approached a group of towers standing as if nothing had ever happened around them. Somehow, the shield generators protecting the center of the base had stayed up, even as those guarding the palace and much of the city had faltered and fallen. Dad had been here, Maeve remembered, eyes darkening. Only that had saved him when so many others had died. *That time.*

Tears welled up again. How could she cry so much? She never cried! Where did all the water come from? Rubbing her eyes with the heels of her hands, powder residue from the shots she had fired burned her eyes.

She knew what her Dad would expect of her at a time like this, but she couldn't help it. She could never be Dad, always strong even when Mom died. She had only found out how much he missed her when she went to his room once in the middle of the night, overwhelmed by her own sense of loss, to find him sobbing, calling her mother's name softly.

But now she had no time to grieve. She needed to concentrate, plan, move forward. With a tremendous act of will, she tried to physically force the tears back.

The bird circled in for a landing atop a medium-sized tower. Maeve, catching movement from the corner of her eye, realized that missile and gun mounts on surrounding buildings were focusing on her chopper. A false move by her pilots and she'd be dead, killed by friends. A mistake by any of the operators of those weapon systems would also end it. She found herself praying, or at least hoping, that everyone did exactly what they should do today.

The chief unbuckled her, before gently helping her down. Priscilla had gotten herself out to wait on the graveled deck. Looking up, she saw a naval staff officer with a squad of Marines headed her way from a glassed-in room about seventy-five feet away. The Marines fell into place around them, weapons pointed out.

The officer, a clean-cut lieutenant commander with the loafer's loops of an aide, whose name tag read *Asroc*, shook their hands. "Admiral Davies is in conference or he would have been here to meet you himself," he yelled over the rotor noise. Pointing toward the waiting area, he led the way.

Why is the commander of the entire Prime Fleet concerned with the orphaned daughter of a midlevel staff officer like my father? She noticed Priscilla lean over and whispered something she couldn't hear in Asroc's ear. When the officer gave Maeve a quick appraising examination and a nod before hurrying them off the roof, Maeve's internal radar went on even higher alert. *What is all this?*

Unfortunately, Asroc didn't say another word all the way to the elevator at the back of the waiting area, or down to the command bunker under the building. Nor did the Marines speak, each standing at the ready in a corner of the car. As they descended, it became obvious they were going a long way down. Maeve watched Asroc. Good-looking, but he seemed to be just an empty suit, a time server. She assumed Davies had picked him to be an aide because the admiral didn't want him doing damage anywhere else.

Maeve decided she needed some information and could now ask safely. Opening her mouth, she didn't even get a word started before Priscilla cut her off sharply.

"Later," came the curt order, shutting Maeve up. She hadn't been a perfect daughter, but Dad had impressed upon her the need for security; a time and place for questions, and times and places not to ask. Dad had been in intelligence and had taught her that the wrong word at the wrong time, or even the right word at the wrong time, might get somebody killed.

Reaching the bottom, the doors opened onto a security corridor and checkpoint. The Marines stayed in the elevator as Asroc motioned her and Priscilla forward. A second surprise hit her as no one stopped them, even briefly, at the checkpoints. They were waved right through.

Sentries guarding a conference room door eyed them as they briskly approached. Asroc pulled out an ID card hanging from a chain around his neck, which they inspected. The sentries came to attention, saluted, then returned to an alert parade rest position.

As they entered the room, Maeve realized that they had walked in on a high-level staff conference. When she made eye contact with the full commander at the briefing podium, he shut his mouth and instantly blanked the screens. Every other person, about twenty plus including the aides, turned toward her. The commander waited perhaps two tics before asking in a nasty voice, "What's this, Asroc? You know this is a secure briefing."

At the head of the table, a bear of a man with thinning light brown hair, stood, causing everyone else to stand. In an affable tone, he said, "It's okay, Simon. I sent Mike up to get these two as soon as they arrived. I'm afraid my business with them will have to take priority for the moment over the after-action report. We'll convene back here in thirty minutes." The others in attendance looked rather stunned but quickly began to pick up their folders and paraphernalia. Rather less patiently, Admiral Davies ordered, steely gray eyes boring into them, "Leave it all. I promise no one will go through your things." Some of the more junior members of the staff glanced up, startled, before springing away like deer being flushed by a hunter. The more senior officers simply left without giving any impression of haste, though a few cleared the room before some of their juniors.

"Steve," Davies called out to a Marine brigadier before he reached the door, "The navy lieutenant here will report to you when we are done. Take care of her business before you return, will you?"

The leather skinned general, giving an appraising look to both Pricilla and Maeve, answered, "I'll get right on it, sir!"

The admiral smiled. "Quietly, if that's possible." The general, with the name tag of *Holmes*, smiled back, nodding before ducking out the door dead last.

Despite the almost thousand years of history covered in the preceding twenty chapters, there is no episode in the annals of the security service that did more to create the conditions for the coup or bring about the current political state of the galaxy than the love between Maude Jackson, Princess of Green Gardens, and then-Lieutenant Robert ap Morgan. At that time, he acted as Emperor Esau Emanuel's best troubleshooter and had gone on holiday of a sort after a particularly difficult mission in what had been Sector Nineteen. Maude and Robert met at an official reception her mother, Queen Euryple, felt forced to give.[1]

1. St. Denis, Peter, *Inside the Imperial Secret Intelligence Services*, Regis, Sector Six, Blauberg City Press Publishers

3

A New Life

ADMIRAL XAVIER DAVIES CAME AROUND THE TABLE and enfolded Maeve uch Robert in a huge hug. Letting her go, he held her at arm's length, examining her. "I am so sorry. Your father had a meeting scheduled with me, had been on the way here, in fact, when you were ambushed. He was very proud of you and enjoyed bragging to me about you."

Maeve felt flustered under the eyes of the most powerful man in the sector and, really, the remnant of the empire. She managed to say, "Thank you," but kept her eyes on his face as her parents had taught her to do in any situation.

Something else struck her—the hug. It had strength but no warmth. She decided he had done it because he thought she expected him to. She judged him to be a cold and calculating man. Dad had taught her to judge people so she could make good decisions. She knew she'd have to do what this man said but wouldn't trust him completely. Dad had taught her that, too.

Davies smiled again, before indicating two chairs. Commander Mike Asroc pulled out one for Maeve while Lieutenant Priscilla Jenks took the other. Davies pulled his own chair forward, Asroc sitting last. Davies waited several heartbeats before going on. "Robert did a very good job training you, I see." Glancing over at his aide, he asked, "Notice how she looked me squarely in the eye, Mike?"

"Yes, sir. You surprised me when thunderbolts didn't immediately fly, striking her down for her temerity to confront your greatness face-to-face."

Davies's face became very stern. "Speaking of which, certain aides need to watch themselves when teasing said august personages. Besides, I'm not as bad as all that, am I?"

Asroc shook his head, face bland. "No, sir. Of course not, sir."

Davies sighed in a resigned way before looking back at Maeve, "He's not such a bad sort, if a trifle disrespectful of his betters. Good help is hard to find, after all, and there is a war on."

Maeve felt a chuckle rise in her throat before it escaped. She felt sure he had said it just to put her at ease, that it had all been an act, but felt much better because he had tried.

Davies smiled. "I'm glad to see you relax a bit." Shifting focus to Priscilla, he asked, "What happened?" Priscilla sat up straight, though her eyes appeared moist. Quickly, she recapped the attack and their flight there.

Davies murmured, sounding surprised, "She got the last one? Amazing." He and Asroc exchanged looks before Asroc asked, "How do you know Morgain sent them? The investigators haven't even begun to trace their back trail."

In a voice filled with all of her loss, Maeve answered. "He said, 'from Morgain with love,' before shooting Dad."

After a moment, Davies just nodded. "Ambushed on the Academy grounds, so we can assume it has been thoroughly compromised." Asroc said nothing, just nodded stonily in agreement. Davies tone bit as he went on, staring at his aide, "I know you think Admiral Efron helped organize the coup. I mostly agree with you, but we don't have absolute proof and, besides, she's dead. It wouldn't have been good business to go in and just boot everyone she ever worked with. But we have to do something else with Miss uch Robert here, just in case there are more rebels there."

"You're the boss," Asroc replied neutrally.

"But?" demanded Davies.

"Are you going to leave the Academy open?"

"After this? I don't see how. I got a flash update that they found a missile launcher on the Academy grounds just a few minutes before the evac ship we sent for these two touched down, so it looks like it is well and truly infiltrated. That being said, we still need to decide where to stash Robert's daughter."

That last statement stunned her. He thought finding where to hide her had a higher priority than a secure after-action briefing or what to do with the Academy? She needed, urgently, to know why. Dad had been a stickler for security so he would never have permitted someone like her to be part of a discussion like this. At least not without a good reason. Why were they doing this?

Screwing up her courage she asked, "Why am I here, Admiral?" She couldn't quite keep all of the jitters out of her voice. Even as she asked, she kept a bit of doubt in the back of her mind to weigh whether he would really tell the whole truth.

Davies smiled reflectively. "You really are quite well trained. Your Dad must have been preparing you to be a spook like him." Glancing at Priscilla, he asked, "Does she know?"

Priscilla Jenks shook her head. "No, sir. She doesn't."

"Good," Davies decided, "Let's leave it like that for now."

Priscilla gave Davies a harsh look but only said, "Aye, sir."

Davies responded with a clipped, "Thank you, Lieutenant." Speaking gently again to Maeve, he went on, "We can't go into all the reasons right now for hiding and protecting you from your sister Morgain, and certainly others, but please accept that they are good ones, very good ones. As far as hiding you, we should give you a different identity. Your father always called you his fairy princess, which is where the name Maeve came from, actually. Your name is an alternative spelling for the queen of the fairies, Mab."

Pondering, he muttered, "Maybe . . ." as he continued to think a moment more. Looking up, he said, "Your father always said *go with your gut* when it comes to black ops. We'll call you *queen of the fairies*." He smiled in a self-satisfied way.

Priscilla stared daggers at him as he basked in his cleverness. After a moment Asroc cleared his throat. "Really, sir?"

Davies lifted an eyebrow over a wrathful eye. "You questioning my brilliance, Commander?"

Asroc shook his head. "Just seeking clarification, sir. Isn't it a bit too dramatic? Might also stand out a bit, don't you think?"

"Of course it does," Davies answered sarcastically. "That's why her name will be Maeve Ellyllyon, which means queen of the fairy folk. Didn't you learn any Welsh history from our visits with Maeve's father?"

"No, sir," Asroc answered. "I thought you both were just making things up." His face reflected the blank innocence of the pure of heart. "That is spelled a-t-h-y-t-h-l-o-n?"

Davies laughed. "No, it is E-l-l-y-l-l-o-n like any good Welsh name. Obviously. But back to our young lady, where to hide her?"

Asroc shrugged. "I think General Holmes should be able to handle the details. You know how much he hates to be micromanaged."

Davies nodded his head. "And I will avoid that as a good commander should. He will figure out the details, after I give him the parameters." Looking at Priscilla, he leaned back before pensively asking, "What training have you received?"

"In addition to proctor and protection, standard Marine field craft, communications subspecialty."

"Good," he said sitting upright, "Have Holmes hide you both somewhere on Beacon. Maeve looks older than her actual age but not old enough to be an officer, unfortunately. Basic spacer rated in electronics here on Beacon should be a good cover, and they can be as young as sixteen, so shoot for that age with her. Train her quick so she can carry out her duties in front of unfriendly eyes, if necessary. Regardless, I want her where I can lay my hands on her if we need her in ten years or so. She should be ready for . . ." Davies paused before finishing, "Well, she'll be ready if we need her and things haven't totally gone to pot."

Priscilla stood. "Aye, aye, sir."

Maeve stood too, feeling awkward. Apparently, she had just joined the navy but didn't know whether to salute as a new spacer, shake his hand, or hug him. He solved the problem by standing and hugging her a second time. She felt no more warmth than the first time but now suspected he cared, just hid it well. A stray thought hit her: he must have lost a lot of people close to him over the last five years. He probably couldn't afford to let himself care too much.

Davies looked at his watch. "The staff'll be gathering back here in ten minutes, Mike. Try to be back by then. I want as few questions about Miss Fairy Queen here as possible, and you being gone too long would probably increase the number of those questions."

"Aye, sir." Asroc's face displayed a brief smile before becoming professionally bland. Maeve realized in that moment that Davies must have been trying for some humor on this black day for himself, too.

Asroc motioned Maeve and Priscilla toward the door. He said nothing until they reached a local-only elevator. Tapping his sleeve as they stepped in, Maeve felt a buzzing in her ears. *Sound dampener,* her mind identified.

Asroc glanced at Maeve before talking to Priscilla, "Lieutenant, what do you need in terms of security? The admiral didn't mention it, but you should have a standard protection detail for this situation."

Priscilla shook her head. "We had a full protection detail out there today. That didn't work so well. The larger the team, the more likely it is to draw attention or be infiltrated. I'd prefer to cover her myself alone at this point."

Asroc shook his head. "The regs are pretty clear on this. The admiral can waive most of them in this emergency, but I know him well enough to be sure he'll insist on at least minimum coverage. For someone threatened like she is, he'll insist on at least six women. Why do you think he picked a commo/electronics team as your cover?"

Priscilla didn't answer, saying nothing else as they finished the ride up three floors to a level nearer the surface. Maeve began to revise her former evaluation of Asroc. Now she saw that the facade of being a kiss-up covered for his being able to carry out the admiral's plans while no one paid attention to him.

Smart on both their parts. The buzzing in Maeve's ears stopped as the doors opened. Thank goodness he'd turned the jammer off; it had started to become very annoying. They stepped out into another corridor filled with military personnel hustling around. She looked about her with new eyes.

Were there men or women here like Mike Asroc, more than they let on outwardly? Probably—no, undoubtedly—true. Some might even be siding with Morgain. A cold shiver went down her spine. Having a realistic view of the world would take away lots of the fun in life and would not be easy to live with. Halfway down to a cross corridor, Asroc showed them into an office on the left where another young man, outwardly as innocuous as Mike, sat.

"He's waiting for you, Mike," the seated man said, starting to get up.

Asroc waved a hand at him, indicating he stay seated. "If General Holmes wants to read you in, fine. He probably will, but I want to be able to tell the admiral that only the general knew about this when I left."

"Like that, huh?"

"Yep," answered Mike Asroc, already opening the door to the inner office, "like that." He motioned for Maeve and Priscilla to enter.

Sitting at his desk, Brigadier General Steve Holmes closed a computer file as they stepped in. "Where's Jack?" he asked.

As she examined him, Maeve became aware of an incredible number of white lines that crisscrossed and pockmarked his face, hands, and arms. *He must have seen so much combat, death, and destruction, he refuses to waste time on niceties. Dad would have said he believed in action, not words or being a politician. So what does that make Davies?* She didn't know for sure and thinking about it made her head hurt.

"I wanted to be able to tell the admiral that only you knew about this when I left, sir."

Holmes looked irritated as he shook his head. "You know better, Mike. That's insulting to me and tells the admiral you think he's stupid enough to believe that nonsense." Slapping the com, he barked, "Get in here, Jack." Not waiting for a reply, he pointed to a red, leather couch. "You two ladies sit while we get this hashed out." Other than that, he ignored them completely.

Asroc didn't answer but bowed his head in acquiescence. Maeve suddenly wished they were back with Davies. He hadn't treated her like a piece of furniture. A moment later, the aide, Major John Deetz, came in with a tray of water bottles and coffee mugs that he put down on a side table before giving the general his own bottle. Maeve felt the hum in her bones of another sound dampener. She hadn't seen it activated, but someone had definitely turned one on. She liked this general's no-nonsense attitude about security, even though he seemed to consider it an unnecessary frill to treat people like they mattered.

As Maeve took a swig of water, she discovered she needed it desperately. She practically guzzled it down and started another. Priscilla sipped a cup of coffee.

"Okay, Mike," Holmes asked, "what does the boss want me to do with these two?"

"You know who this girl is?" Asroc asked.

"Robert ap Morgan's daughter. I should say, the good daughter, the one not running all over trying to bring down the universe like the other three." Both aides chuckled.

Maeve hadn't thought it even the least bit funny. He treated people too brusquely for her taste.

"Vivian's not so bad, sir," Asroc suggested.

Holmes's jaw tightened. "My son wouldn't agree, Mike. He learned the hard way. Word to the wise, stay away from her."

"Yes, sir," Asroc answered briefly.

Holmes nodded at the women on the couch. "Enough pleasantries. What do I do with these two and why?"

Asroc nodded and, in a briefer's tone, ran down the game plan, "Maeve uch Robert is important to plans Admiral Davies has down the road. Lieutenant Jenks is her protector and proctor. She needs an additional five women for security, all with commo/electronics ratings. They are to be stashed as a commo/

electronics team somewhere here on Beacon so the admiral can get her when he needs to. Plan on a ten-year window."

Holmes gave him a piercing look. Asroc nodded slowly in answer to a silent question before going on, "Give her the identity of Maeve Ellyllyon, a basic spacer in electronics. She'll need a quickie course so she can carry out her duties."

"How do you spell that name?" Deetz asked, as he took notes on his pad.

"E, double L, Y, double L, Y, O, N."

Holmes asked acerbically, "You pronounced it Athythlon? This is another one of the admiral's clever Welsh jokes, isn't it?"

Asroc shook his head. "As far as being a joke, I couldn't say, sir."

Holmes snorted, "He's being clever. Tell him for me I'm not amused, Mike."

"Aye, sir."

"We'll take it from here. I'm sure he has other dogs for you to rob."

"Thank you, sir." Asroc came to attention before turning to leave.

As the door closed, Holmes commented to his aide, "Smarmy prick but an excellent aide. You could take lessons from him, Jack."

Deetz leaned back in his chair, chuckling.

Holmes shook his head and smiled before looking at Priscilla. "What do you need, Lieutenant?"

"Proctors will do, sir. As unsettled as things have been, we must cover every eventuality, even the requirement for a new proctor if the need for one should arise. Implacables would be better, but I doubt if that's possible."

Nodding, he looked back at Deetz. "About what I expected from all Asroc's noncommunication." He sighed. "Find five women, the lower actual rank, the better, with close combat skills. Implacables, if possible, as long as they have electronics ratings. Marry them up at Camp Y if you can't find what you need here. Schedule this girl for the training she'll need so she doesn't give herself away."

Priscilla stood. "My team will take care of the training. We'll just need cooperation from Camp Y for rating her and testing."

Holmes nodded. "Do it, Jack. The fewer people who know her the better." Standing, he headed for the door, causing Deetz to jump up, too. Priscilla had jumped to attention when Holmes stood, Maeve clumsily trying to copy her motions a moment later.

At the door, Holmes stopped to face Maeve, extending her his hand. "I knew and respected your father. His death is a great loss." After the quick, solid handshake, he left.

Maeve felt numb inside with everything happening so quickly, meeting these people who were deciding her fate in a moment before they moved on. Would she ever make those decisions for herself again? She didn't know.

Deetz pointed at the door. "Let's go into my office while I get things arranged for you. Do you need anything besides the water and coffee while I get your travel orders taken care of?"

"I could stand to freshen up," Priscilla suggested.

Gratitude surged in Maeve's heart. She really would like a chance to "freshen up," too. A quiet moment by herself would be a real relief. They had been on the go for what seemed like hours, with things piling up one after another.

Deetz nodded, hitting his com. "Need two escorts, female, at my office now." Looking back at Priscilla, he said, "It should be just a minute." He then became engrossed in his computer.

Almost precisely a minute later came a sharp rap on the door, followed by two very fit women stepping in. "You needed us, sir?" asked one.

Deetz, having looked up at the rap, gave directions in a businesslike manner. "Take these two ladies somewhere they can freshen up. After that, they'll need a meal. The girl, Maeve Ellyllyon, will need a full uniform and kit issue for a basic spacer with a specialty in electronics. Make sure the uniform fits properly. After that, take her to personnel for an ID. They'll know what other paperwork they'll need to prepare for her when she gets there. Basic physical only, we don't have time for a full work up. I expect all this done in four hours. They have a transport due out in four hours fifteen minutes. Questions?"

Neither of the escorts answered, but Priscilla did, "We left our gear in the car before it exploded. We were to report into the Academy later after the entrance interview. We'll need some of our things from home."

Deetz thought for a moment. "I'll arrange for your gear to get here from your home. Give these women a list of what you'll want and need. Personnel will be working on her file at the same time, but remember, whatever we bring for the girl will have to be gone through, with all trace of cadet status or family ties removed before you leave this building."

As if punched in her belly, Maeve suddenly couldn't breathe. She had lost her family and then been ordered into hiding until they needed her, like a spare part tucked away for emergencies. Now this. She wouldn't even be allowed to keep a picture of her dad. Then one last, horrible thought came to her: she could not be herself, perhaps never be herself ever again. Maeve uch Robert had become a ghost, just as in all those fairy tales she'd read as a little girl, doomed to forever wander in the cold wastelands. Tears bubbled up; she couldn't stop them. She felt adrift, floating in the universe without rudder, motor, or course.

An arm slipped around her. Priscilla's soft voice whispered in her ear, "We'll get through this together. We'll find a way to keep some pictures. I'll make sure they pack all of yours and your dad's other things for safe keeping while we're gone. It should only be for a short while until things settle down."

Bitterness crept into Maeve's voice as she hugged Priscilla's arm for a moment before letting go. She whispered, "It'll never settle down. The empire is failing, my parents are dead, and I'm an extra . . . something they *might* need. Maybe." Angrily, she wiped the tears from her eyes. "Let's get this over with," she spat out, heading for the door. They were ripping her entire life apart. Minutes ago she had been weepy, but now fury raged inside. They had no problem telling her what to do without even bothering to wait for her agreement, Priscilla apparently going right along with them.

Before the escorts opened the door, they exchanged looks, which she ignored as she headed down the hall. Priscilla caught up in three steps, leaning over to say something, but Maeve side stepped away.

Stopping, Priscilla grabbed her wrist, which dragged Maeve to a stop, fiercely staring back at her. "Listen to me, miss," she hissed angrily through clenched jaws, "I know you lost your dad as well as everything you have that ties you to him. Well, I lost him, too, and I don't want you to die by doing something stupid! I know you need to grieve, but we just don't have time for that, or a temper tantrum either, if we want to keep you alive. Your father and mother both died for you, so the least you can do is to not throw that away. Feel sorry for yourself on your own time. Be the strong girl I know you can be!" With that, she let go and proceeded ahead of her toward, and then into, the ladies' lounge. One of their escorts followed; the other took a position outside the door.

Deep inside, a small voice admitted the truth of Priscilla's words and she hated her for them. Jaw clenching and cheeks tightening as she entered, Maeve turned toward the mirror to survey her reflection. Rummaging through her shoulder bag, she pulled out her brush. She began angrily dragging it through her favorite feature, trying to untangle it. It amazed her what rolling around on the ground, followed by being exposed to a helicopter's backwash, did to it. *What a mess!* "I'll probably have to cut it to get all these tangles out," she grumbled as she stood in front of the vanity mirror.

"If you're pretending to be a basic spacer, that's something we'll have to do next," said the escort, a rather petit redhead standing near her. Till that moment, the escorts could have been mutes for all Maeve knew, but this one obviously felt like she could make personal comments.

"Your long hair will have to go or no one will believe you're a basic."

Maeve glared at the woman. "How short?" she demanded. First Priscilla bossing her around and now this one? Couldn't she do anything she chose to do instead of just being the package to be moved around?

"Short," came the quick answer. "It needs to get not much below the top of your ear."

"No!" wailed Maeve. After all the rest that had happened today, this last demand simply overwhelmed her. At thirteen, she had begun to fill out and get close to her final height, but she didn't think much of her looks. They were all right but nothing terrific. She felt awkward! Her nose, rather plain, lips too thin, mouth too wide. Her green eyes weren't unique, although pretty like Mom's. But her lustrous dark hair? She really liked her hair. It stretched down to between her shoulder blades and swished when she walked. The silkiness gave her a sensory pleasure running it between her fingers. When nervous, she often twisted her pony-tail around a finger. She liked to make a bun, curl it, put it up on top of her head, or braid it in lots of different ways. Her friends often said how much they envied her hair. What could she do with hair that short? Nothing! "No!" she stated firmly, again.

But one look at her escorts as their faces hardened told Maeve they would hold her down and whack it off if she didn't cooperate. She didn't care, she'd fight to keep just one thing the way she wanted it. Priscilla stepped up beside her at the mirror. Softly, she explained,

"Maeve, you have to do this, it's necessary. You can grow it out again later."

Maeve didn't want to even look at Priscilla but saw her plainly in the mirror. She noticed that Priscilla might have been crying just now, something Maeve had never known her to do. Maeve also detected a shadow of hurt in her eyes. *Why? Is it because I let her know how angry I felt toward her? She's not my mother!* Even as she thought that, she felt guilty. This woman had dedicated her life to protecting her, giving up everything else she could ever hope to do. If that didn't come close to acting like a mother, what did? Maybe she should give Priscilla the benefit of the doubt. Slowly, her anger ebbed away and the tears came again, tears for her losses, her hair, her home, everything. Priscilla's soft arm crept around her shoulders, again pulling her gently in. She let Priscilla hug her. She needed someone, if not a mother, at least a friend.

"It'll be okay, honey," Priscilla shushed. "We'll get through this together, I promise." Maeve saw a fresh wave of tears fill her eyes. Letting go of her emotions, she hugged Priscilla back fiercely. Instinctively, she knew she could rely on Priscilla, no matter what.

CNS *Pechnaya*, Ninth Sector
1825 BBMT 30 May 3468

MORGAIN UCH ROBERT SAT TAPPING a finger impatiently on the arm of her chair. Anger coursed through her veins as she waited in her luxurious sitting room in the command cabin of her flagship. The attack on her father should have been completed six hours ago. What had happened?

Generally she had found that decisive action solved problems. She just needed to make sure no trail led directly back to her. For instance, when Commodore Patrick O'Donnell had begun to regret his decision to join the coup, she could have packed up and left. But she would have lost all her hard work and real power this task force gave her. The obvious choice had been how to remove him—and his nosy little yeoman who had never liked her—without creating a mutiny. So they had just disappeared, letting her remove others in turn who she could blame for the commodore's death. Quite satisfactory on two fronts.

Killing her mother had been regrettable, and unfortunately, her father and little sister Maeve, had survived. And the next one. And the one after that. Why couldn't they simply die as planned?

A message dinged on her personal com pad. She noticed no header identifying sender or location. Eagerly she went through the security protocols to open it.

Team lead as well as three subleaders dead. Confirmed Robert ap Morgan dead. No evidence of survival of your youngest sister,

Maeve. She is not registered at Academy or in a hospital, so is presumed to have died in attack.

A shark-like smile wreathed her face. *Finally!* But she did not like the word "presumed." It didn't quite feel like the loose ends were tied up. Plus, with Maeve missing and presumed dead, Morgain still had a problem: she didn't have access to a proctor for the heir she had convinced to join her. *Did Maeve have a proctor when she died?* She didn't know. And, if she did, she didn't know if the proctor survived the attack.

That left her with one option: continue to push forward using the Restitution Movement while claiming to be an heir. At least until she found a proctor she could use.

Pondering, she considered the strategic situation. If only she could convince another task force to join with her, things would go much faster and smoother. Unfortunately, after Commodore O'Donnell disappeared, the loyalist forces in Ninth Sector had kept their distance, although they were not actively fighting her. Perhaps she should concentrate on the mess in Eighth Sector next door? A little judicious trolling? But how to do it? And what bait would be best? Something to think about while she maintained control of this sector.

ARCHIVED IMPERIAL CLASSIFIED DOCUMENTS

Declassified 24 September 3485
Orders in Council—Creation of Implacables
July 15, 3305
Classification—Top Secret/Test of Heirs

In order to avoid a potential breach of the succession as almost occurred in 3271 due to the Qabal incursion, within the Proctors a special unit will be created to be known as the Implacables. To enter the program, candidates must have no living spouse or children. Implacables, both male and female, are discouraged from marriage or having children after induction due to the substantial time and commitment required to fulfill their duties to their heirs, and are usually terminated as Implacables upon marriage. If a female Implacable becomes pregnant, she is removed from the unit, due to danger from her nanites to her unborn child.

Implacables will be activated in the event of an interruption in the ability to administer the standard Test of Heirs, as determined by the Succession Council. The Guardian of the Succession can act on his, her, or their own authority if, in that person's best judgment, it is unlikely the Standard Test can be completed. This decision requires affirmation by two-thirds majority of the Council of Sector Lords, if available.

Implacables will be provided with complete instructions for the administration of the test only accessible by removal of memory blocks once the Full Test has begun. The Guardian of the Succession or designee must initiate the Full Test with appropriate code words.

ON BEHALF OF THE EMPEROR CHARLES ROLAND

4

Safe Harbor

Camp Y, Beacon
0920 Local 30/0020 BBMT 31 May 3468

MAEVE UCH ROBERT STIFLED A YAWN DESPITE the bright morning sun shining on green mountainsides around her. Back home, most of a planet away, the clock had barely struck midnight. Her day had started almost twenty hours ago, however, so she deserved to yawn if she wanted to. Of course, if they had followed Major Deetz's original time schedule, they would have been here six hours earlier, after a fast shuttle ride. Plans had a way of changing, military ones especially, which explained why Petty Officer Second Class Marva Erdogan, one of her original escorts, now stood beside her, as well as Petty Officer Third Class Qi Mai Ling, a petit woman with wonderfully clear skin Maeve envied.

Oddly, most of the women on the team, as well as Maeve, had dark hair, except for Erdogan and Priscilla. Erdogan's hair shone a beautiful dark red that really made her stand out. As for Maeve, she felt lost in the crowd with her dark hair matching the other women with her. Had Deetz planned it this way to help her blend in?

Through the fog of her exhaustion, emotional and physical, random thoughts popped up. The plans had changed because the detail sent to pack her things reported back to Deetz that someone had placed trackers on some of them. That had further impressed them all with the need for more security. After a thorough debugging, Brigadier Holmes decided it would be better for her to be accompanied by her complete team. A further frustrating wait had followed.

With the change of plans, time had been provided for all four of her new guards to get their gear and make arrangements to store personal items while orders were cut, a process that took hours. Maeve understood, but the time passed in an emotional fog as the overwhelming loss of her father made all else nearly meaningless.

Then they had waited for the next regularly scheduled shuttle. Getting a special flight for an electronics team, even one on a classified assignment to a base like Camp Y, would have raised lots of red flags and unwanted interest. So, they had acted just like normal transferees. Exhausted, she simply tried to endure, knowing that not an hour away from Fleet City her personal sanctuary of bed and room sat unused. It seemed so unfair, yet she knew, bone deep, that hiding back home might be the last thing she ever did.

So, finally, they stood on the arrival platform at Camp Y awaiting transport to their billets and training facility, one blonde naval lieutenant and her special electronics detachment; Maeve the lowest ranking person around, being guarded by everyone else. Neither Qi Mai Ling nor Marva Erdogan were Implacables, something Maeve heard them discussing but didn't understand at all. They had taken something called proctor training, however, but that failed to help her figure these things out. The other two protectors, Petty Officers Bonnie Patel and Zeta Marovian, were, however, Implacables. Of course, the team needed, technically, one more woman to be complete. Unfortunately, the only place they could find to hide her allowed a maximum complement of six, including her. So, here they were, one short of the six Priscilla Jenks had seemed to think they needed as a bare minimum.

As for her Implacables, Bonnie and Zeta, neither looked particularly special or different, both dark-haired, fair-skinned petty officers, or so their ranks showed. Personally, Maeve suspected that the only legit ranks were Mai Ling's and Marva's because she had seen them before they were informed of the change of plans.

One thing began to penetrate her gloom, but not in a positive way. A glimmer of understanding dawned on her about the truth in the military maxim *hurry up and wait*, making her even more miserable. As Maeve considered the situation in the midst of her exhaustion, she almost reached up to twist her fingers in her hair, the hair she no longer had. She settled for another yawn.

"Stifle that yawn, spacer," Patel ordered Maeve. As senior enlisted woman in the team, at least on paper, she ran things. Maeve already felt tired of being an enlisted woman after just twelve hours in uniform. Nevertheless, this would all be for nothing if she didn't stay in character. She swallowed the next yawn on the way up. Maeve noticed a glint of amusement in Patel's eyes. She might find this all rather droll, but Maeve didn't. She just wanted a bed and twelve hours sleep. She didn't sleep well in vehicles and hadn't really napped on the way here.

Just then, a bus pulled up and they all grabbed their bags, dragging them on. Maeve looked around for a seat, seeing one beside Priscilla. Without thinking, Maeve stepped toward it when a senior petty officer sat down there instead. This confused Maeve, but she bit her tongue despite the PO being a man and there being lots of women on the bus. Why didn't he let a woman sit? *Not much of a gentleman.* Glancing around, Maeve realized that none of the other women seemed to even notice. Looking closer, she saw that he outranked every one of the other women, including her four protectors that somehow had managed to close in around her.

Reaching a stop, Priscilla stood, heading for the door. Maeve took a step forward, but Mai Ling's hand restrained her. Priscilla looked at Patel, ignoring Maeve entirely. "Next stop is in-processing, so try not to lose the newbie, Patel. See you at our building."

Patel nodded. "Aye, ma'am. If I do lose her, though, I'm sure we can find someone better."

Priscilla just gave her a smile, the same smile Maeve had seen officers giving their lead NCOs for as long as she could remember. "Just the same, the paperwork would be a pain, so try to keep an eye on her."

"Aye, ma'am."

Then Priscilla, her only anchor to the past, disappeared, leaving her very unsettled. Two minutes later, they arrived at a huge building. "Let's go," Patel directed.

Grabbing their bags, they all got off and headed in.

Later, Maeve couldn't really remember much of what had happened over the next two plus hours except standing in lines, having paperwork scanned, walking down interminable hallways, then more lines. By the time they finished, Maeve swayed, dead on her feet and barely awake. She almost fell as they took another bus headed south toward the building that would be their new home. One of the women, Zeta, she thought, though she couldn't have sworn to it, said, "Poor kid's out on her feet."

Patel's voice, deep for a woman, now simply rumbled around in her brain, not making much sense. "A few more minutes. We should get some chow in her before she crashes."

Another voice, slightly higher, answered. Mai Ling? "I don't know about you, but I'm pretty beat, too. Watching for threats while eating is going to be tough for any of us after the last twenty-four hours." A different voice, which had to be Marva because everyone else had spoken, offered a brief agreement.

Not sounding really put out, Patel said, "Right. Sleep first, chow later. I expect the lieutenant will want first watch. If she's half as smart as I think she is, she caught a nap after finishing her in-processing."

"Sleep," came Mai Ling's voice again. "That sounds so luscious."

Maeve had no awareness of going to sleep, since she had continued standing. She wouldn't have believed it possible until someone shook her arm. Awakening with a jolt, she saw the others stepping down from the bus. A voice from behind yelled, "Catch!" Maeve turned barely in time to have her space bag hit her squarely in the chest, knocking her sprawling on the ground. She saw stars briefly as her head made contact with the cement sidewalk. Rubbing her head as she sat up, she saw a crew chief standing in the hatch, grinning at her. "Be sure not to leave your head behind next time," he called with a laugh and a wink. *Did he just wink at me?* She shook her head to clear the stars. A hand, Marva's, lifted her up and handed her the bag. Maeve saw that the other three were watching the area around, each taking a third of the perimeter. They impressed Maeve by doing it in such a seemingly casual way that would deflect potential questions by not looking like a protection detail. Maeve began brushing herself off with her right hand since she needed to carry the space bag in her left while the right stayed free for saluting. She knew that much military protocol, anyway. As for the crew chief, she wanted to deck the guy, but not as much as she hungered for sleep.

"Let's go," Patel ordered brusquely. An amble would have suited Maeve just fine in getting to their billet. Even better, a nap in the warm sun under one of the elms on a patch of grass would be nice, but instead they walked, quickly, the quarter mile to a small building with a sign reading *Signals Communications Detachment 3-77* out front. Maeve stumbled a couple of times on the way but managed to stay upright. A tall barbwire-topped fence surrounded the building, with security locks at every entryway. Maeve could barely move by the time they reached the gate.

Patel stepped up first, presenting her eye for scan, thumbed the pad, and spoke, "Patel." The gate opened briefly before immediately shutting.

Mai Ling prodded Maeve. "You next. You're always second to enter."

Maeve nodded. She had seen her father do this many times, so she didn't fumble around too much, even through her fog. As she spoke, nothing happened. "Uch Robert," she said again, but the gate remained stubbornly shut.

Mai Ling whispered, "Ath-y-thlon" reminding her of her cover name. She had reflexively given her real name, something she absolutely must avoid at all costs from now on.

Miffed and ashamed at the lapse, she carefully pronounced, "A-thy-thlon," after which, the gate opened smoothly. Something else struck her, though she couldn't be sure if she had seen it or just imagined. A light-purple haze seemed to disappear as the gate opened and reappear behind her as she walked into the entryway. Looking back, she saw that haze there again, telling her a shield covered the building.

They really were serious about protecting her! The field seemed to give the other three women a lilac glow. *How pretty*. Abruptly, her mind came fully awake. She now lived in a high-security area with its own protective shield. Why? Unfortunately, she couldn't focus enough to figure it out.

Priscilla awaited them inside with a smile. She indeed looked like she had gotten a nap. Maeve felt a twinge of *not fair* about Priscilla being exempted from the red tape that she, as a supposed enlisted woman, had been forced to go through, but she just didn't have the energy to pursue her emotional pout. Priscilla pointed toward the left hallway. "Take the room to the right. Drop your bag, take a shower, get some sleep. We'll eat in five hours."

Maeve dragged herself to her room. The bag hit the ground in unison with her face hitting the mattress, still just awake enough to hear Patel say, "If someone finds out she didn't shower and make her bunk before dropping off, her cover could be blown before we even get started." She didn't hear the answer.

During the night, Maeve pulled up the blankets that had somehow been spread over her, gradually burrowing deeper to escape her nightmares. She drifted between dreams of her parents dying, her shooting that man, over and over again, and her own death. And she died in many different ways—shot, stabbed, run over, blown up in cars and helicopters—but always dying no matter what she did to avoid it. At last, she fell into a dreamless sleep.

An annoying buzzer began to drag her up from the depths. At first, it became part of another dream until no one died because of it. *It must be a real alarm.* Groggily, she flapped her arm out of the blanket, slapping her hand around across the top of the nightstand beside her bed to turn it off. Nothing there except her robe. Pulling her hand back in, she dragged her pillow over her ears. Finally, the noise stopped. A vagrant thought passed through her brain as she drifted back to sleep, wondering how the pillow and blankets had moved from the end of the bed during the night. She knew she hadn't bothered to grab them as she collapsed.

Then, the world turned upside down! Hitting hard, she landed on her left hip and side. *Ow!* Wildly, she began to look around to see what had happened. Two women towered over her, faces of stone, staring down at her. Patel and Erdogan!

"Two demerits for the basic spacer, Petty Officer. One for sleeping past alert, one for bed not made. It's amazing considering she slept almost eighteen hours," said Patel.

"Aye, Petty Officer," answered Erdogan as she wrote on a pad.

Patel's eyes swept the room before speaking again, "Two demerits for untidiness."

"Aye."

Patel, stared at Maeve for an infinite second. "Waiting for an invitation, vacuum sucker? On your feet! It's morning, the day's begun!"

Maeve had heard the term *vacuum sucker* before, the nickname for a naval spacer, her cover story. She scrambled to her feet and came to attention in her very-wrinkled uniform. "What's your name, vacuum sucker?"

"Maeve uch Robert," she answered automatically.

Then her nightmares became real as Patel, calmly pulling out a pistol, said, "You're dead," and shot her. Between the eyes! She screamed as the shot came flying in. Maeve's mouth gaped open as she realized it had only been a soft dart. It had still hurt, though, coming as it did from a range of five feet.

"That hurt!" she shouted with outrage, rubbing her forehead.

Priscilla stepped into the room as she did. "Good shot, Petty Officer."

"Thank you, ma'am," Patel said with a smirk as she bent to retrieve her dart. Maeve opened her mouth but snapped it shut as Priscilla froze her with a cold look approximately the temperature of liquid helium.

"Sit down, Maeve," she ordered. Maeve, angry, embarrassed, and confused, flounced onto the bed. Why were they doing this to her? This shouldn't be happening! They were supposed to be protecting her, not torturing her! Wasn't imprisonment enough?

Priscilla's eyes softened a bit, but Maeve didn't see even a bit of sympathy in them. "Maeve," she started, "I thought you needed to see what you were up against immediately so you could decide if you are going to live or die. We are here to protect you, but you will be your own best defense. You must forget you're the daughter of Robert ap Morgan, even that you're a native of Beacon. We thought about changing your first name, too, but answering to it is so automatic with most people, you could easily give yourself away without even being aware you did."

Priscilla stopped, waiting, letting the silence grow. It hit Maeve that she needed to respond. "Okay."

Priscilla snorted, "Also, you must forget you are thirteen and civilian. You are now sixteen and a basic spacer from Anglesey, a planet of the star Druid." Priscilla waited again. Maeve nodded slowly. Being sixteen, did this mean she could drive now?

A dart came zipping in, catching her in the throat. That hurt. Again! Patel's hard toned instruction came right behind it, "Dead again, two more demerits. You say *aye* for *I understand* and *aye, aye* for *I will obey*, spacer. Do you understand what the officer said?"

"Aye," Maeve said resentfully, rubbing her throat.

A third dart stung her hand. "Cheerfully!" demanded Patel.

Thunder clouds gathered, anger roiling beneath the surface of her mind. She knew what to say, she had grown up around the military all her life, after all. But things were so wrong, out of kilter. Her father was dead, she now hid a world away from the Academy where she had planned to be starting classes next month, and they expected her to be cheerful? Over her dead body! Gritting her teeth, she refused to say another word.

Patel turned to the second petty officer, Marva Erdogan. "Five demerits, silent insolence."

"Aye. At an hour each, she has a lot of work to clear her slate already."

Maeve gaped. They expected her to take all of this seriously, this military nonsense? "You're kidding. I thought we were just here for protection, not punishment!"

Priscilla sighed before flicking her eyes toward the petty officers. They nodded at the silent order and left, closing the door behind them. Priscilla sat down on the bed before half turning to face her. "Listen to me, sweetie, everything we are doing is for your safety. You have to be able to blend in no matter what happens. We think you'll be okay in this building, but do you want to be locked in here for the next ten years?"

A vision of years of confinement stretched ahead of her, her restriction just as tight as if she were in jail. "Is there any other way to get out of this mess?"

Priscilla nodded. "Of course there is. You can go anywhere and do everything you desire. If you won't work with us, you are free to leave. It means you won't have any protection, so you'll have to watch out for Morgain's assassins by yourself. Other than that, you'd be free."

Maeve felt her throat constrict. She'd be completely alone? Did she have any choice? "So, I have to become an anonymous spacer and stay in what would essentially be a prison?"

"Which would be noticed," Priscilla interjected. "A spacer who never leaves her duty station would cause talk. Even more important, we need to train you and you need to learn how to blend in no matter what."

Maeve nodded but murmured on as the tears began to rise, "Or go out on my own, probably to be killed. Wouldn't you stay with me?"

Priscilla put her arm around Maeve, hugging her tight. "I'd like to, but I couldn't. I'm a serving officer and there's a war on, so what I do and where I go isn't entirely up to me. If you choose to quit and become a target, I'll most likely be assigned somewhere else, to someone else. It's what I've sworn to do."

"Is your oath really so important?" Maeve asked, weeping softly now.

"It is. I promised to be the best person I could be, serve with all my heart, so that other people could be free to make their own choices. If you don't believe in that too, then I'll have to let you go. If you stay, we'll train you hard to make you strong enough to be like us. That kind of training might break your heart, but you'll be happier than you can imagine if you succeed. Do you understand?"

Maeve nodded.

Priscilla waited, causing Maeve to add, "Aye, ma'am."

Priscilla patted her back once more before standing. "Good. On your feet, spacer. Let's eat and then get busy."

Maeve, relying on her vast fund of military knowledge, came to attention, saluted, then shouted, "Aye, aye, ma'am!"

Priscilla came to attention herself, rendered a crisp salute in return, then stated, "You have twenty minutes to shower, dress in your fatigue uniform, and get all of your things unpacked and put away in military fashion." Chow will start at that time. If you aren't there, you won't eat. If everything is not ship-shape, you will spend mealtime cleaning. Am I clear?"

At full brace, her thirteen-year-old body not looking particularly military in her rumpled uniform, she kept her eyes proudly front as she answered, "Aye, ma'am."

"Dismissed," Priscilla ordered. Maeve dumped her bag, grabbing her robe from the night stand and shower things from the pile on the floor, before running out the door as Patel watched her from the hallway.

"Nineteen minutes, spacer." She held a stopwatch. Maeve sped up. Twenty-two minutes later Maeve opened the mess room door to find the food put away, although there were plates and cups for five on the table. Her sixth place sat completely empty. As she gawked, the possibility of not eating began to seep into her consciousness. Especially centered in her stomach.

Marovian stood from her place at the table. "Before we begin your training for the day, you need to clean up, spacer. You have some demerits to work off, so let's get going. Dishes washed, kitchen cleaned. I'll be your instructor for this exercise."

Biting her tongue, Maeve thought rebellious thoughts. *But I'm starving!* Maeve fumed internally. *This isn't fair!* Showering had never taken her long, but her room? She had never been the queen of clean, which made this morning particularly stressful.

Patel stood next. "After you finish here, we'll inspect your room. Following that, we'll go for a run and enjoy some healthy exercise in the fresh air. See you in thirty minutes."

Maeve, even through the haze of rebellion growing inside, noticed Priscilla. She remained silent, watching, observing Maeve. It hit her, the demand that she clean the mess area and her room must combine both training and testing. She could quit anytime she wanted to, but then she would be on her own. Of all the things that could happen today, the thought of being dumped off at her house with a simple *good luck* brought shivers of fear to her spine. She could always quit later. At least she had plenty of time to do these few things and clean up.

Biting her tongue, again, she began gathering things up and taking them to the kitchen. What she saw next sorely tried her resolve to not say anything. When Patel had given her thirty minutes, she should have smelled a rat. Dishes from who knew how many meals waited for her in the sink, as well as on the counters and stove top. It amazed her how much worse dishes looked in the morning after sitting all night.

"I hate dishes," she grumbled under her breath. "This is ridiculous! Do they think I really joined the navy?" she muttered, turning on the water. As she surveyed the kitchen, she saw an apron hanging on a hook. Looking down, she surveyed her work uniform, nice and clean. "If I put that on," she murmured, "I really will be the maid. If I don't, I'll get my uniform dirty and likely earn more demerits." The thought of avoiding more work won, beating pride hands down. She grabbed the apron before beginning to scrub the dried food off the pots from the night before. At least she had access to a dish washer.

One minute early, Maeve made it to her room. Her hair, though now short, lay plastered to her head from steam and sweat, but she'd kept her uniform clean. "Spacer Ellyllyon reporting," she said crisply. If they were going to play games, she'd play along and beat them all until she had decided what she wanted to do. Patel simply nodded, Qi Mai Ling at her elbow. Stepping in, she gave it a quick once over. Maeve felt relieved, she had picked up the floor and made her bed.

Then Patel opened the closet.

"Demerit," Patel stated in a voice that cut Maeve's hopes off. "Clothing not hanging as per standard procedure." Maeve now noticed the neat diagram taped to the inside of the closet door. She had been in such a hurry, she had missed it. Then, as Patel reached for a drawer, Maeve's heart sank farther. A second diagram on the inside of the door carried the label *Drawers*.

Patel's face looked as if she were smelling something particularly nasty as she examined the rat's nest in the drawer. Maeve had just dumped her things in, figuring she could do what she wanted with her personal space. Apparently not. She understood in a bolt of lightning; she had signed on for the full basic training experience, except instead of sharing three drill instructors with forty other newbies, she had the personal attention of five women whose entire mission in life appeared to be the perfection of Maeve uch Robe—Ellyllyon, she needed to remember she had become *Ellyllyon*—or kill herself trying.

Quitting began to look better and better as Patel said in a bored voice, "Demerit, drawer not SOP. Let's go enjoy the fresh air, spacer. Get into your sweats. Five minutes, be outside by the gate."

Stomach grumbling from not eating in over a day, Maeve reached the gate last but on time. The other four women, Marovian being absent, all appeared to be in great shape to Maeve's thirteen-year-old eyes. Their sweats looked comfortable from use but, nevertheless, clean and sharp. Being outdoors would have almost been enjoyable after being cooped up working, if the temperature hadn't been so chilly with the wind blowing. Maeve shivered.

Priscilla smiled at Maeve before nodding at Erdogan. "Lead us in warm-ups, Petty Officer. Then, we'll do our little 5K run. We need to get her training going within an hour. We're behind schedule already with all her demerits."

Erdogan, her long, thick hair tied back with a colorful scarf, started them off with stretches that soon became painful for Maeve. Maeve loved to read and work at her computer, so most of these muscles she didn't use much. Her calves soon began to burn. And then came the run. Not a fast run, more like a jog actually, but it took them up and down hills at the same steady pace.

As they ran, she learned two more things. First, after Priscilla said, "Let's go!" instead of heading off in a single file formation, which Maeve had thought would look silly but meet military standards, four women in a column and one running alongside, they just gaggled. And talked.

Patel spoke first. "So, Marva, find a boyfriend already?"

Erdogan laughed. "Not yet. I plan on using the run to examine what's available."

Mai Ling just shook her head. "Man crazy. You'd think you'd have grown up by now." Maeve realized that these women, these three at least, knew each other very well.

"What about you, Lieutenant?" asked Marva. "Last time I saw you, you were married. Where's he stationed now?"

Maeve noticed a sadness cross Priscilla's face. "Divorced. I'm not sure where he is now."

After a short chill, the talk picked up again, which taught Maeve lesson number two. Marva Erdogan hadn't been kidding. As they ran, she eyed the guys, of whom there were lots, turning it into something of a window-shopping exercise. Not just for her, either, but for both sides.

Maeve understood when some of the men whistled at the other women; Marva with her exotic looks, Mai Ling's perfect petiteness, and Patel's good looks could all turn heads. But as a thirteen-year-old, she had never, to her knowledge, been looked at as a girl by a guy, any guy. Then a spacer running by, a petty officer second class, made eye contact before whistling at her, causing her to blush fiery red.

Jogging along by this time, even up and down hills, had become no more difficult than strolling in the park, which made her embarrassment worse, because she just knew all the guys running by must have been watching her. Then Mai Ling made Maeve's embarrassment worse, commanding in a stern motherly tone, "No dating until you're sixteen. These men are much too old for you."

Even as she blushed more deeply, Maeve took a chance on being cheeky. Joining the conversation, she answered, "I am sixteen. It says so on my ID."

The others laughed as Mai Ling answered, "*Really* sixteen, Princess."

Her father's pet name caused a lump in her throat, momentarily threatening tears, but she buried them deep. Mai Ling had just meant to be nice, after all. Following the run, everyone hit the showers before classes began.

Beginning her first class, Maeve might have dozed off except for her stomach killing her. Lunch couldn't come too soon. It seemed an eternity away that first day. Following the meal, she had kitchen police duty again. With the pile of demerits she had accumulated, she figured she'd be doing dishes most of the next ten years. That night, she also began cleaning the building, a daily chore.

Strangely, no matter how much she worked, her stack of demerits never seemed to decrease, but to multiply like rabbits. Over the next week, she began to wonder if she could possibly have earned demerits in her sleep. Overall, though, between class and work, she didn't really have much time to worry about anything, not even her father.

PRISCILLA SAT RELAXING IN HER chair in the office off the com room, feet propped on an open drawer.

Stepping in without asking or waiting for permission, Patel plopped down in the other chair. "How much fun," she observed, initiating the conversation.

Priscilla just smiled. "A little out of shape, are we, after having all that soft duty around the admiral?"

Patel shook her head. "You just don't appreciate the sacrifices I make for the empire. Pretending to be a petty officer, letting you pretend to outrank me; the list goes on and on."

Priscilla smiled warmly at her friend before sitting up straight and asking, "Pretending to be Bosun June Palmieri for Maeve's benefit? You really think that's necessary?"

Bonnie Patel chuckled. "You asked me to be the one to put your heir through the meat grinder to start with, to see if she has what it takes, so I picked the one person we both hated during proctor training. How's my impression of her so far?"

"I wanted to strangle you, so you're doing a great job. Be careful you don't take it too far or let it slip she's an heir. She doesn't know and the admiral doesn't want her to. She knows there's a price to living up to the oath and she's the one who has to decide whether she's willing to pay it. I remember being thirteen and don't think I could have handled things as well as she has, so far. Just don't make the mountain look so impossibly steep she quits. Because if she does, she's dead."

Concern crossed Patel's face. "You really love this girl, don't you?"

"Like my own daughter," Priscilla stated, a fact she had no reason to evade or regret.

"What if she starts the test and you have to decide she can't pass it? Can you carry out your responsibility in that case?"

Priscilla shook her head. "Probably not, but I told you what the admiral said; ten years at the earliest. I'll be rotated out by then and you can have the duty. I'll just have to cross my fingers till then. Protect her, too, of course."

As Priscilla paused, she shivered. "She may never be ready but will likely have to take the test anyway. As Implacables, we must administer the alternative test if things get more desperate, even when we have no hope for her succeeding. That's why they made us Implacables, for times like these. I wish they'd chosen someone else."

Patel nodded. "Me, too. I like the kid and would hate to fail her, especially if she didn't even have a chance.

"Hey, I remember you volunteered so you could have the nanites repair whatever prevented you from getting pregnant and maybe convince Butch to come back. Did it work?"

Anger clouded Priscilla's face for a moment, but she pushed it away. "No. I started the training thinking I could go back to him and have his children, even though I knew I would be scrubbed from the program when I became pregnant. Funny thing, by the time I finished, I knew I didn't want to have his children. Children, yes. Just not his. He . . . lacked the necessary character I would want in a father to my children. So, I'm still looking for a guy, the right guy."

Patel's eyebrow arched. "Really? Commander ap Morgan didn't fill the bill?"

Priscilla stared hard at her friend. "Don't ever even *hint* about that in front of Maeve. She's having a hard enough time having lost both her mother and father. If she believed I had wanted a romantic relationship with her father, she'd hate me. She thinks of her mother as a saint, and no matter how close we are, I could never see myself stepping into Maude's role.

"Besides," she said regretfully, "he never asked me."

Patel nodded. "I worried about that. You fell in love with the dad and Maeve's the daughter you never had. This can't end well for you, you realize that?"

Priscilla shook her head. "Water under the bridge. Robert is no longer an issue and I need to keep Maeve alive; that means train her so she can hide using this cover story, as well as prepare her for the test if she ever is unfortunate enough to be called upon. So, let's go over the training schedule. What's the focus for this month?"

Patel shrugged as if to say, *It's your heart you'll be tearing out*, before answering the question, "We need to make her look like every other graduate of the basic space and electronics courses before she does something to give herself away. Camp Y has nothing but electronics schools, so we need to work fast before someone notices."

Taking a breath before continuing, Patel pulled out her computer pad. "I am actually going to run her through the officer candidate course program until she is thinking, acting, breathing like a spacer, even in her sleep."

Priscilla felt mischievous as she contemplated that suggestion. "That is evil, Bonnie. I like it. Fortunately, she's a nerd, so she should pick up the technical side fast, which will go the farthest in helping her blend in. Nerds aren't noted for their military bearing, so technical proficiency should be your main focus. Go on."

Patel grinned back. "Bosun Palmieri will ride again, broom and all. After basic electronics, she needs to qualify as an electronics mate, at a minimum third class. That normally takes four to six months, but we can do it faster. The table of organization for this unit calls for all petty officers, with a space for an electronics mate promotable, so we need to get this done before some paper pusher over in admin discovers we have a basic spacer and sends us a regulation replacement. If they do, they'll try to transfer Maeve. Stopping that would get the base commander—perhaps even Admiral Davies—involved, which would blow our cover."

Priscilla felt apprehensive, the threat Patel had identified being one she had been really worrying about. "How long?"

Patel shrugged. "A month, maybe. She has the undivided attention of five very capable women, so it can be done."

"Plus, she's a nerd," Priscilla repeated.

"Plus, she's a nerd," agreed Patel.

Priscilla sat back, tapping her lower lip with her fingernail as she pondered. "Use the training to wire the base, starting with admin, so we can have a heads-up if someone does notice the rank situation. We'll kill two birds with one stone that way, since it will give her practice with a live operation."

"Anything else?"

Patel shook her head.

Priscilla stood. "Very good, Petty Officer. Let's do it."

Patel frowned. "You really enjoy outranking me for this assignment, don't you?"

Priscilla grinned. "Not yet, but I'm sure I will before it's over."

ARCHIVED IMPERIAL CLASSIFIED DOCUMENTS

Declassified 24 September 3485
Test of Heirs Program
Proctor Course revised 2612
Heir Pre-Test Training Objectives

This revision is based upon the experience of four Full Tests of Heirs including analysis of the thirteen heirs who failed.

In order to pass the test, an heir must exhibit good character as exemplified by the Emperor's Oath. Key to that is the ability to understand both how to act properly and why those around the heir act the way they do.

The pre-test for an heir in training therefore has two goals:

1) Practicing a pattern of moral behavior; and

2) Having the opportunity to live in the same society experienced by normal individuals and thereby having empathy for imperial citizens.

It is therefore highly inadvisable to treat heirs as if they are special. They are more likely to be able to pass the test if they have a humble appreciation for the heavy weight carried by the emperor or empress.

5

Intersecting Courses

FORMER MARINE LIEUTENANT AUSTIN CARHART hated paperwork, but he had a screen full of data that needed to make sense, and it didn't. He had never intended to run a business, one of the reasons he had entered the Marines. However, leaving the service . . . irregularly one might say, when he couldn't take control of one of the heirs to the throne, Hugh Cascade, had required him to change career paths. Running a business. That explained why he now sat examining accounts, because somewhere he had misplaced five thousand credits and couldn't find them no matter what he did.

Sitting back, he stared at the screen, wondering if he just shot it the problem would go away. Generally, he preferred resolving issues directly, but unfortunately money didn't react to being bullied, threatened, or coerced. Sighing, he leaned toward the screen again to begin at the top.

An alert icon popped up in the corner of his screen. It broke his concentration, but at the moment he really wanted something else to do. Interrogating the icon, it linked a set of keywords his tap on the Flare system's archeonA array had picked up. The metadata gave the communications channel and security designator of the data he had hacked.

Proctor—Levant system, planet Nebo—1122 BBMT 17 June 3468/Confidential-private.

Msg reads: From Tens Ibramov, former proctor, Nebo, Radiance system, Eighth Sector, To Imperial Navy Retirement Payroll section Beacon, cc Imperial sector capitol Imperial Navy Payroll sections.

Subject: Back pay

The undersigned has not received the back pay he is entitled to from 12 August 3467 to date.

Undersigned is not dead, as listed as reason for non-payment in last communication from Retirement Payroll section.

Am attaching proof of life from local government.

No Imperial Navy representative is available to certify this matter because rebels control the system and undersigned cannot sneak out to an imperial system.

Please forward pay.

Carhart smiled. *Finally.* He hit the screen for the bridge. "Captain Steed, we need to go to Nebo in Eighth Sector to find one Tens Ibramov. There is a standing bounty for any proctor, whatever that is, from Ninth Fleet and apparently this Ibramov fills the bill. We'll need to be careful, very careful. Morgain uch Robert runs Ninth Fleet and has been known to renege on such bounties. All this means I have an appointment with someone who may be worth a lot of money, either by hiding them somewhere safe, or for the bounty, whichever is more."

Argus Steed's bald-domed image filled the screen and he responded worriedly. "You remember what happened last time we visited Ninth Sector, sir?"

"But I'm not going to Ninth Sector, Peer Drunnan is, and we'll be half a sector away from Ninth Sector and Morgain and her fleet."

"That's still awfully close, sir."

Carhart shrugged. "We have an order out for a proctor with a bag, whatever that is, and I now know where a proctor is who needs a ride to somewhere safe."

Steed nodded on the screen. "It's a blind order." Not a question, so Carhart didn't bother to answer. "It could be Morgain."

"We'll just be very careful, then. The early bird and worms come to mind, so let's saddle up and get there soonest. I suggest we hit the core boundary so we avoid Admiral Davies and First Fleet, plus we can go faster."

One of the things he liked best about Steed had to be that he didn't argue. Much.

"Aye, aye, sir. Lifting in about an hour. We are waiting for a few spares the ship's chandler is supposed to deliver today and I'd rather not be caught short without them. Plus I want to top off tanks."

"Get it done, as long as we get going as soon as possible. Carhart out."

CNS *Pechnaya*, Fjord, Verity System, Ninth Sector Capitol
1905 BBMT, 24 June 3468

"PRIORITY DISPATCH FOR HER HIGHNESS," called out the comm tech clearly.

The deck officer shook her head. "You know how she feels about being disturbed at social functions. She's with the sector governor and a bunch of his wealthy supporters."

The tech, Becky Cook, shook her head. "This is one she's been waiting for. I'd pass it up to the ship's captain if I were you. Or Captain Ba Ng on the task force staff. Since he's on Morgain's staff, let him make the decision on telling her."

Lieutenant Commander Beatrice Petronelli smiled, "Or take the hit if he guesses wrong. Open a channel to Captain Ng. He's at this soiree with her."

The tech smiled. "Aye, ma'am."

Turning back, she keyed in Captain Ba Ng's com and sent an alert to him with a secret security prefix. Two minutes later, almost exactly, her board showed that he had opened a channel.

"This is Ng. What's so important?"

His abruptness made her nervous. "Petty Officer Cook, sir. A message came through from Second Sector identifying an unassigned proctor potentially available in Eighth Sector. The instructions on this requires immediate notification of Her Highness for this type of information."

"Then I suggest you follow the Standard Operating Procedure, Petty Officer. Ng Out."

Suddenly her stomach dropped. She would have to contact

Morgain? Desperately she looked around for the deck officer, but she appeared to be in deep conversation with someone in maintenance, and stood with her back toward the comm panel.

Waiting a second longer, she took a deep breath and put in the call directly to the evil witch who controlled their lives. Bracing herself, she waited for the storm to descend.

"What!" demanded Morgain. She sounded furious at being interrupted.

"A priority message for you, Your Highness. A proctor has been identified on the planet Nebo in Eighth Sector."

After a pause, Morgain came back completely calm.

"Male or female?"

"Male, Your Highness."

"Have a destroyer with support ships sent to invite him to join us. Morgain out."

Letting out the breath she hadn't realized she had been holding, Cook looked around to find the deck officer at her shoulder. "Her Highness wants a destroyer and escorts sent to pick up the proctor."

"Thank you, Petty Officer." The deck officer turned and began to work on her laptop again.

Resentfully, Cook wondered why the deck officer couldn't have called Morgain and protected her like a good officer? But under Morgain, bad things happened to good officers, so she really understood and didn't blame the deck officer. Much. She needed to get off this bucket.

And then the questions started coming. Why would someone in Second Sector send a message about proctors, whatever they were, to Morgain? Or were they sending the message to Morgain's friend? Why had Morgain made proctors such a high priority?

She should be able to find out, if she didn't mind the downside of interfering with Morgain's business. Cook decided to just forget it. Satisfying her curiosity could definitely come with too high a price.

* * *

Radiance System, Eighth Sector
2015 BBMT 28 June 3468

COMMANDER'S BELLE SLOWED AS IT came in from solar north. Five years before it had been a corvette assigned to Prime Fleet, before its crew followed Admiral Jeffrey Gladstone in the coup and headed off to Deft to kill Hugh Cascade and then Marine Lieutenant Austin Carhart, among others. Most of the Marines protecting Hugh and the Protector of the Succession Doña Carlota Gonzalves y Rodrigues de Castillo had died, but Hugh and Doña Carlota had survived. Along with bloody Imperial Sergeant Major Sean Ward.

With the empire falling apart, it made sense for an ambitious and smart man to make his move to bring the empire back together using the orphaned son of the now dead Warlord Trevor Cascade. Anger still roiled his gut as he remembered Ward disagreeing with him before threatening to kill Carhart if he even tried. After the battle, he had gone over the hill and found this ship with nothing to do after Gladstone died. Now it was his, running high-value loads and passengers, or trading in valuable information, all while he looked for Hugh and Ward.

"Anything big and nasty in the system, Captain Steed?" Carhart asked. He didn't see anything on the display, but he had people on his payroll with greater expertise than he had, and this situation called for all those talented people to put their skills to use if they wanted to avoid becoming unnecessarily dead. Just as he had taken over this ship on Deft to escape when his plan to take control of the empire blew up in his face, he always looked for a Plan B.

"No, sir. Nothing that looks like a frigate or bigger. This corvette should be able to hold its own against the ships we can see."

And that statement by Argus Steed summed the problem. Any ships or defense facilities powered down or hiding in the gravity shadow of the gas giants or solar primary would be extremely difficult to locate and deal with. Now for the tough call. "Take us in as a merchant—fat, dumb, and happy. And slow. I'll be in my cabin."

Steed nodded. "It'll be about twelve hours, sir."

Carhart nodded before heading out. Standing around the bridge on edge wouldn't do his reputation for having ice water in his veins any good—or his nerves. This could be a big payday, something he simply couldn't pass up.

"MR. CARHART TO THE BRIDGE. *Will begin planetary insertion in five minutes.*"

Carhart scanned his outfit one more time. In his estimation, based upon dealing with numerous wealthy people over the last five years in his travels, he appeared to be a well-to-do merchant, exactly matching his cover as Peer Drunnan.

He stepped out into the hive of activity on the bridge as they slowed for a zero-zero intercept with the planet Nebo. "Where are we touching down, Captain?"

Although he didn't look around, keeping his attention on the screens, Argus Steed answered, "Parson's Springs. It's where the archeonA transmitter is located."

The brown, green, white, and blue ball of the planet grew quickly closer.

A bit later, Steed asked, "Should I put in a call for this Tens Ibramov fellow, sir?"

Captain Steed normally didn't ask permission to do simple tasks like this. Carhart raised an eyebrow.

Steed smiled as he nodded in Mul Muktar's direction. "The bosun is feeling twitchy."

"Mul?" he asked the small mountain leaning against a wall.

"Seems a little convenient. Big bounty out there for a proctor, and suddenly we hear of one out here in the sticks. After five years of fighting, he just discovered that they haven't been paying his pension. He contacts Prime Fleet through an open line, so every sector capital knows about him."

Steed nodded while Carhart thought. Then he said, "I want a team to hack into the archeonA facility, find out where the call came from. Exactly. Plus I want a rumor started that I may be on this mudball and see if that gets a message sent."

"Is that a good idea?" Steed asked, clearly worried.

"I don't want to be the main course at a cannibals' ball, which means we need to know what kind of game they may be playing."

Bosun Mul Muktar broke in. "I'll get a rumor going at a spaceport bar. The three who tapped the Fourth Sector archeonA for you will do this one. It may take some time; we don't want anyone caught . . . or shot."

"Do it. I'll be out trying to sell our moondust and starshine."

Steed smiled. "Good luck. You might actually make a sale this time."

Carhart gave a hard smile in return. "I hope not, because then I'd have to deliver, and what would become of my reputation when we couldn't."

Steed barked a laugh before returning to work.

Carhart began to walk toward the passage that led to the entry port. Mul blocked his way. "Don't you have somewhere to be, Bosun?" Carhart said.

Mul said, "You're not going out without me. This place reminds me of where you picked us up after the Imperial Navy cut and ran. Wait for me to get the rumor mill going or I'll do it later. Either way, you take an escort including me."

Carhart seriously considered ignoring him, but the man made sense, which, when all was said and done, was why he paid the bosun. "Fine, one hour."

Muktar smiled. "Two hours bare minimum to get a good rumor going without raising suspicions."

Carhart stared at him. "An hour and a half, because after two hours in bars, even you won't be able to walk." Pulling out some bills, he handed them to Muktar. "When these are gone, come back. Take a man to watch your back."

The bosun simply smiled. "Being paid to drink, what a great job."

* * *

CARHART WATCHED THE BOSUN STAGGER back to the ship. As he and the spacer second class wavered in front of the entry port, Carhart asked, "Overdoing it bit, Mul?"

Muktar smiled. "Making sure they know I'm drunk, sir. Picked up three tails during the last hour. Figured some would still be watching."

Carhart nodded. "Get in here, because I've got work to do. We'll take the Bulldog"—an armored vehicle that didn't look armored and could pass for a large passenger car on most planets—with a full anti-surveillance package. "Since we need to hide that you weren't as inebriated as you let on."

As they headed for the vehicle bay, Steed called. "We're fueled and I've verified that we have all good food stuffs and water; no animal droppings in this batch."

Carhart nodded. Ship chandlers—those who supplied food and water to visiting craft—talked to each other from world to world. After the first couple of years of knocking about the core, word got around that Peer Drunnan didn't appreciate sharp practices. But Steed's people still remained vigilant in case they ran across a world that hadn't gotten the word. Of course, burning down the establishments of those who had not believed Carhart's reputation had helped encourage the others. The last one had happened two years ago in Eleventh Sector, over four thousand light-years from here.

Two minutes later, the vehicle hatch opened. Carhart sat in back with a four-man team. Mul sat up front with the driver. "Meat-packing district, Antonio." Antonio Petronelli smiled and headed out of the spaceport at well over the speed limit. "Antonio," Carhart muttered, causing them to slow, slightly. Carhart gave up. Good help being hard to find, he didn't want to lose a very capable driver and bodyguard.

"Where are we going?" Petronelli asked fifteen minutes later. The seedy surroundings didn't look like the kind of place Drunnan would frequent as a merchant.

Mul turned around, not showing the slightest sign of being drunk. "Taps in place, I've dropped my hints, and there's not even a sniff of this Tens fellow in the databases around the whole planet. Figured we could see how honest these folks are. From the message we intercepted, we need to meet in this area, but I don't like it. Anything happens in this neighborhood, likely no one much will care."

"Even so, knocking over the local crime boss may not be such a hot idea."

"We aren't going to?" Mul asked with a straight face.

Carhart shrugged. "Did you arrange for a second team to discourage pursuit?"

Mul simply smiled. Carhart leaned back. Now he would see who really ran this planet. Or at least this city. Mul stopped smiling as he pressed his earbud. Turning, he told Carhart, "Advance team says they are picking up heavy weapons signatures and there are armored cars in the vicinity. Three that they can see."

Carhart sighed. The galaxy seemed to be full of so many dishonest people. "Antonio, quickest way back to the ship. Tell Captain Steed we lift, permission or no from the tower, as soon as everyone is back on board."

"Got a tail, boss," Antonio reported as he hung a U-turn in the middle of the block. Fortunately, the street had four lanes.

"Any indication they want to play?"

"Not yet, but it pays to be careful. The captain says he has a couple of sleds ready to provide top cover if things get real."

"Tell him thank you, but no. I want to keep our capabilities secret as long as possible."

"Aye, sir."

The ten minutes back to the ship dragged on. Carhart sweated nervously, despite the environmental systems. As they sped through the gate, a feeling of relief filled him. Forty minutes later, they were off the ground with standard clearance. Carhart felt disappointed, but not surprised, since things that look too good to be true generally were. Obviously, the news about the proctor had been bait, and all it cost had been the fuel to check it out. And Mul's bar tab. He'd just have to find a proctor somewhere else.

Of interest, although David Jones, or Daffyd ap John, gave everything he had in support of the empire, he made Dave Jackson promise to never ask any of his descendants to take the Test. A review of the history of the empire shows that this request protected his family from most of the negatives the leaders of the empire experienced while still allowing his family to serve. At least until Maeve uch Robert and the crisis of the Test.[1]

1. St. Denis, Peter, *Inside the Imperial Secret Intelligence Services*, Regis, Sector Six, Blauberg City Press Publishers

6

The Easy Life

Communications Detachment 3-77, Camp Y, Beacon
0840 Local/2340 BBMT 23 July 3468

BENT OVER A WORK BENCH, Maeve uch Robert peered through a large, articulated magnifying glass as she examined a circuit board with Zeta Marovian at her elbow. Carefully, using her mini-pad, she manipulated a micro welder to the spot of the break and fixed it. "Two minutes, fifteen seconds. Within parameters, spacer," Marovian announced. Maeve nodded. Finally, she had passed this module!

Since she had arrived here over a month ago, her days had been at least eighteen hours long. *Wake up, exercise, military skills such as cleaning heads with a toothbrush, when there are perfectly good domestic bots available! Guard duty, troubleshooting circuits, electronics theory, building networks, basic personal defense and combat, more wonderful military skills such as pulling commo watch when no one ever contacts us, clean up, before, finally, bed.* Then wake up and repeat, over and over again. The days had become a blur. Grousing, Maeve then realized that the good thing about being so busy was it gave her little time to worry about her family or friends.

One by one, she had mastered each task and now she had completed basic troubleshooting! At least she wouldn't have to use these archaic tools in the future, but could do it faster with nanotechnology. She sat back, a pleased glow spreading through her.

"Now remove the weld, Maeve," Marovian said, with a hint of amusement.

"Why?" Maeve asked in surprise. "I thought this circuit formed an essential part of the base security system for this building, linking cameras and mics."

"It is, and, because we don't want anyone knowing what we're doing here, we caused it to fail immediately after we arrived. That being the case, we are going to report that we fixed the fault, but, unfortunately, another fault occurred immediately."

"But we've received a number of demands that we fix it ASAP from the Base Security office. Shouldn't we comply?"

Marovian nodded. "We have repaired the break as requested. When we receive more requests, we'll comply with them, too. Eventually, we'll have our own system in place. At that point, we will be able to feed Base Security what we want them to see." She glanced at her watch.

Maeve felt confused, along with a shadow of dread creeping in. Weren't they safe even here? Couldn't they trust anyone? It seemed wrong to feed false information to people who were supposed to be on the same side. What made things worse, her protectors expected her to figure out on her own why they were doing these things. *Well, Dad taught me to think things through, so I should be trying to use my brain for more than a hat rack, as Dad used to say.*

Marovian smiled. "Tomorrow we'll get back to working on our security system, but tonight I have a date." Standing, she straightened her blouse. "You did really well for a basic spacer. We figured it would take you another week just to isolate the area of the break."

Maeve felt warmed by the compliment. *Ahead of schedule!* Maybe she could get some downtime herself. Teasingly, she asked, "Another week? Didn't you say I would get five demerits if I didn't fix this by tomorrow?"

Marovian smiled wickedly. "I did say that, didn't I? What you need to remember is that we use demerits to spur you. The demerits get you to learn things you wouldn't pay close enough attention to otherwise. On that basis, I award you the five demerits you would have earned if you were going at the normal pace, because I can't think of any other reason to do it. Have a nice evening."

"You rat!" Maeve yelled after her. Despite how hard they were on her, she really liked and admired these women. Pulling up the magnifier again, she carefully removed the weld she had so painstakingly applied not minutes before. Standing, she stretched her back. Checking the time, she saw she had ten minutes until the next class. Her stomach rumbled. *Not very ladylike.* But it demanded food. Sliding toward the door, she carefully looked both ways. No one. She glided out, imagining herself as a wisp of smoke wafting unnoticed down the hall. This game seemed to almost be part of her training: reach the kitchen and get food without being seen.

Silently, she moved along. Two doors, three, past the office. No sound, no indication anyone had noticed her. Slowly, she unlatched the door into the kitchen, peeking through the crack. No one in sight. Striking quickly, her hand grabbed a muffin from the plate near the door.

"Pretty good," Qi Mai Ling said from directly behind her.

Maeve jumped a foot, dropping the muffin as she turned. "You got me!"

Mai Ling smiled. "Always watch your back. Get your dress uniform on and meet me back here in five. You can keep the muffin but won't have time to eat it. Move!"

Maeve stuffed the muffin in her mouth as she hurried to her room and opened her closet.

Everything lay inside neat and orderly, picture-perfect, an adjective that had never applied to her room at home. Pride and the satisfaction of doing things well, filled her heart. On the left, hanging in a place of honor, hung her new dress uniform in its plastic bag. Last week, without any notice, Petty Officers Bonnie Patel and Marva Erdogan had taken her to the naval clothing store. The fitting had been a total surprise. She'd loved it!

Surprisingly, she had been proud to pay for the uniform out of her own pocket. Presents were nice, but it had felt so good to have earned the money herself. She had also earned the right to wear it. For proof of that, she could look back at the pile of demerits she had worked off! Her uniform had arrived yesterday and she had immediately hung it in its place of honor. Taking it out now, a gorgeous white that made her, in her own humble opinion, look terrific, she carefully put it on, nervous excitement causing her fingers to fumble a bit with the zippers and clasps. As she did, she wondered why she had been allowed to get it but had no answer. She hadn't seen anything on the training schedule and no one had said a thing, not even a hint! Being young could be so frustrating, and pretending to be a trainee just made things worse.

Stepping out into the hall, Maeve was surprised to see Mai Ling waiting in her own dress whites. "Let's go, Princess. Are you always this slow?" she teased. Maeve smiled at Mai Ling's quip because Maeve had earned a reputation for being the fastest woman on the team in and out of the shower or getting dressed, and Mai Ling always finished last, the slowest by far.

"Curling my hair," Maeve answered, indicating her short, naturally curly locks. "When it's this long, it takes time." Another joke. Last week, she had been given another haircut to keep her hair just two and a half inches long. Regretfully, she wouldn't be spending any time fixing her hair for quite a while yet. Mai Ling grinned as she headed for the front door.

Patel waited for them there in her work uniform, smiling. Beaming really. "Congratulations! You've earned it. I wish I could be there, but I drew short straw and have to mind the store." Then, shocking Maeve to death, Patel stepped forward and hugged her. As she stepped back, Maeve thought she saw what looked suspiciously like a tear in Patel's eye. Before Maeve could comment, or even ask why the emotion, Patel headed off to the control room.

Outside came another surprise. Lieutenant Priscilla Jenks and Marovian waiting, in whites, also shocked her, but Erdogan in combat fatigues with a sniper rifle raised more questions. "What's going on?" demanded Maeve.

"Your graduation," answered Priscilla. "I'd hate to be late, especially if it's due to you going after that muffin. Let's hurry." Outside the gate sat a car and a jeep-type utility vehicle. Erdogan drove off alone in the jeep while the others got into the car, Mai Ling driving. Maeve, at least once a day, had brought up the subject of her driver's license. Being technically sixteen, according to her official navy ID, and because of navy customs requiring the lowest ranking woman in the car to be the driver, she should be able to get that license. So far, no luck. In fact, the last three times she had mentioned that fact had earned her extra demerits plus comments to the effect that none of her protectors had a death wish.

The jeep disappeared toward the hillside overlooking the administrative quad as the car neared the parade ground. Pulling into a reserved parking stall, Maeve saw the field ahead of them filled with blocks of men and women in whites facing the reviewing stand. Mai Ling called to her as they closed the doors, "Let's go, quickly, to the rear of that second block from the right. We need to hurry, they're about to start."

Priscilla smiled at her proudly. "We'll be watching from the stands. Erdogan is on overwatch from the hills. I'm so proud of you."

Maeve could have sworn Priscilla, like Patel, had a tear in her eye, but didn't have time to verify the observation. Mai Ling set a fast pace for one so small and Maeve couldn't afford to look as if she were straggling along behind. Reaching the back of the second block of spacers, they arrived just in time to come to attention as the ceremony started.

The loudspeaker squealed, "Welcome to the graduation of class 1-02. After today, all of the men and women you see before you will be rated electronics mate third class, having passed all of the examinations necessary for that rating. Following this parade ceremony, your orders will be posted to your personal comp pads."

The band played the anthem, the flag paraded before the graduates, guests, and dignitaries, after which the base commander spoke. Maeve watched the whole thing in a kind of haze as well as awe. Deep down, she felt a strong emotion rising to meet the swell of the music. The whipping of the colors reminded her of her oath, the blazing colors bringing tears to her eyes. The effort to qualify had been worth it. She whispered to Mai Ling, "I thought it took six months to qualify."

Mai Ling, in charge of this detachment of one, smiled, barely moving her lips as she answered, "We cut a few corners to get you here, but you earned your spot on this field. We're all proud of you. You did so well that one of the personnel officers called to see if we would cut you loose. Your scores brought you to the notice of the electronics officer from a cruiser squadron, as well as the admin officer of a supernova. We were offered two trainees in exchange for you. Tempting," she said in a teasing tone, "but in the end we turned it down."

Maeve felt like flying. Finally, she had done something well. "A transfer wouldn't be so bad. I would get to see new places, plus two for one is a good deal," she answered mischievously.

"Nope," Mai Ling answered, "we aren't done with you yet. Five demerits for talking in formation."

Maeve didn't care, her heart floating throughout the hour-long ceremony. Not even the added demerits could weigh her down. Twenty minutes after the graduation ceremonies ended, she jumped back into her work fatigues. On her door, she found posted a new training schedule. As she looked it over, it thrilled her to see that daily inspections were over. Unfortunately, the time saved didn't allow her to relax, just study more. As she examined the following week's plan, Marovian came by dressed stunningly in a beautiful civilian outfit of pale scarf, loose, patterned blouse, and tan slacks with open-toed heels.

"This must really be some date," Maeve observed in awe.

"Yep. Special guy." Her eyes twinkled. "Congrats again, Princess. I've got to go." With a wave, she disappeared.

* * *

Camp Y, Beacon
0759 Local 19/2259 BBMT 20 September 3468

REVIEWING THE LAST TWO MONTHS' records, Priscilla reflected that Maeve's training seemed to be going well. Maybe too well. On one of her monitors, she watched Maeve setting up a security circuit under the instruction of Mai Ling. A second monitor showed the commo room with Patel on duty, and a third covered the gate as Marovian checked in just a minute ahead of her scheduled time. Priscilla suspected Erdogan might be in the kitchen. If she needed to see her, she could change channels on one of the three monitors. Hitting her com, she flashed Marovian to come to her office.

As Marovian stepped in, glowing, Priscilla's heart fell. "Sit," she pointed, continuing. "Want to tell me what's up, Zeta?"

Marovian shrugged her shoulders. "What do you mean?"

Priscilla stood abruptly, stalking angrily around the desk. Pulling up her computer, she showed Marovian a set of pictures of Zeta in what could only be described as *compromising poses* with a good-looking guy. "Explain this. You know we need to be careful because of Maeve. That includes our personal lives. If you were married, this would be bad enough, but this type of behavior endangers the mission, besides being wrong. You know better, Zeta, you're an Implacable. What were you thinking?"

Zeta Marovian's cheeks colored. "We *are* married, Priscilla. I met him soon after we got here and fell in love. I know the rules as well as what's right and wrong. The day Maeve got her rating, we were married."

"Are you crazy?" Priscilla shouted. "I can't replace you here with anyone in the entire Prime Sector, maybe the whole empire. We keep running searches for Implacables, but no luck. There aren't even any female proctors with an electronics background to replace Mai Ling and Marva, much less you. Being married, I'll have to let you go! You know the regs. Opening a real personnel search would set off exactly the red flags we've been trying to avoid!"

Marovian lowered her head, before going on quietly, "I'm sorry, I really am. But it's worse than that . . . I'm pregnant. Probably happened on our wedding night."

Priscilla's mouth gaped open. What do you say to a friend who has just blown her part of a long-term op? What do you say to a friend who has what you've always wanted but can never have? Priscilla managed to ask, "How far along?" as her brain froze. *What should I do?* She had asked the automatic question to give herself time to think.

"Two months. The doctor says I'm healthy as a horse and the baby's fine." Marovian looked back up at Priscilla with a wisp of a smile.

"You don't look like a horse," Priscilla observed, desperately looking for something to say. "You're glowing."

Marovian smiled. "Thank you. I feel like I'm eating like one, though. I'm almost as hungry as Maeve most of the time."

Priscilla smiled back. "I don't think any of us could eat as much as that girl does without adding fifty pounds. So, what now?"

"I'll continue on the team until you find someone else or the baby comes,"

"You might lose the baby," Priscilla warned.

"I don't think so," Marovian answered. "Before I joined up, I lost a baby at three months. This time feels different."

"That's not what I mean. You have the same nanites I do, you received the same instructions, the same warnings. If those little computers decided your baby would prevent you from protecting Maeve, they might just do it automatically."

Marovian's sparkle disappeared at this threat to her child. "That would only happen if you told them to," she answered carefully.

"You know I would never do that," Priscilla said, "but we're undercover. If we are ordered out, and I can't stop it, the nanites might do it on their own. They're only computers, after all."

"I hadn't thought of that," she said quietly, a hint of desperation in her voice.

Priscilla shook her head slowly. "I could never order that, no matter what. Life is more precious than anything, no matter how it happens. But I think you know what you need to do."

"Yes, I am afraid you're right. It's Maeve or my baby. When I started falling in love with Chad, I told myself he could never love me enough to marry me, and, since I would never violate my oath by getting married, I told myself I had nothing to worry about. Then, one night, he popped the question. My mind firmly made up and being totally committed to the mission, as I prepared to tell him, *No, I'm sorry*, I heard my voice saying *Yes, of course*. Ever since then, I've been afraid this day might come," Marovian's voice shook with unshed tears. "I've been trying to find a way to tell you, but couldn't come up with anything that didn't sound selfish. I'm sorry, but I couldn't help myself." Pleading she added, "Isn't this what we're fighting for, babies and families?"

Priscilla wished she could be harsh or stern, but she only felt regret at her own loss, and happiness for her friend. "You're not selfish. Having this baby is the best thing you can do. I wish I could have one."

"I do, too," Marovian said with feeling.

"There is only one way to protect that baby and we both know what it is," Priscilla added in a shaky tone. After a moment to get a bit more control, she continued, "I have been pleased to have you on my team. Good luck, Zeta."

Marovian's exotic eyes gleamed as she stood. "I'm glad you understand." She stepped up and hugged Priscilla.

Priscilla put her arm around her friend. "Let's tell the others. I'm sure they'll be mad at you for keeping this a secret and thrilled for you at the same time. You know they are going to want to throw you a going away party?"

Marovian, smiling happily, said, "I look forward to it."

As she stepped out, Priscilla sat down before leaning back in her chair as she tapped her lip for a long time in thought. *What a mess!*

Sighing, she woke up her secure computer terminal. Typing rapidly, she sent her request for communication.

Two minutes later, a direct link opened. Jack Deetz appeared. "What can I do for you now, Lieutenant?" he asked abruptly.

Priscilla smiled. "Not glad to see me, Jack?"

With a repressive frown, he growled, "I outrank you, Lieutenant, so keep it professional."

Priscilla grinned even larger. It felt good to let her hair down, even if only with a stuffed shirt like Jack Deetz. "But I'm navy, so it evens things."

Before he could get a full mad going, Priscilla held up a hand. "This is more than simply a social call. Zeta Marovian on my team is married." She paused while she watched the cogs turning and real, professional-level irritation begin to show on his face before going on. "She is also pregnant. And before you ask, she will not consent to a termination."

Deetz kept his mouth shut, a sure sign from her experience of his complete engagement in the problem. *What a good officer and a nice guy*, something she would probably never have an opportunity to tell him. He gave her the give-me-more hand sign.

"I think this could work out for the best for all concerned."

Deetz simply shook his head. "How, pray tell? You've been bugging me for months for another female Implacable with a communications background and I can't find one. There are only a few Implacables available at all, and now you need two I won't be able to find? Couldn't you use a weapons specialist or engineer? I can get you two of those tomorrow."

Priscilla shrugged. "They wouldn't fit our cover, so please keep looking. I hear good things come to those who wait."

Deetz snorted, "Not likely. Murphy is a close and dear friend, and he isn't inclined to do favors. So, how is this good news?"

Priscilla shook her head. "I didn't call it good news. I said it could work out for the best. If Zeta were transferred to camp headquarters with a commission from Fleet Headquarters to ensign from her cover rank of petty officer second, we would have top cover and she would be safe to have her baby if anything happened."

Deetz tapped on his keyboard before nodding. "She's *already* an ensign, correct?"

Priscilla nodded.

Thoughtfully, he went on, "A commendation and promotion to officer status for secret and unspecified outstanding actions would answer any snooping. Your cover unit does not have a slot for another officer, so that would explain her need to be transferred."

"Very good, sir. I'm impressed. It only took me fifteen minutes to come up with all that."

Deetz growled again. "Don't get smart with me, Lieutenant. I'm liable to come down there and then you'll be sorry."

Priscilla smiled again. "Ooh, I'm terrified. What do I need to do to get you to carry out that threat?"

Deetz sat back and smiled, too. "Wish I could, Priscilla. I think we'd have fun."

Priscilla's smile became wistful. "Me, too. Talk to you later. Sir."

Deetz signed off, "Deetz out."

Two minutes later, Maeve's head popped up in the middle of a sensitive operation: placing a bug remotely in one of the admin offices. "Everyone report to the mess," ordered Patel on the com. Looking at the screen, Maeve saw her bug sitting exactly where she had left it. She finished parking it where she wanted it, then locked things up. Walking toward the mess, she heard laughter and a bright gush of noise. Opening the door, she found her five companions sitting around the table all talking at the same time. She stood, stunned. She had never seen them this animated or even chatting so freely in all the months she'd known them. They were normally friendly, but that constituted the whole of their regular, feminine, social behavior. Why this? What had broken down the walls they all hid behind? Maeve watched, fascinated, as this team of dangerous, hard women went all gooey.

Zeta Marovian stood up and waved at Maeve. "Come sit by me!" she called excitedly. Maeve stepped around the table where Marovian grabbed her in a tight embrace and kissed her cheeks.

She's been crying! Maeve realized. Grabbing Marovian's arms, she demanded, "What's wrong?"

Blushing and laughing at the same time, Marovian said a bit huskily, "I'm married."

A suspicion hit Maeve. "You married that *special guy* and didn't invite us. I could kill you!"

"You're right, but I couldn't invite you. I had to keep it a secret."

"I'm so happy for you," Maeve said, enviously, and hugged her tightly again.

As they let go, Marovian absolutely glowed as she added, "There's one more thing: I'm pregnant!"

Maeve's hand flew to her mouth, stunned. "What fantastic news!"

Priscilla broke in, "Unfortunately, because of this situation, Zeta will be leaving our happy family and resuming her actual rank of ensign, although it will show up as a promotion when she reports to camp headquarters." Priscilla smiled at her mischievously. "Didn't want you to have to be a petty officer forever."

Zeta nodded. "That's a relief, actually. Hard to make ends meet on a petty officer's pay."

"No problem. We take care of our own." Again facing the others, she went on, "We'll all miss her, a lot, not least because we can't find anyone to replace her. Ships are constantly grabbing sections from this base, sometimes without even telling anyone they've done it. If somehow someone decides they want us, and I can't stop them, we can use her to get help from the admiral. So, making the best of this situation, she is being transferred now before it's too late."

Marovian nodded her head sadly. "I'm sorry, Maeve, but it's already a done deal. My baby comes first. I'll miss you, but we have to do it."

Erdogan hopped in at this point, "Great! The administrative stuff has been taken care of, so now for the important things. *How* did it happen?" Erdogan asked. "I thought you couldn't carry a baby to term?"

Priscilla shook her head. "This shouldn't have happened. I have heard a rumor those little computer nanite packages that the proctors receive could repair damage, but I never knew anyone personally who became pregnant after the treatments."

Marovian gave Priscilla a funny look before answering. "A while ago, for an assignment, I received a nanite treatment. This seems to be a lucky byproduct from that."

Erdogan looked puzzled. "So, if nanites can do such miracles, why don't we all have them?"

Marovian gave Priscilla a helpless look. Priscilla seemed to struggle internally before answering, "It has to do with a planet named Mitteldorf. Good climate, plenty of resources, but no one lives there now."

"Never heard of it," Erdogan said, but a look of horror began creeping over Mai Ling's face.

"Not many people have. Do you want to explain, Mai Ling?" Priscilla asked.

She shook her head violently, so Priscilla went on, "Several hundred years ago, the ruler of Mitteldorf, Long Duc, had trouble keeping his people in line. He had *laogai*, another name for gulags or reeducation camps, but the citizens of Mitteldorf wanted freedom. Their planet being close enough to the empire, they could see the difference between a dictatorship and a free government."

Taking a ragged breath, Mai Ling interrupted, "I'll tell the rest of the story, since my family lived there." Priscilla nodded, sitting back to let her take over. "Nanites were just coming into general use on Mitteldorf about that time and Long Duc knew about their health benefits, but his scientists also discovered that they could be programmed in special ways." Taking a deep breath, she went on, "He told everyone on Mitteldorf of the wonderful life they could have after receiving the treatments. He even promised that he would empty the *laogai* after everyone received the treatment because, with everyone healthy all the time, there would be no more problems. People lined up demanding treatment, almost everyone except a few who did not trust Long Duc. My family avoided the treatments," she said softly.

"Just as promised, everyone became completely healthy. The hospitals closed and things seemed to be great. Then my ancestors began to notice some odd coincidences. People who stood up to denounce Long Duc died from heart attacks, strokes, lots of things. People began to demand answers, so Long Duc told them. Gloatingly, he explained that anyone opposing him would die; the nanites would kill them. Long Duc had emptied the *laogai* only to make the whole planet a giant reeducation camp. The nanites had become the jailors of anyone who had received treatment."

As Mai Ling spoke in a quiet, almost dead voice, horror crept over Maeve. The very thought that someone would use her own body against her almost made her physically ill.

Mai Ling's eyes clouded as she continued, "People stormed the closed hospitals demanding to be cleansed of this plague, but no one knew how to remove nanites. Some found a way to turn the nanites off by using a high-energy archeon pulse at close range. Although it also caused some bodily damage, it did the job. Then they went after Long Duc. Those still carrying active nanites were ordered to kill the rebels. Many died refusing that order, killed by their own bodies. Finally, someone killed Long Duc but, by that time, Mitteldorf had become a slaughterhouse. My family fled early on, stowing away aboard an empire-bound cargo ship, but kept in contact as long as they could, watching as their friends and family disappeared. Few survived, but even they left Mitteldorf. The memories of all the atrocities were just too strong for anyone to want to stay."

Priscilla nodded. "Which is why nanites are only permitted for use inside the body in very special situations. The potential for abuse is too great." After a moment, she broke the somber mood by asking, "So, when are we going to meet Chad?"

Marovian shook her head. "I don't think that's such a good idea. He's such a good-looking guy all of you might try to steal him from me."

Everyone laughed. Erdogan, the plainest of the women in the team snorted, "I'm sure that'll happen." All the others laughed again. "Tell us about him. What's his rank?"

"He's a warrant officer," Priscilla interjected.

"Lucky," Patel said. "He can hang out with officer women as well as enlisted, if the powers-that-be don't watch too closely. Does he know you outrank him?" she demanded.

"Honey," Marovian drawled, "I've always outranked him from the day we were married. That's the way marriage works!" That brought another gale of laughter.

Maeve's heart glowed, grateful to be included and enjoying Zeta's happiness together with these women who were becoming her friends. As for the light she saw in Zeta's eyes, she crossed her fingers. *Someday, I'll have a guy I can feel like that about.*

MAEVE STOOD ADMIRING HERSELF IN front of her full-length mirror. The whites fit perfectly, and the electronics mate, first class rank looked just right on her sleeve. Being in the navy, even just pretend, meant that they had to pay her to protect her cover story. Almost fourteen, birthday still eight weeks away, and not allowed to do much of anything other than study and exercise, money had been piling up, so she had splurged on the mirror. It could extend from a single view to full circle, letting her see herself from every angle. Frowning, she considered her hair, deciding it was still too short. Facing the mirror and standing straight, she saluted. Perfect! She felt ready for the Petty Officer Review Board. Everything fit just right, and she looked exactly as an electronics mate should.

Continuing her self-appraisal, she examined her hemline to make sure the added length, made by taking out the hem, didn't show. In the last six months, she had gained an inch of height, nearing what she suspected would be her ultimate elevation.

Satisfied, she frowned at the other changes that caused concern. If she kept filling out up top and at the hips, she would definitely have to buy a new set of whites. But, all in all, that would be all right, too. The whistles directed her way on their runs were becoming more frequent. *Not a bad thing.*

Stepping into the hall, she came face-to-face with a worried Patel. "You may not be going to the board after all," Patel said bluntly.

"Why?" Maeve demanded. If she were a petty officer, she could leave the building and hang around with the other girls, maybe meet a nice guy like Marovian had.

"Come with me," Patel ordered without explaining, pivoting toward the control room.

From inside the room, she heard Priscilla speaking on the com with Marovian at her new office in Base Security. "Maeve's here now. Do you want to tell her what you just learned?"

"Your sister Vivian just flew into the base with Deputy Base Commander Pax Eckert."

Maeve's heart stopped for a moment. Vivian wouldn't try to kill her like Morgain had, nor hurt her like that sadist Nimue. But she could be bad news, anyway, not least of all to the poor idiots she twisted around her little finger for her own amusement.

"Isn't the commodore married?" Priscilla asked.

Marovian sounded distinctly uncomfortable when she answered, "Yes, he is. I know his wife and she is a good sort. She doesn't deserve this."

Maeve's concern spiked as Priscilla bit her lip. After a moment, Priscilla suggested, "Maybe someone could encourage Vivian to move on to greener pastures."

Maeve decided she needed to speak up since she had grown up with Vivian. "I know her. She won't go unless she's good and ready."

"What if some ladies visit her and suggest she won't like it here?" asked Patel.

Maeve shook her head. "She normally stays until the poor man she is dangling on her string has made a complete fool of himself. I can't think what else could move her along."

Marovian offered, "If it were my husband, and I know Chad would never do anything like this but, if it were, I'd go with him and we'd both let her know she's unwelcome. After which, he'd sleep on the couch for a month!"

"Chad would be a fool to do anything like that," Patel said.

"Men are fools more often than we'd like," Priscilla said softly, "but I think Zeta is right. And since you came up with the idea, Ensign, you get to make it happen."

"What?" Marovian squawked.

"I said, you go talk to the deputy base commander's wife about Vivian. Then the two of you go to speak with him. I hope he's not so far in that an angry wife won't get his attention. If necessary, we can get Admiral Davies involved. I'll let Asroc know you may be calling. Report back in an hour to tell me how it goes. I need to decide whether I am pulling Maeve from the board. We don't want her running into Vivian in the headquarters area accidentally. If I have to pull her and she misses this board, the rules are that she won't be able to try again for another six months. With all the grief I'm getting from admin about being a critical petty officer short, I'd rather not go through that for half a year more."

Patel gave her an amused smile. "Plus, it will be embarrassing to explain why she couldn't make it after you put so much pressure on the board to interview her early in the first place."

"That, too," Priscilla agreed.

The possibility of a delay, and especially its cause, turned Maeve's stomach. She had studied hard for the board and now her sister might be taking it away from her. That Vivian hadn't done this intentionally, to her at least, made no difference. She had messed things up just by being here.

Anger began to course through her veins, which, surprisingly, made her feel better. She wished Priscilla would let her reason with Vivian. That short, sharp conversation would be eminently satisfying, although the galaxy would then soon know her whereabouts.

Taking off her uniform coat to keep it crisp, she stormed around her room in her dress shirt and slacks before opening her study guide. After reading that for a while, she realized she couldn't remember a single thing she had reviewed in the last ten minutes. The loss of this opportunity suddenly mattered more than she had realized. Being promoted would be a recognition of her hard work, of course, but it meant even more.

Every day the team spent ten minutes devoted to one of the points of the Creed and its importance. Judgment, justice, integrity, protection of the weak, sacrifice, virtue, and a willingness to defend the empire to the death had become more than just words she had repeated in school. As her protection team taught her each of the points of the oath; they had personalized and illustrated each one vividly by talking about people they'd known, situations they'd seen. This way of teaching had brought each part of the oath alive for her, while demonstrating how each part fit together as an essential support to the freedom of the citizens of the empire. It now motivated her to want to be a petty officer for real, so she could fight for them also. She found herself wishing that she could do more than be stuck here in hiding.

A rap at her door brought Maeve's head up. "Come in."

"Let's go," Patel said. "It's all fixed."

Maeve grabbed her coat, buttoning it quickly. "What happened?"

"Hurry, girl!" Patel shooed her down the hall. "It takes ten minutes to get there and we only have seven." She began to trot for the car. Maeve did too, book under her arm.

Jumping into the passenger seat, Patel already had the car in gear and moving before Maeve could even buckle her seat belt. "So, what happened?" she demanded, the streets flying by as Patel drove three times the speed limit. Patel blew through a stop sign without even slowing down, something the Shore Patrol really hated.

Patel spoke in a clipped, amused tone, "Apparently, the deputy base commander's wife is a real terror. Zeta had barely started explaining, when the woman, a tiny thing just a mite under five foot, whisked Zeta out the door and into her car. Ten minutes later, they reached the commodore's office and Zeta sat in the waiting room while his wife laid down the law. Zeta said she could hear them yelling through the soundproofing. After a solid ten plus minutes, they, all three of them, went to visit Vivian in guest quarters. Vivian acted nice as could be, shook the commodore's wife's hand, kissed him on the cheek very primly, then gave Zeta a funny look. Turning to the commodore's wife she said something like, *It must be nice to have such good friends watching out for you.* Then, she said she'd be leaving shortly."

Maeve took a deep breath. *Wow!* She'd never have believed Vivian would be so civilized about being chucked out. Seeing where they now were, she realized they would be stopping in seconds. Butterflies flitted inside her middle. An hour ago, she'd been furious at the idea that she might not get to do this and now she wished to be somewhere, anywhere, else.

Patel screeched to a stop, then patted Maeve's hand as she unbuckled her own seat belt.

"Knock 'em dead, honey. Erdogan is on overwatch. Mai Ling arrived at the building before us."

Maeve smiled, or tried to, but she felt scared to death. It steadied her a bit that these women she admired had such confidence in her. Stepping out, she straightened her blouse, then centered her cap as Patel came around the car. Together, they marched in step toward the entryway. As they headed up the path to the huge, white building, a limo pulled past with a flawless brunette sitting in the back. Maeve didn't notice her sister leaving the base.

Recruiting Circular 1 January 3400

Imperial Fleet Academy Entrance Standards
Prime Sector Academy
Entrance requirements circular as of January 1, 3300

- Passage of exam with 125 of 150.
- Age limits: Sixteen with superior marks of 140 or above.
- Eighteen with standard marks.
- Imperial family: Thirteen with superior marks; Sixteen with standard marks.
- Must pass standard mental and physical examination for fleet service. No exemptions.

FOR THE EMPEROR, CHARLES ROLAND

Concurrence by Emperors Raul, Andrik, Cezar, Benjamin, Esau Emanuel, Cyrus

7

Shanghaied

Camp Y, Beacon
0326 Local/2126 24 January 3469

MAEVE UCH ROBERT SHOT BOLT UPRIGHT IN her bed, eyes wide but not really awake. *Alarm? What time is it?* Leaning over to look at her clock, it read 3:26. Irritation blossomed on top of her sleepy frame of mind. "What is going on? Who set my alarm for this terrible hour?" she grumbled.

The sound of the alarm filled the air again. *That's coming from the hallway! It's the emergency alert, not my alarm! What a time for a drill!* Grumbling wouldn't help, so she jumped from her bed, throwing on her work uniform. She did allow herself the satisfaction of thinking *This is dumb! I don't want to play navy right now!* Her mental rebellion made her feel a teensy bit better.

The alarm sounded three more times during the time it took her to throw on her clothes. Dashing for the mess, she hoped she would be there in time. SOP gave her sixty seconds at night to get dressed and into the mess for assignment when not on duty. As she entered, she saw Petty Officer Bonnie Patel, tensely watching the security repeater. In fact, they were alone in the mess. "Where're the others?" Maeve asked.

Patel just shook her head as she concentrated. Maeve stepped into range of the screen and her stomach dropped. The screen showed a heavily armed detail at the gate, led by a commander. He looked ruggedly handsome and Maeve hated him from the moment she saw him.

At the moment, he seemed quite put out. "As I said, open up or we're blowing down the door. Your unit has thirty minutes to be on the transport or you're going in front of a court-martial. That won't be here either. It'll be on my ship. So get in gear and start moving!"

It amused her to see his obvious irritation, waving a tablet carrying some sort of official document. "Your orders from Base Administration are here! You must have received them and claiming you never received them doesn't change anything. Now open this gate!"

What Maeve heard next shocked her. "Just a minute, Commander," Lieutenant Priscilla Jenks said in a calm tone over the intercom. "This is a secure facility, as I tried to explain to you when you first rang. I can't let just anybody waving orders in without proper clearance. Base admin doesn't have authority to send us anywhere, which they know very well. This unit is directly under Prime Sector Fleet Communications Security Office. We aren't going anywhere without their authorization." Priscilla's tone became colder at this point, "Plus, I wouldn't attempt to break in. You'd be leaving with fewer men than you started with, I assure you. The shield is up and we're not bringing it down without proper clearance."

The commander made a visible effort to throttle in his anger. "We are under orders for this mission directly from Prime Fleet Intel. We are authorized to pick up any unit or personnel we need to carry out our mission. But fine, have it your way. Regardless, be ready ASAP. Your orders will be routed here within minutes." The commander then turned away from the gate and began directing his men, including three battle suits, to surround the building, weapons facing in. The battle suits, almost seven feet of faceless metallic menace, scared Maeve as she watched their mechanical movements take them to three points around the perimeter. They each carried a heavy weapon, two laser cannons, and a huge machine gun.

Priscilla walked in a minute later, her uniform having that comfortable mid-shift look it got after six hours or so on duty. She didn't look as calm or collected, though, as she had sounded speaking with the commander.

"Get packed, shower, everything you need to do to move out," she clipped out in an angry tone. "Admiral Davies is off-planet, and I can't get the archeon operator to contact his flagship. Until we get this straightened out, we'll just have to go along with it. Thank goodness we have Zeta to iron things out later."

Patel gave her a raised eyebrow. "When they tried to get us assigned to them, shouldn't a flag have stopped them?"

Priscilla frowned. "Our individual records are flagged, which would normally stop this kind of nonsense, but our unit cover, 3-77, is not protected. Apparently, this Commander Bhat asked personnel for a complete communications security unit and we were the only one nobody had a reason to keep!" Priscilla really appeared exasperated at this point. "Of course nobody wants our unit; we set it up this way to keep a low profile! Now it's come back to bite us in the behind."

Maeve felt a burning desire to know one thing. "I thought our shield and automatic defenses would keep out intruders until Admiral Davies could send reinforcements."

Priscilla shook her head. "These people are supposed to be on our side and can get the codes to disable our defenses. Something smells, though, them showing up in the middle of the night like this. That could be just because Fleet HQ is on the other side of the world and they're getting a late start from there, but it feels very odd. However, the last thing we want is people asking questions. If we arm the defenses, besides being somewhat pointless under the circumstances and possibly killing people on our side, there will be lots and lots of questions asked by people in official positions who will be entitled to answers. Even if Admiral Davies tells everyone to forget it, the rumors of a big fight here on Camp Y will get around to people we don't want knowing about us." Biting her lip, she sighed. "Let's get packed, we only have thirty minutes or so. Move it!"

Maeve ran to her room, her home for the last seven plus months. It looked pretty bare, not much to see, light yellow painted walls, closet door of white pine with her mirror hanging from it, a mirror she couldn't possibly pack, some pictures of her and her friends, the women in the unit. Tears began to roll down her cheeks; she couldn't help it or stop them, as she stood frozen in the middle of her room. The first four or five months, the women who had become her friends had kept her so busy she didn't have much time for nightmares, though they had come anyway. Then, after her promotion to petty officer, third, things had settled into a more normal routine. Still learning, she now worked on lots of things other than electronics and communications. A sob burst out. She wouldn't be here for Zeta's baby!

Petty Officer Marva Erdogan stuck her head in the door. "Hustle, Maeve. We need to move out!" Maeve didn't answer, didn't even turn around. Erdogan stopped in her tracks, then stepped into the room. Maeve's tears were still silently falling, arms loose at her sides. She couldn't face this!

Arms slid around her from behind, a soft voice in her ear, "It'll be okay, honey. Want to talk about it?"

Maeve shook her head, brought her hands up to squeeze her friend's arms in gratitude before letting go. She wiped her eyes with her sleeve. "I must look terrible," she said.

Erdogan gave her a crooked smile. "I've seen worse. Let's get you packed and then you need to take a shower." Maeve nodded gratefully. Together they quickly stowed Maeve's official things. Marva gave her a slap on the shoulder. "Now, get going, girl! We need to hurry."

Racing to the shower and, stepping into one of the two stalls, she began to analyze the situation the way her father had taught her. Her first thought quickly reached the point that somebody needed the special skills of her unit. It hit her; she could use her new skills to help stop the rebellion for real. Wow! She began to get excited. Finished, she raced back and threw her clothes on. She grabbed her bags and headed for the front door. She could even feel a smile beginning to tug at the corners of her mouth. This might be fun, although Admiral Davies would likely have them back here as soon as he found out about this mix-up.

Priscilla looked the team over. Hitting the com, she spoke to the only one of the team not there, Petty Officer Qi Mai Ling. "Anything from the admiral?"

"Negative."

"Disable the special security systems we installed and the defense net."

"Aye, aye." After a pause, "I'm on my way."

Maeve noticed that even Mai Ling's bags stood ready by the door. Priscilla shouldered her space bag. "Let's go. Maeve in the middle. Everyone, keep your weapon hand free." Maeve's incipient smile disappeared as Priscilla's tension hit home. She had misjudged things in her excitement. A potentially dangerous situation and her personal pistol lay at the bottom of her space bag! If shooting started, she'd be helpless! What had she been thinking? Her embarrassment increased her nervousness.

As a tight group, they marched out the door and through the gate. Stepping into a light fog, she saw the commander and his men waiting by a couple of trucks. "Get on!" ordered the commander. His name tag read *Paul Bhat*. Maeve knew she'd never forget him.

She swung her space bag up easily, before preparing to jump in herself. All that daily running and exercise made this easy, which meant she wouldn't look stupid in front of Bhat's men. She knew she looked and acted like a spacer. As she jumped up, one of the men whistled at her. She felt embarrassed.

On a run, the whistles weren't really personal because no one actually knew anyone else. Here, it felt different, more intimate, an invasion of her privacy. The man whistling at her, a big man wearing a Shore Patrol brassard, gave her the creeps with his stare. She waited for someone to do something about this clear act of harassment, an action strictly against regulations. The commander didn't say anything, however. Maeve began to feel even more nervous and uneasy. This might not be as much fun as she supposed. If these men felt they could act like this with the commander around, they would be worse on their own.

There were some things worse than death, Maeve decided deep in her gut, and she'd die before she let any of these men touch her. She had barely taken her seat when the truck jolted into gear, heading toward the spaceport, away from her home since that dreadful day. Suddenly tears welled up, threatening to break out again. *No, I won't let these cretins see me cry.*

Patel jogged her elbow. "Can you pretend to be a spacey nerd?" she whispered.

"Huh?" Maeve, wallowing in her misery, didn't understand. What did Patel want her to do?

"I asked, is there anyone you know that is a super nerd? It may be a very effective cover."

"I suppose so," Maeve answered.

"Getting opponents to underestimate you can be very useful." Patel smiled, teeth barely visible in the passing streetlamps. "Think of that girl in admin, the one without a clue. Whenever you asked her a question or tried to talk to her, she seemed to be in her own world. A lot of times she didn't even answer the question you asked because she obviously lived in her own thoughts. Smart but clueless. I don't think you can act like an airhead and ditsy, so distracted will have to do."

The clear image of the chubby, little blonde came to mind. Even with the protection of Admiral Davies, from time-to-time they still needed to iron out admin problems in person. On the couple of trips Maeve had taken to Base Personnel, the blonde petty officer, who had ignored them while concentrating on her own tasks, had really annoyed her. She apparently knew her business but couldn't be bothered with little things . . . like people.

Back at school, she and her friends, Kai, Mary, Adia, and Nikki, had been pretty cruel among themselves, actually, imitating women in the office, lunch ladies, other girls, and even teachers. None of it had been malicious or done publicly, even though, as daughters of high-ranking court and naval officers, Maeve knew they could have gotten away with it. Some of the other girls with important parents had treated the staff in a truly horrid manner and nothing had happened to them, but neither Maeve nor her friends had enjoyed making others miserable; imitating had just been funny. Plus, after all her experiences with three sisters who excelled in hurting other people, she never wanted to be like them.

As a little girl, she had experienced good and bad times with the other three, though Vivian had been her favorite because she read Maeve stories and helped Mom with her hair. Then they had gone to Grandmother's for an extended visit, almost a year with the travel.

Each had returned from Grandmother's on Green Gardens messed up. Morgain, of course, had been bossy before she left, but she really became pushy after coming home, as well as vindicative if she didn't get her way. Vivian had simply become self-absorbed and kind of wild, ignoring Maeve most of the time, but Nimue? She shuddered as she thought of her next oldest sister. She didn't want to be like any of them, but especially Nimue, who hurt people for fun. It was no wonder that Dad sent them away, one by one, after they returned. Regardless, yes, she thought she could manage copying the little petty officer.

"Won't being annoying make people notice me?" she hissed back.

Patel shook her head. "Just the opposite. If people think they know your type, and it's non-threatening, you'll become part of the background. They'll ignore you, especially if they think you're someone who deals better with machines and problems than people."

Maeve nodded and sat back, pondering. Priscilla leaned across from her seat, a deadly serious look on her face. She ordered, "Start now, Maeve. Remember, no lapses. This is who you are from now on."

Considering for a moment more, she decided her role model would feel unhappy and try to figure out why her perfect little world had been upset. It helped that she felt a bit that way naturally this morning, so she took a deep breath before diving in. "Lieutenant," she whined loudly to Priscilla, "why did you get me out of bed? I don't have duty until 0800. I had those two installations scheduled for this morning. When will I get those done?"

Priscilla smiled briefly before putting a stern expression on her face. "At ease, Ellyllyon. We've been ordered to provide secure communications for the cruiser *Bring It* for a mission to Thirteenth Sector. You'll get sleep when the rest of us do. Erdogan stood watch till midnight and you don't see her complaining. As for the items scheduled to support Camp Y, they'll have to figure it out on their own."

"Humph. I hope they do it right, then. I don't like fixing other people's mistakes." Maeve went on, whining even louder before pouting. From across the truck Mai Ling rolled her eyes but smiled. Maeve jumped into her role with relish. "Remember the last time? It took me *two hours* to straighten things out."

Fifteen minutes later they rolled through the shuttle port gate. As soon as they stopped, they were ordered to get off. Jumping down from the truck, their eyes were momentarily blinded by the light pooling at the foot of a large shuttle. Men and women milled around, loading gear.

A burly man with an SP brassard on his arm loomed out of the darkness. "Hustle it up, gals. We need to get going and you're the last group here." He seemed to have an evil cast to his features. "Captain doesn't like anyone holding him up." Shocked, Maeve couldn't believe anyone would speak to an officer that way, much less Priscilla. She watched as Priscilla's eyes became slits, simply staring the man silently down. A minute passed. Finally the bully came to attention, saluting. "Ma'am."

"Petty Officer Yung," she barely acknowledged, returning the salute negligently.

"I'll have your bags stowed," he offered quickly.

"Thank you. Let's go, ladies," she ordered.

"But their bags," Yung pointed out.

"Yes?" Priscilla asked dangerously. Maeve recognized the tone; Priscilla had loaded up to really let this guy have it.

Yung snapped to attention. "Yes, ma'am!" Turning to some of the ground crew. "You three," he yelled, "get these ladies' bags stowed. Now!" He stormed off, exercising his authority on other people around the shuttle.

The team surrounded Maeve at the entryway while Priscilla watched their bags being stowed. Finally, they followed her aboard. Priscilla pointed to two rows toward the rear on the left with Maeve in the window seat, or what would have been a window seat if there had been windows on this shuttle. Priscilla shared the row with her, leaving an empty seat between them, the other three sitting directly behind. Priscilla dropped her shoulder bag with her personal things on the empty middle seat. A couple of Commander Bhat's men approached them as if to sit in the empty seat, but Priscilla's cold, cutting stare kept the seat free despite the shuttle being fairly full. After the whistle, Maeve didn't want to sit anywhere near these guys. Commander Bhat apparently had boarded the shuttle as soon as they'd arrived, because he now stepped into the cabin from the pilot's compartment up front. Maeve felt him eyeing the situation in the cabin, blank-faced, before closing the door with a clang behind him. She realized with a shudder that whatever else Bhat might be, he didn't appear stupid.

Maeve didn't feel like chattering any more. Fortunately, Priscilla sitting beside her gave her a built-in military excuse for silence.

CNS *Pechnaya*, Taad Ka Ped, Ninth Sector
0650 BBMT 8 November 3469

THE SWIRLING CLOUDS OF THE planet Maidan intrigued Morgain uch Robert. Her supernova, *Pechnaya*, rode majestically above the planet she could kill if she took a fancy to the idea.

Which she just might. "Commissioner Kaur, you must decide whether you will preside over a living planet that forms part of Ninth Sector under my leadership . . . or a dead one."

Actually, whatever he decided didn't matter, when Task Force 9-4 showed up in a few hours to rescue him, she would snap it up and include the survivors in her fleet. Frankly, the constant ambushes and small-scale actions were beginning to erode her strength and she needed to rebuild Task Force 9-1. She had chosen the Taad Ka Ped system to draw in the enemy for two reasons. First, TF 9-4 had become much weaker than hers from fighting with Eighth Sector units. Second, 9-4 headquartered much of its resupply activities on Maidan and couldn't afford to lose it, or so her staff thought.

Ba Ng called from the bridge. *"Many ships entering system, Your Highness."*

She smiled. "Very good. Let's go greet our new acquisitions."

Ba Ng stayed on as she finished. *"In addition to the nova* Incendiary *of 9-4 we have identified nova* Prairie Fire *from TF 9-3. If the sensors are correct, we are outnumbered. Badly. We may not break even if we follow through with the ambush plan."*

Morgain wanted to punish Commander Ng, but her mind coolly calculated that he simply spoke the truth. She could punish someone, however. Calling the captain, she demanded, "Hit all of the TF 9-4 facilities with kinetics."

A soft cough behind her caught her attention. Her guest spoke. "If you do this, they're likely to combine with some other units outside the sector and strike all of your major planets."

He didn't say another word, but he didn't have to. Morgain wished what he said could be ignored, but until she ruled the Core, she would have to wait for vengeance in some cases. She could do one thing, however, for that rat Commissioner Kaur, who must have called for help and now must be laughing at her.

Opening her line to the bridge, she looked at her captain. "One strike only, Captain. The archeonA facility. When I come back, I don't want anything interfering with my finding Kaur and treating him in a way he richly deserves."

"Aye, Your Highness."

Morgain faced her guest. "As difficult as it is to find spare parts for our archeon facilities, they shouldn't be able to rebuild this one anytime soon. Satisfied?"

Her guest smiled thinly. "It makes the point without starting an all-out war of extinction." He then stepped toward her.

Still disgruntled, she let him work her out of her bad mood in private.

Commander's Belle, Delross System, Fourth Sector
2140 BBMT 6 February 3470

FORMER MARINE LIEUTENANT AUSTIN CARHART SAT SWINGING BACK and forth in his command chair as he observed the bridge activity. Normally he preferred to leave operating the ship to Captain Argus Steed, but not today, too much rode on this transaction. Frankly, he needed the money to continue operating at a high level while he looked for Hugh Cascade.

From the sensor station came the report, "Freighter coming in slow and easy. No signature of weapon activation, standard civilian shield. All other shipping in-system over an hour away."

"Thank you. Shield to maximum, just in case Mister Innocent has a friend around we haven't seen. Power up weapons."

"Aye, sir," came from lasers, missiles, and guns, as well as shields. Moments later all reported readiness.

Carhart smiled to himself. Truth be told, he loved action and probably had taken on this commission as much to break the boredom of selling information to the highest bidder as for the money. That the deal would take place in his own back yard, a mere three hundred light-years from his base at Forth Sector's capital, had made it irresistible . . . and possibly a trap.

Glancing over at Argus Steed standing near the weapons panel, he smiled to himself. Steed hadn't said anything after Carhart decided to personally take the job of delivering this Petal Detox vaccine to Levan, but he had been very vocal about this being not a good idea before that. Steed still didn't like it, even with the transfer being made in vacuum to avoid contamination from the virus that currently ravaged Levan.

Which was one of the other reasons why they were taking payment in the rare earths Levan specialized in out here; no one wanted to catch the disease, which made the victim go rapidly senile before the body completely shut down. An organ at a time.

Steed faced him. "Cargo team ready."

Carhart asked, unnecessarily, "Decon ready to go?"

Steed nodded.

The freighter pulled up on their port side just outside shield limit.

"Keep shields up, move package to limit, directly in front of port guns."

"Aye." Carhart watched as the cargo team performed flawlessly. Something they had practiced before arriving several times. Flying to Second Sector for the vaccine had given them plenty of time to go over all contingencies.

"Freighter dropping shield." Carhart didn't bother to acknowledge. The next few minutes would determine whether this very expensive operation had been worth it or not. Or if he had wasted his time and money. And maybe his life.

He didn't bother pretending to be disinterested any longer but leaned forward. A very large palette moved out of the freighter's cargo bay, guided by drones.

"Scan."

"Package contains only the refined products specified."

Carhart gave Steed an I-told-you-so look.

"Drones are armed, though not active at this moment. They are warmed up, however."

Steed gave him the same look back.

Carhart sighed and leaned back. "You were right, Captain. Apparently, these people can't be trusted."

Steed allowed himself to say, "Would you be, with that bug down there? Likely want to know where we bought the antidote and plan on using the *Belle* to get more."

"And infect a whole sector doing it if they're not careful. The same reason no one would bring them the vaccine in the first place: they aren't terribly trustworthy people." Sitting back up, Carhart ordered, "Cargo team, back to the ship, leave package in place. Lasers, begin picking off drones." One blew up a moment later.

Raising an eyebrow at his com tech, she opened a channel without a word. Good to have professional people working for him. "Freighter *Tagus 1204*, this is Peer Drunnan. You just broke our deal, which makes me very unhappy." As he spoke, the weapons screen showed a second drone explode.

"What are you doing?" cried a woman hysterically on his com screen. "We have your payment as requested."

"And armed drones bringing it with weapons warmed up. Here's what we're going to do, double the price. Palette will be placed next to first, drones withdrawn. You take vaccine with your drones after we move the shield back. Any funny business. We blow up the vaccine and then you. Questions?"

The woman agreed. "Okay, but we'll have to go back to Levan for more refined product."

Carhart glanced toward Steed, now standing at the sensor panel. "They're loaded, sir. Probably on their way out-system on a delivery run after getting the vaccine."

Carhart hadn't bothered to mute the channel as Steed reported. The woman's face hardened. Apparently, the panic she had exhibited before had been an act. They had planned the whole thing. The likelihood of this being a trap grew exponentially the longer this took.

"You have ten minutes. And whoever you have coming in on ballistic orbit, tell them to stop before I stop them. Permanently." Carhart sat back to watch the reaction.

The woman now looked haughty. "You can't escape, you're surrounded. Our defense forces are moving in as we speak. Surrender or we'll destroy you and your fast freighter."

Stupid and incompetent, bad combination. "Just to refresh your memory, we set this rendezvous point after you left Levan. None of your ships are close enough to help you."

She smiled again. "You think." Two combat shuttles came around the freighter as she spoke. The sensor tech spoke now. "Bogies. Armed and hot. Must have been hiding in ship's shadow."

Carhart didn't even need to say anything. From the weapons panel the tech reported, "Missile one away, two away, reloading. Lasers taking on shuttles directly."

"Bogies firing. Shields holding," Sensor tech reported, "Bogies down."

Almost immediately, the weapons tech added, "Freighter had laser mounts hidden on skin, lasers and guns firing. Penetrating freighter shield."

The ballet concluded with the sensor tech. "Air escaping from freighter. No evident damage to propulsion."

The freighter came back cold as ice. "You can't get away with this."

Carhart smiled mildly. "Another palette, now. Otherwise I will order your propulsion targeted and then come take what I want. And by the way, that little misdirection play of telling me I'm surrounded when I know there is no one nearby, very amateur. Next time you try to rob someone, be a bit more creative."

"Who are you?" she demanded. "You're not a merchant."

Carhart simply nodded. After a moment, he added, "After your little stunt, you have eight minutes to get me my payment." Looking at the com tech, she cut the transmission without another word.

Leaving the bridge, Carhart felt surprisingly deflated. If things had gone as planned, no combat would have happened. He had expected something to happen, however, meaning he had been prepared for something like the shuttles. In fact, he had been impressed by the way they tried to carry out their hijack, it actually being a smart play on their part. It would have worked if he hadn't suspected such an attempt. Regardless, he could already feel himself coming down from the combat high. And he had unending paperwork to take care of now that the fun was over.

Worse, a little voice in the back of his head wondered if he were wasting his life chasing something he could never have. He hadn't gotten any closer to taking over the empire than when he started after Deft. He shook his head, firmly ignoring the voice. He could and would be the power behind the throne.

MANUAL FOR COURTS-MARTIAL (MCM)

Revised 3277 by Order of the Emperor, Charles Roland

Treason

Definition: Whether intentional or inadvertent, giving aid and comfort to the enemy.

Penalty: Death

8

Nightmare

Secure Communications Section, CNS *Bring It*, Sector Thirteen
1105 BBMT 09 March 3471

DARKNESS ENVELOPED LIEUTENANT PRISCILLA JENKS, stifling her, making it almost impossible to breath. Over the two years since leaving Camp Y, the walls of the cruiser *Bring It* had slowly closed in on her, becoming more and more like a prison every day. One of the few places she felt free, where she could make a difference for the empire, had been here in her tiny Signals section area, a cubicle barely large enough for two people to work in comfortably and three could squeeze into at a pinch. But as she sat here, dread welled up in her heart. What had she done?

She made an unobtrusive hand gesture toward Petty Officer Bonnie Patel. With barely a nod, Patel's hands continued coding and decoding traffic as she hit a switch under her console with her knee. Carefully turning her chair so she wouldn't bump into the two extra women crowded into the cubicle, Patel raised an eyebrow. Priscilla knew a five-minute loop now fed the ship's internal security cams, showing Patel hard at work instead of broadcasting their meeting.

Priscilla looked at each of her women carefully. She never worried any more what her team saw when they looked at her. The last few months had honed down her features, sunken her cheeks. When she had come aboard two years before, Captain Hamilton Pogue had given her responsibility not only for this Signals section, but all of the internal electronics maintenance on *Bring It*, which had suited her fine.

Dedicated and hardworking, now she wished she didn't have

all the responsibility, not since *Bring It* had rendezvoused off Parker's World with the messenger sloop *The Pleasance*. What she knew now, she wanted to forget but couldn't. It haunted her sleep, hiding just behind her eyes, ready to pounce at any moment.

It had seemed like a routine rendezvous with *The Pleasance*, really. After Priscilla's team had first come aboard, they had, just like at Camp Y, installed their own very special security system to monitor every part of the ship in order to protect Maeve uch Robert. As a result, she knew way too much about this flying purgatory. She hated what she knew about Pogue personally. The man treated the women of his crew like his personal harem. But knowing had been a blessing because, forewarned being forearmed, it had enabled her to keep herself and the other women under her command out of his path. That allowed them to do their job, or what they believed to be their job. At least until that fateful rendezvous.

Priscilla shuddered. She needed to concentrate, undo what they had done. Up until Parker's World, Priscilla had believed that Pogue had been gathering intel for the empire by poking his nose into every important system in the sector. That had created a problem for Pogue as *Bring It* snuck around. He needed a way to pass on what he discovered. However, only having a cruiser, he didn't have an archeonA communications system, so all message traffic to recipients more than a few light-years away needed to be by courier.

At Parker's World, as Priscilla monitored the captain's cabin, something she hated to do because of the disgusting things that went on there, she had been surprised to see Pogue receive a coded message on a private frequency, one Priscilla hadn't even known about. Curious, she had copied the message and given it to Petty Officer Qi Mai Ling for decoding. Two hours later, Mai Ling had come back in shock. The message had come from Vice Admiral Traynor, the rebel commander of the sector and former deputy commander of Thirteenth Fleet, thanking Pogue for the information that had allowed him to crush Task Group 13-5 a month before.

Although bad enough, Traynor had then expressed special congratulations to Pogue for his Signals group breaking the loyal task group's private code, making the victory possible. Aghast, Priscilla knew she and her team bore direct, personal responsibility for the deaths of all those men and women fighting to maintain the empire. She couldn't forgive herself, despite not knowing, nor having any way of knowing, what Pogue had intended to do with the broken code. It didn't matter, those deaths were on her soul, their blood on her hands.

Maeve slipped around from behind her. "Sorry I'm late."

Priscilla nodded. They were all here. From habit, she asked, "Status?"

Mai Ling, sitting at the second console, keyed in a request. "Captain Pogue managed to talk another ship into joining his private flotilla."

Priscilla nodded. "Have we confirmed whether the information we've gathered about loyal forces has gone off to Vice Admiral Traynor?"

Erdogan's eyes were deeply hollowed. "As much as I can be sure. Captain Pogue guards his private communications very carefully."

Patel nodded. "You wanted me to verify the loyalty of the various ships Pogue has encouraged to join his little fleet. I can now confirm that Pogue has not changed the command group of the rebel cruisers or other ships that claim to have changed sides. They include the cruisers *Gatsby* and *Smyrna*. As for the *Yangtse*, which had been loyalist, he sent over a couple of his officers to support them. Its former captain and XO are now dead. I have a copy of his private message traffic to the new captain. It is also now commanded by rebels."

Two years wasted. No, worse than wasted. Originally, they had hoped Davies would get them back to Camp Y or somewhere else safe. After the admiral had let them know he didn't see any way to return them to Beacon quietly, they threw themselves into the work to help save Thirteenth Sector. With all their hard work, they hadn't understood how the loyalists kept suffering one disaster after another. But despite their best efforts, a task group here and a task force there kept losing fighting ships, steadily moving the advantage toward the rebels. Now they knew why. They had been helping the wrong side. Priscilla shook her bleak thoughts away. *Focus.* "Okay. We can do something about this. First, Maeve and Mai Ling now belong to the electronics maintenance unit."

"No!" Maeve moaned, "Why?"

"We are about to do some very dangerous things to turn the situation around and you have to be out of the line of fire. Plus, you two are the backup plan if this doesn't work. I'll transfer in two of Pogue's guys, see if we can blame them."

"I want to help!" Maeve demanded.

Priscilla felt both proud and exasperated. A good kid, at sixteen Maeve still had trouble on occasion passing for over eighteen but, since everyone on *Bring It* knew her age, no problem. *Why did she have to be so dedicated? Heirs are supposed to act like this, but really! Couldn't she be normal at least once in a while?*

Maeve didn't know, even now, the secret of her being an heir, although she acted like one in every way. Priscilla eyed her, waiting for her to back down, Maeve simply smiled back, waiting. That girl really had a most disagreeable habit of doing her own thing. *Teenagers!* "You can try the waiting game on me, but it won't work. We'll keep you informed, but you *are* going!"

"Yes, Mother," Maeve answered nasally, obviously unhappy. If Maeve only knew how much Priscilla wanted to be her mother for real. The way things were going, she'd never even have a chance to get her safely back to the admiral, much less have that kind of relationship. She realized she had lost focus. *Keep it together!*

"After we move you two, we are going to reverse the trap. Vice Admiral Traynor thinks our intel is letting him prepare for Commodore Bogart. Maybe with our help Bogart can cut him down to size."

"Where?" Patel asked.

"Vistula Reach."

"When are you planning for us to send out the corrupted data to Traynor and the real thing to Bogart?" Patel asked.

"Now. It's time. I'll set it up."

Patel negated the thought, "It's a two-woman job and you need to stay in charge, try to keep them off our backs, if possible. Besides which, you know your responsibility for Maeve as well as I do, and she takes priority. If this goes south, you need to be out of the line of fire, too." Priscilla suddenly felt helpless, torn in half. She needed to do this herself to relieve some of the guilt, but she understood Patel's point.

Petty Officer Marva Erdogan, a feral edge to her voice, spoke up, "I'm in. I'll help Bogart, Patel can misdirect Traynor. Getting the false information into that channel looks like a bigger challenge."

Qi Mai Ling raised her hand. "What about Traynor's request for a complete personnel roster."

Priscilla tapped a fingernail on her lower lip. "I don't know. Pogue always leaves people intentionally off that list, but I have no idea why. For instance, he's left us out." She shrugged her shoulders. "Rebels are such trustworthy creatures, who knows. Let's think about doing it after this next battle. I'm still not sure." Her eyes shifted briefly to Maeve, the one person she didn't want Traynor to know about. Patel nodded and pointed to the door, indicating they should all get out of there. Priscilla saw her tap the switch, cutting the surveillance loop. As she exited, her heart felt lighter than it had been since Parker's World. Maybe they could repair some of the damage they had done accidentally.

PRISCILLA STOOD BRACED AT ATTENTION in front of Pogue's desk, literally *on the carpet*, because a gorgeous, deep pile covered the deck in his main cabin, its luxuriousness matching the rest of the suite. None of that touched Priscilla as she devoutly wished to be somewhere, anywhere, else. Cleaning sewage tanks in hydroponics came to mind as being infinitely preferable.

From behind his desk, Captain Hamilton Pogue sat examining her, slit-eyed, silent. To his right stood Commander Paul

Bhat, stony-faced, radiating anger. Both wore blue working uniforms, but Bhat's fatigues were covered in oil and dirt. Whatever else you might say about him, he acted every inch the working executive officer. He must have been in an engine room when Pogue called this impromptu gathering.

Priscilla, on the other hand, didn't look as crisp as Pogue, though. According to the logs and security surveillance in the corridor, she had been officially off duty, sleeping, when he had called. In reality, she had been spying on Pogue with Patel, watching his reaction to Traynor's message following the thumping administered by Bogart and his task force. From Priscilla's perspective, that had turned out even better than she had hoped. Bogart had taken the advantages they had given him and run with them as hard as he could.

She knew Pogue didn't agree with her elation, his reaction best being described as undeniably furious. She almost smiled as she remembered what an amazing crash that pile of ceramic shards in the corner had made as its previous form, an antique vase, impacted the bulkhead less than ten minutes ago. Beautiful blue and white pieces still lay glistening to her right on the carpet.

Priscilla didn't smile, however; she didn't even think loudly. If her life had been the only one on the line, she might have told this quisling exactly what she thought of his treachery, as well as his lechery, and then attempted to kill him or die trying. She didn't have that luxury, unfortunately. She had to protect the women who had passed on the information under her orders, as well as Maeve. *Especially* Maeve. So, here she stood, pretending to be a cabbage or some other vegetable, inert and clueless, waiting for Pogue to drop the hammer. Priscilla ground her teeth in frustration.

"Do you know why you're here, Jenks?" Pogue asked in a silken tone.

Acting with every ounce of her ability, she answered with a question, trying to look confused, "My section's responsibility for some recent imperial victories, sir?"

Pogue glanced at Bhat, who shrugged his shoulders. Looking back at Priscilla, he appeared to visibly make up his mind. Sitting up, he said simply, "Somebody in your section has hacked into my personal mail. If their messages to me got out, it might be embarrassing to certain women on this ship," he said as he leered at her, trying to make a point, she supposed, about their content.

Priscilla's skin crawled. He now expected to use his low-life and illegal relationships with women under his command to cover-up his betrayal of the empire, and he wanted her to help him! If she had been carrying a pistol, they'd both be dead right now, but his bullyboys at the hatch always frisked her, ensuring she didn't have that option. Those searches added one more thing he owed her. Those men enjoyed their job way too much and, despite being an officer, she couldn't do anything about it. Priscilla's heart shriveled into a dying sun, cold heat compressing it as it came closer and closer to going nova. She wanted to reach out and remove that smug look, but she just couldn't. She prayed she'd be there when Pogue received his accounting and be able to do it herself, but the way things were going that didn't seem likely. A rap on the hatch interrupted them so she didn't have to make up a lie.

Zane Weston, a huge, blond man, stuck his head in the hatch. "Cross-checked the duty logs against the corridor surveillance tapes, Captain. The only two people actually in the com office when the communications went out were two of her women, Patel and Erdogan. Somehow, they fiddled with the tapes of the office, but they definitely were there at the time. What do you want us to do with them?"

Priscilla cringed inwardly at the evil light in his eyes. She had tried to help Patel and Erdogan cover their tracks, but not well enough apparently, which meant two of her friends would likely pay with their lives. She cried inside for her friends but couldn't let the tears show.

Bhat looked down at his boss. "I'll have them questioned."

Pogue approved, "Good. Do that." Bhat stepped around the desk, heading for the hatch.

"As for you, Lieutenant Jenks," Pogue said in that charming way of his, as if she could possibly have forgotten the current unpleasantness already, "I want to see more of you. Set up a time with my yeoman so we can get to know each other better."

Priscilla forced herself to smile as if she would ever, *ever*, do that. "Thank you, sir, I'd like that." *As long as I have a pistol when I come. Extra-sharp knives would be even better!* That thought really did make her want to return.

Whether due to her apparent eagerness or his own galaxy-sized ego, he smiled warmly.

"That'll be all, Lieutenant."

Priscilla pivoted, heading for the hatch. She maintained a regular walking pace under the watchful eyes of Weston and Nantz, the enforcers standing guard on Pogue's door. She prayed that Patel and Erdogan had been watching and would try to escape, or at least not be taken captive. She shuddered as she considered what they would face before they died if captured, because die they would. To be accused of a crime against Pogue on *Bring It* meant one thing: to be found guilty. Turning a corner and out of sight of Pogue's hatch, Priscilla tapped the emergency code into her com to alert the team. She wanted to run, be there to help when Bhat arrived, but would never be able to explain her presence if she did. To keep Maeve safe, her highest duty, she had to sacrifice Patel and Erdogan, and herself and Mai Ling, too, if necessary. Agony tore at her heart, because she knew what Patel and Erdogan were about to go through if they were captured, both as individuals and as women. The fact that Maeve might be exposed by them scared Priscilla even more. Patel's nanites would kill her if Bhat got too close to the truth, but Marva Erdogan lacked the additional protections and blocks Implacables received. If she broke, a not likely but remote possibility, they were all dead. Including Maeve.

Dropping down a shaft two levels, she hurried as much as she could. In order to keep Maeve safe, heaven help her, she might have to kill Erdogan herself. Gunfire, echoing from up ahead, caused her to break into a run. As she turned into the corridor leading to the communications office, she screeched to a stop, a large crowd preventing her from getting closer than twenty feet. Craning her head to find out what had happened, relief washed over her as she saw that she wouldn't have to kill a friend. Ashamed to feel so relieved, she nevertheless rejoiced. Stretched across the threshold of the room, black smoke curling above her, Patel's bullet riddled body sagged lifeless. Just behind her she could see Erdogan lying dead. Priscilla felt a wild battle pride when she saw that they hadn't gone alone. One of Pogue's goons lay dead in front of them, while the ship's doctor, Harrison Davison, treated a second, badly wounded one.

As the doctor worked, Bhat got the attention of the crowd. "Listen up," he shouted over the hubbub. "These two were rebel moles that have killed many of our comrades through false information. Go about your duties so we can clean things up."

Priscilla could hardly believe how well he lied. She stepped on that thought, too. Smoke curled from the gun Bhat held, one she hadn't even been aware he wore, which meant he must have been involved in the shooting. Bhat stared at her, his eyes gun barrels. "Find out what else they sent out, and to whom, in the last twenty minutes, Jenks," he ordered.

Priscilla nodded. Stepping gingerly over the remains of her friends, women loyal to the end, she brought up the duty logs. "Just a response to a routine personnel request from *The Pleasance*," Priscilla said calmly, inwardly rejoicing. Patel, knowing her time had just run out, must have decided that, since Pogue didn't want Traynor to have the full personnel roster, she would make sure he got it. That act could have been almost the last thing she ever did. Turning, she saw Commander Bhat suddenly turn a ghastly pale. "Apparently it included the entire morning report for the flotilla that came in today," she concluded.

As she watched, he tapped his com. "Traynor has our personnel roster, sir. The complete one including *all* ships' companies." After pausing apparently to listen, he added, "We do have that request we have been putting off."

She couldn't hear the response, although she could pull a

recording later if she wished. Whatever Pogue said got a huge reaction from the XO as his voice came over every loudspeaker in the ship. Speaking through his lapel mic, he said, "Now hear this, all hands ready for departure as soon as ship and flotilla are prepared for a long sortie. Section heads, report on what needs you will have for a long intel mission outside the empire. Staff, inform flotilla of the mission parameters, Plan Baker Two. This is no drill."

Priscilla smiled, watching Bhat hurry off down the corridor as if his tail were on fire. Patel had hit the bullseye on this one. Pogue didn't want Traynor to know something, something serious enough to get them running. From beyond the grave she had really kicked over the ant hill. *Good for you, girl, wherever you are.*

Waiting while a couple of Dr. Davison's orderlies carried Patel and then Erdogan away, she stood stone-faced as, inwardly, her heart ached with grief. She wished they could be given burials with full honors, but no one would ever know of their heroism, could ever know, at least until she got Maeve safely off this ship, something looking less and less likely all the time. The doctor seemed rather dour, she decided, doing his duty but not saying anything as he finished his tasks in prepping the bodies for spacing.

She wished she could recruit someone from the crew to help her watch over Maeve, just in case something happened to her and Mai Ling, but she simply couldn't take that chance. And when they headed out of the empire, there would really be no way to get Maeve back to Admiral Davies. Regretfully, she imagined what might have been but would never be now. Maeve would have made a good empress. If only given the chance.

MANUAL FOR COURTS-MARTIAL (MCM)

Revised 3277 by Order of the Emperor, Charles Roland

Desertion

Definition: In time of war, failure to report to duty station or leaving duty post without permission in a potential or actual combat situation.

Penalty: Death

9

Alone in the World

CNS *Bring It*, Nighthawk System
1720 BBMT 13 June 3473

MAEVE UCH ROBERT CRAWLED THROUGH THE DUCTWORK checking connections for this new system Lieutenant Priscilla Jenks needed. She hated getting dirty, but this work had to be done right, and there were only the three of them.

Following Patel and Erdogan's deaths, Petty Officer Qi Mai Ling had become Signals chief, more or less. Likely, Maeve decided, it came down to not having anything on Mai Ling, but Captain Hamilton Pogue really didn't trust her, either, so putting her in a dead-end spot made sense. As Signals chief, where she had no outside contact and she used the standard codes to com the other members of the flotilla as they patrolled Nighthawk watching for another TechMech attack, she had little or nothing to do. Normally that would have given Mai Ling lots of time to do this sort of work. Unfortunately, Pogue had been keeping Mai Ling under surveillance since Patel and Erdogan had sacrificed themselves.

As for Maeve and Priscilla, they'd had airtight alibis when everything went down. Which meant she and Priscilla needed to personally do this dirty, filthy, probably useless job because they had survived. Regardless, the TechMech would probably kill them all if they stayed here long enough. The TechMech's first attack had caught the flotilla by surprise, costing them the cruiser *Yangtse* and several destroyers before the fleet succeeded in turning them back. And the flotilla had gotten even smaller since then from the follow-on attacks.

Maeve wiggled around a tight corner before moving on. As she passed air vents, she held her breath, moving slowly to avoid anyone in the cabins or other spaces noticing her. She inched around another corner and then up to a main shaft. After that, she climbed using the ladder set in the shaft's side for maintenance.

Memories haunted her as she moved invisibly through the darkness. In the little more than two years since they had reached Nighthawk, ships had come in from the empire identifying themselves as carrying heirs. Pogue had informed the flotilla that they were fakes, pretenders to the throne. Once they arrived, the men on them had disappeared into Pogue's private hell that no one ever returned from. Priscilla had been convinced they were legitimate, but how could you tell? Well, Priscilla seemed certain enough to insist on doing something about it.

Which meant Maeve found herself clambering and squeezing herself through the innards and maintenance spaces of the ship. She snorted to herself. *The last thing in the world a sane person would call what Priscilla intends to do now is* maintenance. Finally, she reached the midship fan platform. Priscilla sat waiting for her, not exactly happy, but at peace, Maeve decided. *She hasn't been happy since Patel and Erdogan died.*

"Everything check out?" Priscilla asked.

"Yep," Maeve answered, "all lines are hidden, clear, and connected."

Priscilla just nodded. "Good. I'll place the final charges. You head back to your quarters and make sure you're seen in case something happens. These last scuttling charges are going in locations where someone might see me, and we need to keep you safe if that happens."

"And if we need to blow up the ship?" Maeve asked softly.

"We'll try to get off before we do. Regardless, we need to protect the next heir that comes through. I'm afraid the empire won't last long if we don't."

She knew Priscilla believed in the empire with every fiber of her being. After all, she had dedicated her life to saving it. Intellectually, Maeve believed the same but found it harder to keep the faith. Her father and mother had died serving that ideal, Patel and Erdogan, too. And Priscilla's words now made her face the possibility that Maeve might lose her, too.

No! She couldn't! But Priscilla hadn't offered her any choice. Losing her would be much too steep a price to pay for any ideal, but she hadn't been able to argue Priscilla out of doing this. If she warned Pogue or Commander Paul Bhat, the XO, even anonymously, that might not prevent Priscilla from trying, but, even if Priscilla didn't do anything, those two would search until they found the threat to their ship. Either way, Priscilla would be dead. At least letting her go ahead left a small chance of survival.

Maeve sensed Priscilla watching her intently. "It'll be all right."

Maeve shook her head. "Sometimes I just don't know if it's worth all the death and destruction." No tears came despite the bleakness in her voice.

"We've been over this a dozen times," Priscilla said softly, reaching out to squeeze Maeve's hand. "One thing I've learned, Princess, is that it doesn't take two to make a war. If you don't stop people like Pogue before they're in charge, they won't be satisfied with just running things, they'll keep coming until they have your soul. The only way you have a fighting chance of saving your soul, living an honorable life, is to prevent men like him from winning."

Maeve squeezed Priscilla's hand back. "Is an honorable life so important, then?"

Priscilla gave her a bittersweet smile. "Everything I've seen tells me all other choices are frauds. Believe me, it's worth it."

With that, Priscilla turned to go, but a strange bag fell out of her blouse as she did. As Maeve stared at it, it seemed to shift color and shape in a constant state of change. Priscilla snatched it up quickly.

"What's that?" Maeve asked. She had caught a glimpse or two over the years of the strange sack, but Priscilla had never offered an explanation and Maeve had never asked, respecting her privacy. However, if things went badly, this might be her last chance to know what Priscilla had guarded so zealously over the years. She needed to know what Priscilla held so dearly that she carried it with her most of the time.

Priscilla gave her a bittersweet smile. "This represents everything I believe in, but now it's nothing." As she began to stick it back in her blouse, she abruptly pulled her hand back. Showing it to Maeve clearly, she explained, "Maeve, this might have been yours one day, if things had been different, but now it looks like it never will. I want you to put your hand on it with me and repeat the oath. Maybe it will bring you luck in the days ahead." Her voice choked up a bit as she made her request, surprising Maeve. Priscilla rarely showed emotion, so this really mattered to her. Reaching out to touch the bag, a tingle ran up her arm. Together, they recited the oath, "Protection, Integrity, Judgment, Justice, Sacrifice, Virtue, To the Death."

Priscilla smiled, more relaxed than she had been in months. Awkwardly in the confined space, Priscilla moved forward and hugged Maeve. Maeve embraced her with everything she had. Gently, breaking the hug after a moment, Priscilla patted Maeve's hand a last time as a tear trickled down her cheek. She then tucked the bag into a crack beside the fan before muttering, "Jenks three one seven one niner five whiskey." The bag suddenly burst into an intolerably bright orb before slagging into a molten plug in the crack. A moment later, Priscilla crawled away.

Tears flowed as Maeve headed back toward her quarters through the maze of ducts. She also felt something changing deep inside as her doubts melted away, replaced by a steely resolve. She had no idea what all that with the bag had really been about, but she rejoiced that Priscilla had shared it with her.

Approaching the vent into her room, she slowed. As a section leader now, she had her own room. Peeking around the edge of the vent cover, she scanned to make sure no one had come in. Opening the vent, she slid in quietly before replacing it. Taking her shower things, she headed out the door. She needed to get this grime and oil off before someone noticed. Thankfully, she saw no one in the corridor on the way to the showers.

Singing softly, she lathered up her short hair. Getting clean always made her happier. Gradually, the foreboding about Priscilla receded along with the physical dirt. As she scrubbed her hair, she considered the fact that she could barely remember what it had been like longer.

FROM THE SHADOWS OF THE duct, Priscilla paused to watch Maeve go. Would she ever see the girl again, one she secretly cherished as the daughter she would never have? She knew her emotions were out of control, but at the moment, she didn't care. She might not have another opportunity to mourn.

Simply put, if someone found her before she placed the last charge, she would have no excuse, no plausible way to explain why she was carrying explosives to hydroponics in her satchel. *I hate the broccoli and want to wipe it out?* The dark humor brought a shadow of a smile. Carefully she crept forward.

As she neared each grate, she pushed a skinny eye forward to scout for anyone who might see or hear something in the space beyond when she passed.

Keeping weight off the middle of the duct, she crawled slowly, carefully placing each knee and hand. Using the skinny eye again and seeing nothing, she continued crawling forward.

Boom. Somehow she must have pushed the duct out of shape behind her. Glancing back fearfully, she didn't see anyone at the last grate, the only one in a straight line to her present position. Taking a long, slow breath, she moved on and turned a corner. Only two more grates to go and she would be in hydroponics. One more.

Finally reaching the grate in hydroponics, she extended the skinny eye through the grate, carefully examining all she could see of hydro. Letting go of a breath, she sighed. Things were going well.

Placing her satchel back out of sight, she disconnected the grate from the inside using the clips she had tied it down with earlier. She hadn't wanted even the slight sound of an electric screwdriver as she entered the most ticklish part of the operation. Sound could echo in funny ways, back down the duct or even through hydro into the corridor.

One more look, all clear. Sliding open the grate, she backed quietly out of the duct and began to dust herself off as it closed. She would grab the bag with the explosives still up there after she verified she was alone.

Strong arms grabbed her before she could turn. In her ear, hot breath spoke. "I like to take a break in here where nobody ever comes." The man chuckled, his arms like steel. "I've wanted to get to know you better, Jenks, and here you came straight to me."

She knew who had her now, Petty Officer Wally Welks, a truly disgusting man. "Release me, Welks. I'm an officer!"

"Too good for me? I don't think so." He squeezed tighter, now nibbling on her ear.

Suddenly desperate, Priscilla managed to thumb her com with her right, trying to call anyone who would answer, while finding a nerve junction with her left and stabbing hard.

The combination of pain and a voice coming through the com must have startled Welks, because he pushed Priscilla violently away. As she stumbled forward unexpectedly, she threw her arms forward to keep herself from hitting the steel deck. Even as she did, her head rammed against a steel pump cover.

As she hit, the pain caused her to scream. Falling onto the deck, she heard footsteps disappearing. Sliding into unconsciousness as her head hit the deck, the thought followed her into oblivion, *Maeve* . . .

As Maeve enjoyed the hot water coursing over her, the loudspeaker blared, startling her. "Dr. Davison and medical team to hydroponics. Casualty in hydroponics. Lieutenant Jenks. Report stat and take her body to security per SOP for examination."

Maeve's hands dropped. The shower pelted her, suds dribbling across her face, as she cried. Priscilla, the woman who had taken the place of her mother, gone. *I never told Priscilla how much I care.* Regret overwhelmed her as the tears streamed unchecked, loneliness threatening to crush her.

Standing there under the stinging pelt of the shower head, she vowed that she would strike back as long as she could, the best that she could. First, she would finish setting the scuttling charges Priscilla had died trying to place. Then, at the right time, she would blow this ship, and every evil creature on it, into pieces so small no one would ever find them. *And then . . . ?* Well, the possibility of anything positive happening for her seemed very unlikely from what she could see right now. *If* she survived—a big if—she would do what she could to straighten out the rest of the universe.

Finishing her shower, she headed for her room. As she walked past the petty officers' mess, she became aware of eyes following her. Her back became stiffer. Hairy, ugly, disgusting creatures, those men in there. Not a one held a candle to Dad. If she ever decided to like a guy, he would have to meet that standard.

1220 BBMT 12 September 3473

COMP PAD IN ONE HAND, roll of wire in the other, Ensign Maeve Ellyllyon hustled down the corridor on her way, ultimately, to missile control. *Why did I let them promote me?* she chided herself. *Especially since they think I'm completely oblivious to people and what is happening around me.* Of course, that might be the reason. After dealing with seriously smart and competent people like Patel and Priscilla, Pogue and Bhat apparently wanted someone they could control in charge of electronics. *If they only knew, they wouldn't sleep well at night; not at all.*

The last month of sixteen to twenty-hour days had worn her pretty thin, but it hadn't left her much time to worry or to mourn for Priscilla. The first month after she had died in that mysterious accident, things had been pretty rough. On pins and needles, she had expected a massive ship-wide search when security discovered the scuttling charges. When that didn't happen, she knew the explosives hadn't been found, and she moved them until she could place them herself.

Still, it had been darkly amusing to watch the frustration of the command group which, in its own way, acted as a tribute to Priscilla's death. Pogue and Bhat had been obsessed with determining what happened and why Priscilla had been in hydroponics when her log showed her being on the opposite side of the ship. Because of that, choosing a new divisional officer hadn't happened right away. During that period, the com and electronics section chiefs reported directly to Bhat, but, because he had trained in propulsion, he had only a vague idea as to whether they were doing what needed to be done. The electronics and communications petty officers, without an effective officer in charge, had generally let things go.

All except her. She felt a little smug about how she had made sure all of her section's responsibilities were squared away. On a cruiser, something always needed to be repaired, something always required maintenance, plus thousand-hour checks, upgrades, and modifications. Here in the back of beyond, without proper spare parts, you constantly had to figure out a way to replace things you couldn't repair. If you let things go long enough? Well, the cruiser wouldn't fly, couldn't fight, and would become uninhabitable pretty quickly. Smart people didn't let their ship fall apart and she didn't. The downside had been that appearing to be more concerned with the job than her people took real effort, a real chore. But she would do what she needed to do to maintain her cover.

Because only her section had been even close to being in good shape, Pogue had finally tapped her to fix everything else. Before being designated as the new divisional officer, Maeve had figured it wouldn't take long to catch things up. Wrong! Apparently, when things were let go, it took a geometrically longer time to correct them. *Let things go a day, you might get caught up in a day. Let things go seven days it might be possible to catch up in fifty days. Let things go four weeks?* Well, by her calculations she might just catch up by the heat death of the universe. She walked faster. After she dropped these supplies, she needed to be on the other side of the ship in ten minutes.

Stepping into hydroponics, she paused to let her eyes adjust to the leafy green dimness. Heading for the wall section where she had assigned a team to remove a coupling connecting a nutrient sensor to the feed switches, she couldn't see anyone but the petty officer.

"Welks, where's your team?" she demanded with a hint of annoyance. And he really did annoy her, so she had no need to act.

Wally Welks, a fat mound of flesh who didn't bathe often enough to please Maeve, simply smiled at her hungrily. After a moment, he lazily drawled, "On break."

"I told you to have everyone ready when I got down here. The XO told me we can't afford to have these controls off-line for more than forty minutes. If they are, he'll chew me out again. Get your people back here right now!" she snapped, anger rising.

Welks pushed himself off his chair. "I told you, you jumped up little tramp, they're on break. When you called, I sent them out." He smiled even more evilly. "That will give us some time alone."

Maeve's mind refused to recognize or believe this could be happening. Petty officers didn't threaten officers; he would be spaced for that. *How could he think he could get away with it?* But even as those thoughts swirled in her head, she remembered rumors about other crew women who had gone missing. Red anger exploded as she prepared to fight, but her momentary disbelief had been all he needed.

In that moment, Welks's arms were around her, his face, his breath, on her. She struggled, but her arms were pinned. For such a huge pile of flesh, he had amazing strength. Trying to kick him, she found her legs were pinned by his. Digging her thumbs into his sides, the only thing she could move, she screamed out, "Let go of me! I'll kill you, Welks!"

He chuckled, a sound of deep satisfaction. "No, you won't, but I'll kill you when we're done, and no one will ever know the difference."

Suddenly, he woofed, letting go of Maeve except for a hand clamped to her right wrist. Maeve saw him turn away, giving her the chance to break free. She had been straining against his grip so hard that, when she broke free, she fell to the ground. From the deck, she could only see his back as he brought his hands up ponderously before taking a swing at someone she couldn't see very clearly in front of him. Maeve knew the power in those arms and hands. Whoever he connected with, when he did, would be dead or seriously injured. As he swung at a shadow, she watched the punch go wide, missing completely.

Then he shouted in pain. A counter punch must have been thrown by his opponent, obviously connecting. She dimly saw Welks's attacker deliver a snap kick to the knee that brought him to a standstill. A moment later, a punch to the throat left him gagging. Then a kick aimed at the top of the legs made contact. Although she couldn't see exactly where that kick connected, from Welks's reaction it appeared to be somewhere extremely sensitive.

He hit the deck, retching, his left leg sticking out at an unnatural angle. By the time she got to her feet, ready to help, Welks had already toppled to the floor. Maeve realized he wouldn't be getting back up. Without Welks blocking her view, she finally recognized her rescuer. *Mai Ling!* So short and petit, if Welks had connected even once, she would have been done, but, instead, he lay moaning on the deck. As he lay there, Qi Mai Ling hit him twice more in the face. Maeve heard a bone crack as the second strike landed.

"That's enough, Mai Ling," Maeve ordered. "He's down and injured, you've hurt him enough. After Captain's Mast, they'll space him and that'll be that."

Mai Ling just shook her head. "You know what Pogue is like," she answered, breathing heavily as her right foot slammed down, like as piston, breaking his left arm against the deck. "He's likely to get a promotion and you'll come to Pogue's attention as a possible bed companion. Do you want that?" She kicked again.

Panic rose in her throat. In her opinion, Pogue treated women as badly as Welks, which meant Mai Ling might be right. Whether true or not, Maeve didn't know for sure but didn't want to find out. "Fine. Let's get away before someone finds us here."

Mai Ling gave one last kick to Welks's face, which might have dislocated his jaw, before standing upright. "Okay. Let's go. Remember your things."

Maeve realized she hadn't even given her com pad or other items lying on the deck a thought. She had just wanted to run, needing desperately to get away from this already ugly memory. Grabbing her comp pad and shoulder bag, she began stooping for the wire when she decided. *I don't care if they do find out about me having been here because of the wire. This job has to be done and I don't want to lug it down here twice.* "Let's go."

Together, they headed back toward the code room. "How did you happen to stumble on this?" Maeve asked, a question that hadn't occurred to her in the heat of the moment.

"I keep tabs on you and knew you were headed down here. I happened to be in the mess when a couple of Welks's guys came in with big cheese-eating grins on their faces talking about how they were glad for this unexpected break. They'd apparently been told not to come back for an hour."

An hour, after which she would have been dead, never to be seen again. "Thank you," she said fervently, reaching out to touch Mai Ling's arm.

Mai Ling patted her hand. "It's become something of a habit, watching over you all these years. We need to keep moving before someone stumbles on all of this."

Tears prickled at the edges of Maeve's eyes as they headed up-ship together. After a few steps, Mai Ling slid her arm around Maeve's shoulder. Maeve slid her arm around Mai Ling's waist, grateful for her nearness and love.

MAEVE PICKED AT HER FOOD while she waited for Mai Ling. Over the last week they had gotten in the habit of meeting for lunch. Today, Maeve had been waiting for forty-five minutes, but no note had come from Mai Ling explaining her tardiness.

Unfortunately, Maeve couldn't wait much longer. A glitch in one of the pumps feeding a hydroponics vat had developed an intermittent fault and almost killed a large portion of the carbon dioxide recycling system in hydro two. Enjoying breathing as much as the next girl, nothing except lunch with Mai Ling could have interrupted her diagnosing the problem.

Worry began to tie her stomach in a knot. Did Welks say something implicating Mai Ling in his accident? If he did, he would need to explain about assaulting Maeve. He couldn't be that stupid. But what if? What if he'd concocted some story? Was she next? Could she do anything to find out? No, not even make discrete inquiries. That would be the fastest way to join Mai Ling, making her possible sacrifice worthless. The reality of being the last of her team began to grow in her chest, along with a sense of awful aloneness.

Just then, two women on Mai Ling's team walked in, talking in low voices. As they looked at Maeve, she waved them over. Looking at each other, they slowly moved in Maeve's direction.

"Hi, I'm waiting for Mai Ling for our lunch. Do you know how long it will be before she can take a break?" Maeve waited anxiously while the two looked at each other and seemed to come to a decision.

"She never came in this morning. Don't ask around if you want to stay safe. Keep out of it," the shorter one hissed.

"Thanks," Maeve murmured to the back of the rapidly departing women. She felt sick inside. Looking up, the chronometer on the bulkhead showed she needed to be on her way. Leaving three-quarters of her food untouched, she took her tray to the disposal area for recycling. Her face hardened. Whatever had happened to Mai Ling, Welks undoubtedly must be involved. *I will make his life so miserable for this, he'll wish he had died last week.*

CNS *Pechnaya*
1020 BBMT 11 October 3473

SEATED AT THE CENTER OF CNS *Pechnaya*'s spacious flag bridge, Morgain uch Robert bathed in the almost sensuous feeling of power flowing around her. This supernova—*her* supernova—counted as one of the most powerful ships not only in Ninth Sector but the entire empire, which meant the galaxy. The men and women around her obeyed her immediately, catering to her every whim. Her task group counted as the strongest single fighting force in the sector.

She glanced about at every station. And if anyone failed to comply? That man or woman would never make another mistake ever again. When her strength in men and women dropped, her task group would capture other ships and give the crew a simple choice. Very few rejected her offer to join her, none twice. What could be better?

The sudden startled movement of a communications rating caught her attention. The woman printed out a hard copy before placing it in a high-security envelope. Morgain felt the entire business of maintaining some things highly secure silly, but the military would do things their own way. The rating handed the envelope to a lieutenant, who passed it to a commander, who then brought it to her. "A high-security message, Your Majesty."

Opening the envelope, disbelief and a thrill of purpose coursed through her. One of Trevor Cascade's sons had somehow survived! And, he had a proctor. Her moles within Prime Fleet were definitely paying off. How convenient. She could kill two birds with a single stone.

Plus she had a good idea where they might be going outside the empire for this test. When your grandmother reigned over an independent planet, you learned all sorts of interesting things, one of which she would put to good use now.

Focusing, she noted the commander still standing at rigid attention in front of her. Of course, she had not dismissed him. Rising from the command seat, she ordered. "Plot a course for Alpine. My ships will refuel there before beginning a search for a stealth ship, the *Ambrose B*."

Leaving, she barely heard the "Aye, aye, ma'am."

* * *

Jeffco Secondary Command Post
0930 Local/0330 BBMT 20 October 3473

VICE ADMIRAL NGAIO TRIED TO focus on the fleet logistics download displayed on the screen, but his mind kept wandering to the boy out there. Hugh and his ship had left nine days ago and were beyond the boundary of the empire. He was safe from interference now. A window popped up on his screen further distracting him, his bosun Wendy Yu. "Your archeonA call to your mother through the planetary archeonA on *The Crossing* is connected, Admiral."

"Thank you, Bosun. Make sure the line is secure and no listeners, please."

Wendy nodded, her face replaced by a weathered woman who appeared to be at least eighty. "Duong, my son!" The old woman's voice sounded strong although she looked as if a stray breeze would blow her away. "So good of you to call."

Behind her, Admiral Ngaio could see the shrine she kept to her son lost not long after Deft eight years earlier. "Quong Ngaio how are you?" he said.

His mother cocked an eye at him. "Why won't you call me mother as you used to?"

Duong Ngaio smiled. "When you stop asking when I will give you grandchildren."

"Humph," she snorted. "Not likely."

"Then I will not stop calling you 'phoenix.' That is what your name means, after all, and the meaning of the name tells us who the person really is." Before she could say anything else, he went on, "I have great news. Chi did not protect the heir in vain on Deft. He would be so proud to know this news."

Suddenly Quong Ngaio's eyes shone with a special intensity. She could only utter, "What?" before choking up.

"It is secret, but I know you will tell no one. The boy Chi died to save has entered on the Test of Heirs to become emperor. I thought you should know; Chi's sacrifice may be partially responsible for saving the empire."

Tears began to flow down his mother's face. "Now I know he made an especially noble sacrifice. Thank you for telling me."

"You are welcome, Mother."

A bit of strength returned to her voice with a hint of asperity. "The only better news I could have is that you will provide me with a grandson, firstborn!"

Duong chuckled. "Are not your eighteen grandchildren enough, Mother?"

"No! Not until I have one from you!"

Treadle Communications Array
0340 BBMT 20 October 3473

BASED UPON THE KEYWORD *Deft*, an electronic tap on the central archeonA processor node recorded the entire conversation before disconnecting itself. It dutifully bundled the entire message for transmission to its master on planet Treadle in Sector Four. Three days passed before it could piggyback the message unnoticed. When it arrived, an alert chimed on *Commander's Belle*, a non-military corvette in Treadle orbit. The communications tech sent it unopened addressed to the ship's owner, Austin Carhart. Although it arrived after 3 a.m. local, the receipt chime woke him instantly. His wolf-like features sharpened as he listened to the conversation.

Opening his strictly prohibited and very expensive database, he located Duong Ngaio, listed as an officer in Seventh Fleet. "So that's where you went to hide him, Doña Carlota," he muttered.

Doña Carlota Gonzalvez y Rodriguez de Castillo, the Protector of the Succession, had evidently taken Hugh Cascade to Jeffco ten years before. After all these years spent eluding rebels and fleet alike, this gave him a chance to get back on top. Now he knew where Hugh had been.

The only question the man once known as Austin Carhart needed answering now was where to go to find Hugh at this moment? He intended to find out, be there when Hugh arrived, and take up where he left off back on Deft. And with any luck, Sergeant Major Ward would be there, too. He looked forward to initiating his long-delayed plan. And getting payback for being thwarted so long ago.

ARCHIVED IMPERIAL CLASSIFIED DOCUMENTS

Declassified 24 September 3485
Implacables Training
Top Secret—Medical Department Only
Synopsis of Information to be Protected

A candidate for the Full Alternate Test will need to take one of two courses in order to allow complete evaluation. The regular course passes through the same planets Joe Jackson used as supply points when he and his task force headed to the core, as well as on his return to Earth for the Final Battle. They are as follows:

Nighthawk, a thieves' paradise; Alpine, hegemonic despotism; Deveroe, slave market; Pi Nu, the perfect anarchy of a planet without agreed legitimacy of authority. All of the characteristics necessary to pass the test can be examined by stopping on these planets in sequence.

The secondary course is a single planet, code name Lorelei.

All information on the intersection of the test with these planets must be protected by memory block until needed.

10

White Knight

FOCUSING ON HER DUTY PAD and the listed tasks, Maeve blocked out everything else, even ignoring the com panel. She didn't expect any message traffic from any of the other ships in Captain Hamilton Pogue's pocket fleet. He discouraged unnecessary messaging between ships. Commander Milton Jay, Pogue's second officer, never bothered her since she kept all her systems operating. He only cared about efficiency when it involved this ship. Nor did she expect anything to come in from the planet Nighthawk, either. Besides, Tavares, sitting beside her, could handle anything that came up. She had more important things to do.

After all these years of her acting like a nerd, the rest of the crew expected her to ignore anything except a nearby exploding supernova and would be surprised if she noticed that if it weren't on her schedule. This allowed her to remain deeply focused on Wally Welks, a look of wariness in her eyes as he hobbled about checking electrical connections as per the monthly SOP.

She had included a monthly check of every connection in the ship for corrosion in the new SOP and made sure that former Petty Officer Welks always got the duty. Of course, she had gotten the XO to believe that the idea for the SOP had come from another of her section chiefs, but it had been all her. Giving the credit to someone else kept her from appearing too competent, which gave her an added benefit: she avoided bringing herself too much attention.

She felt hatred and loathing churning in her guts for Welks.

His broken bones hadn't knitted properly from Mai Ling's beating, which made this type of duty particularly difficult for him. She didn't care. Correction, she *did* care. She had chosen him specifically for this duty to keep her vow as part of her debt to Qi Mai Ling, whatever had happened to her. Maeve's discrete questions about the disappearance produced exactly nothing, not even getting her a visit from security. Just nothing.

She hadn't been able to break Welks in rank for, or even say anything about, the attempted rape. So, in order to punish him, she had been forced to get *creative*. Surprisingly, Welks had been standing by in hydroponics when a control valve, a repair he signed off on, broke loose. Maeve smiled darkly. The valve breaking loose didn't constitute an offense that would generally get someone broken, of course, unless it happened as Admiral Pogue came through inspecting the area and liquid "fertilizer" soaked his uniform. As he screamed at Welks, she hadn't been completely sure that Welks wouldn't end up being spaced. Unfortunately, that particular fantasy hadn't come true. Instead, the admiral had busted him to electronics mate second class, which kept him crawling all over the ship from morning till night. For now, it would have to do.

With half an ear she heard the com chime. Probably one of the corvettes with some fanciful reason for a supply run down to the planet so they could see girlfriends or something. Without even bothering Pogue or Bhat, ninety percent of the time Maeve could have told them the answer. *No, you cannot make a run for toilet paper at this time. A flotilla run will be organized in due course. Submit your needs on this and all other consumables by 1800.*

Normally, Commander Bhat said exactly that after she took the message pad to his office for him to review, sign off, and take action, but it saved her an hour when she did it herself. Plus, if she took the message pad, she wouldn't be able to gloat over Welks suffering through that mindless duty. However, if she blew the requester off in a particularly absent-minded fashion it would enhance her reputation as a complete geek.

She prepared herself to be annoying when Tavares flipped the autoresponder, a demand sent to incoming ships that they identify themselves and then leave the system. Turning toward him, she felt a quiver of alertness. Who could be coming in? On Tavares's board she saw a red warning light showing a ship approaching on preon drive. Although an imperial ship, it was obviously not one belonging to Pogue's squadron. *Too far out.* TechMech came from that far out, but they only had graviton drive. So who? She prayed it didn't carry another heir, fake or otherwise. The duty laid on her by Priscilla before she died had been clear: if another heir came through, she must blow up *Bring It* to stop Pogue from torturing him or her. She couldn't decide if she wanted to do it and, if she did, to escape and survive the explosion. *If I can.*

"Nighthawk, this is Core Naval Ship Ambrose B *on recon,"* came the response.

Maeve took over the com. "You're who?" she asked. A real imperial ship might give her a chance to get off this death trap.

The woman responding spoke very clearly and somewhat slowly, offending Maeve deeply. The crew and officers might snicker about her single mindedness, but they respected her competence. *"CNS* Ambrose B. *We are scouting for Task Force 13-6. We would like entry as a neutral power for refuel and provisioning."*

"Wait one and hold at the heliopause," she replied. *Liars!* Maeve despaired. Task Force 13-6 had been blasted to pieces years before through Pogue's treachery. Her momentary hope flickered and died. She'd never get off this ship. On the positive side, as if it mattered much, she didn't need to decide whether to blow up *Bring It* today. The tactical board showed the ship decelerating toward the heliopause, the recognized legal limit of the star system.

Maeve keyed Bhat. "Sir?"

"Yes, Ensign?"

"A ship coming in claims to be the *Ambrose B* scouting for Task Force 13-6."

Surprising her, the line went dead.

After a minute Bhat came back on. *"Ask for proof of identity."*

"Aye, aye, sir." Changing to the outbound com, she asked, "Can you prove who you are, *Ambrose B?"*

The response from another female speaker came back both snippy and irritating. *"We could wait for the task group to arrive and blast their way in but thought the friendly approach would be better. We are asking nicely, after all."*

"Wait," she ordered again. *That seemed like a pretty confident answer. Maybe they are who they say and can back that attitude up with some real firepower.* Flipping back over to internal, she passed on the answer, exactly as she received it. Staying in character, she added, "Sounds like they need to be taught some manners, if you ask me."

Killing the circuit from his end, Bhat didn't even bother acknowledging.

Behind her, she heard "Attention! Admiral on the bridge!" Turning and standing, she was momentarily stunned as both Bhat and Pogue entered. Generally, only one or the other appeared, and then not often. Commander Jay normally ran the ship, especially in combat, these two being worse than useless in battle. In Maeve's opinion, the ship would have been destroyed long ago with them in command of combat ops.

Ambrose B must be the real thing. She watched Jay huddle up with Pogue and Bhat but couldn't quite make out what they were saying. From the intensity of the whispers, however, they were definitely not happy, none of them.

Jay stood abruptly before facing the com station. "Execute Plan Snare Three focused on the *Ambrose B,*" he ordered. Tavares sent the code group immediately. In the holotank at the Ops station, three ships at the opposite side of the system from the *Ambrose B* quickly headed off for deep space. Maeve knew the Snare series involved surrounding an unsuspecting ship with massive firepower. Because the ships springing the trap had to fly all the way around the system on low power to avoid detection, it would take a day to get everything in place. The basic trap had worked on two small craft carrying men saying they were heirs taking something called the test, a lone non-imperial destroyer fleeing the TechMech destruction of its home world, and some cargo vessels. A few others had gotten away, obviously wary of just such a maneuver.

Should I warn them? Thankfully, Pogue ignored her as she thought. After considering the pros and cons for a moment more, she decided against contacting the *Ambrose B* for two reasons: If they were for real, they'd see Pogue's trap far enough away to take action to protect themselves. Second, she might give herself away, and the risk outweighed the small benefit.

A change-of-status flag popped up on her panel, one she had never seen before, a white diamond surrounded in blue and other colors of the rainbow. Looking closer, she saw that it resembled the imperial flag. Running her cursor over it, since she didn't want to interrogate the flag aloud so someone like Tavares could overhear, she sat back stunned after reading *King's code database retrieval underway.* What did that mean? She queried the operating system. A red *clearance denied* symbol appeared. A flicker of hope rose, reborn in her chest as the possibilities became obvious as well as practically endless. *Maybe these people are the real thing. Maybe I have a chance of escaping this abyss after all!*

Maeve concentrated on her com panel. After listening to a few minutes of general small talk among Pogue and his friends, she completely tuned them out. She began a subroutine that should allow her to bypass the block on the query she had run. So absorbed was she in trying to break through the block, the chime indicating another incoming message from the *Ambrose B* actually made her jump in surprise.

"CNS Bring It, *this is CNS* Ambrose B. *Please patch me through to Pogue."* The second woman spoke again.

Startled, Maeve's voice came out a bit squeaky. "Who are you and how did you know who we are?"

"Bad com procedure, spacer. Now either patch me through to Pogue or a duty officer who can. This is Fleet Commander Gail Felt, commanding, on imperial business."

Tavares jumped in from his console, disrespecting her. His attitude went with her cover but proved bad for her self-esteem. She sometimes regretted the cost she paid to stay safe. "You have no business on this net and are unauthorized to call this ship!" he yelled.

Another voice cut him off. "This is CNS *Bring It*'s com officer, Lieutenant Albans. Can I help you, ma'am?" She turned and saw Pogue himself at the command station. *He decided to answer? Who were these people?*

"Hamilton," the woman on the other end gushed gaily, apparently recognizing Pogue's voice, *"I thought you were dead. We all did after you disappeared into that mess in Thirteenth Fleet. As far as helping me, none of the memories I have about your so-called help on Gilthorpe would lead me to believe that accepting your help would ever be a good idea."*

Maeve wondered if a commander with a fleet-confirmed rank could really be as vapid as this woman sounded. Probably not, she decided. Which prompted the question, what did Pogue think? Did he buy it? She watched him surreptitiously.

He laughed in return. "You're Gail Felt all right. Or at least an excellent simulation. You maintained the same untrusting attitude at Commander's Course, as I recall. Got close to lots of your girlfriends, but never you."

Gail gaily laughed right back. Maeve now had no doubts about it being fake. Good acting though, she admitted as one professional to another. Maeve stared blankly at her panel as she concentrated on the conversation. Disappointment grew, however, when Gail requested a secure channel and Pogue agreed. He gave Maeve a severe look before pointing *out* with his thumb. "Security lock the com panel, then both of you leave," he ordered.

Maeve obeyed, taking Tavares with her. "Go to secondary in case they need your help," she told him with a pout, pretending her feelings were hurt by being excluded from something like this.

"Aye, ma'am," Tavares replied.

As he disappeared, she activated her earbud before tapping her link into the secure channel. Hopefully, she hadn't missed much.

Interesting. They accessed the logs with something called King's code and Pogue believes them implicitly! They must be the real deal, so what now? They sound like they can handle themselves. Good for them. So this really looks like my ticket out. She listened with only half an ear as Pogue and Gail Felt chatted over past history. She had almost arrived at her cabin when a man called Ward confirmed they had an heir aboard. She almost came to a complete stop.

Her promise to Priscilla stared her abruptly in the face. She must blow up the ship to protect the heir. But maybe she ought to give Ward a chance? Pogue sounded almost afraid of him, so perhaps they could get in and out safely? With her too? No matter what else happened, she had a duty to warn them. If she did, would Pogue suspect someone tipped them off? Maybe. And Pogue believed in guilty until proven innocent. With her past association with Priscilla, Patel, and the others, she'd be the first to be questioned. *Better not to do anything just yet.*

As she entered her cabin, her com beeped, calling her back to the bridge. Turning, she headed back up-ship. Stepping through the control room hatch, she had to squeeze around all the division officers crowded onto the bridge to get to her station.

In the center of the bridge, Pogue stood smiling that charming smile he had, the one that only appeared as he proved, one more time, his brilliance. "Another false heir is coming in," he said. "I want his ship, so we have to do this very carefully. Until we have the command group, don't anyone do anything to tip our hand. If they send a group aboard for resupply, detain them, quietly. No breakage!" He glared at his security officers as he said the last. Those guys tended to get exuberant at times like these.

Maeve tapped her com. "Tavares, get back here. I have a headache coming on."

Tavares appeared in five minutes, allowing her to slip out. Unfortunately, it did nothing to get the *Ambrose B* there faster.

To fill the time, Maeve decided that she needed to be ready for any eventuality. She could blow up the ship anytime she hit the self-destruct switch but, if they really had an heir, she wanted to go with them. Should she pack just in case, or not? If she needed to leave in a hurry, she'd need a bag ready. If, on the other hand, things went sour, she didn't want it to look like she had been ready to leave if Pogue had her quarters searched. *Safe, not sorry,* had been her motto for five years. She had become a good spook, just like Dad and Priscilla had taught her. So instead of packing, she grabbed a meal and a shower.

Finishing that, she still had time before they arrived, time to think, time to brood. She tried to distract herself playing a video, but just couldn't focus. She activated her feed from the monitors at the entry port. *Maddening* described the situation perfectly. The clock seemed to crawl almost to a stop.

She tried to imagine what this heir might look like. Would it be a girl or a guy? Tall or short, dark or blond, handsome or ugly, she couldn't decide. As *Ambrose B* drew ever nearer, she found herself wanting to scream, *Run!* Too late! *Bring It* and the squadron now covered them with their missiles and guns. They were trapped.

I should have told them, not waited. She scolded herself as she second-guessed her decision. Pogue would kill them all. She should blow up *Bring It* now but couldn't quite make herself do it.

Pogue looked smug standing in the entry area in his dress whites, a four-man team with him at the reception port and six-man ambush team in the cabin across from his own. A three-man bully squad waited in supply for whomever went down there. The people from *Ambrose B* didn't have a chance, she knew it without a doubt, and yet she couldn't turn away. On pins and needles, her stomach cramping in a tight knot, she stared at her private security screen, waiting for the first glimpse of the heir.

The boarding tube connected as Pogue and his command group waited impatiently. She noticed motion in the tube, then it stopped! Were they having second thoughts, changing their minds? Too late now.

"Come on, come on, come on," she found herself chanting under her breath. Suddenly, two Marines stepped in, weapons out, professionally checking the port area. One stood shorter than average with red hair and the other quite ordinary in every way except being somewhat old for a Marine in her opinion. Both came in alert. This might not be an heir, but these two obviously hardened warriors apparently thought so. If they thought they had an heir with them, it could be, it *must* be.

Run before it's too late! All sorts of crazy scenarios suddenly flooded her mind on ways to help them escape. Subconsciously, she slid forward on her chair, nerves taut, barely breathing.

Then a man stepped through the entry port wearing the dove gray uniform of an officer cadet. Not handsome, exactly, but tanned, fit, and rather rugged with black hair and gray eyes. But so young!

She didn't know what she had been expecting but this, this *kid*, no way. The other heirs Pogue had claimed were pretenders had looked dangerous, older, experienced. This smooth-faced boy looked so *normal*, lacking that hard edge she had been expecting.

Three women came through next, one tall, thin, and brunette, another shorter and dark, and the third—obviously used to command—with graying hair. Beside the commander came a man slightly above average height that looked like a real hard case. Slightly balding, actually, but she wouldn't ever want to meet him in a dark alley. Finally came a Marine who definitely looked like a player, good-looking in a shallow way, along with a black mountain of a man. Both were just as tough looking as the first pair of Marines.

Then the boy spoke and Maeve's jaw dropped. He sounded like an idiot aristocrat from a bad space drama out on some pleasure cruise! She watched as he flummoxed Pogue with a few well-chosen words and a capitol city accent. *What a complete and total fool!* There he stood, soon to be fighting for his life when the iron jaws of Pogue's trap snapped shut on him, and his only concern seemed to be about getting a more comfortable suite than the *Ambrose B* could provide? Pogue would be doing the galaxy a favor by getting rid of him. Despair hit her. *I'll never get off this ship!* Hopelessness threatened to swamp her as faith died.

It's too bad. Those men and women with him are definitely first-rate, much more dangerous, sharper even, than the people who came with the last two. They deserve better than to die for a numbskull like him.

Then she noticed the reaction of the short Marine by the airlock. His face had frozen in shock. Why? Had he just discovered that he had backed the wrong horse? Maybe, but what were the others thinking? She focused on the women. The blonde definitely believed this Cascade fellow to be putting on an act. Maeve could see her biting her cheek, her face a study in concentration at keeping it straight. The brunette didn't have as much self-control. She could barely keep a smile off her face and Maeve could see her struggling to keep herself from laughing. The oldest woman simply watched blandly with interest. They all were in on the joke!

Rerunning the film on Pogue, she saw that indeed this pup had gotten him off-balance from the first word. Watching Pogue's face, she realized that Pogue had gone from being unsure to supreme self-confidence as this kid did a terrible impression of a spoiled aristocrat. *Amazing!*

While Pogue and Bhat confidently directed this apparently clueless young man toward the commander's quarters, she had time to focus on the heir's team. On the way down-ship, the kid's security team proved exactly how expert they were, and they were very good indeed, taking no chances.

Two of them effortlessly blocked the four men Pogue had detailed to provide the heir with *security* at the entry port. Like the last two times, that foursome had the assignment of taking down the heir's security team before they reached the cabin. That wouldn't happen now. She had a pretty shrewd idea that if

those four tried to overpower the two facing them—the giant
Black man and the good-looking white guy—those two would
be the only ones walking away. Pogue's guys apparently thought
so too, because they backed off after just one look.

Rerunning the entry port tape and listening carefully, she
noticed that, as he spoke, the kid had used two different accents,
even acted differently at times, and Pogue had completely
missed it. She had too, she admitted to herself. He had drawn
them all in, got them leaning in the direction he wanted, and
now he headed for Pogue's quarters. He didn't realize his danger,
but how could she warn him? Frantically, she tried to come
up with a plan as they neared the captain's cabin, but nothing
came. The two in the rearguard caught up before they got there.
Anxiously she watched to see what would happen next, knowing
things were about to get interesting when the six men Pogue had
stowed across from his cabin jumped out.

But nothing happened. Nothing violent, anyway.

She felt strangely disappointed by the anticlimax as the rear
detail sealed that cabin door before Pogue's backup team even
had a chance to make a move. Did the kid's men know or were
they just being thorough? Regardless, they weren't leaving anything to chance. She relaxed, just a teeny bit, at the thought.

Switching to her camera in Pogue's cabin, she tuned in just
in time to see Pogue suddenly get angry. *Uh-oh. He just figured
out he's been made a fool of in front of his officers. That boy is in
real trouble now.* Pogue always treated obstacles and problems
the same way: step on them hard and fast so they couldn't fight
back. *What will this kid do, what can he do? How can I help?*
Pogue liked to leave the dirty stuff to his bullyboys but would do
the rough stuff when necessary. She had watched him personally
gun down an officer loyal to the empire in the shuttle entry port
when he refused to order his ship to join Pogue's pocket fleet.
One shot, dead between the eyes. Bhat shot just as well.

On the edge of her seat, as if she were watching a horror
movie slowly unfold, she waited for the end she knew had to
come. Pogue never lost; he always had an edge. She sat glued to

the screen, hoping against hope. Even so, she knew any chance of that boy winning could only be called slim at best. She had seen Pogue easily break others, and he would do the same with this overconfident boy or kill him like the others. A dark hand clamped itself over her heart as her attention remained fixed in dread on the scene.

Her com board blinked. Unauthorized signal originating from somewhere on board. This group had secure communications! Adding another window, she quickly scoured the ship to see where the women were being held hostage. *What? It's not possible!*

The three women all carried weapons now and were headed back to the entry port with several carts of supplies, food mostly, by the look of the boxes. Switching to a camera in the stores area, she found the goons sent to tie them up pretty well out of commission. From the camera angle they appeared, besides being banged up, to be tied up securely in the storeroom where the women had left them. *Who are these people?*

Switching her attention back to the drama going on in the captain's cabin, she saw that Hugh's security had their pistols leveled on Pogue, having already disarmed both Pogue and Bhat. She watched as Hugh and the others relaxed. She wanted to scream, yell, warn them. *Those two are snakes! Don't turn your back on them, ever!*

The old, tough Marine tapped out a message, his action splitting the attention of the heir between him and his prisoners. Although the other two Marines had their weapons pointed at Pogue and the XO, they looked more relaxed also. Maeve bit her lip in an anguish of terror. And then it happened.

As if in slow motion, Pogue drew a hideout gun from under the arm of his chair and Bhat came up with one from the chair's back. They began firing before anyone could react! The average looking Marine guard in front of Pogue went down, clean shot right between the eyes. Pogue now shifted his aim toward the second guard. Bhat shot the old man in the head. Bhat's aim then shifted toward the woman, the ship's captain who apparently knew Pogue from before. *She should have known to never trust Pogue!*

Unexpectedly, it ended. Bhat lay on the carpet, blood gushing but obviously already dead. Pogue had slid to the ground clutching his stomach, hands red from the blood welling up from a deep wound. *Who shot them?* Had she missed seeing someone in the room? She found herself breathing again, but what had happened? A small feeling of pleasure popped up as she realized that that scum Paul Bhat lay dead. With a little luck, Pogue would die too. She had wanted to be the one who killed him for the sake of Patel, Erdogan, Mai Ling, Priscilla, and all the others, but this would do. That he had died, when he thought he would be the one doing the killing, felt glorious.

Rerunning the tape, her understanding of the scene changed. Her focus had been on the dead, which meant she missed the key element, one she had never expected. Neither the crusty, old Marine nor either of the guards with them had shot Pogue and the exec. It had been the kid, the cadet. She could hardly believe it, but there he stood, a curling wisp of smoke rising from his pistol barrel. She focused on his eyes. They were a steel gray with no give in them. Through them she could see his will, undeniable, irresistible as a black hole. At that moment, she could almost believe that he would overcome all odds, any obstacle, to achieve his goals. *He must be a true heir.*

Sitting back, she tapped her lower lip with a fingernail, watching. She had consciously adopted tapping her lip from Priscilla. Initially she had used it to tease Priscilla, but now it reminded her of her friend. Doing it really distracted her, often breaking her concentration, but it kept Priscilla alive in her heart. So she tapped while watching the unfolding scene. If she had been down there, she would have gladly let Pogue bleed to death, but they didn't. They were smart enough to try and keep the captain alive as a hostage, which appeared to be their plan.

Let him die! Maeve's shout echoed in the halls of her mind. That dirty old man held direct responsibility for uncounted innocent deaths, including her friends. *Let him die!* The cry vibrated in her heart.

Ignoring her, they called for the medics instead. Thankfully, it appeared that that old Marine might live, too. Maeve used the cameras to follow the young man in gray. Hugh Cascade, Pogue and his own captain had both called him. She just couldn't really think of him as *Your Highness*. As he headed out into the corridor to get the medics, surprisingly, the boy staggered slightly and looked like he would be sick. *He might not be a cold-blooded killer after all.*

Changing her camera to see the corridor beyond the hatch, her veins went icy; Zane Weston and Gene Nantz stood at the hatch. They were medics, true, but also some of Pogue's worst enforcers. They not only would do anything he asked them to, but they liked to hurt people. She knew of a couple of occasions when Pogue's fun got too rough, they had been standing by. They could fix problems. Or end them.

Maeve's stomach began to hurt again, constricting into another ball of anxiety. The man mountain in the corridor, the one Hugh called Jebet, stood focused on the far hatch, away from the one Nantz and Weston were entering. At that hatch stood just the good-looking one, Peterson, with Hugh, and the solidly muscled pair coming through the hatch individually stood taller and easily outweighed either Hugh or Peterson.

Then it happened. Weston pulled a gun out of his bag as he followed Hugh to catch him by surprise, while Nantz did the same to Peterson. Priscilla's security tapes included an incident where Weston sliced three loyal crewmen to ribbons and one of them had a gun. What chance did Hugh have alone?

Then Weston hit the deck, hard. *How?*

She'd have to go back to the tape later to see, but now Hugh kneeled atop the brute on the deck and didn't seem to be even sweating! Vaguely disappointed that it had been so easy, she realized that Hugh hadn't been fooled for a minute. He'd been waiting for just such a stunt.

Moments later, Hugh took Weston into the cabin. Hunching

forward, she watched as Weston began trying to save Pogue's life and then called Doctor Davison for help. She considered jamming the signal but decided it might reveal her presence. She'd have to find another way to finish Pogue off later. What happened next froze her into immobility. Hugh in a very matter of fact way said *"Listen, Zane. Be sure the doctor knows not to bring weapons other than his knives. If he does, you'll be needing a new doctor because I'm losing my patience."*

"I'll tell 'im," he sneered. *"Who do you think you are, anyway?"*

"The heir apparent," Hugh answered with a hard smile, one she wished she could match. Weston's head snapped around, giving Hugh a hard stare.

Hugh just smiled more broadly, but the short Marine's enthusiastic agreement really caught her attention. *"Better believe it,"* he said, total conviction in every word. That Marine—named Dunn, according to his name tape—believed in this kid younger than him and had followed him into what might have been a death trap, as had the older and supposedly wiser man, the captain of the ship, and the other three Marines. Come to think of it, the women on the supply run had done the same thing. They had been alert, ready to react at a moment's notice, and confident. She had seen it in every move they made.

But they had one thing more, something that had given their actions an edge. *They believe in him.* The possibility of surviving began to flicker back to life. Maybe he *could* be her way off the ship. Hope grew, beginning to replace the despair she had lived with for too long. Still, she couldn't be sure if she should hope, because they were a long way from getting off alive. Perhaps wanting to believe in Hugh blinded her to the impossibility of ever escaping, but for now she'd rely on the faith his people had in him.

What could she do to help? As things stood now, there were simply too many variables to come up with a plan. She sat back again to watch, but seeing so many of Pogue's people, the ones she had been most afraid of, dead, out of the picture, or humiliated, exhilarated her all by itself. Looking around for something to munch on, she found only a small bag of stale popcorn. Sighing, she stood up to get a snack from the mess.

This probably would take hours, so she better pretend to be busy before Jay sent someone to find her. Setting the system to record, she closed the special security application on her com screen before heading down-ship. She had work parties in Engineering and laser three and needed to make sure they were doing what she had told them to do. After that, she should check up on electronics and signaling. Last, she'd step onto the bridge and make sure Tavares had the watch. She wanted to saunter, but found herself almost running when the corridors were clear. She checked the time. To get to all these places and supervise normally would take her an hour, often longer if Pogue or Bhat were prowling around. *Thank goodness that wouldn't happen.* Today, she barely stuck her head through the Engineering hatch before heading off to laser three.

"Ensign," Petty Officer Marley called to her there as she prepared to duck back out, "we have a little problem." Maeve gritted her teeth but stepped back in. If she left now, Marley might be sharp enough to notice her acting abnormally. Maeve always took a personal interest in every project, especially if a problem cropped up. Soon she found herself deep into the innards of the control panel with two techs, talking electronics. Unexpectedly, someone kicked her boot. She backed out of the cramped space to see what they wanted.

"Commander Jay wants you, Ensign," Marley said. "Apparently, they're having trouble communicating with the captain's cabin. Wants you on the bridge now."

Cold sweat sprang up on her back. Maybe her active recorder had blocked incoming calls. "Tell Abercrombie to get up there and handle it. I need to finish this up and I have some other things to do."

Marley looked doubtful but nodded. Abercrombie, although useless, looked impressive as he messed around. His attempts at fixing things would give her time to return to her cabin and take the recorder off-line. Maeve tried to concentrate but recognized she had become more of a hindrance than a help right now. After a while, they found the glitch, no thanks to her, but every moment had been an agony not knowing the current state of events in the captain's cabin.

She pounded off to her cabin, by way of the Signals room, fortunately nearby. Tension almost made her ill as she hurried. She didn't know what had been going on in Pogue's cabin and Jay wanted her up-ship! She couldn't stand it. *What's happened?*

Nerves taut as piano wires, she locked the hatch to her cabin before opening her security application. The usual time delay necessary for opening the channel physically pained her. Then it opened and showed Hugh standing there, pointing a pistol at the doctor!

Opening a quarter-screen box, she ran the recording at high speed. Called doctor, doctor came, doctor operated on Pogue. *Saved him too, drat.* Doctor on his normal high horse, this time demanding Pogue be moved. *Oh my!* The doctor demanding that they move Pogue had almost gotten Davison killed and certainly scared him to death. *Ah, that's what's bugging Jay.* When they called, Hugh had kept the screen blank.

Maeve felt relieved. Her communications tap hadn't caused the problem after all. She knew that the camera on the com could only be authorized from Pogue's cabin. He didn't want anyone seeing what went on in there without his permission.

She smiled evilly. *Abercrombie will be even less useful than normal. Jay will probably be calling for me again soon. Better send reinforcements so Jay won't miss me.* Hitting the com, she called Signals.

"Have Welks and two more ratings go to the bridge to help Abercrombie."

"Aye, aye, ma'am," came the laconic answer. That should keep Jay off her back a while longer. Now to enjoy the show some more. Her stomach grumbled. *I didn't stop for a snack!* she realized, and she simply couldn't go now; things were becoming too interesting.

Interesting, indeed! This boy appeared to be the son of the

last Fleet Overlord, Trevor Cascade. Before today, Pogue certainly had thought he'd killed all of Cascade's sons, but Davison knew the warlord personally and believed in Hugh Cascade, too. That brought up a fascinating question, *Where has he been hiding all these years?* They didn't explain it to the doctor, so her curiosity would go begging a while longer. The doctor appeared convinced, though.

Now what? Suddenly apprehensive again, Maeve wondered what they would do. Dunn, the little Marine, dragged Weston out into the main cabin. She just stared, not believing what happened next. Hugh, the boy who'd fooled Pogue into thinking of him as an overbred snob, who'd proved to be a dead shot but treated the doctor with kindness, now threatened to cut Weston to little pieces personally, and Weston believed him!

How did this kid really stack up, as a good one or bad one? Truly confused, she simply couldn't decide. But what followed drove all thoughts about Hugh from her mind as Weston admitted to atrocities she had suspected but never could have proven. The things he described she never wanted to hear again. The doctor's reaction showed he agreed with her. If she succeeded in getting off this ship, she'd take the doctor with her. He didn't belong with the rest of the crew.

So, what should she do? The answer came simply because she knew what she must do, no question: help Hugh, his men and women, and then go with them. This floating nightmare must be destroyed once and for all before it ruined any more lives. She activated the cursor on Pogue's computer screen to flash in a series of colors . . .

NAVWAR OFFICER COURSE

Introduction to Military Technology Sensors

Naval Officers Basic Course issued 3411 with revisions

There are three general types of sensors used by CNS units: light speed, gravitonic, and preon. The successful midshipman will be able to integrate incoming data from all three for use by the tactical officer. The student will be able to determine whether gravitonic sensor data comes from a natural or man-made source. The student will be able to pinpoint to within one light minute the location of a ship using preon drive. The student will be able to determine whether integration of light speed sensors is appropriate based upon speed and distance to target.

11

The Escape

CNS *Bring It*, Nighthawk System

0115 BBMT 25 October 3473

MAEVE'S NERVES HAD BEEN ABUSED so much today that waiting for someone, anyone, to notice her flashing cursor became torture. *Look at the computer screen!* Then, a miracle! Prince Hugh, or whatever he called himself, noticed.

Finally! Hallelujah! She waited as they decided whether it might be important. *No duh!* Could he really be that dense? *What can I do to convince them?* She entered a command to activate the camera icon. Now maybe they'd all get a clue! She wanted to scratch someone's eyes out! She took this huge chance revealing herself, and they were deciding whether they wanted her help?

Fools! Without me you'll never leave the ship alive!

Then Ward, the old Marine, faced the computer as he spoke to Hugh. "Whoever it is wanted us to notice them by making us aware by enabling a camera icon while blinking that cursor at us. They could have continued to monitor in secret, so what do they want?" Maeve turned the cursor amethyst purple, the imperial color of protection. That should be obvious enough for even these two.

"Sergeant Major?" Hugh began, "if someone can monitor the captain's day cabin secretly, I would guess they have set up a monitor in the bedroom also."

The cursor cycled to white against the black. Impatience filled Maeve. *That would be yes.* White stood for virtue or truth.

"Also, they haven't transmitted any threats or demands, which indicates what to your mind?" Hugh asked.

Ward suggested. "We need to get Captain Felt in here."

Maeve almost came off her seat. When she finally seemed to be making progress with these people, they bring in someone new, so she had to start all over? The doctor stayed with Dunn in the other room when he went to get the woman. At least Davison wouldn't know too much if things went badly. Ward now lay slumped back into his seat. In moments, Gail stepped in, before heading directly to prop Ward up. It warmed Maeve's heart to see the concern Gail had for Ward. Hugh, the only other person in the room, sat facing the camera.

For a minute, Gail busied herself making Ward comfortable.

Indicating a chair, Hugh ordered Gail, "Grab that and sit so you can see the monitor better. Someone has been watching us secretly and just let us know. Let's see what they have to say for themselves." As soon as Gail settled into the chair, Hugh asked in conversational tone, "Can you hear and see us okay?"

Maeve typed *Yes*. Their lack of expression indicated that they weren't quite sure about her motives, but they all needed to hurry things along. They didn't have time for this. Tick tock, tick tock.

"I take it you are in a private area but still need to be careful?"

Yes! Obviously. That didn't mean she could be careless, though, duh.

"You are not the acting commander or a member of the command group?"

No.

That Hugh seemed surprised by something this basic unsettled her a little. She needed to remember that he could make mistakes, something good to know.

"You've been listening in. Do you have a suggestion for our little predicament?"

Surrender?

Hugh's look of disgust with her answer amused her.

She typed, *Can't take a joke? I will have the sensors in the Oort cloud simulate a full on TechMech assault. The other ships will head to the cloud to pick up leakers that get through.*

"Then what?" asked Hugh.

Elmira Hayes *stays here under* Bring It's *guns, which is standard procedure. Admiral Pogue doesn't trust Lieutenant Brennan.*

"And?" prompted Ward.

You tell Commander Jay you are taking Pogue to your ship. He will follow the security cameras showing you moving the admiral to your ship, so everyone will back off. Jay won't do anything to harm Pogue. As soon as you're aboard and away, I will take a shuttle to the Hayes *and follow you out of here.*

Hugh asked, "How do we keep *Bring It* from following us or just blowing *Ambrose B* up as soon as we're off?"

They won't be able to. Trust me. Maeve held her breath, hoping they wouldn't ask how she would prevent *Bring It* from intervening, because she absolutely wouldn't tell them. She couldn't. If they were captured, she needed to keep her ace in the hole secret.

Hugh turned his back on her to face Gail and Ward. Obviously, he wanted their private, honest opinions. *Smart boy*, she thought approvingly.

Gail and Ward's incredulous expressions spiked her agitation. Maybe they wouldn't accept her help. Then what? Gail finally answered. "It's crazy. Trust someone we don't know to do things we can't monitor and hope to get away."

Maeve typed furiously. *Do you have a better plan?*

Hugh turned back. "Captain Felt," Hugh asked formally, "what do you have from your team?"

Gail became stubborn, refusing to speak.

Hugh glanced at Ward, who shrugged as he caught Gail's eye. Hugh then added, "If this person has eyes in the captain's quarters, there are probably eyes and ears everywhere. I would say it is even possible our com channel has been identified, even if the signal hasn't been decrypted. All they need is a fix on the transmission site to find the team. So, where are we?"

Although still not happy, she answered, "We have the supplies and fuel on board, but *Bring It's* guns and missiles are live. We have no way of turning them off at this point, as we are stuck far from all the control lines and nodes, which means we can't get away without being blown up."

Hugh leaned toward her, intently. "Without help, you mean."

"Yes, Your Highness," she answered formally. "Without help."

Maeve let out a breath she didn't even know she had been holding as Hugh turned back to the screen. "Why should I believe you and rely upon you?"

Why not? she typed. Frustration filled her. *Stop wasting time! Make up your mind.*

"Because we may create so much havoc for *Bring It* that they are glad to see us go."

And blow you up as you sail away, anyway, she answered as he talked.

"Maybe yes, maybe no. But, again, why should I trust you?"

She changed the cursor back to purple. *Get a clue! I'm here to help.* Indecision gripped her. If she explained any more, Commander Jay could easily identify her. *Well, in for a penny.*

She began typing again. *My team and I were accidentally assigned to Pogue's ship. We decided, while we were here, to monitor the situation and keep our heads down. By the time we figured out which side Pogue supported, our only option would have been an IED within the ship. It would have been suicide. We watched as Pogue carefully transferred out or killed every loyalist he and his men could find. I've lost my entire team because of that.*

Maeve paused, feeling the deep pain again, before continuing. *He filled their slots with mutineers, which makes this ship completely loyal to him. Almost. I don't know of anyone else besides myself for sure. I have almost blown up the ship several times, just to have it over with. This is the first time I have been able to see a way off while still carrying out my plan.*

Hugh nodded and then asked Ward, "Suggested actions?"

Ward's lips tightened before answering, "Stupid tactically but apparently the likeliest way out. I'd flunk a cadet who chose this course. Too many guns, too many ships, too many people who think we're the bad guys."

Gail nodded agreement. Maeve had to admit that she agreed, too. Amazingly, they were all on the same sheet of music. Doing what she suggested would be stupid.

Hugh turned back toward the screen. "Start the ball rolling," he ordered formally. "How long?"

Even as she typed, she activated one of the messages she had prepared long before. *It will take hours for the signal faking an attack to get to the cloud, without being detected, and then back. Can't send out an archeonB signal without Commander Jay knowing.* Mentally she added, *Or my Signals team, for that matter.*

While she worked on her end, she watched as they got everything ready to move. Maeve then settled in to listen with half an ear while she checked on her teams. It wouldn't do for one of them to stumble across her spy system at this late date. Hugh had brought the doctor in to talk to him, so she tuned in on the bridge to find Welks, Abercrombie, and the other team members she'd sent being yelled at by Jay to get the cameras working in Pogue's cabin. Smiling, she checked her other cameras. Clicking back to Pogue's cabin, she approved of Hugh's offer to take Davison with them. If Davison agreed, it would be very crowded on that small ship Hugh had come on, but, after all this, they couldn't leave him behind.

Surprising her, Davison refused to go with them. *He has a family on Nighthawk?* She leaned forward. Davison deserved to live and so did his family. She started the cursor to blink white again on the blank screen to get their attention. Hugh asked, "Which shuttle are you taking?"

Indecision gripped Maeve. *What do I do?* If she told them and they were captured, she would have no way to escape. But she couldn't get away, anyway, if Commander Jay stopped them. At that moment, her inability to choose became irrelevant.

Hugh leaned intently forward. "If Davison has a family he won't leave behind, at least some of the people on the corvette will feel the same way. You could have a mutiny if you don't get a civilian transport and take them with you. Which shuttle?" Hugh insisted.

She had to think about that. She brought the cursor to green while she weighed the question trying to decide what she should do, the right thing to do. She hoped he understood the color scheme. She decided to tell them. She had already thrown safety out the airlock, anyway. She typed *port* in green. After a moment she went on, *I will take him if you'll rendezvous with the corvette and take me with you.* She hoped she had made the right decision, because the whole situation tied her stomach in a knot.

She caught Ward shrugging. What had she missed?

She saw Hugh shaking his head. "Thanks for the help, Sergeant Major."

Ward smiled back. "Comes with the territory, Your Highness, comes with the territory. If you can't make simple life-and-death decisions for a few hundred people, how will you be able to do it for billions?" Although said lightly, Maeve saw the truth in his answer. He meant it.

Maeve relaxed as Hugh ordered Ward, "Ward, get on the com and make arrangements for safe passage to the *Ambrose B.* Doctor Davison, you accompany the medics to sick bay, after which, you are on your own to get to the shuttle. The corvette will be on its own to get the crew's families and then go home, and I mean to Seventh Fleet, not to Thirteenth Sector, the best way they can." Taking a breath, he faced the screen and formally declared, "On my honor, we will rendezvous with the *Elmira Hayes* before we leave the system and pick up our unknown benefactor before continuing on our way to Earth." He had made her, an anonymous stranger, a promise. From what she had seen the last few hours, he would likely move heaven and earth to keep it. She'd trust him to keep his word.

She went back to checking on the status of her teams, as well as any surprises Jay might be setting up. Angry voices coming from the screen quadrant showing Pogue's cabin snapped her attention back. *What now?* Ward seemed to be arguing with someone over the com screen. *What could make him so angry?*

"I don't care if you are the next most senior commander of this flotilla. Get off the line so I can speak with Commander Jay."

And then she heard it, a voice she never thought would make a difference in her life, the captain of one of the cruisers in the flotilla. "Sergeant Major," drawled the overbred voice of Wilby

Dent, "you don't understand. You have no choice but to surrender. You are in the middle of that ship, in the middle of this fleet, in the middle of this solar system. So, if you would be so kind?"

Maeve had no idea why Dent would be calling; Jay took charge when Pogue wasn't available. Like now. Then bits and pieces of conversations she had overheard between Bhat and Pogue suddenly made sense. In a way, they must have been hiding Dent and keeping his importance secret. Hugh taking over relieved her a bit, while greatly amusing her when he started by downgrading Dent's rank of lieutenant commander and putting on his snob act. "Lieutenant, why are you giving my man here trouble? We are leaving, of course. I am the heir apparent, and I will be obeyed! Now put Commander Jay on."

A thrill of pleasure ran up her spine as shock crossed Dent's face showing on the monitor screen in Pogue's cabin. "Warlord?" he whispered.

Just as at the entry, Maeve watched Hugh take the advantage and run with it. "Your name, Lieutenant?" he demanded imperiously.

Dent visibly shook himself before getting control. Sneeringly, he answered, "I am Wilby Dent. My father was wrongly convicted of treason, when it was that usurper, Emperor Cyrus, who was the traitor. He killed my father. And so I helped start the Restitution Movement to remove the usurpers and return my family, as descendants of Emperor Benjamin, to their rightful place as rulers of the em—"

Then another call broke in, splitting the screen as Dent remained online. An icon on her screen indicated that this had been relayed by the planetary archeonA facility, not from a nearby ship as Dent's had. With a gasp she recognized her sister, Morgain uch Robert. A cold sweat broke out on Maeve's forehead and she felt deeply grateful she couldn't be seen.

Morgain said with her huge smile. "What a pleasant surprise, all of us on this call together. By the way, good to see you, Sergeant Major." She flashed him a blinding smile. "I understand you have made a bit of a mess there but are stuck." Her face hardened into a mask of fury as she turned her attention to Dent. "As for you, your usefulness to me is at an end. I am on my way to claim my prizes even as we speak." Dent's transmission abruptly ended. She refocused her attention on Ward. She gave that blinding smile again, but watching Hugh's face, Maeve felt pleased that Morgain now appeared to repel him. Morgain continued, "Here is my offer: surrender. I might even let Cascade's boy live if you do it quickly. But decide now. I want you and the bag, and yes, I know about it because when I was an heir, one of my proctors talked before you pulled her. You have ten seconds." A smug look crossed Morgain's face as she said this.

A flash of insight came to Maeve. Morgain must have sent Pogue out here. It explained some other conversations she had overheard between Bhat and Pogue that had made no sense before.

Gail cut the incoming feed abruptly. Hugh didn't appear upset to Maeve, so he must have given Gail a sign she hadn't seen. Knowing Morgain, she had no doubt her sister would be furious about being cut off, something she would love to see. She also regretted that Priscilla hadn't known who Dent really was. No question she would have found a creative way to pay him back, something impossible for her in the current situation.

Breaking into her thoughts about her sister, she heard Ward ask her, "Can you get your diversion going now?"

She typed in blue, indicating her best judgment, *It'll be awhile. The Oort cloud sensors are a long way out there. Before I can tie into the archeonB sensor net, I have to use old-fashioned light speed radio. It takes hours for radio to hit the first relay so it won't be detected.*

Dent's a pompous, arrogant little prick. He commands one of the cruisers and it's heading toward solar north on my screen. My guess is that he decided he should make himself scarce before Morgain shows up. As for Morgain, though, she's a totally different story. Don't underestimate her power. I can personally attest that she is pure evil.

Watching the camera feed, she saw the raw hate on Davison's face and sympathized deeply. With half an ear, she listened to them as she made sure nothing new got in the way of their escape. She heard Ward say, "Good thought. Dunn and the others have rebreathers as part of their protection detail kit, so we have just enough with Kennion's."

"What?" asked Davison.

Maeve disagreed about Jay trying to take them down with gas, but they were being careful and professional.

As time passed, she realized that Hugh felt as nervous as she did. He paced like a caged tiger. The countdown clock on her screen showed over an hour left. So slow! What could she do to not pace like him? Pack! She had time. But she couldn't risk being seen carrying a space bag anywhere on the ship with the current alert. Worse, she had no time to go to her private cache, the things she most wanted to take with her, where they lay hidden in hydroponics. She couldn't take the chance of getting them because she'd probably be forced to get involved in a technical issue she couldn't easily come up with an excuse to avoid. In the event that Jay happened to be there, she would really be up a creek without a paddle. Extremely unlikely, but you couldn't plan on something not happening. She had to stay in contact with Cascade and his people.

She began stuffing small essentials into her duty uniform pockets as a small tear slipped down her cheek. She had left almost everything tying her to Mom and Dad back on Beacon and now she must leave the rest. When she did, what would be left of her?

She stuffed her little pistol into a pocket. Out of character, but she had to be on that shuttle when it left, and she'd shoot her way through if necessary. Going through her closet another time, her eyes settled on her whites, remembering the day she'd earned them. Another tear fell, taking with it this additional piece of her life. She had always been a bit vain about how she looked in her formal uniform but, unfortunately, had absolutely no way to bring it.

Looking around, she saw various items strewn about, things she couldn't possibly take with her. As she did, she permitted herself one spark of rebellion. For five years, she had kept every-thing in its prescribed place so as to keep her cover intact. After today, that wouldn't matter; she'd either be dead or gone. She shoved everything left on the floor helter-skelter into the closet and slammed the door.

Sitting, she set herself to waiting again. Just to keep busy, she uploaded a worm into the ship's targeting system to keep it off-line during the escape. It wouldn't prevent fire under local control, but it might keep Jay off-balance long enough for her to blow the ship up while getting safely away.

Suddenly, an icon began flashing, catching her by surprise. An alert message had just come in from the cloud! *A real one.* She watched Commander Jay competently order the response. Why not? He'd been doing all the real tactical work for years; he didn't need Pogue or Bhat to do this job. As per standard pro-cedure, he kept *Elmira Hayes* and *Bring It* as a reserve while the others headed for the cloud. She'd been half afraid Jay would order all of the ships to go, even with the crisis on board. Thank goodness they were staying. Getting a shuttle safely away in the middle of a battle would be dicey at best.

Sitting at her desk, she typed, *That's for real! My message didn't have time to get out there and back.* Then Hugh surprised her again. He changed the plan so *Elmira Hayes* could meet the ship carrying its dependents from Nighthawk to enable them to get safely away, people he didn't even know. Plus, to top it all off, he wanted to go out to fight the TechMech alongside the mutineers. *Complicated guy; clearly a believer in "duty first."*

Maeve waited as Hugh decided what he would do. At last, he faced the monitor. "Get to the shuttle. Wait for the doctor as long as you can. We're on our way now."

Maeve didn't pause for a second invitation. Tying the scuttling charges to a proximity sensor that would only go off when both the port shuttle and *Ambrose B* were safely away, she headed for the infirmary. On the way, she wrapped her arm in a sling.

Reaching the infirmary, she found no one there, so she sat in a chair and waited. Foot swinging nervously, she almost left twice without the doctor before sitting back down. She felt sure Hugh and the others must be off the ship by now. What if she reached the shuttle too late, after the *Ambrose B* took off or blew up? In an agony of indecision, her mind froze for a timeless instant. Breaking the grip of fear, she checked the time. Only seven minutes had passed. It seemed like hours. *Breathe.* Seconds sluggishly blinked along. *What's taking the doctor so long?* A sudden clatter in the passageway alerted her. They were here. Davison gave her barely a glance as he ordered his patients to be placed in berths.

"Doctor?" she asked.

"What do you want, Ensign? Can't you see I'm busy?" In fact, he appeared to be anything but busy to Maeve's eye as he kept glancing around in a distracted way.

"Sorry to bother you, Doctor, but I hurt my arm over at the port shuttle and need your help."

Davison shook his head. "Can't go now. Waiting for someone. I'll send a medic."

Maeve grabbed Davison's arm. "Port shuttle, Doctor, now!" she repeated, forcefully.

Sudden comprehension dawned in his eyes. "Oh . . . Let's go." She nodded and looked around to see if anyone had paid attention. What could Davison be thinking? He made a terrible conspirator. Thank goodness no one had noticed.

Davison took one last look around at his sick bay, a melancholy expression on his face, before speaking to the chief orderly. "Take care of the patients, Hathaway," he ordered before heading out.

Maeve just shook her head. How oblivious could a man be? If Hathaway figured things out, he might call Jay and then they'd never get off this ship. As soon as they were out of sight, she threw off the sling, before grabbing Davison's elbow. "Run, Doctor! We don't have much time."

Living on a starship, no matter how large, didn't require a high level of physical conditioning. She could have exercised more like many of the crew, but walking around checking on her teams should have been enough, at least in her mind. But both were breathing hard as they neared the shuttle tube entry hatch. Catching her breath, Maeve drew the tiny pistol hidden in her pocket. Inside the circular entry port a single guard stood watching the access hatch, a woman Maeve barely knew. Pointing the pistol as they approached her, Maeve ordered, "On the deck."

The woman stared back, uncomprehending. "Down, now!" yelled Maeve as she fired a round that spanged off down a passageway. She could feel her father standing at her shoulder, approving of her tactical choice.

"You'll never make it," squeaked the woman as she dropped down.

Maeve didn't bother to answer, just motioned Davison into the shuttle connector, following him down the tube and then aboard. Dogging the hatch, she disconnected the tube before heading for the flight deck. For someone to get to the hatch, they would need a vacuum suit and she'd be well gone before that could happen.

"Where's the man?" Davison asked in confusion as he followed her. "The one who arranged all this? And the others? There must have been others."

Maeve didn't have time to explain. Strapping in, she said, "Just me, Doctor." She began powering up. One good thing about being in charge of the electronics: you had to test all the systems to make sure they worked, like the flight simulator, for instance. She set an autopilot course for the *Elmira Hayes*. "Strap in, Doctor."

"Can you fly this?" he asked incredulously.

An imp peaked out of her as she answered, "We'll see, but I hear there's a first time for everything. Now strap in; we're going."

Davison began to sputter, but the clamp holding them to the side of the cruiser let go at that moment, throwing him to the side. Hastily, he dropped into a seat.

"Port shuttle," came Tavares's alarmed voice. *"Shut down and open your hatch. Security is on the way there at this time."*

"Negative, Control," Maeve answered, "going for a little joyride. Out." She switched to *Elmira Hayes*'s frequency. She really didn't have anything to say to the people back on *Bring It*. Besides, speaking to people about to die because of her felt a little ghoulish. Blasting away, she checked to see how far they were from the ship. Minimum safe distance for the charges passed quickly, but they hadn't blown. She hoped that *Ambrose B* had made it, because she had no time to wait. She needed to activate the backup plan. She grabbed the manual initiator from her left, side pocket. Just as she powered it up, a blast wave hit the shuttle, throwing them about. As close to the blast zone as they were, the shuttle's stabilizers weren't sufficient to dampen all the effects of the explosion. That answered her concern about *Ambrose B*. It must have just barely cleared the safety threshold, allowing the automatic destruct to engage.

Watching her flight screen, she unlocked the autopilot, setting a course for *Ambrose B*. Minutes later, while approaching rendezvous with *Ambrose B*, she keyed in a delayed auto-course to *Elmira Hayes*. Unstrapping, she grabbed the doctor's hands. "Good luck."

Not waiting for a reply, she ran to the suit locker to throw one on before heading out the airlock. She stepped out into blackness, slowly spinning until *Ambrose B* came into sight, waiting just as Hugh had promised. Kicking off, she had barely started when the shuttle shot off behind her.

Too fearful to allow herself to hope even now, she more than half expected *Ambrose B* to head out-system, leaving her to drift away until she ran out of air. The distance between the point where she'd stepped off the shuttle until she reached *Ambrose B* required only a ten-second hop, but it seemed to last almost forever. A ping warned her as she neared the ship, perspective being unreliable in space for judging distance. Flipping to present her boots to the hull, she clanged down safely. Clomping in her magnetized boots to the airlock, she felt strangely let down. They had waited for her and she had arrived safely, so why didn't she feel relieved?

Opening the airlock, she shrugged out of her jet pack. She stepped into the airlock, hung the jetpack on a hook, and began the cycle to re-pressurize. Finally, the hatch opened. On the other side, two Marines stood armed, alert. Then it hit her, relief washing over her, she had escaped all those dangers! The fear, the loneliness, the darkness. Joy exploded in her heart. Entering, she smiled, a dazzling bubble of happiness filling her to bursting. *Safe at last, after all these years!* Removing her helmet she almost laughed to see Hugh off-balance. *By me? My, my.* She wanted to giggle. Up close he looked even younger than he had on her monitors, and better looking.

"You are?" he asked, sounding befuddled.

She kept herself from laughing, barely, at the heir apparent. Automatically, from engrained habit, she responded, "Maeve Ellyllyon, Ensign, reporting as ordered, Your Highness."

ARCHIVED IMPERIAL CLASSIFIED DOCUMENTS

Declassified 24 September 3485
Test of Heirs Program
Proctor Course revised 2612
Procedures Upon Acclamation of Heir and Placement of
Gems in the Galactic Starburst

The proctor of the successful heir becomes Imperial
Protector with duties detailed in that section when the
heir becomes emperor or empress. The successful heir
achieves this status by 1) receiving all gems, 2) being
acclaimed, and 3) placing the gems into the starburst.

All other unsuccessful heirs, except for a co-ruler
as described in that section, cannot be allowed to go
forward after either partial or complete receipt of the
gems. An heir who has repeated the oath while holding
the bag is included in this procedure. There can usually
only be a single carrier of the Galactic Starburst. As
a result, the Guardian program will deactivate any
unsuccessful heir's medibots and commobots. The proctor
will then return the body of that heir to his, her, or
their family for interment with honors.

12

Passenger

CNS *Ambrose B*, Nighthawk System

0610 BBMT 25 October 3473

HEIR APPARENT HUGH CASCADE STOOD a moment collecting his wits. Weariness weighed on him. He had only this one last task before he could eat and then crash. Since before entering the Nighthawk system more than twenty-four hours earlier, truthfully, zero six hundred yesterday, he and the crew had been on high alert. Between preparing for all foreseeable eventualities, followed by flying in extra slowly, the day had already been way too long even before reaching *Bring It*.

Behind him, he heard Sergeant Peter Petersen speak into his com, but couldn't quite make out the words. Giving himself a mental shake, he gave the ensign a crooked grin. "Let's go talk in the gym." Half turning toward his men, he ordered, "Dunn and Peterson, with me. Have Fleisch meet us there."

Before he could take a step, Petty Officers Karen Hall and Pam West came double-timing it down the corridor. "Your Highness, forgive the interruption, but we are going to need some time with the ensign before the two of you speak," Pam said.

Hugh raised one eyebrow questioningly. "Protection protocols require us to make certain the ensign isn't a threat," Karen answered.

Maeve looked at her, surprise showing on her face. "Me? A threat? I just blew up an entire ship to protect all of you."

Karen spoke up. "Exactly. You just blew up a ship with hundreds of people. You are clearly capable of violence. For the moment, we're going to treat you as the dangerous person you are."

Maeve looked stunned. Hugh couldn't blame her. He hadn't anticipated his team would be this cautious. He realized now that Sergeant Kevin Dunn had called the women to the hatch when he realized their "guest" was female.

"I'm sorry, Ensign EL-Y-Lon," he pronounced slowly as he read her name tag. "But even I—in fact, especially I—don't get to argue with royal protection protocols."

The ensign grimaced. "It's pronounced Ath-y-thlon, not Ell-y-lon, Your Highness. It's Welsh."

Stopping halfway through his turn, Hugh's mouth screwed itself up into a frown almost unconsciously. "I'll try to remember, Ensign A-thy-th-lon," he pronounced slowly but distinctly.

Pam stepped forward with an apologetic smile. She didn't even look at Hugh as she spoke to the girl. "If you will accompany us into the facilities, Ensign? This shouldn't take long." Hugh caught a sideways look of Maeve's face and thought he detected fleeting anger and embarrassment.

He'd had no idea.

Maeve's face hardened into anger in her voice, as she asked, "What if I choose not to be *examined*?"

Pam shrugged. "Regretfully, you'll be returned to the airlock and required to leave. We'll let *Elmira Hays* know where you are, but I can't guarantee they'll be able to come back and get you before your air runs out."

Maeve nodded as she pondered for a moment. "I never even considered what might be necessary in order to protect an emperor. It has been so long and I was so young when Cyrus died." Giving a sour grimace, she took a step toward the facilities and shrugged her shoulders, before saying, "Let's get this over with, ladies." Carefully looking directly ahead, and especially avoiding any eye contact with Hugh, she moved quickly.

Maeve being escorted away with blank-faced guards served as just one more reminder of how his life had changed. He watched Maeve march resolutely into the head, followed by her escort. Her cheeks flamed scarlet, but she held her head. Hugh blushed, too, as he realized what kind of search they would be conducting.

He didn't like this at all. In a bolt of clarity, he got it. His life wouldn't ever be his anymore, it belonged to everyone else and would be treated that way. He wondered if girls he dated, if that ever happened, would be subjected to the same intrusive search? Checking out people his protectors hadn't fully vetted before, like their passenger, must be a special case; there had to be a limit, didn't there?

To distract himself, he returned to his quarters. Opening his screen, he accessed the sensors that let him follow the battle at the fringes of the system. It seemed to be almost over, but at a terrible cost. Pogue's squadron appeared to be down to just three ships under drive, but they had won. Those were chasing down a couple of TechMech survivors. Hugh, recognizing their gallantry, wanted to salute them. Hopefully, most of the other ships could be refitted and their crews saved.

Strange thing to be feeling guilt for abandoning traitors he would otherwise have had to order executed, he reflected.

A rap came on the hatch. Through the com, Hugh ordered, "Come."

Dunn entered and announced, "The ensign is waiting for you in the gym, Your Highness."

Hugh's cheeks colored, but he commanded his face to remain impassive. Hugh refused to spend more time thinking about anything except the business at hand. In his hands lay a girl's life. A woman's life, really, for what she had done indicated her to be fully adult regardless of her age.

Stepping across to the gym/mess, he found his way blocked by Gail, looking quite stern. "Captain?"

Captain Gail Felt looked into his eyes as if searching for something before she answered, "Her name is Maeve uch Robert, not Ellyllyon. We ran a DNA scan through the proctor's database."

"Thanks." He tried to step past her, but Gail didn't move. "Why didn't you just space her, then, if she lied?" he asked.

Gail frowned. "She might have a good reason. Don't be hasty, but I suggest you try to get her to tell you her real name on her own. One other thing, Your Highness, she is barely eighteen years old. She's just a teenager."

"*I'm* just a teenager. And I'm out here trying to prove I'm worthy of being emperor. And *she* just blew up a ship full of people. Seems to me that we're both quite a bit more than 'just teenagers,'" Hugh growled before pushing past her. Walking into the gym, he saw Peterson waiting with sidearm drawn as Dunn and Gail followed him in. At the far end of the room waited the ensign, freshly showered and wearing a new uniform, standing between Pam and Karen. He couldn't help but notice how remarkably crisp and clean she looked. *Pretty, too.* After the last several, stressful hours he knew he could have used some time in the head and a change of uniform, too.

Straitening up to a full brace, the ensign saluted and said, "Your Highness," in a beautiful alto voice. Hugh hadn't even thought about her voice the first time they'd met, but he liked it.

Recovering, he returned her salute before indicating a chair and saying simply, "Sit, Ensign." He paused, staring stonily at her. Gail sat also, but none of the others did. They stood guard to protect him. A pointed reminder, if he needed one, that he had surrendered control of his life and that this liar might be dangerous. She settled easily into her hard-backed chair.

"So, Ensign A-thy-th-lon," he pronounced again carefully, "tell me how we came to meet out here in the sticks." The line came from a particularly bad novel he had read last year, but it seemed like a good impersonal way to start. Gail had told him to get her to tell the truth and he'd give her a chance. One.

"Well, Your Highness," she began, a serious look crossing her face, "I am the daughter of Robert ap Morgan, a relatively little-known member of the intelligence community. Intentionally so. My family has guarded the emperors for a thousand years as their unseen shield and sword against those who strike from the darkness. Since the days of Constantine Jackson, Your Highness." Her serious look gave way to a small smile.

She's proud of her family and its service to the empire. With a nod, Hugh acknowledged that she had just volunteered her true identity. Hugh's misgivings had begun to give way as she spoke, but he recognized that she could merely be well trained in gaining the trust of others. Hugh leaned back, evaluating her. His life, not to mention the existence of the empire, could depend upon his decision here.

Eyes narrowing, he examined her even more closely. *She's nervous.* Hugh began to catalog the signs like a check list. Her hands looked tense, fidgety, her left hand squeezing the fingers of her right so tightly the tips were almost white. Every minute or less she crossed then uncrossed her ankles. When crossed and if the right foot lay on top, it wriggled like an eel, nonstop. Could she be scared? *Probably terrified and because of me or what I might do.* He realized that, if this interview went badly, she would have a long space walk to the nearest ship, much less planet. Despite those minor tells, she amazed Hugh with her ability to convey calm from her shoulders up. Did it all constitute an act to manipulate him or simply for survival? If survival, he could easily understand and appreciate her behavior. If she did it for some other reason, then he and she would have a problem.

He glanced at Gail, but she wore an unreadable poker face. As he looked back at Maeve, he became aware that the silence had already stretched well beyond social convention. However, he knew it could be a very effective weapon, having been stood tall on more than one occasion for transgressions minor and major back on Doña Carlota's estate on Jeffco. Having experienced the impact of long silences, as well as used them to avoid responsibility, he sat and thought some more.

"So, tell me a little more about your father, Robert ap Morgan," he demanded finally.

As he examined her closely, he noticed her fingers intertwined in a death grip, but otherwise she maintained her composure. She acquiesced to his request by nodding slightly. "He belonged to Imperial Counterintelligence as well as liaison to the Imperial Succession Council. He escaped the initial coup, but they gunned him down afterward. This happened about five years ago, on the Imperial Academy grounds. Right in front of me, as a matter of fact. I personally shot the assassin."

Her clipped sentences only accentuated the deep grief he detected in her voice and on her face over these events. What she said here had the ring of truth. If not, he might as well give up now because otherwise he would never be able to trust his judgment.

"What happened then?" He began to feel intrigued by the story, but also knew the more detailed her story became, the easier it would be to detect a lie.

"I was thirteen at the time and one of the youngest persons ever accepted to the Academy," she added proudly. "Dad pulled strings to get me in. He thought I would be safe there. I had been accepted to the last class before the Academy closed and was on my way for the entrance interview when they killed him."

"I'm sorry you didn't get to go. So tell me, how did you come to be called Maeve Ellylon instead of Morgan?" he prompted.

"My name, in the proper Welsh, is Maeve uch Robert. Admiral Davies changed my name to keep me safe. When he closed the Academy, he hid me away as an electronics mate and faked my age as sixteen. His people trained me in everything I needed to know to make that cover work. Then my team accidentally ended up on Captain Pogue's cruiser. It shouldn't have happened, but we didn't have a choice. We had been together for two years, between training and Pogue's ship, when we found out which side he really supported. That would have been about three years ago. Since that time, I have watched each of those women, my friends, caught and killed. I am the only one left," she finished quietly, but with a hint of determination in her voice. He knew she must have passed through fire to get here.

Pausing to add up thirteen, two and three, he asked sharply, "How are you an ensign at eighteen? Shouldn't you only be enlisted?"

"Remember, my cover made me three years older. On top of that, I did a petty officer's job pretty well for about four years on that ship. With all the purges to get rid of loyal spacers, they lost lots of competent people and leaders. After my superior died trying to set up scuttling charges, there weren't many competent petty officers left, which meant I didn't have much competition for the job."

Swept up in her story, he nodded at her to go on.

"It's also possible that Pogue just wanted me around in case he got bored with his current harem." Hugh's eyes went up and he glanced at Gail. Fury filled Maeve's eyes. "Pogue was a pig and used his position to bribe, blackmail, or simply force women to join him in his cabin. My team leader had wired Pogue's suite after a fleet action damaged that part of the ship. I—I can't," she struggled to remain composed. "Some of these women were never seen again." A shudder ran through her as she clearly contemplated that she could have eventually been one of those women.

Hugh recognized that he had stopped attempting to be objective as anger filled him. Pogue's actions were directly opposed to everything the Creed called for in any citizen, never mind a senior military officer. That this young woman had witnessed his actions and, feared that she might one day find herself alone with the man to suffer a similar fate, turned his stomach.

"As I explained, my team leader died, I don't know how, trying to complete our plan for scuttling the ship. A number of heirs had come through and been killed. She wanted to prevent that happening again. After she . . . ," Her voice cracked with emotion. "After her death, I finished setting up the charges and waited for the right time."

Hugh looked around the room. Gail looked angrier than he'd ever seen her. The other two women had tears in their eyes. Dunn seemed to be clenching his jaw. Only Peterson looked unmoved. He turned back to the young ensign and nodded. He had a decision to make. If this woman *wasn't* loyal to the empire, she'd gone to extreme lengths to prove she was. And her story, based on what he'd heard about Pogue from Gail and Sergeant Major Sean Ward, rang sadly true. Plus she had saved them.

Hugh nodded once more to himself. But a small doubt kept poking him, sounding remarkably like the sergeant major. He needed to look objectively at all the options. Maybe the next question would finish clearing things up. "Did anyone get off *Bring It* with you?"

Maeve nodded. "Doctor Davison is with *Elmira Hayes*, sire, as requested. We're still within archeon range, so you should be able to verify that."

Hugh saw that, although still tense, Maeve had stopped fidgeting, her foot now hardly tapping at all. Obviously full of anger and grief, she no longer appeared nervous. Her emotions had a tight focus, but were no longer aimed at him, as far as he could tell.

Hugh decided. Leaning forward, he looked directly into Maeve's eyes. "What you've been through, no one should have to suffer. And certainly not someone as young as you. I believe the empire owes you a debt of gratitude, and I have no doubt that your father would be very proud of you." Tears filled Maeve's eyes.

Looking at Gail, he saw her appraising him. *I think she approves.* Looking over at Karen and Pam, he ordered, "Please set the ensign up with a bunk." Standing without another word, he left the mess.

WAITING UNTIL HUGH HEADED UP-ship, Gail stepped out of the mess and quickly walked the opposite direction on her way to a cabin on the far side of the main deck. Her mind chewed over what to do about Maeve as she went. No one could see what she did after she made the right-hand corner into the short aft connecting corridor. Speeding her step a bit, she passed the turn that led to the engine room and engineer's cabin, getting to the next corner quickly. Those ten steps seemed enormously long but, glancing to her right as she hit the corner, she verified that the corridor behind her remained clear. Looking ahead, she saw no one in this longer corridor, so she slowed a mite as she took the four steps to the aft port cabin. Turning the handle before giving it a quick yank, she stepped into the dimness. Closing the hatch behind her, she felt confident that no one had seen her. As she closed the hatch, she took care to keep it from slamming.

Ward might be asleep, but she couldn't tell. After almost getting killed, he certainly needed the rest.

"I'm awake, Gail, you don't need to be so careful. Besides, that hatch clatters like a drawer full of pans even when it's closed carefully."

Her eyes found him sitting at the desk watching the com screen, though uncharacteristically slumped. "You should be in bed asleep," she observed, before sitting on the other chair. "Back there on *Bring It*, I thought a time or two we'd have to carry you back."

"Fat chance. This little scratch won't cause me any problems."

Gail's heart went out to this man who could never slow down, never give less than his best, even if it killed him. She also knew that arguing wouldn't make a difference. Besides, if she did, it would just irritate him and then he'd spend precious energy proving his fitness for duty.

Men! But she really just meant one man. "So what do you think? How did he do?"

"Do you really need me to answer that? I saw that look you gave him."

Gail sat down on the bed near Ward. "I won't pretend that wasn't impressive. He showed good judgment, maturity, and empathy there that I'm not sure I'd seen in him before."

Ward nodded. "I agree, though I worry he might be a tad *too* empathetic. She pushed all of his buttons. She may have saved us, but now he wants to save *her*."

Gail chuckled. "So he reacted as any red-blooded male would when he discovers he has just rescued a beautiful damsel in distress? My, how awful."

Ward gave her a severe look. "It's not a laughing matter, Gail. This situation is tough enough already."

Gail shook her head. "In my opinion, he just earned the sapphire for judgment with how he handled Maeve. What's more, it's obvious you're also going to award him some other gems for this last little escapade. I think you're worried things are going too well."

Ward's eyes betrayed his anxiety. "He is doing very well and, you're right, it *is* making me nervous."

Gail smiled sweetly, noting that he didn't discuss whether he intended to award Hugh anything or not for his actions on *Bring It.* What had happened there hadn't even come close to being a normal part of the test, but then, nothing they had done so far had. Reacting to the situation, as the heir found it, became the test.

"I'm glad you're happy about Hugh. Did you happen to read the rest of the report Guardian kicked out when I ran Maeve's DNA?"

Ward groaned. "Yes, I saw that she's an heir. Still qualified, it seems. Only one of the four daughters who is. But based upon what her sisters have done since the coup, I would have a tendency to not trust her."

Gail nodded. "Admiral Davies himself hid her. Why would he have taken a personal interest in her if she couldn't be trusted?"

Ward just shook his head. "That was five years ago. And what are the odds that we would end up with another heir on board, especially one of Robert's daughters and the sister of the woman who just threatened us all?"

Gail grimaced. "The odds are long, I won't deny that. But we have a DNA sample. She is Maeve uch Robert and I detected active imperial nanites, which makes her an heir. Serendipity occurs all the time, even when we don't recognize it. Personally, I'm grateful she's an heir because we may need her."

Ward snorted, "But if she's anything like her sisters . . ." He let the thought trail off.

"We've seen zero evidence she is; quite the opposite, in fact. I'll watch her, of course, but I think she survived a situation that would have twisted other people into psychological pretzels, and she looks normal to me. Relatively, anyway. If she passes the psych examination, she'll be good to go."

Ward didn't even try to hide his alarm from Gail. "You intend to administer the oath, don't you? Regardless of the results of the psych eval, you've already decided she's mentally fit, haven't you?" Rushing on, he fixed her with a steely eye before adding, "Having two heirs together on the same ship is probably a very bad idea, don't you think? You know what happens if one succeeds."

Gail stared him down. "It might be bad or it could be the best thing for both of them. A little competition and support might not hurt. But it is, as you noted by not giving me an order *not* to give her the oath, my decision. I'll let you know when I decide."

Gail knew Ward well enough to be sure he wanted to make the decisions regarding *both* Maeve and Hugh, but couldn't decide if arguing would change her mind. It wouldn't, of course. In the end, he surprised her a bit by ignoring the issue entirely. He only said, "Better get my game face on," as he forced himself out of the chair. But he couldn't keep himself upright, teetering forward to lean heavily on the desk.

Stubborn old fool! Gail's face tightened with anger. "You're kidding! You're going to see him like this? You know what handling the stones takes out of you when you deal with them."

Panting, Ward disingenuously asked, "Who said anything about presenting stones?"

"You're an idiot, Sean Ward! You know that, don't you?"

He managed a small smile, then whispered, "It's why you love me."

Gail snorted, then stood and went to him, getting a hand under his arm. "When you pull this kind of stunt, I wonder. Call me when you're done and we'll get someone to help get you back here."

Ward just nodded as he leaned on her, shuffling to the hatch . . .

The Core Planets

Nicholas Armbruster, PhD, April 4, 3555
Part V, Chapters 13 through 16

Part V covers the Dissension Period from 2880 to 3103. Only three emperors and two empresses ruled during this era, but the active interference with the Test of Heirs, by not only the three main lines of the Jackson family but other parties as well, became so significant that many heirs went into hiding and refused to participate. The empire itself fell into a very fragile condition as a direct result, with entire sectors acting essentially as independent nations.

The best estimate of the carnage suffered by the Jackson family is that 101 heirs died in the test itself and as many as a thousand died from other than natural causes during this 223-year span. Historically, a number of groups have been identified that arose for the sole purpose of ensuring the success of specific branches of the family by any means necessary. As a result, public acknowledgment of official membership in the Jackson family became very bad for one's health.

13

Heart or Head

Ambrose B, Norma Arm
0735 BBMT 25 October 3473

AFTER VISITING THE BRIDGE, HUGH CASCADE returned to his cabin. Flinging himself back onto a chair, legs splayed out in front, he felt exhausted. He still needed a shower. And the conversation with Maeve Ellyllyon or Uch Robert had been emotionally draining. Knowing what he knew now of her time under Captain Pogue, he felt guilty they had ever doubted her. Putting a hand over his eyes, he shook his head, he tilted his head back against the top of the seat back and wondered if he could just fall asleep in the chair.

A hard rap at his hatch made his head snap up, interrupting his funk. "Come," he growled into the communicator.

Sergeant Major Ward shuffled in, sitting without waiting for an invitation. Without preamble, he began harshly, "I watched the whole thing from my cabin. Are you out of your mind, sire?"

Hugh's bad mood boiled over. "Sergeant Major, I have just shot two men and threatened to torture another to death. At my orders, we let a small flotilla take on an unknown number of barbarians, alone. We left Sergeant Kennion's body behind like so much garbage, instead of being laid to rest with the honors he so richly deserved. I condemned to death a ship full of people I've never even met, while having no way of knowing if all of them were guilty of treason, or even most of them. Most likely, some were not. To top off my day, which has not yet reached oh eight hundred, I just grilled a girl, a young woman, who helped us escape near certain death, in order to decide whether or not to have her pushed out the airlock. So, I guess the answer would be a nearly unequivocal *yes*." By the end, his anger had led him to stand and begin shouting.

"Your Highness," Ward stated firmly but with restraint, "sit down and listen."

Still shouting, he stared down at Ward as he answered, "Sergeant Major, I am out of patience, besides being just a little tired of having to act like an emperor all the time."

"That's part of the problem, Your Highness. You're trying to *act* like you think you should. You should be trying to do what's right, of course, not just trying to look like some playwright's image of an emperor." Ward managed to push himself upright in order to stand toe-to-toe with his charge, even though the effort drained the blood from his face. In a pale imitation of his parade ground voice, he ordered, "So, sire, sit down and shut up!"

Shocked by Ward's attempt at volume, as much as the sergeant major treating him like a cadet, he sat abruptly. Almost immediately, his anger and pride began to shoot up as he realized he had followed the order. He again began to get up out of his seat. Fortunately, a little voice barely got his attention before he could. He knew that Ward really had it right.

It reminded him of a time Doña Carlota had interrupted a truly volcanic eruption by a corporal who had been dressing down a private. The private had made a rather common mistake with a duty log. That error had nothing to do with the corporal's loss of control, but arose from the denial of the corporal's request for transfer to a fleet assault force, receiving orders instead to remain at the estate. The corporal had chosen to vent his vexation with the universe at large on the private because he could.

Doña Carlota had made it clear to the corporal that taking advantage of a position of power to make oneself feel better constituted an unacceptable abuse of authority both in the Imperial Fleet and Marines, as well as on her estate. Hugh realized, as the memory flitted through his mind, that if a corporal shouldn't act that way with a private, then an emperor certainly shouldn't with a sergeant major.

Taking a deep breath, Hugh stared at Ward. Voice still hard and intense, Hugh spoke carefully, "I won't yell at you like I want to, but unless you have a really good reason for giving me an order, Sergeant Major, you and I will have a problem." His eyes softened as he really looked at Ward, suddenly realizing how his bullet wound had truly drained him. "Now sit down before you fall down. You look terrible."

Ward gave him a half smile followed by a half bow. "Of course, Your Highness." With a grunt, he dropped back into a chair.

Hugh sat back. "Go ahead, Sergeant Major. Before I interrupted you, you were inquiring after my health, something about my mental stability, I believe?" He did such a perfect imitation of Doña Carlota that Ward smiled briefly.

"You always have been an impertinent young pup; you know that, Your Highness?"

Again Hugh mimicked Doña Carlota. "It is lèse-majesté to accuse your imperial liege of an act of impertinence, which is clearly something of an impossibility, by definition." Continuing on in his normal tone, he said, "And don't try to make me feel better. I would rather be mad at the universe just now. But as to my sanity?" he reminded Ward.

Ward just shook his head and smiled a bit more. Hugh actually felt like he had achieved something of a victory getting even that much out of him. Ward hadn't laughed at his smart aleck behavior since he'd turned twelve. "Your Highness," followed almost immediately in his initial acerbic tone, "as I said, *were you out of your mind*? That woman is the daughter of Robert ap Morgan. She told you that."

"And?"

"Her sister is Morgain uch Robert, the woman who demanded we surrender." Ward waited while that sank in.

Hugh blanched as he connected the two. Admiral Hollister and his staff considered her bad news, on the level of a supernova, and they were sisters? Add to that the fact that Maeve had been on the ship with Pogue, who had been a traitor. Plus Maeve had come aboard this ship because he approved it! He might as well have opened a vial of Virgilian night sweat fever on the ship and killed them quickly. But then Hugh remembered his gut instinct. He waved Ward to continue.

Ward took a deep breath, let it partly out to regain strength, then plunged on. "She has two more sisters, Nimue and Vivian. I often saw or heard of Vivian at court with one powerful man or another. Generally, these normally self-controlled men followed her around like drooling idiots. Something about her mesmerizes men. I never knew what she really wanted with them, because she never stayed with any one of them for very long, after which they all imploded. Or their careers did."

Ward paused to regain his strength before continuing. "Nimue, from everything I've heard, is worse. After the coup, she disappeared into Sector Three."

He shook his head. "But they're not in the same league as that witch, Morgain."

Gathering a deep breath, he went on, "No one could explain why the three older girls turned out that way. Everyone who knew him and his wife, including me, couldn't blame them for the girls' behavior. Sure, he was a somewhat superstitious man, but that wouldn't have had such a catastrophic result. Claimed to be descended from the Druids, an ancient Lost Earth bunch of sorcerers and wizards. If you let him, he'd talk your leg off about it. His library, from what your father told me, filled rooms with reproductions of thousands of Lost Earth books, every bit of it copied on cubes and stored in several secure locations in case something happened to the hard copies. Unbelievably security conscious. He even claimed that his ancestors had helped set up the Test of Heirs for Dave Jackson and kept it safe ever since. I suspect that is why Morgain had him killed, to ensure he took whatever secrets he had to his grave so she could do what she wanted to after that."

Hugh's mouth wanted to drop open, but he firmly commanded his jaw to remain closed. "Morgain killed her father? Ensign Ellyllyon, or more accurately uch Robert, claims to have been there and shot the last of the assassins."

Ward nodded. "There is no doubt that Morgain had her father assassinated. From what I heard at the time, the ensign killed the last assassin. It is certainly true she dropped out of sight immediately afterward and that Admiral Davies, a good friend of ap Morgan's and a member of their odd little Welsh Society, absolutely refused to talk about her, even when Doña Carlota tried to track her down while looking for all four sisters. So, it is possibly true that he stashed her away. It is also probably true she blew the ship up." He held up a hand to forestall any objection. "Although the fact that we couldn't have escaped without her seems to answer it."

Hugh felt troubled but said nothing. Ward shrugged, continuing, "Five years ago, I received a one-year assignment from the regency council to be Maeve's tactical officer once she reached the Academy. I would have been leaving Doña Carlota and you to take the assignment because Doña Carlota thought I needed to be at the Academy. It killed two birds with one stone. I never went, because that Academy class never happened. Shortly after her father's assassination, the Academy closed. There being no obvious heir, even five years after the coup, the regency council fell apart about that time, so I took over from Daniels to become your proctor."

"So why, if her sisters were so overwhelmingly power mad in one way or another, did she choose the Academy?" Hugh asked thoughtfully.

Ward shook his head. "I never got a chance to evaluate her, so I can't say. However, it is always better to keep unstable nuclear devices away from critical facilities, which pretty well describes the two of you at this time, Your Highness."

Hugh gave him a sour smile. Ward had hit entirely too close to the truth, especially since they'd just blown up a cruiser together. Softly, in a thoughtful tone, he asked, "Which is which, I wonder?" Continuing, he added more firmly, "Well, what do you think I should have done, and what do I do now?"

Ward gave him a wicked look before answering in his best court manner, "How should *I* know about either of those questions, Your Highness? As to the second question, it *is* Your Majesty's decision, Your Highness." Ward's act reminded Hugh of stories he had seen filled with particularly annoying courtiers.

Not to be out done, he answered in kind. "Why, *thank you*, Sergeant Major, you have been *most* helpful."

"I only live to serve, Your Highness."

"Of course you do," snorted Hugh, returning to ponder the situation seriously for a long moment. "I'll do what you taught me to do, Ward," he declared with a glint in his eye.

Hugh's change of tone, indicating his intention to take full responsibility, brought a crisp response from Ward, "Which is, sire?"

"Follow my gut, of course. I think she's solid."

"Even after all I told you, sire?"

"Even after all you told me."

Ward gave him a speculative look. "So what do you want to do with her?"

Hugh replied, "Same answer. She has been helpful, and the gut says keep her."

"That feeling may be based on her being a beautiful girl for whom you feel sorry, Your Highness."

Hugh chuckled. "Yep. That could certainly be true, but we're going with my decision for now. Just keep an eye on her, Sergeant Major. Like you do everyone else."

That seemed to surprise Ward a little. "Sire?"

"Sergeant Major, we both know, now at least, that for the last ten years you had one purpose: keep me alive for this test. I also remember, now that I've had time to think about it, a number of occasions you were where you really had no business being when I, regularly, got myself up a creek without a paddle. So, all in all, I assume that you constantly worry about me, as well as everyone who comes into my vicinity, especially someone who could kill me or compromise the test."

Ward smiled but didn't answer Hugh's assertion directly. "I will certainly keep an eye on her."

"Good. I will, too."

At this, Ward's eyebrow rose in a question. Hugh grinned. "Well, Sergeant Major, she *is* quite pretty."

Ward shook his head. "This is neither the time nor the place for romantic distractions. And that comment is not amusing under the circumstances. She is dangerous and you need to keep that in mind, and nothing else. Even as a joke."

Hugh's turned serious. "I'm well aware of that." Then he grinned again. "But it was entertaining to see that look on your face."

Ward's eyes crinkled at the corners, but he didn't smile back. Instead, he studied Hugh for a minute. Hugh could feel his eyes examining him, something he had experienced often. Mostly in the past, it had been to see if he measured up, and other times because of some particularly spectacular prank or mistake. But today, Hugh found Ward's expression inscrutable.

Ward cleared his throat, gaining a little time, before answering. "Unfortunately, with the galaxy trying to kill you, combined with the challenge of raising a very rambunctious and precocious boy so he could have a chance of taking and surviving the test, finding you a nice girl, one that could stand up to the challenges of being an empress, has been way down on our to-do list. We concentrated on the first two priorities." Ward smiled as if reflecting on memories.

"My own marriage made me someone I couldn't have been otherwise, the best thing that ever happened to me. Fireworks and supernovas at the start that developed into a deep friendship. It really hit Ann Marie hard as our boys died, one by one. Being a service family, you see lots of families lose fathers or mothers, sons and daughters, but the way my boys died, in accidents and illness, seemed worse. I'm just glad she didn't have to deal with the loss of the little one, but stood there with him at the end. I miss her very much."

Hugh watched Ward struggle with hidden emotions for a moment before he continued, "But from my general observation, marriages that start with those kinds of emotions don't last long. I lucked out. Too many of my buddies started the same way I did and were divorced within a few years. I'm absolutely certain that it is better to start out as friends with the woman you marry, before the fireworks go off. That way, you'll have a firm foundation to withstand whatever comes your way."

Ward's emotional sharing of this advice took Hugh by surprise. He'd been trying to get a rise out of the sergeant major and instead got a life lesson on choosing a wife.

After the silence stretched for a minute, Hugh asked the obvious question, "How do I get that kind of friendship with a woman while I'm living inside the bubble of being the heir? That seems impossible, Sergeant Major," Hugh's bitter frustration overflowed a little. He would likely never experience what Ward had just described.

Ward just shook his head. "I honestly can't tell you how it can happen; I can only tell you that it does. It did for Emperor Cyrus. For a few years, anyway. It can happen for you. Just have faith and don't settle for anything less."

Hugh nodded, thinking. *I had female friends. At least I think they were friends.* His mind drifted to Liz and Bettis . . . but his train of thought ended, when Ward solemnly continued, "Hugh Cascade, please stand and extend your hand." Hugh raised a questioning eyebrow, then stood and held out his right hand, as he had back on Jeffco when he took the oath. Ward tried to stand also but sank back into the chair, puffing a bit from the exertion. Pulling out the bag, he stated firmly, "The heir acts with integrity."

The golden topaz rose through the odd nanite bag. Hugh took it, a sudden fierce glow of pride spreading through his hand to his chest, warming him. Letting it go, it sank back through the bag, the glow remaining in his arm.

"Integrity is acting rightly, even toward those who are powerless to require correct action, as well as to those who would never know if they were treated poorly. Integrity is doing right because it *is* right. You refused to endanger people you did not know, for safety or convenience's sake. Most people lie, rationalizing their actions in situations much less life-threatening than the one just past, yet you would not. Lying is addictive and you refused its seductive allure. Remember that the temptation will always be there and avoid it. On Nighthawk, it would have been convenient and easy, and might have condemned the system to destruction. You chose correctly, in spite of potential personal cost."

As Hugh started to sit, Ward commanded a second time, "Hugh Cascade, please stand and extend your hand." Startled, Hugh hesitated a moment between sitting and standing, something a person watching might have found amusing. He needed to earn all seven stones in order to win the Galactic Starburst and become emperor, but he had felt sure it would take a very long time. Was it possible Ward believed he should receive a second so soon? Gathering his wits, he straightened and put out his right hand for the second time.

"The heir executes true and merciful justice."

Hugh felt stunned as the perfect emerald emerged. Reflexively, he grasped it. Unlike the first time he held it, a singing, vibrant chord seemed to take his whole body, a chord of perfect pitch and harmony. He knew the nanites approved of his choices, whatever they had been. At that moment, Hugh didn't want to, wouldn't, let go. He literally *couldn't* release it. Slowly, the chord softened, almost disappearing. But not quite. Hugh heaved a sigh of longing and regret as the unearthly sound became part of the background. Now he found letting go hard but possible. The emerald sank back into the bag.

Hushed, in a tone of awe, Ward spoke, "I have never seen such a reaction, although I've heard of it. Your eyes were the same color as the emerald and not their usual gray. I can't believe what I felt from you . . ." More firmly, he said, "Justice is a hard thing to administer. It tries the soul of the judge as well as the person brought before the bar, but it is essential to the life of the empire. You demonstrated true justice two times here in Nighthawk: first, when you allowed the crew of *Elmira Hayes* and Dr. Davison to retrieve their families, and second, in rewarding Maeve uch Robert for her sacrifices. But remember, not all justice turns out well. Justice must always be its own reward."

Hugh didn't know what to say nor could he speak. He had felt exhilarated a minute ago. Now, the weight of an endless series of decisions stretched before him. Each decision would be critical to someone, each would affect the existence of the empire for good or ill. Why would anyone want such a burden? But he had chosen this duty, had volunteered. He had felt the emerald's nanites giving him strength, but the decisions would still be his alone to make. And to live with alone.

Ward struggled to his feet. "Now that that's done, let's call it a day. We all need some food and rest. We've earned it after the last twenty-four hours."

Hugh put a hand under one of Ward's arms while sliding his other arm around Ward's back to help him to his quarters. Ward weakly tried to push Hugh's arm off. "Not proper, Your Highness," he protested, without force.

Hugh didn't fight him, but let him slide back into the chair. Apparently, Ward had had just enough strength to carry out these duties, and no more.

"I'll be fine. Have Pete or someone help me. Dunn needs to be on guard outside your door, but any of the others will do. Tell Captain Felt I'm on my way back to my cabin, because she'll want to check on my wound. She really fusses if we don't keep her updated on little things like life-threatening injuries."

Nodding, Hugh called Peterson to come get Ward before comming Gail. He then headed to the mess for a snack, to be followed by a shower. After the last twenty-four hours, he really stank.

Although none of the other members of the crew were present when he walked in, a program ran on the monitor. Someone had prepared a memorial to Kennion: *Timothy Kennion, Sergeant First Class, born August 17 3429 on Baker's Moon, Silicon System, Sector Eleven. Joined the Imperial Army May 31 3447. Selected for Fleet Elite Marines January 12 3453 for unspecified heroism above and beyond the call of duty. Rank at time of transfer,*

Staff Sergeant, Elite rank, Master Gunnery Sergeant and Technician Second Class, Weapons. Awards include Imperial Starburst, Second Class; Order of the Core, Third Class; three wound stripes, Bronze and Silver Stars, one award each, as well as other lesser ribbons. Widower, one daughter, Maurine, living on Jeffco.

Kennion had a daughter? How had he not known that? Feeling very still inside, he wished he had suggested they do this but appreciated the fact that someone did, knowing Kennion well enough to put in the personal details. This man, the bare bones of his life and service scrolling through on loop before him, paid the price so Hugh might, just maybe, turn into a decent emperor and fix things. He couldn't ignore that sacrifice.

CNS *Pechnaya*
2250 BBMT 25 October 3473

MORGAIN UCH ROBERT SAT BOLT UPRIGHT. SHE normally paid scant attention to the bridge repeater in her quarters, which included the destination and time of arrival of her task force at their next port. Most of the time it had been meaningless.

Generally, she had kept her task force in a single system over the past nine years for two reasons. First, the most important thing she had learned from Commodore Brian O'Donnell was simple: concentration of force made winning battles easier. She had proved that piece of advice true a number of times and now lived by it. Second, she had noticed that ships detached, either by themselves or in small groups, frequently disappeared, never to be heard from again. And often not due to enemy action. Keeping everyone under her guns avoided that slow attrition. Besides all of that, she liked seeing her power filling a system on the holodisplay. Now, though, they had to abandon that practice to pursue the bag of nanite impregnated gems and a proctor.

But the repeater said they were headed for Alpine and would arrive in nine days. *Why aren't we headed for Nighthawk? Grandmother had just reminded her that the test went through Nighthawk, which was much closer than Alpine, which she remembered from her visits to Green Gardens.* Gnashing her teeth, she regretted the two days it had taken to get her task force organized and on the way out here because they might have already arrived in Nighthawk.

Calling the bridge, a lieutenant, Richards, responded instead of the captain, as she had expected. Without any introduction, she demanded, "Why isn't the captain on the bridge, Lieutenant?"

Richards answered in a neutral tone. "I'm the night duty officer, ma'am. I can call him, or perhaps I can answer your question?"

Stifling her anger, she decided this man looked competent, so perhaps he could fix things now. Otherwise, she would have to wait for the captain to come on the line and put up with all of the other time wasted in military protocol until they did what she wanted. "I thought we were headed for Nighthawk."

Richards nodded, tapping on his comm pad. Then he stood at attention as he reported. His obvious fear made her a bit happier as he did. "Yes, ma'am. You asked the captain how quickly we could arrive in order to capture the stealth ship *Ambrose B* there. The astrogator calculated it would take two days. The captain commed Nighthawk an order to relay instructions to *Bring It* to hold *Ambrose B* until we arrived. The planetary archeonA array relayed that instruction. Later, it reported that *Bring It* had exploded and that they had lost track of the stealth ship. Also, most of your flotilla in-system has been destroyed by the Tech-Mech. The planetary communications team reports that surviving ships from the battle have already fled. Being now defenseless, the planet begs for help. The captain decided that with everyone gone from the system by the time we arrived, we would be unable to trace the movements of the stealth ship. Since we will be in Alpine in under nine days and likely ahead of it, a search for *Ambrose B* from there would be more likely to succeed."

As Richards spoke, her mind emerged from the cloud of anger and kicked into gear. The captain had obviously made the correct decision and avoided wasting her time on a simple math problem. Fruitlessly adding days by going to Nighthawk would cause her to miss *Ambrose B* in Alpine, too. Frustrating, but it couldn't be helped. Losing Dent and the others in that flotilla really didn't matter to her, either; she could kill Wilby Dent anytime. The important thing was to find the *Ambrose B* and get that proctor and bag. She could almost taste her victory . . .

Graciously, she nodded, as she gave Richards one of her blinding smiles. "Thank you, Lieutenant. Well done. Alpine will be the perfect place to set up a search."

Closing the screen without signing off, she began contemplating how to keep Ward and his bag from slipping by her.

ARCHIVED IMPERIAL CLASSIFIED DOCUMENTS

Declassified 24 September 3485
Test of Heirs Program
Proctor Course revised 2612
Determination of Heir's Readiness to Take Test

The two most difficult tasks for a proctor are: first, to determine when a candidate is ready to take the test, and; second, determining whether the Heir has failed and must be removed from the test procedure.

In many ways the decision that will require the most evaluation is whether a candidate can even be allowed to take the test. Most candidates fail, which means that the proctor will be condemning an unsuitable candidate to death by admitting him or her to the test procedure. For this reason, deciding whether to administer the oath should be unhurried and careful in the extreme. Only the most qualified and experienced candidates should even be considered.

14

Teenagers

Ambrose B, Norma Arm
0630 BBMT 26 October 3473

HEAD ACHING SLIGHTLY FROM LACK of sleep, Maeve Uch Robert picked at her breakfast. Her rest had been interrupted by nightmares, a jumble of events and scenes from the past as well as *what ifs* from yesterday. The sounds of laughing and talking from across the mess made her head ache even more. The female crew— Sally Carr who hadn't come aboard *Bring It*, a slightly tanned lieutenant that appeared motherly, plus Petty Officers Pam West and Karen Hall, she thought they were called—shared her table. The Marines shared another one.

Just then Hugh Cascade walked in, looking like his night's rest had equaled hers. He scowled at the Marine sergeant named Pete Peterson when he loudly called out "Deadeye." Dropping into a seat after choosing oatmeal from the buffet, he studiously ignored the lively discussion going on. *He has the right idea.* Maeve returned to chasing her food around the plate as she tried, unsuccessfully, to ignore them as well.

Talking louder than before, Sergeant Kevin Dunn insisted, "You never saw anything like it. His Highness here drove those scalpels into the carpet so hard I thought they would go right through the deck plates, but they snapped off instead. Zane took one look into those cold, gray eyes and really believed what His Highness said about torturing him to death. Never would have happened, but that goon believed it."

At that, Maeve glanced up, feeling slightly sick, and abandoned all pretense of eating.

Then Peterson took up the story, waving a piece of toast in his hand like a sword, stabbing it for emphasis as he spoke, "You didn't see what he did in the corridor. Ask Jebet. He saw it too. His Highness looked ready to puke his guts out when he came out of the cabin after shooting those guys. I thought he might faint!"

Maeve glanced up at Hugh and found him looking back at her; she quickly dropped her eyes in embarrassment at having been caught looking at him. Peterson seemed not to have noticed either of them as he went on, "Jebet had to watch the far hatch. I wanted him to help me handle the medics instead of Hugh, but they showed up just then, so we had to get on with business. I just hoped he could help get the medics to Captain Felt before keeling over. Well, just then the one in the rear decided to get frisky so I just hoped Jebet would be watching the lead medic, since I had no doubt His Highness would be useless. First combat does that to you if you have time to think right afterward."

Out of the corner of her eye, Maeve watched Peterson take a bite of his toast, smiling like a Cheshire cat, slowly chewing as if he had finished talking. Sergeant Tabi Fleisch, a woman standing above average height with very dark hair who had remained on the ship during the whole thing, snorted in exasperation. "So, finish your story," she demanded.

Peterson just smiled more broadly. "As I said, both of them medics tried to get cute, pulling hideout guns, but I expected something like that. I screwed my pistol into my guy's eye, getting his full and complete attention, so he dropped his gun real peaceful like. Not used to people who know how to fight back, I guess."

Taking another bite of his toast he chewed slowly, seeming to be really eating up the attention, especially now that Pam, Karen, and Sally had turned toward him, obviously listening intently. Maeve turned her back to them, so none of them could observe how all of this affected her.

She heard someone, Dunn probably, slap Peterson, growling in exasperation. "Get on with it!" Dunn ordered.

Peterson continued, "So, I looked up and couldn't see a problem with the other medic." He paused again, chewing.

As Maeve glanced back, she saw Fleisch lean over the table, as she said, "I'll ask Jebet to tell the rest, if you don't."

Peterson just continued, smiling, "There's nothing much to tell. His Highness had the medic face down on the deck with his knee in the middle of the guy's back. Big brute, too. His Highness had the medic's wrist twisted back so tightly I thought it must be broken."

Sergeant Vincent Klostermann, a big man who looked almost like a door, broke in, authoritatively. "So did the kid throw up? Of course not. I trained him; he's strong inside. If you don't freeze up the first time, you'll be okay. End of story." Maeve was confused by the look of obvious relief on Hugh's face when he heard this.

Maeve looked down at her plate, unseeing, lost in her own thoughts, as the Marines started laughing, before going over the entire thing again, bit by bit, this time with Hugh adding some details. Pam and Karen joined them as Sally walked out of the mess.

Maeve began fuming inwardly. They had hardly mentioned her part in it. Without her, where would they be? *Still there, or dead!*

Grudgingly, she had to concede, at least if she wanted to be honest with herself, that his reflexes were great. *He took down Paul Bhat and Hamilton Pogue just like some gunfighter, and then Zane Weston, as easily as if Weston had been a raw recruit. But what else does His Majesty have?* He had brutally threatened Weston, but would he have tortured him? Weston had believed it, and he should know, the pig! But the Marines, talking among themselves, said Hugh would never have tortured and killed him in cold blood. She just didn't know. She didn't notice Gail slide in next to her with a tray.

"So, Ensign, how are you feeling this morning?" Gail asked lightly. "Sleep okay?"

Grateful to Gail for dragging her attention away from the Marines she'd been working so studiously to ignore, she smiled brightly. "Not bad. Anywhere away from Hamilton Pogue is wonderful."

Gail nodded, Maeve noticing how Gail's hooded eyes examined her. "I meant to ask you yesterday, but between arranging new quarters, allowing everyone some much-needed rest, and getting things settled after our hasty exit, we had no time. Who led your team? I might have known her."

Maeve's eyes clouded, reflecting the sadness filling her soul. "Priscilla Jenks. She had been assigned to help my father after mother died. She just kind of took over caring for me after Morgain killed him, too." Tears began to prickle at the edges of her eyes, threatening to burst out at any minute, however a sudden huge burst of laughter by Hugh quelled them.

Looking up into Gail's eyes, she saw compassion and understanding.

"It's okay, I understand what you're feeling, really I do," Gail murmured so no one else could hear. "Just don't be too hard on the Marines, either. They need to blow off steam like this or they'll explode. Remember, they lost a friend yesterday, so they need to handle the loss, and this is how they do it. I've known them a long time and they're all good men, especially Hugh." Pausing, she went on, "A long time ago, I knew Priscilla well. I am sure she loved you as deeply as if you were her own daughter. She couldn't have children, you know."

"I didn't know." Suddenly, Maeve couldn't speak, a lump forming in her throat as she fought emotions she'd never acknowledged. "She never shared anything about that."

Sadness filled Gail's eyes, too. "She suffered a lot of pain because of that. I think that might be part of the reason she went to work for your father. She saw a little girl with no mother and, as a woman who could never have a daughter, well . . ."

"Dad told me she did more than just assist him, and I could tell she liked me. He said he couldn't tell me anything else until I grew a little older, though."

Gail half nodded, as if in partial confirmation. "Maybe so. Did Priscilla ever show you a strange bag?" Maeve's eyes narrowed in suspicion. Gail just smiled, in response. "It appears that you and I need to have a little talk. Privately. Come along to my cabin."

After finishing breakfast quickly, they dropped their trays in the kitchen and left the mess. Down the corridor, Gail opened her quarters, ushering Maeve in before her. A red icon, warning of a gravity change coming in the common areas, flashed on Gail's com. With a corner of her attention, Maeve saw Gail tap it in acknowledgment that changed it to a steady orange. Gail then sat on the desk chair while pointing Maeve to the other. After a pregnant pause, Gail asked neutrally, "Are you descended from any of the emperors?"

Maeve paused to think. *Why did she ask that?* After considering it for a moment more, she said, "Dad always said we were directly descended from Constantine Jackson."

"Then are you one of Dave's descendants or Joseph's?" Gail asked.

"No, Dad said he came from another line, a granddaughter."

"I never heard of that line before," Gail answered pensively.

"Dad used to smile about it, but didn't go into more detail. He said he'd explain when I grew up a little more."

Maeve carefully watched Gail as she said this. Gail seemed to be struggling with a decision. Maeve tensed as she saw Gail apparently decide. "You don't have a bag with you. Did you ever have one?"

"No," Maeve answered truthfully. She ordered her face to be innocent and sincere.

Gail smiled sadly. "You really can't fool me. Your face agrees with what you just said, but your eyes tell me you're hiding something."

As Maeve began to protest, Gail held up a hand, stopping her. "I know you don't have it, since you came aboard without it. I'm also sure you know exactly what I'm asking about. Priscilla received training to be proctor, just like Ward and me. We all were trained to test the heirs of the empire. Ward is here with Hugh. My last heir assignment focused on a sweet girl named

Anna Beth Fitzgerald. She died off Yak Peak, where my ship got shot to ribbons rescuing Ward. A long time ago."

Maeve saw that Gail's eyes glistened with tears. She felt tears welling in her eyes, in empathy for Gail's loss and in what she could only think of as a delayed reaction to all of her own. Nevertheless, it had been so long since she had let her true emotions show, it seemed wrong somehow, and dangerous. With an effort, Maeve composed herself so she could focus on Gail once more.

Gail gave her an off-kilter smile as she patted her hand. "We'll talk about this some more, but you must be an heir if Priscilla stayed with you."

Maeve's thoughts froze. Deep inside, it suddenly all clicked: discussions with her father, her sister trying to kill her, the assignment of Priscilla and her team to a young orphan girl. Maeve's heart pounded as her emotions cascaded from fear and dread to elation and back. But a shadow of guilt hovered over everything else in the background of her thoughts. The price to keep her alive had been so terrible. Did she deserve—had her life been worth—the deaths of her father, Priscilla, and the others? She forced herself to appear attentive, trying not to reveal her inner turmoil. "So, what does this all mean?"

"I have no idea why you ended up on Pogue's ship, but we can sort that all out later. I feel certain Admiral Davies didn't intend for this to happen, though." She shook her head, apparently trying to chase the question away like an annoying fly. "Anyway, report to Sheila, as I'm sure there are electronics to work on. There always are. Did Sally go through the clothing locker we use when running ops, the extra uniform storage, and the supplies yesterday? She told me you didn't bring any clothes and only a few personal items. You undoubtedly could use a few things."

Smiling wanly, Maeve said, as she stood, "She did, thank you. I really just needed a few basic items and pieces of clothing."

Standing, she headed for the door. As she opened it, Gail shouted at her, "Stop!" Twisting her head to look back at Gail, Maeve felt a sudden tug from the corridor. A huge gravitic hand grabbed her. Clutching the door jamb as she spun, she couldn't quite stop herself, but continued the turn she had begun, which brought her down painfully with a thump on her behind. *What the heck?*

"What idiot cranked up the gees?" she demanded in outrage. Through the open hatch, she saw Gail stabbing a button violently and felt the gravity return immediately to normal.

Gail answered as relief hit, "The Marines train in two gees."

At the same moment, the Marines in high-pressure suits, Hugh in the lead, rounded the near corner at a slow trot to find her plopped in the middle of the hall.

Stopping beside her, Hugh asked, "Can I help you, Ensign?" He bent over carefully, as if still under two gees, extending a hand toward her. Although jogging in two gees, he obviously hadn't even started sweating hard, while she had barely been able to move.

"No, thanks." Maeve muttered, "I can take care of myself." Rolling over, she got to her knees before slowly standing up. Using her palms, she steadied herself against the wall, aware of Hugh watching her silently with a puzzled look on his face.

Face flaming with embarrassment, Maeve headed gingerly down-ship toward Engineering. Unconsciously, she rubbed her aching posterior, bringing a gust of laughter from Peterson and a couple of the others. Snatching back her hand, she turned her head to give Hugh a dirty look. As she continued away, she heard Hugh mutter, "Stow it, Peterson." Glancing back a second time, she saw Hugh stab an amused Peterson with a dirty look. Peterson smirked.

Klostermann spoke up, "Okay, gentlemen. Fun's over. Back to work. We'll let her get to her cabin before cranking it back up. So, in the meantime, pick up the pace!" Turning away from the direction Maeve had taken down the corridor, they jogged off.

Maeve saw Hugh twice that day, once in the mess/gym, the other time as he came from the bridge after a lesson. Both times she ducked from sight. She hoped he hadn't noticed but feared he had seen her both times.

By the next day, Maeve's pride, as well as backside, felt much better. Pam and Karen had teased her so unmercifully the night before about her pratfall that she had come to the conclusion that she had only two choices: either kill Pam and Karen or get over it. She decided to let it go. Besides, Maeve had begun to discover that Pam and Karen teased and pulled practical jokes pretty regularly. It helped everyone blow off steam. They were beginning to make her feel like part of the crew, and as if she had friends again, something she'd been without for a long time.

By the time she reported for a simulation with the Marines later that day, she actually felt cheery, almost bubbly, which definitely didn't feel like the person she had pretended to be over the last five years.

In the scenario, they had to rescue hostages. Seeing Hugh walk in, she gave him a welcoming smile. He didn't smile back, didn't say hello. Nothing. He seemed to look right through her, which oddly disappointed her and deflated her bubble, as he headed over to Ward sitting in an armchair. Hugh asked, "You up to this, Top?"

Top? Marines don't usually call a sergeant major that. How involved is Sergeant Major Ward with everything going on? Like a first sergeant? How else were they different? This group could only be called interesting.

Ward just smiled, "I'm fine. Brief the troops and get going, cadet."

Cadet! Hugh began to formally address the team. *Stuffed shirt.*
"Today we are going to rescue hostages on a hostile vessel. These are the teams. Dunn, you're with me . . ." He ran through the standard mission brief. Occasionally, she felt his eyes rest on her, perhaps longer than might have been expected.

Two hours later, the entire team dripped with sweat but had rescued the hostages. Wrapping up the post-op evaluation, Hugh complimented her, "Ensign, you particularly impressed me by your rewiring of environmental without orders. It's what needed to be done, but I couldn't figure out what to ask for. You just did it." He said it in his perfectly proper standard military manner, back straight, face impassive. Finishing, he said, "Good job, Ensign. Good job, team."

Waiting for the laughing and joking Marines to clear the corridor, she ducked back into the mess to use the showers on the far side. Two minutes later found her luxuriating in the hot water. The delicious feeling seemed to melt away her bad mood. She really had done a good job. And Hugh had noticed and said something about it. Over the last few years, most of the times when she had done good work, her superiors had taken credit while she received the blame for their mistakes.

She heard the door from the gym open. *Did I put up the "Women Only" sign?* Alarmed, she couldn't remember. Then, she heard a man humming. "Get out of here!" she screamed.

The humming broke off. "I'm sorry. I didn't see a sign on the door."

Hugh? Oh, my gosh! "Get out! Right now!" she yelled.

"I'm going. I just need to pull on my clothes."

Hiding behind the shower curtain, she hoped Pam and Karen didn't find out or she'd never hear the end of this. The door slammed. Quickly, she dried and dressed. As she stepped out into the mess, she saw Pam sitting with a cup of coffee smirking at her. Maeve colored all the way to her roots. Again!

GAIL AND WARD SAT SHARING a snack at a small movable table in the mess, alone except for Dunn. Gail let the peace of this quiet moment together seep into her bones, one of too few they had been able to enjoy the last five years. Leaning forward to examine Ward's wound carefully, and his look, she asked, "You really think you should put yourself back on full training duty tomorrow?"

"He only shot me in the head, and it *has* been four days. You think I'm malingering, Captain?"

Ward's bland expression truly impressed her. Only somebody like her knew him well enough to get his humor. She didn't find him funny, not today, anyway. "No, I don't, but you do, Sean Ward. If you want to know what I think, which you don't because you haven't asked, is that you should take another week at least."

Ward just shook his head, "If I did, what would happen to my reputation?"

She just stared at him, grinding her teeth. He could be so exasperating!

Ward gave her a sidelong look. *Uh-oh. Here it comes.*

"What did you decide about Maeve?" he asked bluntly, but quietly enough that Dunn couldn't hear.

"Ran her through some unobtrusive psych evals. She's pretty solid."

Ward frowned. "You know the old saying about too many cooks?"

Gail's face hardened. "As I said, she is qualified as far as we know. I seem to recall we were bemoaning the lack of heirs when we started on this little jaunt, so quit whining." Although said in a whisper, she managed to pack her statement with impressive intensity.

Ward sat back and gave her a rueful smile. "Okay, okay, you're right. An heir and a spare makes this quest more likely to succeed." He chuckled at his play on words.

Gail didn't find that comment even a little amusing. "She's not a *spare*, she's an heir. If I decide she should take the test, then she will."

Ward's face became just as hard. "You think that's a good idea? You know what could happen." He said this loud enough that Dunn turned in their direction.

Gail gave a sharp nod, making an effort to answer as quietly as possible. "Yes, and I think this could end better than anyone could have foreseen."

"Or become a total disaster," Ward insisted.

Gail nodded again, "Or become a total disaster. We'll just have to make sure it doesn't turn out that way."

"Amen," Ward answer fervently.

They both ignored Dunn's questioning look as they changed the subject.

* * *

Commander's Belle, Treadle System
2010 Local, 1610 BBMT 28 October 3473

Captain Argus Steed knocked on Austin Carhart's open hatch. His boss had been deep in reviewing something on his screen, which he closed at the interruption. *Something's off kilter.* "Boss, we have nearly finished supplying, though why we need to have 50 percent extra for the simple run to pick up a load just five days away seems unnecessary."

Carhart leaned back in his seat. "We're not taking the load at Francine. We're headed to Pirate's Shoal."

Steed felt his eyebrows rise; he couldn't hide his surprise. "It's the best paying load we've seen in a while, and no strings. Take three people to Beacon from Fifth Sector who have no other way of getting there. Plus, Pirate's Shoal can be very bad for your health. Especially after what happened last time."

Carhart tapped his desk, an obvious signal of displeasure, but Steed simply maintained eye contact. After all these years, Carhart should know better than to try these games with him.

Carhart smiled. "Good points, but we're going. I need some information and it is one of the two places I can get it." Pausing, he added, "Maybe."

Steed nodded. "And the other is more dangerous," he guessed.

"And the other is *much* more dangerous."

"We'll be loaded and out of here in an hour. But we are flying careful all the way."

"Whatever makes you happy." Forestalling Steed from saying, *then we'll head to Francine*, he added, "As long as we go to the Shoal."

MANUAL FOR COURTS-MARTIAL (MCM)

Revised 3277 by Order of the Emperor, Charles Roland

Good Order and Discipline

Following the breakdown of military obedience to the lawful representatives of the empire in 3271, upon the death of Emperor Burt, the importance of emphasizing not only the role of "Good Order and Discipline" but the necessity of strict enforcement by commanders has become glaringly apparent.

Good Order and Discipline includes all behaviors of each and every service man or women, on or off duty, which supports the mission of the military.

Breach of Good Order and Discipline

Interference with the mission through active or passive acts, including inefficient performance of duty, inattention to assignment details, harassment of personnel, and any other action a commander finds has interfered with maintenance of morale.

Punishment: Commander's discretion up to and including death by spacing.

15

Character

Ambrose B, Galactic Space Between Norma and Crux-Scutum Arms

2305 BBMT 1 November 3473

As Maeve's eyes flew open, she recognized the bulkhead, closet, desk, all in her cabin on *Bring It*. Had she ever left? Had she just imagined Hugh? Had *Ambrose B,* a ship exactly like she had wanted to rescue her, imagined in every detail, been a dream? Dressing quickly, she checked her discrete sensor net for a status update. She couldn't find anyone anywhere!

Stepping out, she headed for her office, running through the empty corridors. Passing sickbay, a ragged corpse stepped out, grabbing her. Corpsman Hathaway. "What did I ever do to you? I didn't rebel. You never even asked before you killed me!"

Wild-eyed, Maeve broke away, now desperate to get to the shuttles and away. Behind her, a murmur of sound grew into a roar. Glancing back, she saw a crowd gaining on her, Welks in the lead, followed closely by Weston and Nantz. All were torn, bloody, missing limbs, faces gashed, but catching up to her. She would never be able to escape.

"Why?" they demanded. She had no answer.

"What right did you have to kill us? We weren't all rebels." Their piteous cries ripped out her heart.

"Murderess!" The accusation hit home, stabbing deep. She had killed them, all of them.

As she ran from her guilt, her side caught in a stitch and her breathing became ragged. The hatch into the shuttle bay came into sight, just ahead. Relief flooded her; she would make it!

Reaching out her hand to grab the latch, it opened. Her

entire section stood on the far side, waiting for her, just as hideous as those following. "What did we do?" they demanded in chorus as their grasping fingers grabbed her wrist and began dragging her forward. "You were our officer; you should have taken care of us."

Paul Bhat, a perfectly round hole in his forehead, stood beside the airlock, a hungry smile on his face. "Spacing for you. You betrayed your ship. Worse, you sentenced your shipmates to death without even knowing if they were guilty."

The open airlock came closer and closer. Just as they shoved her inside, she screamed.

"WAKE UP, HONEY. YOU HAD another bad dream." Lieutenant Sally Carr sat on the edge of her bed in her Class B uniform, obviously just come from watch. Sally's hand gently stroked her face.

Reflexively Maeve reached out, clinging desperately to Sally, squeezing as hard as she could. She'd had that dream again! The realization that she wouldn't be spaced filled her with enormous relief. "Sally, thank you for rescuing me."

"Sure, but can you talk about it?"

Maeve shook her head, violently. "I can't. I don't want to think about it."

Sally stroked her hair for a bit, before speaking again, "You really need to tell me. Nightmares express your deepest fears, and I could tell this one terrified you, the worst you've had by far. If you talk about it, maybe we can keep the dreams from coming back."

Maeve shook her head again but less strongly. She felt so ashamed, so guilty. But the possibility of the nightmares coming again terrified her even more. She couldn't ignore them any longer. After a moment, she whispered almost inaudibly, "Do you think we live after we die?"

Sally nodded. "Yes, but I don't think the dead bother the living. What did you see?"

Maeve sighed into Sally's shoulder. "My old ship." Sitting up, she stared down at the deck, not wanting comfort. She didn't deserve it after what she had done. "I killed them without a trial, without evidence."

Sally gave her a crooked smile. "The ship rebelled, you know."

Maeve grabbed the lifeline, then shuddered and pushed it away mentally. "I know, and Pogue killed the loyalists brave enough to stand up to him, but still, not all of the crew remaining on the ship may have been rebels; some must have regretted joining Pogue, like Dr. Davison. Did they deserve death?"

Sally rubbed Maeve's shoulder. "Honey, you know the regulations. If you're consorting with rebels, what does Charles Roland's law say on that?"

"Death," Maeve muttered softly, "but I'm not a judge. I shouldn't have made that decision."

Sally shook her head very briefly. "The regs say it is the duty of all loyal spacers to fight mutineers, up to and including executing them."

Maeve could feel some of her angst draining away. "But not all of them may have been rebels."

Sally sat back, studying Maeve for a moment. "Did any of them try to save your friends or the other loyal spacers killed by Pogue?"

Maeve shook her head.

"Did any even try to stop the traitors, besides Priscilla and her team, that you know of?"

Maeve's head jerked in a hard shake. They had fought their hopeless battle alone. With her access to the entire ship with her personal security network, she would have known if anyone else had tried.

Sally smiled sadly. "The truth is you will never know for certain. Maybe some of them were like the doctor, just keeping their heads down. Others may have wanted to do something but couldn't. Every loyal crewman or woman would have agreed with you and wanted to end this rebellion, no matter what it cost." Sally squeezed Maeve's shoulder before pulling her in for a hug. "And that is the truth. You did what you had to, the right thing for the empire and your oath. It isn't easy to realize some innocent people might have been hurt, but we'll never know. I think they understand."

Maeve hugged Sally back just as hard before letting go. She couldn't think of anything to say but, "Thank you."

Sally stood up and handed Maeve her sheets and blanket. "We both need to get some more sleep. Tomorrow will be a long day."

Maeve quickly made up her bunk and lay back down. She knew she wouldn't be able to sleep but didn't want to keep Sally up longer. Surprising her completely, the alarm awakened her hours later out of a sound, and dreamless, slumber.

BY NOON THE NEXT DAY, even though the nightmares still floated in the back of her mind, Maeve began to feel better, although not in the mood for company. She waited until everyone else had probably finished eating lunch before slipping quietly into the gym/mess area to get herself a tray. Finding a corner, she sat facing the wall, feeling lonely but safe.

Absorbed in her private misery, just nibbling at her lunch, she didn't even hear anyone enter. Suddenly, someone, a guy, slipped in beside her on the bench, but she didn't look up from her plate to see who. If she ignored him, maybe he'd go away. A bump from someone's thigh against hers brought her head around.

"How ya doin', Ensign?" Sergeant Pete Peterson's handsome face smirked just inches from hers.

Maeve's heart leapt into her throat. She had been here before! On Pogue's ship the men preyed openly on any woman without a *friend*. And some of the men, for that matter. Suddenly her fear turned to anger. She didn't want a *friend*. Why did she have to constantly deal with men like this? Maeve gave Peterson an icy glare without answering, letting the moments build up until a minute passed. Most guys couldn't stand the deep freeze but, apparently, Peterson happened to be one of that rare minority completely impervious to hints. *Too bad for him.*

Then Peterson, keeping that same knowing smirk, slid his arm around her lower back, followed by a squeeze. No enlisted person had ever dared to try something like this in public on her as an officer.

"Why don't we go and *talk* somewhere?" he suggested, assuming in his supreme self-confidence not only her willingness but eagerness to spend time with him.

Initially stunned and off-balance, Wally Welks's face flashed in her mind. Anger blazed, preparing to erupt at his complete and utter disregard of the possibility she might not want to *talk* to him. Or even have anything to *do* with him. Welks and Peterson were cut from the same cloth. She felt sure her face reflected the fury she felt, yet he remained as smug as when he slid that arm around her waist. She'd give him one last chance to back off before she beat him to a pulp. As she opened her mouth to tell him well and truly off, along with dumping on him all of the misery, disappointment, hurt, and anger she worked so hard to hide over the past three years, a whip-crack voice cut through the room. Stunned, she froze.

A FEW MINUTES EARLIER HUGH CASCADE STOOD. TRYING TO FORCE himself to concentrate on multi-dimensional math and maintenance procedures, two things he didn't do well at in the best of times, had become a lost cause. Memories kept jumbling together, one after another, of Maeve and the botch he had made of things. After accidentally walking in on her in the shower, Hugh had tried to apologize several times, but she had run off every time. Of course, Petty Officers Pam West and Karen Hall had noticed and begun calling her Rabbit, which apparently caused Maeve to make herself even more scarce. Worse, even Sean Ward found the situation hilarious, and let him know it.

But the worst teasing, and something that had embarrassed him immensely, had occurred at lunch the day before when Pete Peterson suggested that he had missed a golden opportunity walking in on her in the shower. Back on Jeffco, Pete had caused no end of trouble with his skirt chasing. Hugh had been on the receiving end of more than one fist from an older brother or father, on behalf of some girl Pete had wronged. Twice, Hugh had ended up in full-blown brawls because of him and he still hadn't completely forgiven Peterson for his jackass behavior.

Maeve, or Ensign uch Robert as he ought to think of her, didn't deserve the Peterson treatment. She was a member of the crew and needed to be treated as such. These women onboard were not the kind Marines like Peterson found on leave.

Giving up on the math, his stomach rumbled, making him stand almost without thought. A moment later his feet brought him to the mess/gym. Stepping into the mess, he took the scene in at a glance. Peterson had an arm around Maeve, while she looked ready to deck him. Peterson, as usual, seemed to be completely unaware of her reaction. Hugh had seen him in action before, scoring on an unbelievable number of women and girls with that same supreme self-confidence. But Pete hadn't considered one minor point that Hugh felt pretty confident about: Maeve had watched Pogue and his crew of womanizers in action and hated everything about that type of behavior. Hugh knew Pete believed every woman found him irresistible, but Hugh had observed enough females make themselves scarce when he showed up to know that not to be true. Regardless, Peterson, being Pete like always, just bulled ahead. Hugh needed to do something about it before someone got hurt . . . most likely Peterson.

Hugh spoke with steely decisiveness, no give at all in his voice, "Peterson! Find someplace else to sit." He spread his feet a comfortable distance for fighting, ready for anything Pete might do. Peterson had a tendency to not think above the belt in situations like this.

Peterson's head snapped around, a grin on his face, evidently ready to say something smart.

Hugh spoke before he could, voice firm and unyielding, "Peterson, you're an idiot. She's an officer; you're enlisted. Strike one. Two, I'm the heir and I just gave you a direct order."

"And strike three?" Pete responded with a half sneer. The first two reasons obviously didn't impress him, either of which could land him in the brig if he continued to ignore them. Or dead, for that matter. Disobeying a direct order in a combat zone rose to an execution-level offense.

"I'm tired of your behavior toward women in general and the women on board this ship in particular. Also, I'll beat you black and blue if you don't move."

Peterson's jaw dropped, Hugh's challenge coming at him completely unexpectedly. It surprised Hugh a bit, too, but Hugh knew he meant every word. Hugh could see him measuring and reassessing the situation.

Hugh waited, clearing his mind of everything but Peterson. He knew Pete liked to explode in a single motion, taking out his opponent with a quick, unexpected blow. However, Hugh intentionally chose to stand off to the right and about ten feet behind the chair where Pete sat, preventing Pete from using most of the moves he liked. If he tried to kick the chair at him to foul Hugh's movements or distract him, Hugh planned on sending it right back at him while attacking in a single motion.

Hugh smiled a little grimly. "Go ahead and stand. I'll wait for you to prepare your sucker punch before I lay you out."

Hugh watched thoughts percolate through Peterson's mind until he realized the obvious: Hugh had actually taunted him. Hugh knew precisely when it hit him, because Pete reddened, before drawing his arm back to his side, ready to fight.

Glad the tactic worked, Hugh really didn't care which insult did the job as long as it had. He judged Pete now teetered on the verge of going berserk, thereby losing every last remaining spark of fighting smarts. He'd seen that a time or two, and Peterson had found himself in big trouble in those fights until his buddies had bailed him out. Well, no one would help him today.

Surprisingly, a single spark of caution appeared to be keeping Pete from wildly charging at Hugh and getting slaughtered. Pete had been there when Hugh took down that medic on *Bring It* with no problem whatsoever. Standing carefully and slowly, Pete put the chair to his right side and began to step under great control toward the hatch, giving every indication of leaving as requested. Not fooled, Hugh, tense and still, kept his entire attention on Pete, knowing the blow would soon be coming. At that moment, the 1MC, the ship-wide public address system, blasted, freezing them both.

"Peterson," Ward's voice blasted through the com, *"report to me! Now!"*

The shock of Ward's voice broke the coiled tension in the room. Nevertheless, Hugh kept his attention focused on Pete, knowing he might still ignore the sergeant major and take his chances with him later. Pete just gave Hugh a venomous look before stepping out.

As the hatch slammed shut, Hugh turned his head to Maeve. "You okay?"

Maeve nodded, a little shakily. "I could have handled him, but thanks anyway."

Hugh smiled. "Pete doesn't take no for an answer. Before you came on board, he got a bruise or two trying to put the moves on some of the other women." Stepping toward where Maeve still sat, Hugh prepared to join her, glad of having a chance to be on her side for once.

But Sergeant Major Ward interrupted this golden opportunity to apologize to her by calling him through the com, *"Your Highness, please join me in my cabin."*

"Be right there, Sergeant Major," Hugh responded formally. *This is likely to get official and sticky.* Just what he needed, another lost chance to apologize and talk to her.

"I'm sorry for that," Hugh muttered before hurrying out, leaving Maeve all alone in the mess.

SERGEANT TABI FLEISCH, WEARING A sidearm and standing at attention beside Ward's hatch when Hugh arrived, knocked. The intercom announced, *"Come."* Fleisch opened the hatch with almost robotic precision before resuming her position of attention. Walking in, Hugh saw Peterson at attention, white as a sheet. Hugh recognized this as an official hearing despite the lack of paperwork on the desk. Ward, normally a stickler for regulations, apparently had decided to pass on it this time.

Ward stood before saluting hand to breast, as did Peterson. "Your Highness!" they shouted in unison.

Hugh returned the salute. "At ease," he ordered. Ward relaxed into his seat, but Peterson remained at attention. Hugh decided not to take notice and left him that way. *He must really be nervous.* Looking at Ward, he asked, "Sergeant Major?"

"I happened to see what Fleet Marine Sergeant Peterson did and we have a little problem. Assaulting, or threatening to assault, the heir apparent is a capital crime. Refusing to obey the heir is a capital crime. In time of war, while in a combat zone, initiating what might be construed as a sexual assault on an officer by an enlisted person is a capital crime. I just reminded Sergeant Peterson of these facts from *Rocks and Shoals* that he seems, momentarily, to have forgotten."

Hugh perfectly understood what regulations Peterson had run afoul of in the mess, but never for a moment believed Ward would seriously think about implementing them on any of these men whom he had known so long and worked with closely. Hugh had been wrong. He gave Ward a questioningly look.

"As the heir apparent, which includes being commander-in-chief, Your Highness, you are the one who must determine whether he lives or dies. It's your call."

Hugh studied Peterson's face as a series of questions hit him with a shock. *Can I condemn him to death? Should I? For the good of the ship and crew, must I?* His mind shied away from the thought of what duty demanded. *What does good order and discipline require?* He had never seriously considered that before. "Suggested punishment?"

"Airlock," came the immediate response. Peterson's face grew even paler, if possible, but he did not move. Explosive decompression qualified as an especially gruesome way to go. A person's blood boiled away, after which internal organs might burst from the body, a truly ghastly death. A hard punishment for extremely serious crimes.

Hugh pondered a long moment before speaking. He should have Pete executed. There were, and they all knew it, no extenuating circumstances. But it felt so much like murder. On the other hand, an empire could not exist in a state of anarchy or arbitrary enforcement, the only law being the whim of the leader. If he failed to require that the law be followed to its fullest extent now, what incentive would there be for others to stay inside the lines? What should he do? Could he find a middle ground? He wished the nanites would take over, it would be so much simpler.

He took a deep breath before speaking.

Facing Peterson directly, he pronounced his doom, "For threatening the heir, for refusing a direct order, for initiating unwanted sexual contact on a commissioned officer in a combat zone, I condemn you to death, Sergeant Peterson, by ejection from the airlock." Peterson's sudden intake of breath spoke volumes. He remained silent and still, however, his personal discipline impressive. Now, at any rate. He should have thought earlier. Hugh continued after a long three heart beats, "I hold the sentence in abeyance due to services rendered. Sentence will be carried out immediately should you violate these portions of *Rocks and Shoals* again. Dismissed." Peterson gave him an almost uncomprehending look before saluting robotically, doing an about-face, and leaving stiffly.

As the hatch closed, Ward sagged back into his chair, still apparently feeling the effects of his wound. "Should you have done that?" Ward asked.

"I should have handled it differently in the mess," Hugh answered ruefully. "After all the guff I have taken from him, on Jeffco as well as here, I wanted to beat him senseless. I lost control, but just shooting him out the lock would have been my fault as well as his. He's a good man in everything except where women are concerned. Hopefully, this won't come back to bite me."

Ward nodded. "Hopefully. Elite commandos are a funny bunch. You may have gained a friend for life, or he may decide you aren't worthy of serving because you didn't space him; too weak. We won't know until later."

Hugh shrugged. "I couldn't think what else to do, but now I need to go."

Ward smiled. "Not quite yet, Your Highness. Step forward."

Hugh noticed the gem bag on the desk. As he focused on it, the sapphire rose up. Ward paused as if catching his breath. "Take the stone and touch it briefly to your lips." As Hugh did so, Ward said, "The heir exercises fair and impartial judgment."

The sapphire, or more precisely, the nanites impregnated in it, again swept through his mind, clearing it while creating a burning warmth that felt almost painful. Hugh suddenly understood that judgment would always be painful no matter how he decided. He must exercise it but never desire it.

"You have exercised judgment that has been stern, fair, and impartial, fearing no man's censure, taking no man's gift. In Nighthawk, you sought to balance competing goals, providing a way for those who have maintained their loyalty to the empire to protect their families while returning with honor when you could just as easily have ordered them to come with you for your safety and convenience. Often there are competing needs, you balanced those with Doctor Davison, which could have turned out badly, as well as with Ensign uch Robert. Judgment is also rarely simple nor is the final result always known, and you have demonstrated that you know you are not infallible. With Peterson, you have truly shown you can handle difficult decisions and understand the competing interests when you make your choice."

Finishing, Ward suggested, "Continue to act wisely. Place the gem back on the cloth."

Hugh reluctantly let the sapphire go. The desire to make good choices and his newfound knowledge of how badly things could go really concerned him. With a sigh, he forced his hand to release the gem onto the bag, watching as it appeared to be absorbed.

After leaving Ward's cabin, Hugh hustled back to the mess but found it empty. Checking her cabin, no one answered, neither Maeve nor Sally. Scratching his head, he decided to follow the old soldier's maxim learned as a very young man on Doña Carlota's estate, *Eat when you can.* He went back to the mess for a snack.

THERE HE GOES. MAEVE FELT an odd emptiness as Hugh strode purposefully out to do whatever the sergeant major needed him for. *Why did he interfere? I could have handled the situation! I've been taking care of myself since . . .* The fact that Pete had completely ignored her attempt to do just that quietly undermined her bold assertion, but she firmly suppressed the niggling doubt.

I would have! The whole scene began to play itself back in her head. The mere memory of Peterson's arm around her made her flesh crawl. She never again wanted to feel that trapped and scared, seeing his leering smile just inches from her face and feeling his hot breath on her cheek. Neither her ice-maiden act nor her anger had chased him away, leaving her only the option of physically fighting back, but would that have worked any better?

Priscilla Jenks and the team had taught her some moves, enough to defend herself physically against most of the spacers. Then, after Welks's attack, she had really applied herself to learning how to defend herself physically against most men. Until now, until today, that had seemed enough to keep her safe. But against Peterson or any of these men? Elite commandos? She could have been in real trouble, she miserably acknowledged to herself. Depressed but honest with herself, she didn't think she would have had any chance at all.

Staring at the wall, though not seeing it, she felt a warm arm go around her shoulder. Shocked, she jerked back and spun, only to see Sally's concerned eyes. "Are you okay, honey?" Sally's depth of caring broke a dam inside of Maeve. Her pent-up wave of despair, fear, and loss overwhelmed her defenses. The intensity of the release caught her off guard, sweeping her away in a flood of feelings she couldn't control. Wrapping her arms around herself, she desperately tried to control the tears threatening to surface. Sally scooted closer, putting both arms around her. A long-forgotten feeling of safety swept over her as Sally held her tightly, patting her back softly. A flash of Priscilla holding her just this way when her father had died crossed her mind, something buried since the day Priscilla had died on *Bring It*. She missed her so! And all those others: Dad, Mom, Qi Mai Ling, so many more. Why couldn't she control her feelings better? She didn't want anyone to know how vulnerable she felt right now.

Evidently seeing her struggle to control her emotions, Sally whispered to her, "Let's go talk in the observation dome. No one will disturb us there." Maeve nodded, willing herself not to let go of the tight hold she kept on her emotions. Unobserved, they made their way to the deserted nose.

People didn't like the observation dome. The universe looked decidedly odd seen directly from a ship flying relatively faster than light. Far ahead, the stars shone clear and cold, all the galaxies, nebulae, and the glories of the universe a riot of colors, with yellows and whites predominating, laid out on display against the black emptiness. But closer? The stars ahead blue-shifted as they drew near, fading into an odd purplish haze before becoming red to disappear behind. This violent dance of the stars could be deeply unsettling to someone watching it play out against the unmoving celestial backdrop. Maeve plopped down on a soft chair with Sally taking another. Maeve gave a quick look outside, catching a reflected glimpse of her green eyes in the dome before turning away. Both of them then ignored the outside. For a while, they just sat in silence. Maeve's thoughts became tears, trickling softly down her cheeks.

Finally, Sally asked gently, "Do you want to talk about it?"

Shaking her head hesitantly, she said, "I'm not sure I can. Life is so hard sometimes." The tears came harder and Maeve let out a quiet sob as this admission overwhelmed her defenses.

After a seeming eternity, Maeve broke the silence, "I'm so sorry for all the tears. I just don't know what has come over me. I haven't let myself go like this since Priscilla died. After that, I locked away my feelings deep where no one could touch them." She breathed deeply, trying to get control over her emotions. "It simply wasn't safe." A surprising realization hit her, causing her to murmur softly, "Until now."

Sally's eyes teared up at that as she whispered softly in reply, "Honey, you truly are safe now. Talking can really help but can be tough, too. That's why the floodgates opened, because inside you knew you could let them. You can talk about it with me if you want to."

Maeve nodded. "I'd like to talk a bit about my dad and my mom." Maeve sniffed. "And Priscilla and Mai Ling and the others." With that, she put her head down on her arm, resting on the arm of the chair, and let the hurt, anger, and darkness wash over her. Her eyes burned, but no tears came as bleakness filled her.

Maeve thought a moment, terrified of the dark place she looked into, but she couldn't ignore it any longer. If she tried to, it would eventually swallow her up like a black hole. Slowly, hesitantly, she began by explaining about her mom, "My mother's name was Maude. She braided my hair and sang all the time. She loved me and my father very much. She might have been a princess, but when she left her home world, her mother, the queen, took away her title. She'd tell me how she gave up everything because she loved Dad so very much.

"One day, we were on the way to a conference of some kind at a naval building with Dad. Suddenly, a bunch of cars and a truck ambushed us. They killed one of Dad's escorts right off. Mom, Dad, and the other escort started firing back. They bailed out of the car and pulled me out before it blew up. It must have been on fire, but I honestly don't remember much. We could hear sirens and help coming, but the attackers kept getting closer. Mom shielded me with her body. Suddenly, she went limp, gone, just like that." Blindly staring at her hands, she could again see her mother's blood covering them.

Bit by bit, Maeve told the rest. How her dad taught her to shoot, how he had died, how she'd killed the last assassin. "If Morgain had been there when Dad died, I would have shot her without a second thought. When I thought back about it later, I knew I couldn't do it, but I wish I didn't feel that way. Now I just want to stop her for Dad and Mom's sake. Vivian—everyone liked her—but she had always been so vain and self-centered; I don't miss her. Nimue? How can I hate a sister enough to kill her? She's just plain rotten and mean." After a few more minutes talking about her sisters, she drew a deep breath and sighed. "You probably think I'm horrible, feeling about my own sisters this way?"

Sally simply shook her head. "We all have demons; yours are worse than most."

The bleakness in her voice matched the void beyond the dome. Sally hugged her tightly and Maeve hugged her back. Discussing what had happened to Priscilla, Mai Ling, and the others opened the wounds even more.

Quickly, Maeve talked about how she had to personally take over keeping tabs on Pogue after she'd lost all of the others, how dirty she felt knowing what went on in his cabin. Finally, she descended to her darkest place, the weeks just before they'd arrived, when she had lost all hope.

"So, I decided to blow up the ship after the next TechMech attack, if those barbarians didn't kill us all first. But you came." Almost inaudibly, she whispered, "With Hugh, an actual heir. After all of the supposed fakes that came through, I still can't believe it. And, he agreed to let me come with you . . ."

"What happened in the mess?" Sally asked gently.

Just as softly, almost emotionlessly, Maeve told her. Maeve barely noticed Sally's expression of deep concern. Peterson's story led to talking about Welks and Hamilton Pogue, although she kept the details sparse. As she wound down, she asked plaintively, "Why do I attract men like that?"

"Honey, it's not your fault. There are men who are pigs, but not everyone is that way. The other men on the ship are real gentlemen. Even Peterson generally is okay, just sometimes stupid. But the others are the best."

Maeve sat motionless, neither nodding nor shaking her head, as if she had not heard Sally. Then she spoke very softly, barely above a whisper, "I feel so alone, as though no one understands what I've been through or can relate to what it's like to have your childhood ripped away and adulthood forced upon you."

Sally nodded, then said, "I can think of one person who can understand all of that." Maeve looked up and Sally went on, "Let me tell you about Hugh. At least, what I know." Sally described the little boy who had been five or six when he lost his mother, a little boy whom a fleet and an army had tried to kill on Deft, where he had been taken to avoid exactly that just before the coup. Maeve's heart began to ache for the loneliness and terror he must have surely felt then, and how it must have felt being raised by the military on Doña Carlota's estate, because she had experienced the same feelings when first Mom, and then Dad, had been shot down right in front of her. How could Hugh stand it all? Then Sally explained, "Hugh had been hunting back on Jeffco when a nuclear strike hit the manor, trying to kill him. It almost did, too. After getting back safely, Admiral Hollister and Doña Carlota told him he could become emperor if he passed this test. Or die if he failed, and that the empire needed him—*we* truly needed him—to try."

Sally ended by adding, "Since then, he *has* been trying. Trying to learn, trying to show he can do this, and most importantly, trying to meet the expectations of everyone around him. He's your age, Maeve, and if what he's been going through isn't being forced into adulthood, I can't imagine what is."

Maeve sat for long moments as she absorbed the things Sally had told her. She and Hugh had a lot in common. Both damaged by the cruelty and greed of a few, scarred inside where no one could see. Both stood alone, without their families or much of anyone in the universe. Of all the people in the galaxy, Hugh might best understand how she truly felt because he had suffered just like her. The idea of what it might be like to have a friend who truly understood her, what she had been through, brought a gentle smile to Maeve's lips. By the time they finished talking, midnight had long passed. Silence filled the ship as they headed back to their cabin to get some sleep.

CNS *Pechnaya*
1155 BBMT 3 November 3473

READY TO SIT DOWN AND enjoy her steak Milanesa, something Morgain uch Robert had been looking forward to for several days, her com dinged. Irritation rose at the interruption.

Sighing, she laid down her fork and said to her dinner companion, "Will you excuse me? Apparently, the ship can't function without my personal intervention."

Her guest chuckled. "Of course. I look forward to trying this with you when you return."

One of the things she liked about him was his superb manners. Giving him a genuine smile, she nodded and rose to take this call in her command cabin. Sitting comfortably, she opened the channel to see a com tech, Becky Cook by her name tag. A *tech* interrupted her? That would be the last mistake this tech ever made. "Yes?" she demanded.

"The planetary government is calling and demands to speak to the fleet commander. They call themselves the Enlightened."

Simply nodding, Morgain recognized that she did, in fact, need to speak to these individuals. Her supply people wanted to refuel and access the out-system weapons cache Ninth Fleet had established over a century earlier.

Adopting an interested look, she opened the link. A trio of rather self-important people, two men and a woman, replaced the com tech's face. The man in the middle didn't even give Morgain a chance to greet them. "By what right do you enter our peaceful system with your warships? We don't want you here; you're not welcome. Get out right now, Admiral!"

Morgain sat back, letting a bit of silence descend. She'd give them one chance to act appropriately, and then she would find a way to make their lives difficult. "We are from Ninth Fleet, and we have a port and resupply agreement with your government."

The man to the left nodded. "Fine. One day for resupply and then leave!"

Morgain sighed. She had tried to be reasonable and this is where it had gotten her. The system had a huge amount of mining and commerce and would have made a comfortable place to control the search from, but that didn't look like a possibility now. "Although that appears to be a breach of our porting agreement, we will comply."

The three smiled back smugly without even saying anything. They had *expected* her to do whatever they said? On top of interrupting her lunch, they clearly didn't understand that she could destroy this system without even blinking. And apparently didn't care.

Too bad. I gave them a chance. Some people are just too stupid to live. Smiling, Morgain asked, "Is there anything we can do for you while we're here?"

The woman on the right leaned forward. "Now that you mention it."

Morgain smiled even more broadly. They would now tell her exactly how to hurt them the worst. It almost made up for her steak cooling.

Zeta Tau Alpha Debris Field
0250 BBMT 5 November 3473

"SLOW AND STEADY, HELM," DIRECTED Captain Argus Steed as he stood glued to the holodisplay in the middle of the deck as *Commander's Belle* pushed her way, at just a fraction of her potential speed, into the mass of deep space rocks. Former Marine lieutenant Austin Carhart watched silently from the command chair for this maneuver.

Since the area didn't belong to any specific star system or quadrant, officially at least, in his persona as owner of the *Belle* Peer Drunnan, Carhart had ordered Steed to carefully take his very expensive and somewhat illegal private corvette into the zone near the intersection of sectors Prime, Two, Seven and Eight.

Zeta Tau Alpha 773, the official designation of this mess, but better known to people who visited it as Pirate's Shoal, lay ahead.

He hoped he could find what he was looking for because coming here had been a gamble. The information he needed had to be classified Top Secret, Imperial, perhaps higher, which made it very risky to even look for it, but he absolutely had to have it. His other sources remained dry after that single, lucky hit telling him about Hugh Cascade. No one knew where he had gone.

The rating in Tactical hit the alert button. "Cruiser near the shipfitter's dock, Captain."

Carhart sat up as Steed nodded with an unnatural calm.

"Are its guns and targeting systems hot, Petty Officer."

The PO shook his head. "No, sir. Seems to be pretty badly shot up, actually. Air is escaping from at least three hull ruptures." After a pause, he added, "The cruiser is *Pontus* from Task Group 8-2. Admiral Perdot commanded the task group at the time of the coup."

Steed glanced tensely at him. "Sure you want to go in, sir? You remember what he said the last time you met."

Carhart simply nodded before relaxing back into the chair once more.

Steed fixed the helm with his eye. "Proceed to dock at the Shoal. Contact control for instructions. Liberty for the crew by watches."

Carhart stood and stretched. Reflecting wryly, he admitted to himself that approaching the Shoal could best be described as an adventure, one not to be taken lightly. Dealing with dishonest people meant always being on your toes, and the current management of Pirate's Shoal, this hollowed out planetoid, proved that point in spades. But he needed information, regardless of price, in money or peril. After all, he played for none but the highest stakes at this point, the empire itself.

Stepping off the bridge he entered his cabin in three steps. Normally the commander's day cabin on a warship, he used it as his suite because, for all intents and purposes, he commanded her, as a would-be mutineer had learned to his surprise six years earlier. People who knew Carhart never tested him.

Carefully he picked a solidly respectable outfit with a hideout gun, vibro knife, and openly strapped on pistol. Now ready, he commed, "Captain Steed, I'll need the bosun and three men with me, all armed with pistols and rifles."

"Aye, sir." Steed rarely said much, which he appreciated. Good man, too. Like every man aboard, he owed his life to Carhart and paid that debt in loyalty.

He stepped into the entry port, the two guards there saluted sharply, as did the three common spacers waiting to go with him. The bosun, Mul Mantar, simply nodded, almost imperceptibly. Carhart didn't care, because nothing and nobody resembled a space rock more than Mantar: short, massive, and immovable when he decided to be. He inclined his head forward before heading down the docking tube to their assigned entry bay. He could have docked directly to Pirate's Shoal on a docking collar but preferred to be able to leave swiftly, if need be. A docking collar could all too easily become a trap by simply increasing the gravity at the point of contact. At the station side of the docking tube, he paused to speak into his almost invisible head piece. "Soft lock on docking tube, keep the power plant hot. Things feel a little off."

Steed responded, "Let's break off and head somewhere else, sir."

His eyes narrowed as he examined the concourse through the glass in the secondary airlock hatch. Pirate's Shoal consisted of a warren of corridors, most wider than ships' passageways. Even so, the concourse seemed much busier than he had expected. A steady stream of men and women jostled each other in both directions.

Mantar put a massive hand on the secondary lock that would let them into the concourse, keeping it closed. "Sir, those are Perdot's people out there, at least many of that crowd. I think we should go."

Carhart stared icily in silence for a moment, but Mantar refused to move. "Open the hatch, bosun," he ordered. To Steed, he added, "Cancel liberty plans until I return."

"The last time we ran across Perdot, he promised to gut you

and then space you." Mantar remained unmoved. "I heard him say it and I believed him."

He smiled at Mantar with a brief second of warmth. "So, let's give him his chance. That is his personal cruiser out there in a repair slip. It is shot up so badly I don't think it's going anywhere anytime soon. On the holo, there were only two destroyers, a frigate, and some sloops docked that I know are his, and a cruiser, *Gatsby*, that belonged with 13th Fleet and has been missing for five years. I think being here will be quite instructive."

Mantar didn't move.

"Now, Mul."

Reluctantly, Mul Mantar opened the hatch. Pointing to the men on the left, he ordered, "You two ahead." To the other one, he jerked his head. "Behind, with me." His voice seemed to come from some deep cavern in the earth. "Where are we going, sir?"

Fully Drunnan now, he glanced right and left, judging the flow. Most of the officers seemed to be heading left. "Follow the big fish, bosun. See where they take us, but I'd guess the ship's chandlery."

Without a word, the lead security men headed to their left. Surprisingly, the corridor soon became less crowded, but the percentage of officers and senior petty officers shot up until there were very few enlisted. The majority of those few, however, were steel-eyed shore patrol who definitely did not greet the appearance of Drunnan and his armed retinue with anything approaching welcome.

He turned toward Tomaguchi's Careen and Ships Chandlers. A knot of Shore Patrol blocked the entrance. A particularly large man with the rockers of a senior petty officer on his arm stood facing them with a sneer, not saying anything. Mantar attempted to step around.

Carhart simply smiled and turned his head to look at him. "I'll handle this, Bosun." As he faced forward, his right hand seemed to leap like lightening, grasping the left wrist of the roadblock, a man outweighing him by an easy hundred pounds. In another half second, he pinned the man's arm painfully up against his back and Carhart's left hand had his pistol out and pointing at the balance of the patrolmen.

Mildly he said, "I would like to have a little chat with your boss, and I am sure Admiral Perdot would like to speak with me." His eyes were lasers focused on the stunned knot of guards. He then suggested quietly, "If you would please step aside?"

So stunned were the patrolmen that he doubted they even noticed his four men had their pistols out, too. Three of his men, except the bosun, moved quickly, pushing the frozen men blocking the door to the sides. He stepped through the door, his team closing it behind him. And his stomach dropped. As he took in the scene, he wondered if the accustomed hard-shouldered arrogance he had forced on the universe around him the last ten years might have just gotten him killed.

At the counter straight ahead stood the black-hearted proprietor of the chandler's shop, Enzo Tomaguchi, with Gene Perdot to his right. Zo, as people called Tomaguchi, not affectionately, had a ghostly pallor, a most unusual state for him. The bullyboys he normally surrounded himself with were nowhere to be seen. Perdot, sometime vice admiral of Eighth Sector and self-proclaimed sector lord, also seemed to have lost his usual self-possession.

If they were as frightened as they seemed to be, a man who ran a successful business in this lawless outpost and the leader of a fleet not much better than buccaneers, a visitor like Drunnan had to be in real trouble. In that instant, he understood why. Facing them, he saw a person he had never expected to meet this side of eternity, a rumor who had supposedly died in the early days of the rebellion, Wilby Dent.

From what he had heard, Dent had been at best a minor character in Morgain's orbit no one knew much about. Turning, he was at a loss to understand why these two were cowed by Wilby Dent. Then, he took a closer look. Older than the last picture he had seen, something about the eyes chilled Carhart to his very marrow. Coming face-to-face with a crazed, human-sized cobra would not have been more terrifying. This man was definitely unstable. And more importantly, in charge.

His and his men's survival depended in this moment on how he reacted to Dent. He needed all of his faculties fully online at this moment. Including his charm, trying once more to be the innocuous merchant, Peer Drunnan.

He gave a self-deprecating smile and shook his head. "I can see I've come at a bad time. I'll come back later." His attempt at charm seemed to have no effect on Dent, who coldly demanded, "Who are you and why are you here?"

"Peer Drunnan, at your service. I have a little information to trade and looked to get some in exchange. But you gentlemen appear busy, so, if you'll excuse me?" Turning to leave, he ran hard into a chunk of humanity who had stepped up unnoticed behind him. To his left, a gun held Mantar against the wall. Carhart couldn't believe this had happened without a sound but couldn't deny reality, either. Turning back toward Dent, he knew he now faced someone much more dangerous than he could ever have expected to run into. Zo and Perdot had obviously come to the same conclusion.

Dent leaned toward him, his breath rancid. "What information do you have that is worth your life?" he asked softly.

"I know where the heir Hugh Cascade and his proctor were two weeks ago," he stated levelly.

Dent appeared amused. "So do I, Hamilton Pogue's cruiser *Bring It* in the Nighthawk system. If you had provided that information to me a month ago, that would have been worth something to me, but now? Anything else, anything of real value?" Carhart's stomach dropped as Dent took Peer's high card and casually trumped it. Now what?

Before he could come up with anything more, Perdot cleared his throat. "This *person's* name is actually Austin Carhart."

Dent blinked blankly at this. "Which means what, to me? And remember, when I contacted you to join me after the coup, you were not, shall we say, receptive? You made it clear to me that when Bartleby Quadros died . . . and as a result I lost control of Twelfth Fleet . . . that you had no further use for me. The others said the same thing. Me, the one without whom there would have been no rebellion. The one who planned every step of the way. A few like Garrison Traynor even wanted to kill me. I plan on fixing the problem with Twelfth Fleet myself immediately and then take care of the others personally, so be careful what you say because I have not decided what to do with you. Yet."

Perdot paled even further, before going on. "He helped save Cascade's son on Deft."

Dent's coloring changed spectacularly from red to purple to white anger. "Is this true?"

With a deadly certainty, Austin Carhart knew his next words might be his last. So he told the truth. Almost. "I served there, a Marine lieutenant fighting under Doña Carlota Gonzalvez y Rodriguez de Castillo, the Protector of the Succession, and Imperial Sergeant Major Sean Ward. When Morgain demanded we turn over the boy, I argued that we should. I have been on the run from the empire ever since." After bending the truth without quite breaking it, Carhart imperceptibly held his breath. What happened next scared him more than Dent's apparent anger just moments before.

In a calm, almost disinterested voice, Dent asked, "So you would like to kill Ward and the others, would you, if given the chance?"

Carhart most assuredly would love to kill Ward. As for Hugh? That could be negotiable.

"Absolutely," he said, mustering all the sincerity he could.

Dent smiled slightly. "Good. I will give you that job."

Perdot desperately broke in. "But he's a liar, a thief. He can't be trusted!"

Dent's anger returned, and he began almost screaming at Perdot, "And you can? You who betrayed me when I could have become emperor overnight? Why shouldn't I have you executed right now?"

To Carhart's experienced eye, Perdot seemed about to faint from fright. Stuttering, he got out, "B-b-but I know where another heir is." Dent simply raised an eyebrow.

"It is Robert ap Morgan's daughter Maeve. He's the one that really kept the coup from succeeding. When I took Periastron, we captured Admiral Davies's aide, a commander named Asroc. Before he died, he told us Davies had hidden Maeve at Camp Y. Pogue picked her up accidentally and Davies couldn't get her back after Pogue went to Sector Thirteen."

Dent's entire attention now focused on Perdot. "Her alias and proctor."

Perdot fell all over himself as he answered, "He hid her as Maeve Ellyllyon. Priscilla Jenks proctored her."

Dent gave Perdot a sidelong glance as Carhart saw a thought take form on his face. "I had Maeve uch Roberts within my grasp all that time while she hid on *Bring It* and didn't know it? Perdot, you just gave me very useful information." Nodding toward the guards he added, "He can live another day. Take him out." Two of them grabbed Perdot and dragged him away.

Turning his eyes like gun barrels to train them on Carhart, he continued to speak, sounding perfectly rational, "Based on that information, and as nearly as I can tell, Maeve must have been the one who blew up Pogue's ship and helped Cascade escape. I want you to find a way to control her and bring her to me. She may be of use in dealing with her sister Morgain, who is a thorn in my side. If not, she will die, very slowly. But be sure to kill Cascade and Ward." Then, with emphasis, he asked, "Do. You. Understand?"

Carhart, for the first time in his life, felt like an insect under the microscope of Dent's gaze. Figuring that a positive reply would be his best ticket away from this rabid dog, he said, "Yes, Your Majesty." Using that title on Dent couldn't hurt and might keep him alive. "I'll do it. Where are they?"

Dent shook his head as if shaking off an annoying fly. "I don't know, but a clever fellow like you should be able to figure it out. They're headed farther out, though, than Nighthawk, where they were last seen. Someone should know, you just need to ask the right person. And the right questions." Dent refocused on Carhart. "Now, go."

Carhart had never been so glad to leave anywhere in his life, not even Deft. Even as he turned and headed back to his ship, he expected a shot in the back at any moment. One thing he swore, if he ever saw Dent again before the heat death of the universe, it would be too soon. An idea hit him as he reached the ship. Maybe one of Maeve's other sisters would be of use in controlling her. Morgain had been one of the original conspirators, but he had no chance of separating her from her fleet. Nimue? Bad news from what he had heard, but, by all accounts, the second oldest sister, Vivian, could be quite charming. She would be his target.

Which meant the information he needed could only be found in one place, a planet where he didn't want to go.

The Core Empire

Part VI, Chapters 17 through 22

Part VI examines the Middle Empire Period from 3103 through 3232. Great internal unrest marked this period due to the continued dynastic battles between Dave Jackson's descendants, through Crystal Marris and Yvonne Sabonis, as well as Elsie Jackson's Paracletes descendants. During the eight Tests of Heirs in this period, fifty-four heirs died, including six after completing the test but before the acclamation of the eventual emperor. Two emperors died in battle, one suffered assassination, and another died under mysterious circumstances. Interestingly, not until the end of this era did a descendant of Elsie, Joe Jackson's sole surviving daughter, successfully complete the test for the first time. Clara Peacock became consort of Ira Jandon, a descendant of Dave's second wife, Yvonne, the first of the two examples of joint rule. We will focus on the dynamics that led to this unusual solution to the empire's political problems.

16

A Talking To

Ambrose B, Entering Crux-Scutum Arm
1400 BBMT 7 November 3473

HUGH SLID INTO HIS SEAT on the bridge the day before reaching Macanak 52, more than a thousand parsecs farther out from the galactic core beyond Nighthawk, but his mind hadn't accompanied his body. Even under normal circumstance, astrogation held little interest for him. But the atmosphere on the ship had changed with Sergeant Pete Peterson's near spacing. The female crew were freezing Peterson out and the male crew were wary of spending any time with him other than on duty. He could feel morale suffering. On top of that, Maeve had been keeping herself scarce, often down in Engineering or somewhere else with her head buried in junction boxes and wiring cabinets. He still felt he had to apologize to her for what had happened with Pete.

He suddenly became aware of Captain Gail Felt and Lieutenant Sally Carr's somber expressions, which caused his stomach to churn with worry. *What have I done now?* Astrogation and his other bridge subjects were coming along fine, generally, if not quite four-star, and a quick review of what else he could have done came up empty. He had no idea what might be bothering them. Hugh hated not being in control of a situation. Regardless, Imperial Sergeant Major Sean Ward and Doña Carlota Gonzalvez y Rodriguez de Castillo had drummed into him a simple general rule: facing a problem early beat, by far, ignoring it until it became a major event. Sitting tall, he looked Gail straight in the eyes, and barked, "Cadet Cascade, present for training."

Gail didn't smile at his attempt to cut the tension by clowning a bit, a sure sign of things being far worse than he feared. "Your Highness," she began. The knot became painful. Things must really be serious, Gail never addressed him formally on the bridge. During training they preferred for him to be simply Cadet Cascade, not the heir apparent, so by calling him by his title she had chosen to make this almost a matter of record.

Barely missing a beat, he answered, "Yes, Captain?" equaling her demeanor. If she thought they needed to have a serious discussion, it must be important, so he would respect her judgment and treat it that way too. Sitting on the edge of his seat as a good cadet should did not comport, in his mind, with the proper way for the heir to act, however, so he leaned back a little.

Gail sat up straighter as she began, "There is a small matter of friction between members of the crew that needs your attention."

"Go on," he said.

Gail nodded to Sally. "You tell him, you were the one she talked to."

"You seem to keep Ensign uch Robert at arm's length. You are purposefully shutting her out and it is likely to affect how the others treat her, too."

"No, I'm not!" Hugh said defensively. "If anything, she seems to be avoiding me. Is she mad about my saving her from Peterson?"

Gail smiled. "There is no doubt that Peterson's behavior triggered a lot of emotions in her. But I don't think she's mad. You have to remember that the two of you are the youngest crew members and about the same age."

Where is this going?

"At school you got along with guys and gals. The girls all came from good homes and were safe and protected. Even the girls in the surrounding towns lived in a civilized environment, with help always nearby. But not Maeve." She paused while Hugh digested this, before going on, "As a teenager, a *young* teenager, Captain Hamilton Pogue swept her up onto his ship where she suddenly had to deal with adults and pretend to be one. It must have been terrifying, even with Priscilla Jenks and her team there to protect her. Pogue and his crew acted toward the women on board much worse than Peterson did, but no one tried to stop them. She lived with the constant knowledge that someone could prey upon her at any time, and she could do very little to protect herself."

Hugh tried to imagine that but couldn't.

"On top of that, she and her team discovered that their hard work in code breaking unintentionally ended up killing loyal spacers, and that they were trapped on a rebel ship. I heard about your little flash of brilliance back on Jeffco that almost blew the operation when you queried the attacking fleet's transponders to identify them. It didn't, but how would you have felt if it had?"

His stomach fell. If that had happened, he would have wanted to die. Had Maeve reacted that way when she found out?

She went on, "Your Highness, as emperor, how you deal with women may be even more important than how you lead men. Men have physical advantages in strength, but women are the glue that holds society together. Or women can tear everything apart. The same is especially true on a small ship like ours."

A sudden stillness took him as thoughts and questions hit him. How had she survived, especially at the end with no friends, no support? For him on Pogue's ship, would it have been easier or less scary? Probably less terrifying in most ways.

Breaking into his thoughts, Sally answered, "It might help you to understand how to work with her if you knew some more about Maeve, Your Highness." And without even waiting for him to agree, she began to explain what Maeve had gone through. Some of her experiences Hugh understood only too well, but then there were the differences. While his family had died early in the coup, also, Maeve had actually been there when both her parents had died. And what Maeve had gone through on *Bring It* really shook him.

Sally continued, "The really sad part in all this is that Maeve has no idea how to act in a normal setting toward normal people, which is why her defenses are always up. She has learned to be tough." Leaning forward, Sally earnestly smiled before patting his knee, a sincere action that made him wince. "Since her father died, she has been able to rely on only a few men. Then you came on the scene, the dashing prince who rescued her, and she has no idea how to react to you. Without her help, we wouldn't have been able to get away from that ship alive and she knows it. She also knows, gut deep, that without us, without you, she couldn't have escaped from that ship either. *Ever.* She knows she needed to be rescued but had lost all hope. The problem is that her emotional wall keeps her from being at ease with the reality that she is safe." Then Sally surprised him. "You have a wall, too."

Hugh opened his mouth to disagree, but Sally's stern look stopped him. Almost as if she could read his mind, she drove on relentlessly, "You have one, so don't argue. Why else did you put on that stone face when we started this conversation, if not to keep anyone from seeing what you were feeling?" Sally crossed her arms and sat back, waiting for a response. Hugh bit his tongue, refusing to answer. If he denied having a wall, she'd take that for proof it existed and, if he agreed, she'd probably give him a triumphant smirk. That left shutting up and waiting her out.

After a moment of silence, she quirked up the left side of her mouth and went on. "As I said, she acts the same way, too. Also, unlike you, she desperately needed the illusion that she could handle any situation on her own, something you caused to crumble. Can you understand how, rational or not, this makes her feel vulnerable and terrified? Based upon her past, any hint of weakness would have been blood in the water to the sharks she lived among."

Almost against his will, Hugh nodded.

Sally gave him an understanding smile. "When she came on this ship, she felt deeply and completely humiliated in a way only a vulnerable woman can. Then, afterward, you didn't even give her a throwaway *thank you* for her part in the escape. Bottom line: you hurt her feelings by interrogating her, by not trusting her."

For Hugh, it all seemed too much. "*Interrogating* isn't what I'd call it. More like an interview or a debriefing."

Gail smiled at that. "Ward said you reacted the same way when he talked about that opening *interview* with you. But, yes, you did *interrogate* her. If you're honest with yourself, you'll admit it, plus you know you needed to do it. You simply performed your duty as the heir apparent." Before he could argue more, she glanced at Sally before continuing, voice soft but compelling, "Later, the Marines sat in the mess, talking and joking about the mission. She felt you were all a bunch of insensitive clowns. She *knew* those people who had died on that ship and, even if she hadn't liked most of them, laughing about them dying offended her. She's even been having nightmares about them dying."

Hugh's eyes opened a little wider in surprise. Then Sally added another factor for him to consider, "Besides which, and most importantly, she is the one who actually blew up the ship, something she is really struggling with. Being the one who pulls the trigger is always tougher."

The memory of his own feelings and nightmares after shooting Pogue and his XO popped back into his mind, bringing him up short. He hadn't even considered how she might react. Based upon what Gail and Sally had just explained, she understandably took it even worse than he had. How could he have missed the obvious?

Gail went on, "Since then, several unfortunate things have happened that have compounded her discomfort: her embarrassing pratfall in the corridor, the simulations where she feels far less capable than the rest of the team, you walking in on her in the shower, and last of all, Peterson." Hugh opened his mouth to protest, but Sally quelled his attempt at self-defense before he could utter a word. "You have been respectful and proper and tried to do the right thing at all times."

"Then what's the problem?" Hugh asked dumbly, now totally confused

"Maeve needs time to adjust to being a part of the team, and after what she went through on Pogue's ship that may take a while," Gail said. "Until she does, you need to treat her less like Sally or Karen and more like the girls at Doña Carlota's estate. You just need to be nice to her and patient with her. Especially patient," Gail stressed.

"But—" Hugh began.

Gail shook her head. "I know this is hard for both of you. One more thing, I'm going to give you the same advice all young officers get from their sergeants: *If you don't know what to say, listen.*"

Taking a breath, she paused in thought for a moment. "She wants desperately to be included; give her a chance. You're the heir apparent, so she isn't supposed to start conversations. Besides which, you are at least a little intimidating to those who don't know you. You have loads of charisma. Both your father and mother had it, too. Men and women felt his power, believe me. I sure did, and you got his genes in spades. Maeve certainly feels the pull of your personality. She also admires what you're doing and why you're doing it. She wants to believe that you can fix what's wrong with the universe, but is utterly terrified of what will happen if she does begin to believe in you and you fail like everyone else in her life."

Maeve believes I can save the galaxy? She had a higher opinion of his abilities than he did, to be honest. His darkest nightmares were about his all-too-likely failure. Knowing how much she believed in him helped him feel he might be able to succeed.

An errant thought flitted through his mind. *Does everyone on board feel that way?* In that instant, the mere possibility of all those hopes and fears centering on him almost crushed the life out of him. He felt, for that moment, an overwhelming urge to run away, hide, and never come back. The memory of that dark meadow back in the mountains flashed before his eyes. He sometimes found himself wishing he had taken the other path back on Jeffco. After the nuke hit the estate, he had run deeper into the mountains for dear life. Resting at the meadow, well ahead of the fire, he relived his decision to either continue ahead toward the towns on the far side where he could disappear or race the fire along the left fork toward the secondary command post where no one might be waiting for him. He had gone to the left, chancing the danger of the fire coming over the mountain, because he knew his duty.

Sitting up a little straighter, he stiffened his spine. Doing one's duty didn't guarantee success or that right would always prevail, but it made success possible, if only an unbelievably small chance. His resolve to continue doing the right thing stiffened, too.

Drawing in a huge lungful of air as if he had been swimming deeply and just now broke the surface, he focused on Gail and Sally. Then taking the plunge, he asked the question he dreaded now more than any other, "Does everyone feel that way?"

Gail and Sally exchanged another glance before Gail answered with quiet sincerity, "I guess we do. *I* certainly feel that way. You're our best hope, just about our only hope."

Sally nodded, adding with a quiet intensity, "I do too, Your Highness. For Maeve, it is even more of a leap of faith. For years, she has lived in the bottom of a black pit surrounded by demons we can only imagine. During all that time, she has undoubtedly asked herself late at night, why she should go on living? Did she have a duty to try and save an empire she had no idea still existed? She had nothing to comfort her as she sat all alone in the dark. I'm sure you can understand that. All that changed when you came along: handsome, able, dedicated, charismatic, decisive, restoring a glimmer of hope and peace. You need to help her so that she, too, sees how she can make a difference. Feeling helpless feeds despair, so give her hope by including her."

"I don't know if I can do anything about this, but I'll try," he stated with a firm nod.

Gail added firmly, "It's simple, really. For her to trust you, she has to know it's the real you."

Hugh nodded. He had no idea what else to do. He couldn't say no, but he didn't know exactly what to do next about Ensign uch Robert. "Thank you for the insights. Now let's get back to something easy, like astrogation," he said half clowning trying to divert them back to the astrogation instruction. Something he knew he didn't do well on.

Gail and Sally laughed, but the look they exchanged said they thought he was headed for trouble at light speed.

Galactifacts for Kids 3500

Parsec. One parsec equals the distance of 3.26 light-years. It means one parallax arc angle second. It is based on the radius of Old Earth's orbit around its sun. In other words, it is how a star seems to change position as Old Earth orbits the sun due to parallax. You can see an example of parallax by staring at a faraway object while closing first one eye and then the other. The object will seem to move, although it remains still. Star distances can be measured in the same way.

17

Choices Behind the Scenes

Ambrose B, Entering Crux-Scutum Arm
1505 BBMT 7 November 3473

AS HUGH DISAPPEARED FOLLOWING THE tactical simulations, Gail noticed Sally watching her. Deep in thought, Gail ignored her. After a good five minutes, Gail audibly sighed, before turning her seat to face Sally. "So, what do you think, Sal gal?" Gail asked as she searched Sally's face.

Sally disappointed Gail, but didn't surprise her, when Sally answered blandly, "About what?"

Gail pursed her lips in exasperation. "Why, is the star La Crescenta 52 a pure diamond or rhinestone, of course? Tell me what you think about Hugh and Maeve."

Sally snuck a grin. "Just checking. For the record, I think that star is rhinestone. Bardingham is the real deal."

Gail restrained herself from smiling. She really did need to know what Sally Carr thought about their heirs but agreed about La Crescenta. As for Sally's judgment about Hugh and Maeve, Gail knew Sally loved the people around her with all her heart, which gave her a special insight into what they thought and who they really were. "And?"

"Hugh is a real smart-mouth and Maeve is uptight. If they opened up to each other, they could really help heal each other. If not, they will deeply hurt each other."

"Do you think Maeve would make a good empress like Clara for Hugh?"

Sally did a double take before answering, "Really cutting to the chase, aren't you? Personally, I think it's a bit premature to think about matching them up. Hugh has to complete the test and we all have to live to get to Earth, so I'd let it go for now." After a moment, an even bigger realization hit her. "Clara . . . as in good Emperor Ira and *Empress* Clara, the double heirs? Maeve's an *heiress*?"

Gail didn't answer the last question. "I need to make up my mind about something right now. Leave it at that. With everything coming up, especially Alpine, I need your opinion on my original question." Sally didn't know everything Gail did, and Gail couldn't explain it to anyone. Well, anyone except Ward, and maybe an heiress, until both heirs, not just one of them, completed the test.

"Well, before we marry up the love birds, don't you think we ought to let them decide if they even *like* each other?" Sally's face echoed the disquiet she felt talking about this.

"Valid point, but not what I asked. How do you think she'd do as empress?"

Sally sat up after a moment more of thought. Confidently, she asserted, "She could make a great empress. I'm probably biased, but there is something special there, steel under all her defenses, which would match him."

Gail nodded. "Thanks. I agree, but the only real way to know will be as nature takes its course. It may turn out they hate each other." She paused, making a decision. "Let the girls know they'll be providing Maeve with a protective detail when she's off the ship."

Sally quirked an eyebrow but left her question unasked.

"She is not taking the test . . . yet. But she is an heir. And keep that last part quiet, please."

Without another word she stood, leaving Sally with the controls.

A RAP ON HIS HATCH brought Ward's head up with a snap, out of his deep concentration.

Hitting the com to the hatch, he simply said, "Come."

Gail poked her head in. "Have a moment?" she asked.

Ward couldn't read her expression, so he responded with a question, "Personal or professional?"

Gail shrugged. "Professional for sure; could be both."

Ward's eyes narrowed. There would be lots of coming and going in the corridors with dinner time near, so why had she come here now, taking the chance that she might be seen entering his cabin? "Come in and sit. I just finished reviewing Hugh's progress." In front of him, a series of graphs and notes filled the computer screen.

Gail perked up. "How's he doing?"

"He's on track." Saving the file, he closed it. "I know you didn't come to discuss Hugh, though, so what's up?"

Gail gave an impish grin. "But I did come to talk about him. Him and Maeve, to be exact."

Ward suddenly felt like he had walked into an ambush. Gail wanted to talk about both heirs, while seeming to dangle personal time as a carrot to get what she wanted. She had never manipulated him before, but they had never faced a situation like this one either. "Uh huh," he answered noncommittally.

"I've just had a chat with Hugh, and I had one with Maeve, earlier. I've never seen two teenagers more confused about their feelings, honestly."

"Feelings?" Ward asked. "For each other? I haven't seen it. I mean, yes, Hugh seems to have noticed she's female and in his age range, but no more so than any of the women on Jeffco."

"From what you've told me, you kept him far too busy to even think about dating."

"He wasn't exactly locked in a monastery. He met girls. Mostly who had fathers who didn't approve. Remember, they all thought he was an orphan being given a scholarship, not an heir to the throne."

"So, what we have is a young man who has been alone most of his life, other than a pair of authority figures who undoubtedly loved him but never shared it, and some Elite Marines with all the manners of a wildebeest. It's a miracle he's not feral, never mind being clueless about women."

Ward started to speak, but Gail cut him off. "And on the other hand, we have a young woman who lost both of her loving parents, whose sisters would just as soon see her dead, and who also grew up not just surrounded by the military, but by those who are the worst part of it: the misogynistic, egotistical filth, the very embodiment of 'conduct prejudicial to good order and discipline,' who commanded *Bring It*. It's astounding to me that she could even *imagine* a romantic relationship with a man after all that. Yet, if I were a betting woman, I'd say Hugh has caught her eye."

Ward raised his eyebrows and asked, "You done? Or is there more to this lecture?"

"I'm done."

"Good. Now let me say this: Yes, Hugh isn't as experienced as some his age when it comes to women and dating. But Doña Carlota absolutely drove into him the need to be a gentleman and to treat women with respect. In that regard, he may have been the most civilized male on Jeffco. Yes, Peterson provided the worst kind of role model, but Hugh recognized that he was trash when it came to women and demonstrated that by standing up to him when Pete behaved inappropriately with Maeve.

"Further, even if he is smitten with Maeve—and I'm not saying he is—he has far more important things to worry about than whether or not to pass her a note in homeroom."

Gail just shook her head. "Oh, ye of little faith. First, Hugh actually doesn't need my help. He understands that Maeve has been through a lot—more than any woman her age should have—and needs him to just be there, being normal and aware that what she's been through makes it difficult for her to be trusting of men, in general. Second, I am still a little concerned about her emotional stability, but I think Maeve is about ready for the oath."

"*What!*" thundered Ward, shooting to his feet. Glowering, he made an effort to contain himself as he sat back down, slowly. Gail really knew how to push his buttons when she wanted to! "Don't you think we ought to discuss giving her the oath *before* you create a potentially fatal competition?"

Gail pursed her mouth, anger beginning to show. As a betting man, he would have laid long odds against *any* personal time after they finished the professional part of this meeting.

He watched quietly, forcing himself to become still inside, as she glared for a moment before speaking, "Female heirs are the responsibility of the Amazon proctors. As I'm the only one left that I know of and, especially since I am the only one on this ship, she is my responsibility. I'll make my own decisions about giving her the oath, Sean Ward." She growled as she finished, a deep, feline warning. Her using both his names reinforced his opinion as to how this meeting would end.

Muttering, he glared darkly. "You know what can happen when two heirs compete, only one can place the gems and the other dies. The last time was Theodore just 450 years ago, and that didn't end well. I've watched Hugh for ten years, waiting in order to avoid this, and you want to put them both at risk this way." Sitting back, he stared at her.

Then an alternative occurred to him, the potential option that could only occur when the heirs had romantic potential. Ward sat bolt upright. "You're not suggesting we arrange the consort alternative?"

Looking at him as though he'd finally guessed the answer to a riddle, Gail sat back and relaxed. "It *has* happened, albeit only twice in the entire history of the empire, and both times were more than two hundred years ago, Ira and Clara, and then Christos and Keiko right after them."

"The first pair did calm the family feuds, but the second almost started them again," Ward answered belligerently.

Gail's cheek dimpled as she laughed at him. "I think it would be romantic. Besides which, this entire venture is such a long shot, two arrows in our quiver gives us, what, a geometrically better chance of success?"

"No, no, no! I won't agree to this! I won't allow it!" Ward stormed at her, unsure of exactly how he had gotten to his feet but aware that he had, and that he felt a little woozy as a result. "I don't want heirs competing on this ship, hurting each other's chances, undermining each other. If the two of them don't accept the consort alternative, I don't know whether either would be willing to put their gems into the starburst and kill the other one. Then where are we? No heirs and no emperor."

As he shouted, he knew Hugh couldn't, wouldn't, do anything to hurt Maeve, or anyone else, to get power. His desire to rule didn't run gut deep, a major reason Ward wanted him on the throne. Hugh considered the throne a sacrifice, not his innermost desire. And that, more than anything, exemplified why the test existed: to find someone who would become the living embodiment of the test.

Gail's face hardened in return, leaning forward, growling out her response, signaling a final warning, "You don't have *any* say in what I do or don't do as the Amazon proctor. I think we ought to let it play out, personally, so I'm just letting you know that whatever Hugh gets involved in, Maeve must be there too."

Her intensity surprised him, as well as her commitment, knocking him back mentally. Ward dropped into his chair as he stared at Gail, a question forming behind his eyes. "You really think they could work it out? Because if both survive and don't choose the alternative, things could get really messy."

Gail eased back in response, not answering except with a small hint of a smile.

Ward dropped his head into his hands. "I knew having you along would be trouble," he mumbled.

Gail had halfway left her chair to leave before he looked up with a half smile of his own, holding up a hand in a gesture of surrender. "You really think they have a chance?"

Gail shrugged. "If they both survive, if they both complete the test, if they find the template, then manufacture a new Galactic Starburst, if they get there together, and if they agree, yes. Then they make a second one. Pretty unlikely, but at least it'll be interesting."

Ward just stared at Gail, amazed at his luck in finding her. "Okay, we'll try it. I'll enter you into Guardian as proctor for Maeve officially, which will tune the nanites in your bag to her. After I do, you will be more in tune with her feelings so that when—*if*—she is ever ready to take the test, you'll know. Something interesting I learned, surprising me really, is how much feedback I got directly from Hugh as his official proctor."

Ward realized that he had not only promised to activate the nanites for Maeve, something Gail could actually do herself without his permission, but had shared more about his experience with Hugh than intended. Apparently his subconscious agreed with Gail. Maybe it would work out. As a great covert operator, Gail often had unique insights into people, as well as situations, and could really surprise him. Like now, for instance, as she began to smile very intimately at him.

She definitely could be full of surprises.

Beacon Astrographic Society

Circular 10-2658
Significant Systems
Based upon Admiralty Sailing Instructions

Main inhabited planet:	Planet Alpine
System:	Macanack 52 (local name Solidarity); G2V star type output 99.95 percent of Sol
Cluster:	Macanack
Arm Crux:	Scutum
Location (Galactic Standard Coordinates):	11,074, -3619, -225

Alpine is an inhabitable planet .98 of standard gravity. It's orbit averages 1.1 AU. Alpine weather is approximately 5 percent cooler than standard as a result of orbit and solar output.

Government is a socialist combine. Deficits are made up through heavy export of systemic rare earths from Kuiper Belt to several surrounding manufacturing systems with healthy economies.

Despite its governmental system, it has built a significant space-based industry that is generally well-maintained. Most non-empire space industries have much higher accident rates than those within the empire. Alpine's is only 15 percent above the empire's average.

Fleet units are reminded that this is a watched planet under Imperial Council Order dated March 7, 2491. As a result, no interference except to maintain status quo is permitted.

All supplies are to be paid for out of funds banked on Belmira which are accepted on Alpine. No extradition treaty exists between Alpine and the empire. Alpine does not recognize the empire as a legitimate government because of the Jackson Monarchy. Ship's companies are therefore subject to local laws and regulations when dealing with the local authorities.

18

Desolation

Macanak 52 or Solidarity System
0610 BBMT 8 November 3473

AMBROSE B CAME STEALTHILY IN from Alpine's solar north, unchallenged. System traffic control seemed dead, but as they could see no traffic, the approach appeared quite safe. *Ambrose B*'s sensors swept the system around the planet but detected no high-energy signatures anywhere. If they didn't know better, they could have been entering the system of a pre-space culture, except for all the high-tech space junk.

Hugh sat in his usual jump seat on the bridge, nerves taut as he performed sensor tech duties. His eyes remained focused on the screens, but his mind kept trying to sort out his earlier discussion. He tried to focus on the tactical situation, but found nothing to concentrate on, nothing to do. No ships, no com traffic, no active orbital facilities nor extra-planetary energy signatures, just a few indications of life on the earthlike planet, Alpine, ahead of them. He ran scans for weapons systems. He ran scans for sensor arrays. Nothing. When he ran scans for remains of installations and ships, however, the sensors went crazy, picking up space junk and debris. About one hour out from the planet, he shook his head before setting up a net call. He pulled in Lieutenant Sheila Kirk from Engineering, Gail Felt the captain, Sergeant Major Sean Ward, and Maeve uch Robert.

"I am picking up lots of space junk but nothing else, no traffic or active extra-planetary facilities. The survey logs showed this to be a very prosperous system for this far out in the arm from the core. What do you think?"

No one answered for a moment. Finally, Gail stated the obvious, "Somebody apparently took them out."

Ward agreed, before adding, "There's not supposed to be anyone in the neighborhood big and nasty enough to do this. We left the TechMech more than a thousand parsecs behind us. Not good if there is another band of crazies roaming around out here."

Hugh harrumphed grumpily in response, "That much I knew. Suggestions?"

Ward had decided, apparently, to ignore Hugh's bad humor, letting it roll off him. He suggested evenly, "Take it slow and easy, all guns hot?"

Maeve added, hesitantly, "The main energy signatures are far from the former major population centers. Someone really stomped on them and didn't leave much. No one's broadcasting and the planet doesn't seem to have an archeon array of any kind for communication anymore."

"Okay." There didn't seem to be much more that could be said that would help, so Hugh put on his official persona and took charge. "Things are a mess down there, so bring us down at the largest remaining population center with an active energy signature, Captain."

Gail nodded before cutting the conference call line. She and Lieutenant Sally Carr carefully wove a way through the space junk surrounding the planet, the remains of a once-huge space presence. Smoothly, they brought *Ambrose B* down on what remained of a minor spaceport. Ruins were a better description. Kinetic strikes had leveled much of the area, although a few facilities of what would have been a moderately large port on most other worlds, had survived. Somehow.

His mouth taking on a sour smile, Hugh hit the com switch. "Sergeant Major, I'll need the team. There is no radio traffic, so any planetary communication must be taking place by landline. Ensign uch Robert may be able to hack into it for us. Add her if you think she can help and it won't be too much of a risk. See you at the entry point in ten."

Hopping up, he headed for his cabin to grab his gear. No nonsense today, simple military protection and the equipment to stay alive. Jacket to prevent projectile penetration, cap/helmet that did the same, chameleon camouflage uniform, sidearm, knife, personal long-range weapon, water, and rations, as well as odds and ends of additional equipment. It took several minutes just to dress and then another couple to saddle up the gear. As a result, Hugh reached the entry port last.

Sergeant Kevin Dunn looked him over and commented, "Perhaps you need a keeper, Your Highness. Last man here and you still look like Joe the Ragman."

Everyone, both women and men who were there, laughed at the old Marine joke. Even Maeve, but her laugh sounded forced.

Chuckling, Hugh said, "Lead on, Sergeant Major, let's go make contact."

At which point, Ward threw the first monkey wrench of the day into the gears. Looking straight at Hugh, he pointed out, "Maeve should stay here, Your Highness, and perhaps you should, too. This could easily be a hot LZ and we need to lock it down first. *Ambrose B*'s armor is more protection than chameleon skin. After all, your job isn't to be a bullet stopper."

Hugh nodded, feeling mutinous. "I think you're right about Maeve staying here if we can find what we need without her. But I'm going."

Ward prompted, "What is the mission, sire?"

"Get fuel, get food, get intel, take the test, get out." Hugh had reviewed the parameters a dozen times for this mission in the preceding two weeks.

Then, Ward threw the second monkey wrench. "The expected portion of the test for Alpine, Judgment and Justice, seems to have been blown away by whoever carried out this kinetic weapons strike, Your Highness. Equally, Nighthawk did not focus on Integrity in the way I expected, but to this point, events have definitely created the conditions for a complete test anyway. As a result, it might be an excellent idea, and safer, for you to stay here. As for Maeve, her expertise might come in handy if we need to get access to any local com channels, but Jebet could probably do it just as well. That means she should stay here, too."

Hugh took a deep breath, trying to figure out why Ward wanted to change things at the last minute. As the heir, did he or did he not need to take the test here on Alpine and face all the obstacles? He had thought so when Ward initially explained things to him, and all the simulations were designed around him. That meant he must go, didn't it? Just as Hugh started to speak, Gail came over the com, *"I agree. If he stays, Maeve has to stay. If she goes, he has to go."*

Maeve stared at the com near the hatch. "I have to go! I'm really the only one who can tap into their systems. Jebet is okay, but not if he hits a surprise."

Ward nodded. "So you go." Turning to the camera, he asked, "You're serious about both going? What happens if we lose them both?"

"You and I had this little talk already. Hugh has to go because he is the heir apparent. You know the rules and you're being obtuse about it. He has to face the dangers as he finds them, no matter what form they take. You also know why she has to go."

Hugh noticed that Maeve seemed equally as curious about this little byplay between Ward and Gail. She didn't know, or at least didn't seem to know, what they were talking about either, he realized.

Ward ignored them, his face seemingly chiseled from bedrock as he stared at the camera.

"You really are going to be difficult about this?"

"We both know what our duties are. By this time, you should know I will always do my duty to the best of my ability, just as you'll do yours, so stop arguing. Either both go or both stay."

Ward's face didn't soften at all. He just motioned out the door with his head. Dunn and Vincent Klostermann led off. Hugh noticed as they set off across the tarmac that, oddly enough, he didn't stand alone in the center of the group. Maeve walked with him. Neither talked to the other despite being side by side. Hugh, in fact, took great pains to ignore Maeve, who seemed to be returning the favor with interest. Ward took right wing, closest to Hugh, while Pam West and Karen Hall walked to their left, weapons up and hot. Sally followed them, Tabi Fleisch and Jebet bringing up the rear. Hugh passed an uncomfortably silent fifteen minutes marching across the tarmac to the nearest intact buildings even though the day felt pleasant.

To no one in particular he commented, "Feels good to be breathing real air again after so much time cooped up." A cool wind blew in off the far peaks, some of which looked taller than most mountains back on Jeffco. *Much taller*, Hugh judged with a practiced eye. It would be real work to get to the top of one of them.

As they neared the buildings, Hugh commented to Dunn, "Take a long time to climb one of those."

Dunn agreed, "Maybe a week or more. Those are pretty rugged peaks. Need oxygen near the top."

Hugh's eyes were glued on them. "I bet you can see forever up there. Certainly be worth it."

Maeve broke in dismissively, "Why not fly up there and save yourself the walk."

Hugh stared at her incredulously for a moment. "That's not the point. The effort is what gives it value."

"Is it? Not to me. If I want to see the view from the top of a building, I can take a lift; I don't feel the need to take the stairs."

Hugh just shook his head.

As they reached the building, Maeve asked, all business, "What now?"

Hugh ordered, "Find a hardwire link. We'll check the fuel pods." Quickly scanning the area, he finished, "Over there. There even seem to be some water trucks with the fuel trucks."

Spinning away before she could say another word, he set off toward the trucks. His four-man team stayed with him, while Ward remained behind with Maeve and the three Amazons. Hugh supposed Ward could replay whatever he did later for the test if he needed to from their suit cams. As they reached the first fuel pods, Dunn stepped in front of Hugh while Klostermann and Fleisch began to check them for booby traps. Hugh tried to step around, but Dunn stayed between him and the trucks.

"Move, Kevin. I can do that as well as they can and, with all four of us, it'll be finished faster."

Dunn shook his head. "You're the heir and Sergeant Major threatened to skin me alive if I let you anywhere near unnecessary danger. Personally, I believe him, so you're staying here."

Hugh wanted to order him out of the way. He wanted to help and, more importantly, he didn't want any more deaths like Tim Kennion's on his conscience. He didn't want anyone dying for him but knew he had to follow the rules and stay away if he wanted people to follow his orders. Following orders really could be described as a two-way street. He watched, helpless, as the others completed the check and set up a robot remote to drive a fuel truck. The water truck could wait because they could use recycled water if necessary; they often did. But they couldn't lift without fuel. Hugh felt useless as he watched his men check for every type of bomb in either the pod itself or its pumping equipment. Behind them at the ship, Pete Peterson waited with Sheila to get the lines hooked up when the truck arrived.

Everything moved along normally, boring Hugh to death, until the crackling of the com startled him, "You better get over here, Your Highness." It sounded like Sally Carr.

AFTER THE MARINES LEFT, MAEVE walked into the operations building and found . . . nothing. No desks, no computer terminals, no fiber optics. Just trash. The building stood bare, completely stripped, not bombed but torn apart by vandals. Stepping back outside, she luxuriated in the breeze. It had been so long since she had felt wind ruffle her hair, she wanted to simply enjoy it. Combined with the sun peeking out from the occasional cloud, it felt like heaven. She closed her eyes for a moment, savoring it all. She could even hear insects buzzing around or chirping. She loved being on a planet again. Opening her eyes, she looked around for the next best option for com terminals. A ten-minute walk away stood what looked like a maintenance hangar. Heading off with Ward beside her, Pam and Karen sliding ahead, and Sally bringing up the rear, she blocked the others out mentally, enjoying a sense of solitude. With no one talking and open space extending in every direction, a peace she hadn't felt in years soaked into her bones. Because she hadn't really paid close attention as they walked, she accidentally piled into Pam and Karen, who had stopped and stood tensely just inside the hangar door. Curious as to what could possibly be the matter, her eyes began searching the shadows ahead. Suddenly, she took a half breath before involuntarily screaming.

Hanging from the rafters she saw men, women, and children. *How did this happen?* Morbidly, she couldn't tear her eyes away from so much death.

Ward, as if from a great distance, ordered, "Pam and Karen, cut them down. We still need to check the building for com lines." Maeve noted in the same detached way that Pam and Karen moved right in to get it done.

Pounding feet began to rouse her. Hugh stepped in front of her, grabbing her shoulders, demanding, "Are you all right? What happened?"

Hugh's physical contact snapped her out of the fog protecting her from the horror around her. Maeve covered her eyes with her hands to shut out the horrible scene. Leaning against his chest, she began to shake. "Dead, they're all dead . . . Children, women . . . hanged. It's so horrible, I can't . . . can't go back in there."

She desperately wanted, needed, protection and comfort. Then she felt Hugh tentatively, gingerly wrapping his arms around her back. In the long-ago past, Priscilla had provided that feeling and, more recently, Sally, but Hugh's protection just felt right. She felt safe and the last man to make her feel that way had been her father. She could barely recall what it felt like to feel so completely safe. Dad wrapping her in his arms seemed like ages ago.

His voice steady, a clear promise, Hugh softly said, "It'll be all right." Letting go of her, he put a hand on each of her shoulders, causing her to drop her hands to look up at him. "We need to find a com line, though. We'll be with you when you go in, but right now I need your help to get the mission accomplished. Will you be okay, Ensign?"

Hugh using her rank snapped her out of her emotional state. Maeve nodded, gaining strength from Hugh's calm words. Surprisingly, a wisp of resentment added to the mix. With Hugh, duty came first. Always.

Abruptly she jerked away, glancing around, almost panicking. The others were watching and had seen Hugh holding her! Most of the Marines had completely blank expressions, but she knew they must have watched her break down and Hugh put his arms around her. Dunn gave her a slight grin, embarrassing her. Hugh wiped it from his face with a sudden glower, though.

"Clear the building; find a com link," Hugh demanded brusquely to no one in particular. Maeve watched him turn away and begin scanning the area, apparently searching for threats. He didn't look in her direction again.

She noticed Dunn and Klostermann begin a sweep around the perimeter of the huge hangar while Jebet and Fleisch kept watch over Hugh. Sally stayed with Maeve as she took a deep breath, before reluctantly stepping back inside. The dimness made Maeve nervous, a deep uneasiness stoking her fear of what she might find in here next. She heard Ward following.

Twenty steps in, Maeve stumbled in the dusky interior. A sickly-sweet stink enveloped her, overwhelming her senses. Fighting a desire to gag, she stopped to let her eyes adjust to the dimness. As things became lighter, she saw, beneath her left foot, a little hand. She had stumbled over a dead child. Her stomach heaved and she threw up, her vomit splashing onto other bodies seen only vaguely in the dimness. A warm arm encircled her shoulders, Sally's this time. She hoped Hugh hadn't seen her lose it like this.

"You've received a nasty shock," Sally murmured to her, reassuring. "It is hard to see people do things like this to each other. Let's go back outside."

"No," Maeve disagreed, "I don't want him to know I can't handle this. Let's find the landline."

Sally didn't say anything for a moment or ask who Maeve meant by *him*. Finally, she let go of Maeve's shoulders and handed her a canteen. Taking a quick sip, Maeve swished some water around in her mouth to get rid of the sick taste before spitting it out, careful to avoid hitting a body when she did.

After Maeve finished, she looked up to find Sally scanning the huge interior, a much bigger building than it had appeared from the outside. Maeve stood still another minute, breathing as shallowly as she could through her mouth to lessen the stench. She watched as Pam and Karen lowered the last of the bodies, petit Karen undoing the ropes and the much taller and more robust Pam gently guiding the bodies to the floor. She found it difficult not to fixate on the ghoulishness of the scene, but forcibly broke her gaze away to see what else there might be to help them in the hanger. As her eyes adjusted, Maeve made out an office area in an obscure corner. Pointing, she suggested, "Let's try there." Using her peripheral vision as she walked, so she didn't have to look too closely at any one body on the floor, she managed to not step on any more strewn about.

Grabbing the latch on the office door to open it, she discovered it wouldn't move. She rattled it in frustration until Sally laid a hand on her arm. "You might want to step back. Sometimes you get flying splinters." Maeve stepped back, then drew her sidearm and raised it, being sure to keep Sally out of her line of fire. Sally nodded, then raised her leg before driving her heel into the door next to the lock. The doorframe splintered and the door flew inward.

Sally went through the door, weapon raised. Maeve followed on Sally's heels. Just inside the door, Sally stopped and looked back at Maeve before angrily demanding, "Stay outside!" Maeve hastily retreated. As one of the most even-tempered people Maeve had ever met, the shock of Sally acting upset with her made compliance almost automatic.

She had been focused on Sally, not realizing that Pam and

Karen now stood to either side of her, Pam facing the door Sally had just gone through, weapon up, and Karen facing the warehouse behind them.

"Coming out!" Sally yelled, then exited the office. She took in the scene and said to Pam, "There are about a dozen," she hesitated, "survivors in there."

Pam called back, "You and Karen search them and send them out one at a time after you're sure they're unarmed. I've got Maeve."

Sally nodded. A moment later, she and Karen stepped through the door, weapons at the ready for any surprises that might await them.

I've got Maeve? Since when do I need a babysitter? Before she could explore that thought, Sally spoke through the com, "His Highness better get in here. I have prisoners that need to speak with him."

THE SOUND OF RAPIDLY JOGGING boots echoing across the hangar accompanied Hugh as he ran up to the office area. As he arrived, he found the team covering a group of people who now sat on the floor outside of the office in which they had been hiding. Hugh noted with almost subconscious approval that Pam and Karen took up positions covering the group from opposite angles so that, if they needed to fire, only the targets would be hit.

But what an odd group: three men, in what must have been very fine and expensive clothes before they began living in them, mussed now, and filthy; four women plus half a dozen kids huddled closely behind them, cowering near the wall. All of them looked to be in the same condition. One of the men, a somewhat stout man of medium height, stood up when Hugh and the team arrived.

"You there!" He pointed at Ward. "I demand you let us go and leave Alpine immediately," the leader blustered. He apparently assumed that Ward, being the oldest and male, had command.

Karen simply said, in a normal tone of voice, "Shut up," while motioning with her rifle. His jaw immediately clamped closed, the rest of him deflating as he did.

Stopping, Hugh felt good, not winded in the slightest. His two-gee runs had gotten him into great shape. "So, what's up?" Hugh asked, looking at Sally.

Sally answered, "I found these people hiding in an inner office. From what they told me, I believe they are some sort of planetary authorities."

Hugh nodded to Sally, acknowledging her report. Speaking to the leader Karen had verbally slapped down, he said, "I am Hugh Cascade, heir apparent to the Core Empire. Do you know what that is?"

The man puffed his chest out before answering, which made him look remarkably like a bullfrog to Hugh. "I am Basil Paddon, magistrate of Spreitenbach. And of course I do. You people killed our planet. Isn't that enough? Now get out of here."

"What did you say?" Hugh asked, confused. "You're saying *we* did this?" He pointed at the bodies lined up in neat rows across the floor.

"Not that," sneered Paddon. "Those were all members of the Enlightened, like us. The masses killed them after your people knocked our monitoring stations out of orbit. We're the only Enlightened left here in the city of Spreitenbach."

This confused Hugh. "So your own people attacked you and executed all these people, but you blame us? Who knocked out the monitoring stations, whatever they were?"

"Imperial Navy, just like you, shot them out of orbit. Ninth Fleet, she said. She had a lot of huge ships; I don't know how many." For a man who had been cowering in the dark minutes before, Paddon's arrogance seemed to have diminished little.

Maeve's voice broke in, her face a stony mask, "Did the woman who led them have blonde hair?"

Paddon's voice quivered in reply, "Yes, a witch named uch Robert. Our planetary government offered to trade them fuel and food in exchange for their help in identifying the discontented—"

Hugh raised a questioning eyebrow. "The 'discontented?'"

With a look of disgust at his lack of knowledge, Paddon said, "Yes, those making life unpleasant here on Alpine. Some of the masses seemed unsatisfied with the perfectly balanced lives we provided for them. Ungrateful!" he spat out as a curse. "What more could they want? Never having to worry about bad choices, never having to worry about failing. Envious of us, who were always working for their well-being!"

"After your fleet landed and resupplied, it left without doing as they promised. Before they left orbit, they destroyed all of our own ships, as well as the monitoring stations in orbit that were designed to prevent things like this." He pointed at the windrow of bodies.

By this time, the toad-like man's voice had risen almost to a shout. Hugh judged that he must have spoken like this many times before in public. He sounded much like any number of dictators Hugh had studied in school.

The squat little man leaned forward. "When the monitoring stations went down, the fail-safes kicked in. The orbiting kinetic weapons all fired at once, everywhere. The Enlightened, the masses, even the malcontents, all of us, had known what would happen if the stations went down." Hatred seethed as he finished, "No one except your fleet commander; she destroyed our Eden! Things were perfect. People had enough to eat, everyone filled a job they were fitted for, we ensured social harmony for all of our people, and the stations kept it all in balance. Life couldn't have been better. And you people destroyed it!"

Hugh felt thunderstruck. Maeve looked like she would be sick and he couldn't blame her. "Magistrate Paddon, I'm confused. Are you saying you programmed the stations to destroy everything on your planet if the masses rose up in opposition to your government?"

Magistrate Paddon huffed, "Of course! The people knew that upsetting the harmonious society we had created depended on each of us knowing our place. The Enlightened governed and the people worked to provide us with what we needed."

Hugh boiled with anger. These people, these Enlightened, had used the threat of instant death to keep the masses they despised in line, their network of weapons stations nothing but a glorified dead man's switch guaranteed to lay waste to the planet if the people rose up in opposition to their government.

Hugh's eyes narrowed as his jaw clenched and shoulders tensed. His hand subconsciously moved to rest on the butt of his sidearm. Everything became clear, sharp, in focus like they did when he hunted. A corner of his mind noted Maeve's eyes widening in alarm. *She's probably a little concerned about what I'm going to do with these people.* He could practically feel Ward's eyes on him. He stilled his heart, forcing himself to pull back from the anger he felt. Judgment time had arrived. Again.

Hugh spoke, confidently, without anger, "We will pay for our food and fuel. We will be gone in two hours." After a pause, he continued in a stern voice, "We will punish Morgain uch Robert and her rebels. I swear on my honor. They shouldn't have destroyed the monitoring stations that caused this destruction. For that, they will pay."

Paddon's face took on a look of vulpine anticipation, his pleasure evident at the vengeance that would be rained down on Morgain and her people. Then, Hugh went on, "She needed my permission for that, which she did not have." His prisoners blanched as the meaning of his words sank in. The realization that this tall young man standing before them could just as easily have done the same thing hit them hard.

He bored on, relentlessly, "I would have destroyed both the monitoring stations *and* the kinetic weapons platforms. But as to this?" Here his arm swept out to include the windrow of bodies behind him as well as the whole planet. "This could never have happened without you threatening to kill your own people for simply objecting to your governance. Taking away choice makes a person an animal. You have been punished by your own evil, so I won't do anything else to you. Now. However, if I come back and find you have rebuilt this abominable system, I personally will hunt down every *Enlightened*," the word sounded like a curse as he pointed at the bodies, his voice barely containing his fury, "and *that* will be the best you can expect."

The magistrate and the rest of the survivors in his group blanched, their lack of doubt in Hugh's willingness to follow through on his promise clear on their faces.

Hugh barked, "Sergeant Klostermann!"

"Your Highness?"

"Kindly supervise the magistrate and the other adults here in collecting the remains and building a funeral pyre. There's been enough death and destruction here. They don't need disease, also."

"Yes, sire!" He turned to the magistrate. "You heard the man. Get moving!"

At first, Hugh's reaction stunned Maeve, but as he spoke, understanding dawned on her. Her face took on a fierce light echoing the fire in his eyes.

Destroying Morgain, who had spitefully caused this destruction, was a given, but freeing men and women from bondage to the Enlightened? He felt so strongly about freedom he would come thousands of parsecs from the empire to protect people he didn't even know?

As he ordered Vinnie Klostermann to supervise the building of the funeral pyre, she went over what he'd said. The decisions he'd made weren't simple. On *Bring It*, there hadn't been many options. Circumstances drove actions. Today, he could easily have finished the job the people had started, executing the Enlightened for their role in the destruction of the planet. Or he could have offered to help restore their government, in the belief that a benevolent dictatorship superseded anarchy. But Hugh had thought the choices through like a chess problem. She couldn't help but admire the judgment he had demonstrated.

Pechnaya, Kari System
1405 BBMT 8 November 3473

"This is system control. Please identify yourselves," came an impersonal voice.

Listening from her cabin since she rarely dealt with the basics of running her fleet, Morgain uch Robert idly wondered if these people would be as tiresome as those in Alpine. If so, they would suffer the same fate.

"This is *Pechnaya*, flagship of Her Majesty Morgain of the Core Empire. We require berthing and resupply while we run a rescue mission in this quadrant."

Morgain almost believed the lie herself as the comm officer played his part. A moment later, a different voice came on. "Tell Her Majesty she is welcome here. We would like to host her at an official reception after you land."

Well. Unexpected but I can use the diversion. Hitting her comm, she ordered, "Arrange it. I will bring a plus one."

Her guest smiled at that. "How thoughtful. Of course, I would love to come."

FLEET OPERATIONS DECISION PAPER

11 May 3308
Standard Imperial Fleet Table
of Organization—Task Force
As per Order in Council December 12, 3307 approved by
Charles Roland

- Supernova
- Nova
- 4 Cruiser squadrons—4 ships each
- 8 Destroyer squadrons—8 ships each
- 8 Frigate squadrons—16 ships each
- 8 Corvette squadrons—16 ships each
- 40 Sloops
- 8 Fleet Colliers
- Additional ships as fleet commander determines necessary for mission

19

Extreme Similarities

Spreitenbach Spaceport, Alpine
1320 Local/1420 BBMT 8 November 3473

"ARRANGE FOR PAYMENT, SALLY," HUGH CASCADE ordered before turning away, disdaining to have anything further to do with these *people*. Lieutenant Sally Carr, as second officer and purser, paid for the ship's needs. Hugh marched quickly out before he changed his mind and shot the pathetic lot standing speechless behind him. It wouldn't be right but most assuredly would feel good.

Stopping upon reaching the sunlit tarmac, he began to breathe deeply, trying to clear his lungs and mind of the stink he had left inside. The bodies, after a day or more of hanging, reeked of decay. Worse, a different kind of odor clung to the surviving members of the Enlightened, now begrudgingly doing the work of gathering their dead friends and family. Petty Officer Pam West had gathered the surviving children and brought them outside, also, and had found some energy bars to feed them.

They haven't learned anything from their losses! Frustrated, helpless, he wished he could find a way to make them understand the evil, not just the stupidity, of their entire society.

Sergeant Major Sean Ward stepped up close. "We need to talk, Your Highness," he said softly.

Hugh struggled to keep his seething anger out of his voice as he answered. An emperor needed to be in control of himself at all times. *Being in control* would not accurately describe his current mental state. "On the ship, Top. On the ship."

With that, he stepped off briskly, trying to physically excise the anger from his system by hurrying. He really wanted to kill someone right now. Full contact, hand-to-hand training would be a good substitute. A ten-mile run under full field gear would also serve. He would have to settle for a fast walk of about three-quarters of a mile, unfortunately with Sergeant Kevin Dunn, a head shorter than Hugh, almost running to keep up.

Commander Gail Felt's voice came over his earbud, "Trouble's coming from all around the spaceport. Looks like a couple of thousand people, and I don't think they're friendly."

"Great," muttered Hugh thoughtfully. Maybe he could kill some of *them*. He didn't know who they were but didn't feel particularly picky just now. A question rose from his training. Into the com, he asked, "Do we have enough food so we can lift and go somewhere else?"

"Negative. Worse, we sent drones out to what seemed to be the storehouses nearby, but they appear to be empty. Pretty thoroughly looted, I'd say."

As he scanned the edges of the port, Hugh could see a wave of humanity coming on. Sergeant Major's comment about *Ambrose B* being better protection than chameleon skin suits came back full force. "Warm up the guns, Captain. We need to keep this mob away till we can take care of business."

"Guns are already hot, Your Highness," Gail responded in a neutral tone.

He supposed he had offended her by telling her to do what any experienced special operative knew by instinct. Oh well. "I'm sorry. Of course they are. Warn them before we shoot them, though."

"Roger," Gail answered, voice not noticeably warmer than before.

He watched as a drone launched from the ship and then heard her voice projecting from the drone as it hovered over the heads of the crowd. Where he stood, he couldn't understand what she said; to the crowd, it must have been deafening. The sound of the guns rotating on their gimbals and locking onto the crowd echoed across the tarmac. Even from Hugh's limited vantage point on the side of the mob, the message appeared to pierce through the anger standing in the way of their sense of self-preservation. Most of the mob did an about-face and began running for the fences. Not everyone, though, exhibited such good sense. A few hundred, moving in compact groups, kept coming on. Unlike the others who wisely began running away, they appeared to be armed. Hugh heard the boom of Gail's voice, this time without a doubt laying down the law and where the line would be if they came any nearer. They stopped but didn't retreat. The closest bunch stood about half mile from Hugh. He turned toward them, slowing a bit so Dunn could keep up by walking quickly.

"Ward," Hugh spoke into the com, "I'm heading for the nearest group to talk to them. We need to stall for time until we can find food and load it on. Send Jebet and Fleisch to meet me."

"Roger, Your Highness. We need to hurry, though, in case Morgain uch Robert comes back."

Great, one more thing to worry about. If she showed up with a task force, or even a task group, he, and the *Ambrose B*, would be in big trouble. Or even a destroyer would be enough to ruin his entire day.

Ward didn't argue any further, which surprised Hugh, but he did feel grateful, especially after Ward had made such a point initially of not wanting Hugh in harm's way. Ward's simple *Roger* and warning were enough of a goad to motivate him. Hugh, turning toward where he had last seen Sergeants Abdul Jebet and Tabi Fleisch, saw them double-timing. The very tall and dark Jebet running toward him full speed truly impressed Hugh, since Jebet carried the laser rifle and its support equipment that weighed over one hundred fifty pounds. Pressing on, Hugh and Dunn arrived at the biggest group just seconds before Jebet and Fleisch.

"Anyone here in charge?" Hugh asked the mob pleasantly. There were enough guns in this mob of fifty or sixty people that, if a firefight started, he'd be toast, so he figured he should keep things cool until *he* decided to start the shooting. From the desperate look in their eyes, he decided few in the mob had much in the way of self-control. Unfortunately. Avoiding a firefight might not be possible. Still, he'd try.

The other thing he clearly saw as he looked over the mob shuffling about with uncertainty: most of these people had no idea what to do when confronted with a new situation. The Enlightened had taken so much self-determination from these people that they couldn't think or make good choices for themselves. He'd have to be very careful, so he didn't accidentally encourage bad decision-making with these people, at least until he lifted off-planet.

Regardless, in the end it wouldn't matter to him in the least if one of them shot him for a good reason or a bad one. His job today would be to encourage or persuade these people to do what he wanted them to without bloodshed. He hoped Jebet had his laser rifle pointed in an *encouraging* direction, making Hugh's job easier. From the reactions of the people on the side of the mob nearest Jebet, those to Hugh's right, he figured they recognized what a laser rifle looked like and what it could do, and they wanted to be somewhere else if it started burning people down.

They were edging away. Good, the mob had begun to settle down, meaning that in another couple of minutes it wouldn't be a mob any longer, just a collection of individuals acting on their own, each sure any gun Hugh and his people pointed in their direction had his, her, or their personal name on the bullets.

Sergeant Vincent Klostermann, having set the pyre detail to their task, joined them just as a mousey woman stepped to the front of the crowd, wearing a fancy dress two sizes too small. *Looted from the Enlightened?*

"I'm Zilda Wilniak, Secretary of the People's Committee. You will surrender your ship to my men and stand trial for crimes against the people of Alpine."

Zilda's authoritative tone and the words she used all seemed to mean something, at least to her, but Hugh figured she had watched way too many melodramas and other bad holos.

Hugh's com chirped in his ear. Ward spoke quietly from about fifty feet behind him where he had apparently taken up an overwatch position. "Remember, these are civilians, and based on their clothing, poor ones at that. They are simply out of their depth. Don't treat them like military or equals, and they won't act like military."

"Roger," Hugh said out loud into his com. Apparently, Zilda thought the acknowledgment was for her and that she had just won. She smiled broadly as she turned back toward her people. Hugh watched her, images of the dead hanging from the rafters in the building behind him swimming in front of his eyes. *She thinks she's in charge but is really a psychopath.* Hugh spoke harshly, interrupting her before she could declare victory. "I didn't agree to your terms, lady; just telling my crew that I understood what a crazy person you are. How are you out on the street without a keeper?"

Spinning, she stared at Hugh, eyes bulging, her face rapidly turning an alarming shade of red. Hugh wondered idly if she might simply drop dead from apoplexy. *That would be too much to hope for.* He had no doubt that she had played a role in the hanging of the Enlightened, including the women and children.

"Why, you—" but she couldn't blurt out another word, momentarily at a loss for something to say. Spluttering, she went on, "We outnumber you hundreds to one, thousands to one. You don't stand a chance."

"Think so?" Hugh said in an offhand way. *Careful*, he warned himself. *She's stupid enough to get lots of these people killed.* "You'll never live to find out if you try something. Better drop your weapons before you get hurt. Jebet, prepare to fire on these people. Her first."

From the direction of the ship, he heard a dorsal mount move up and down, then back and forth, before it settled into place pointed at the crowd, its rock-solid immobility probably more menacing than the previous motion. Without warning, the deadly rattle of five hundred rounds fired from *Ambrose B* cracked unexpectedly overhead. Actually, aimed three hundred yards away, Hugh estimated. Regardless, most of the crowd hit the ground and threw their hands over their ears. Others screamed as they ran in every direction. All except four men and the woman. The men looked terrified, eyes darting about wildly, forgetting they even held weapons in their hands, but not the woman, Zilda. She simply frothed at the mouth, furious.

Klostermann stepped forward, twenty years of hardened Marine behind his bellow aimed at the four men still standing. "You heard the man, drop your weapons! Guns, knives, everything you've got, then move fifty feet back and fall on your bellies. *Move it!*"

Hugh noted that Klostermann's approach—treating the mob as if he were inducting new boots for training—worked exactly the same here as it always did back on Jeffco. Those on the ground obeyed instantly, throwing away weapons as if they were poison. Hugh realized that Klostermann hadn't needed to say *or else* or explain what would happen if someone failed to comply. His mere bearing and confidence had been too overwhelming for these people to even think of ignoring his order. Pistols, knives, rifles, all clattered to the ground as the mob—everyone but the woman and her four companions—began worming away as fast and far as possible from anything the terrifying figure in the pattern-shifting uniform might consider a weapon, some not stopping fifty feet away, but continuing to crawl toward the perimeter fence.

As he watched Klostermann, he realized he hadn't heard anything from Maeve's team. An icon popped up just at that moment indicating that they had returned to the ship, but no bugs placed. Not surprising; everything not bolted down had apparently been stolen. Focusing again, it surprised him that the five were still there. He examined them more closely.

Of the five still standing, four were plainly scared, but they all held their ground. To them, Hugh judged, the odds might seem to be three to five because two of the Marines, Dunn and Fleisch, seemed to be watching over the terrified people on the ground. They seemed to have forgotten about Ward standing well behind Hugh; he could read it in their stance. These five thought they had the edge. The tension built as Hugh watched them gather their nerve to act. Even so, the sound of a single shot ringing out took him by surprise, almost causing Hugh to jump as it echoed off the buildings at the edge of the field. In front of him, a man who had been cradling an old-fashioned hunting rifle like he knew how to use it, slowly crumpled to the ground, blood gushing from a stomach wound, his rifle clattering away as he fell. Hugh didn't need to look to know who had taken the shot, sure that Klostermann had resolved the problem, since Dunn and Fleisch were occupied and Jebet's laser made a very distinctive sizzling sound when fired.

"Saw him bringing the muzzle of his rifle up with his finger on the trigger," Klostermann commented phlegmatically.

Hugh nodded. About what he had expected to happen when you dealt with amateurs. Hugh didn't bother to look around at Klostermann, but kept his eyes on Zilda. When you were face-to-face with a mountain lion, you maintained eye contact if you didn't want to be eaten. As for Klostermann, he would focus on the three remaining men and not the dying man. Living threats took priority over the dead.

But Zilda, his personal problem now, went wild with fury, "You're all dead! Killing a member of the People's leadership carries an automatic death penalty."

Out of the corner of his eye, he saw Jebet train his laser on her, ready should she make any move toward pointing her military-grade rifle in Hugh's direction. Hugh decided she had either reached the point of being beyond reasoning with or had become actively suicidal. He didn't know which, and didn't have time to figure it out, so he ignored her. *Jebet can take care of her if she does something extra dumb*, he consciously decided. As for the other three men, they were showing uncommonly good sense, dropping their weapons and raising their hands, two of them backing off, slowly.

The remaining one, a small guy with a sharp nose, remained

next to the dying man. "Can I see what I can do for him?" he asked. "I'm a doctor."

That impressed Hugh. He heard no quaver in his voice at all, simply a request to provide help. "Certainly. I'm sorry that your friend made a poor choice. We warned him, but I still wish it hadn't been necessary."

The little man didn't answer, just dropping to his knees to apply pressure to the wound. The blood flow slowed, then stopped. Although the doctor's arms were red to the elbows, his help had been too little too late. Only the immediate attention of a full trauma center might have helped, but even that likely would have been insufficient.

The body lost all tension, the life gone. Hugh didn't feel sick like he had on *Bring It* or even in the hangar behind him. Hugh couldn't decide if he felt so little emotion because the man had brought it on himself or if he himself had become more hardened. He hoped for the first option. He didn't want to get so used to death that it didn't bother him anymore.

All this time, as he watched and thought, the woman ranted on, making increasingly lurid threats against Hugh and everyone with him. Hugh absently noted that she carefully kept her weapon pointed away from them, however. At least her sense of self-preservation still functioned. He ignored her, focusing on the little man. As the man stood back up, unconsciously wiping his hands on his pants, leaving red smears without doing much to clean his hands off, Hugh spoke.

"I'm sorry you couldn't save him."

The man shrugged, hooded eyes hiding his emotions. "He died of bad judgment. Zilda's. She signaled for us to open up on you. Harry here unluckily moved first, which unfortunately got him killed."

Hugh weighed the man's fatalistic attitude. Did this come from growing up in a place like Alpine or had he lived such a brutal life he didn't know any different? It raised a question whether he had been too merciful back in the hangar. If people acted this way because of the government, he had no idea what to do about it. He just knew he rejected it on a gut level. It also made the man's desire to help his dying comrade a testament to his spirit, his ability to overcome his environment even here in the blackest pits of despair. He cared, cared despite the misery he lived with. Hugh's mind clicked. This man he might be able to work with. Nodding to the doctor, he introduced himself, "I'm Hugh Cascade from Jeffco in the Core Empire."

The man took a step forward to shake hands, before ruefully realizing they were still covered with blood. Dropping the hand, he said, "Vintner Jacques. Doctor, but I'm also part of this People's Committee now."

Zilda leaned forward, face red, screaming, "One more word, Jacques, and you're dead! Only I can speak for the Committee."

Hugh looked at her, considering, as he counted to fifteen silently. Ignoring Zilda, pale and shaking by the end, he told Jebet in an off-handed way. "One more word out of her, shoot her."

THE CORE EMPIRE

Chapter 26

This chapter focuses on the genius of Charles Roland in putting the Core Empire back together, or at least Sectors Prime through Sixteen. Asked how he could get many thousands of worlds and hundreds of billions of people to do what he wanted, he famously answered, "First, you get them pointed in the right direction. The rest is easy."

As we examine how he rebuilt three-quarters of the empire in a mere thirty-two years, we will evaluate the accuracy of his statement.

20

Unexpected Allies

TURNING BACK TO THE DOCTOR, Vintner Jacques, Hugh Cascade saw that the doctor had turned a shade whiter than before. Whether in reaction to Hugh ordering the woman's death or Zilda's threat, he didn't know. Jacques appeared to be a good man and only that mattered at the moment. "We need food before we lift off. We can pay."

Dr. Jacques smiled wryly. "Money's no good just at the moment. Trade or swap. We wanted your ship so we could get out of here, actually. That's all I really wanted, anyway. We've been at the mercy of the Committee, which means Zilda Wilniak, to get food for our families since the whole place broke down."

Hugh heard the woman practically jumping up and down but saying nothing. Hugh almost smiled. Abdul Jebet's rifle must have really terrified her. Returning his attention to the doctor, he asked incredulously, "You were going to lift out thousands with a little ship like this? Somebody can't count very well." Jacques looked like he wanted to answer, but Hugh kept on talking, "If you are at the mercy of others for food, maybe we can help each other. Where is the food in the city now?"

Vintner Jacques gave him a measuring look. "I don't think the few of you can get to it. The Committee has most of the warehouses, but they're pretty empty by now and guarded by the most fanatic of Zilda's followers. The Association for Understanding and Harmony also has a set of warehouses."

"The Association for what? Who are they?"

Jacques goggled at Hugh for a minute as if he had two heads. Cocking his head, he thought out loud, "You really don't know much about Alpine, do you? What kind of place do you come from?"

"Just a normal place in the midst of an all-out civil war. Tell me more about these Association people."

"They're the Enlightened's secret police. There are about a thousand of them, very well armed and trained in riot and crowd control. Even before the monitors were destroyed, they had lots of experience with that, more since then."

Hugh smiled sharply. "If they're organized, they may be easier to reason with, or at least deal with, than Zilda. As you just saw here, mobs are unpredictable. They might run away, or they could fight to the death; you never know beforehand. We may be able to deal with this Association because they are used to following orders and have something to lose. And, if they're not reasonable, well, my friends are Marines, so that won't be a huge problem either. If you can come up with a group to help us," his smile disappearing and becoming a frozen wall, "not including Zilda or anyone like her, this becomes pretty simple. We will get food for you and us. Otherwise, we'll do it by ourselves and burn the warehouses to the ground when we leave."

Jacques stood unbelieving for a moment, mouth slightly agape. "You really are a hard case. I thought I'd seen it all before I met you. Killing and compassion, all wrapped in one package." He paused for a moment, then nodded, "Fine." He seemed to have joined Hugh in ignoring Zilda, even though she stood close by, chest heaving, barely restraining herself. As if she were a million miles away, he said, "Zilda always acted too radically for my taste. Before the monitors went down, she led many of the discontented here, always trying to bring down the Enlightened. Not a dime's worth of difference between them, from what I've seen of the People's justice since they took over most of the city."

Zilda obviously couldn't hold it back any longer, regardless of the threat Jebet posed with his enormous rifle. Growling low in her throat, she promised, "You're dead. When they leave, you'll face the People's justice, and then you'll be dead."

Sergeant Kevin Dunn broke in from the side, "Jebet didn't shoot her, Your Highness, so can I?"

Hugh wearily shook his head. "If I went around the galaxy killing everyone who needed killing, I'd die of old age before I even got off to a good start." He stared at Zilda as he spoke, watching the color drain from her face while he calmly discussed her death.

He decided to speak directly to her one more time, "Against my better judgment, I'm going to give you the same chance at learning some sense that I did for some of the Enlightened I met earlier. I am letting you live, on the condition that you don't rebuild the space monitors and kinetic strike systems, as well as allow people, individuals, to make their own decisions. A *people's* anything sounds like an excuse for tyranny to me. If I find you have replaced the Enlightened with your own form of tyranny or the monitoring system—either one—I will come back here and kill you. That is not a threat but a promise by the heir apparent to the Core Empire."

"Royalty!" she screeched. "You're a tyrant and you threaten us for doing the same things you do?"

In a detached voice, Sergeant Vincent Klostermann spoke to him, "She really can't be reasoned with, sire. Let me resolve this."

Hugh's eyes had not left Zilda for an instant. "Tempting, but no. It would be neither justice nor good judgment."

"You *would* mention the Imperial Creed," Dunn muttered.

Hugh smiled grimly. "If we don't live by the Creed, what are we? Along with other instructors, you taught me that." His eyes kept boring into Zilda's soul. "Get out of here. If I see you anywhere near me, and that means within a good mile, my friends are authorized to help you join your friend on the ground there. You have ten minutes to get a mile away and that building there," pointing to a tall building well beyond the spaceport fence, "is about a mile. Get going."

"You can't do this!" she screamed. "I am the head of the People's Committee!"

Dunn spoke up, "Nine minutes, fifty-five seconds. I get first shot." Zilda stood dumbfounded.

"Nine fifty," Klostermann answered. "I'm senior; I get first shot."

Jebet joined the party, "Klostermann already got to shoot somebody today. I've been lugging this heavy monster all over and, besides which, you already said I could shoot her."

Zilda, reminded when Jebet spoke that he carried a laser rifle, turned without another word, and sprinted for safety.

"Should I watch her?" Klostermann asked.

"No," Hugh answered, "we need to take care of business." Hugh slowly turned to survey the area to see what had changed. It surprised him to see Sergeant Major Sean Ward standing ten feet behind him.

"So, Sergeant Major, you heard the whole thing?"

"Yes, Your Highness. Would you mind if I planned the assault on the warehouses and you stayed out of harm's way?"

"I think I need to be there, Top, but I promise to be a good boy and not lead the assault myself. Will that be acceptable?" Hugh asked in a relaxed way. Calmly, he waited for the response, knowing what he would do regardless of his proctor's approval. He had to go, his word and this mission were on the line, and that trumped any other concerns.

Ward gave him a crooked smile. "Probably the best I'm likely to get under the circumstances." Glancing at Vintner Jacques, Ward waved him forward, before tapping his com to project a map of a portion of the city five miles away. "Based upon what you've told His Highness, I think we know where the Association is located. Take a look at this 3D holographic map and show me the best ways you see to get into the warehouses."

The map had been color-coded by function to make examination easier. The warehouse complex consisted of four rows of five huge warehouses marked in blue, the whole surrounded by a concrete wall topped with guard towers, broken glass, and wire, highlighted in red. Inside the wall, a one hundred-yard-wide pavement separated the wall from the warehouses, indicated by a large white stripe on the map. Each warehouse measured about one hundred yards wide and two hundred yards long with a one hundred-foot-wide street between each, also in white, making the area almost half a mile wide by three-quarters of a mile long.

Hugh commented as he examined the compound, "We should focus on taking just one warehouse, the area is just too huge to secure in an hour. If we have to fight for every building, it could take a week and we would likely end up burning the whole place down in the process, something that would make this whole operation pointless."

Jacques, surprise showing in his eyes both at Hugh's quick analysis and his confidence in command, turned quickly back to concentrate on the map. Touching a section of the area accidentally, it suddenly expanded, causing him to step back involuntarily as trucks, men, and weapons grew before him in stark clarity, equipment tan, men yellow. Jacques, overcoming his obvious surprise, leaned closely over the more detailed projection. "How'd you get this information?" he wondered aloud.

"Mapped the whole city on the way in," Ward said. "Didn't know what would be useful, so we captured data on everything from the surface to about fifty feet underground. You never know when sewers and service tunnels will become useful."

Ward pointed with two fingers at a portion of the map. Several of the tunnels on the projection, ones leading to the warehouses, then flashed in green. Jacques smiled. "I can see that. What do you want me to do?"

"Get a mob around the outside of the wall and make lots of noise. We'll take a warehouse from the inside. I'll give you two hours before we hit them to get your people together. That should be near sundown. We'll hit them here, at this warehouse."

Jacques nodded. "What about my people here? What do you want from them?"

Ward just smiled, before answering, "We'll need some help taking and holding a warehouse until we can move trucks in, ten to thirty people will do. We'll train your people enough that they don't accidentally shoot either themselves or each other. Or us, for that matter."

Turning to Klostermann, he said, "Want to get that show on the road, Gunnery Sergeant?"

"No problem, Top." Turning, he faced the crowd whose heads were up watching the goings-on while still lying on the ground. "Okay, you people. Those who liked things under Zilda, you get the same ten minutes to go join her off the field. Any one of you who leave, be sure I don't see you within a mile of us again. Get going." A few, a very few, got up and ran after Zilda, which included one of Jacques's two remaining companions. Everyone else stayed put.

Klostermann walked up and down among the bodies on the ground, measuring those who stayed with his eyes. Every so often, he tapped someone with his toe. Hugh watched, fascinated.

"Those I tapped, stand up and make a line to my right." After they began milling around, Klostermann bellowed, "To my right, idiots. Spread out a little, arm's-length apart. The rest of you stand up and get behind one of the people in line. Move!"

Chaos quickly became an approximation of order. A formation of sorts appeared. "Now, listen up!" Klostermann bellowed. "The people in front are squad leaders. The rest of you will follow their orders. If you don't, either they will shoot you or I will." He let that sink in. "We are going to get food for you and your families, something that so-called People's Committee couldn't do. Dr. Jacques will be in charge of you." Klostermann faced Dr. Jacques. "Where do you want your troops to assemble?" he asked.

"Dubois and Nietzsche in an hour. Tell them we are going to be fair and do what's right, not follow some crazy agenda."

Leaning forward so only Jacques and the other man nearby could hear him, Klostermann said in a quiet voice, "Tell 'em yourself. If you want them to follow you, you have to give them a reason to. They're not soldiers, so duty has no meaning for them, not yet anyway."

Vintner Jacques nodded before stepping out in front of the group. Surveying the faces in the formation he said, almost yelling, to be sure they heard him, "People, my friends and fellow citizens of the city of Spreitenbach, you have heard what Hugh Cascade said to me and Zilda. He told the Enlightened, our former masters, the same thing. He wants us to be free to choose, free from others telling us what to do. He threatened—no, promised—the Enlightened and Zilda, with her People's Committee, that if they rebuild the space monitors, he'd kill everyone involved. Because of their distrust of us, of what we might choose, the Enlightened threatened us with destruction if we disobeyed them. We were destroyed anyway. Zilda and her so-called *People's justice*, her reliance on informants just like the Enlightened, tells us there is no difference between them. We must have the opportunity to make our own choices. Being *forced* to be good isn't good at all. We are only free when we can make choices, good and bad, and then choose good. Our friends here," Jacques said, pointing at Hugh and the others, "need food, just like we do. They'll do the most dangerous fighting but need our help. If we help, we get to keep the warehouses when they go. We, then, will be free from both the Committee and the Enlightened. If you will join me, we can build something new on Alpine, a city built on choice and consent. Who's with me for freedom?" he shouted.

The volume in response from the group of about forty attracted others from the mob who had stayed on the spaceport and started them walking in Jacques's direction. It looked like another hundred or more from what Hugh could see. Jacques spoke well, from the heart, Hugh thought. After what the doctor said, Hugh wanted to join them himself. A sudden thought hit him. Walking about twenty feet away, he motioned Ward to join him.

"Yes, sire?" Ward inquired, solicitously.

Hugh grinned at Ward's quietly mocking tone. "You sound as if you think I'm about to do something nuts, Sergeant Major."

"Of course not, Your Highness. I am sure everything you do is carefully thought out and the risks are weighed against potential reward for maximum effectiveness. Although, if memory serves, there were times I remained completely in the dark and baffled as to what, or whether, you were even thinking. Like when you free-climbed a three-hundred-foot cliff, the times you were speeding up to fifty miles per hour over the limit on winding mountain roads, or just two weeks ago when you changed our plan on *Bring It* on the fly just as we were about to meet with Captain Hamilton Pogue, to mention just a few of many, perhaps hundreds, of examples."

Hugh's grin got even bigger. *This is fun. Risking everything to win everything really is a giant rush.* "I will grant that many of the things I did when young and foolish could have been better thought out and were somewhat riskier than they needed to be, but I am older and wiser now." Hugh could see that Ward didn't buy his explanation or excuse, whichever it might be, but Hugh pressed on, "Which is why I am talking to you first. This time."

Hugh, seeing Ward's body language, figured that Ward expected the worst. *Might as well tell him.* Jumping right into his plan, he said, "I know you may not like this, but here is what I want to do. Captain Felt, Sergeant Peterson, and Lieutenant Kirk, keep the ship safe. If things get out of hand, they fly over and strafe the heck out of everyone and everything before picking us up. Otherwise they sit tight there. Sergeants Fleisch and Dunn do a soft recon to verify the right warehouse. You lead a team, including a squad or two of Jacques's troops, and hit the food warehouse from the inside." Hugh noticed Ward tensing up, waiting for the other shoe to drop. "I will take Ensign uch Robert for commo with Lieutenant Carr as our guard. We'll also be in the middle of Jacques and all the people he can find to create a diversion, so we should be safe. The operation doesn't work unless he and his troops show up to help, and if I don't go, they won't believe we intend to share. Even if I go, they may not trust us, but going with them is the best way I can think of to show them we'll keep our word."

A thought hit him. "Do we have air sleds?" Some of the simulations Ward had put Hugh through had required air sleds, armed and unarmed. He needed to know if they were theoretically available or actually in the *Ambrose B*'s inventory.

Ward nodded slowly as he gazed straight into his monarch's eyes. "Yes, armed ones, sire."

Hugh nodded in satisfaction. Ward's body language relaxed a bit, becoming cautiously neutral instead of adamantly opposed. *This will work!* "Then Petty Officers West and Hall will ride them in as top cover. Let's delay this op for another two hours so we get maximum benefit from the dark. That way, the defenders will have less of an idea of how many of us there are. Since Jacques's group only has to sit still, making noise and diverting attention, they should be able to handle that without too much supervision. The inside of the warehouse should be lit. If it is, the locals with you won't have a problem, and if it's not, the defenders won't stand a chance."

"Can you clarify for me again, Your Highness, exactly what the purpose of your mission is, just so we are clear?"

"Jacques's people need to see me there keeping my promise to them. I'll be staying with them as a hostage, so to speak. I also intend to offer the defenders a chance to join Jacques before we massacre them. I'm pretty sure most of them are just there to take care of their families."

Ward just nodded. "We better hurry then, sire. It'll take Klostermann two hours to get these locals minimally ready to take with me, plus Fleisch and Dunn shouldn't rush the recon if they don't want to give the plan away. After that, it'll take me two more hours to get in position if we want to do it quietly." He hit his com. "Did you catch this harebrained scheme, Captain?"

"Yes, I did. Frankly, even your plans are generally saner than this one seems to be. I'll get Maeve and the girls back here so we can get their side of it ready."

Hugh heaved a sigh, with great emotion. "It is so good to have the confidence of one's subordinates."

Ward gave him a steely look. "Just be glad I'm letting you out to play at all. You almost got shot by these crazies once today.

Remember that this whole trip's been wasted if that happens, even if it's just by accident."

"That's another reason for the sleds. They can scan, watching for Zilda and any friends she might round up to try and sweep the board after we take the warehouses."

"Good thought, sire. I will assume you didn't just think of that excuse as we've been speaking, but included it as a fail-safe the entire time. Captain, can you set up a drone loudspeaker system, so it can be heard all over the city?"

Hugh just grinned. He refused to tell Ward one way or the other about when he'd decided he needed the air sleds. Truthfully, he now really regretted not having shot Zilda earlier. The thought of what she might do to the plan began nagging at him.

Gail came back all business when she replied, *"Sure. Just need to run calculations on focal points. What do you want to say?"*

"I'd like that speech Dr. Jacques gave rebroadcast for everyone in the city. Splice together Hugh's speech to the Enlightened and the one here. Leave out the objective, have it ready to go as soon as possible. Then, start broadcasting it with some intro about the free city of Spreitenbach or something. Call it whatever you want. Add a call for the inhabitants to throw off the Enlightened, the Association, and the Committee."

"And done in half an hour, I bet? Don't want much, do you?"

"Not much at all, Captain, just peace and justice for all the people of the galaxy, and by tomorrow, if possible. Raspberry mousse for dessert would be nice, too."

Gail giggled, a most uncaptainly sound, before whispering, *"Raspberry mousse,"* and signing off.

Hugh vaguely wondered about the raspberry mousse before returning to Jacques and his people. They had been waiting patiently while he cooked this up. One of the bad habits of a sheep culture seemed to have worked out in his favor this time. Hugh explained to Jacques, "We're going to start announcing your new free city of Spreitenbach within an hour. I found your speech pretty inspiring, so we are using that. If nothing else, it should keep Zilda busy holding onto what she has. I'll meet you at the assembly area in four hours with my com specialist. Sergeant Major will need two of these groups, about twenty men, to go with him into the warehouse. You pick them and have them stay here with Sergeant Klostermann. He will give them a quickie course in how not to shoot their friends. It's something the sergeant major is really worried about." Hugh smiled so as to take the sting out of the comment. Jacques's return smile let Hugh know that no offense had been taken. He apparently found the mordant humor amusing. *Doctors, like soldiers, probably joke about death so its constant presence doesn't destroy them.*

Looking around, Hugh and the Marines found themselves in the center of a circle of over a hundred men and women who just minutes before had been a mob thirsting after their blood. Now they were just a crowd of people docilely standing about, watching them with curious expressions on their faces. "If you'll talk to these people, I've got to get going," Hugh said to Jacques.

Reaching to shake hands, he stopped short. Dr. Jacques's bloody hands repelled him. Jacques's discomfort and embarrassment as Hugh paused were also plain. Standing still, uncomfortably, for a moment, Hugh said self-consciously, "I'll be there in four hours." Looking into Jacques's face again, he knew what he needed to do to cement their alliance. Grasping the doctor's bloody hand impulsively, he shook it firmly before letting it go. The sticky gore clung to his hand, but Hugh stared firmly into Jacques's eyes, so he knew Hugh meant it.

Sudden gratitude, and something more Hugh couldn't explain, shone in Jacques's eyes as he nodded back. "Four hours."

IMPERIAL MILITARY TRAINING STANDARDS

Army Cadet Training Course
Imperial Staff Operations Paper
Supporting Document Appendix J-1
Urban Warfare

Urban warfare, also known as street or city fighting, is the term used for the bloodiest form of combat engaged in by organized forces. It is not only house-to-house but often room-by-room. Dimlot Harold, a pirate chief involved in the destruction of Rigel Base in the War of the League of Humanity, is quoted as saying, "If we go down there and fight, everything we might be able to use would all be worthless by the time we're done. Why not just drop a rock on them?"

Many military theorists agree with Harold's basic premise about city fighting, if not the method he employed to avoid it. On Old Earth, the Siege of Stalingrad, resulting in the near total obliteration of the city, as well as the Battle of Fallujah, which resulted in 60 percent of all buildings damaged or destroyed, are excellent examples of what happens to a city when it suffers an all-out assault.

Military historians agree that the only justification for such risk is an overwhelming need. Generally, urban warfare destroys any benefit the victor seeks from the city, as well as complicating further operations by creating a near impassable obstacle in the rear. A commander who begins a campaign in a city has picked a course of desperation because he has no other choice.

21

Stepping into the Dark

Spreitenbach Spaceport, Alpine
1420 Local/1520 BBMT 8 November 3473

HEADING BACK TOWARD THE SHIP, Sergeants Kevin Dunn and Tabi Fleisch scanned for threats while keeping pace with Hugh. Hugh Cascade supposed Sergeant Major Sean Ward had decided he needed Sergeant Abdul Jebet and his laser rifle to keep things under control if something went wrong back there. Those trainees were only fifteen minutes removed from a ravening mob, after all.

A broad smile broke out on his face as he heard Sergeant Vinnie Klostermann's bellow, herding the people who had just wandered over to hear Jacques talk. The best speeches were from the heart and Doctor Vintner Jacques had certainly sounded like he believed what he had said.

After getting back to the ship and washing the blood off his hands, Hugh wanted a meal, followed by some real planning. The idea he had come up with on the tarmac felt too seat-of-the-pants even for him. *Prior planning prevents poor performance* qualified as more than just a cute military axiom. It could save his life or that of somebody with him. He'd seen too many dead people today to think that death cared who you were when it came for you.

After washing up, he stopped by the bridge, where he found Lieutenant Sally Carr already there with Captain Gail Felt. "Where's the ensign? I need to let her know what she'll be doing tonight."

Gail gave him a hard look. "I have her getting a mobile com control board together, as well as a virtual screen to keep track of all the units. Anything I've forgotten, sire?" Her tone made it clear that she didn't need any reminders.

"Um. No. Sounds good, thanks."

"I'm glad you approve." Hugh didn't miss the sarcasm in that. "Also, Ward called while you were on the way over. One more condition before you go: we're not letting either of you out to play unless you're both wearing medium armor, including face shields."

Hugh groaned. Medium armor weighed the wearer down and could pinch and itch. Luckily, the cool Alpine weather helped, since armor could also be very hot, even with the internal environmental controls. Each suit weighed forty to fifty pounds, depending on the size of the person wearing it. For all of these reasons, Hugh had no intention of wearing it here or anywhere else. "You're not *letting* me out without it?" he asked with an edge in his voice. His temperature began to rise as he thought about what that implied.

Gail stopped working on the com board, her eyes drilling deep into his. "That's right, *let* you and the ensign out. We are in hostile territory, and we won't let you go without reasonable precautions. Besides which, you won't be running, ducking, or sneaking around. In other words, you'll be targets. Ward, as proctor, can veto anything he thinks is unnecessarily dangerous, so guess where he comes down on this subject, Your Highness? If you'll excuse me, I need to get out this message Ward asked me to put together as soon as possible, before we can finish planning."

She returned her attention to her work as Hugh left the bridge. Dropping down to the mess, he grabbed a bite in sullen silence and then headed for the armory on the bottom level. Sergeant Pete Peterson sat waiting for him with a cheery grin on his face, the kind Hugh remembered seeing much too often in the past, when Peterson got his way.

"I've been expecting you, sire. Let's find a suit that's just your size," he suggested happily.

Hugh kept his mouth shut. Peterson enjoying himself while fitting him for this mobile coffin just made him madder. Having no choice in the matter simply made things worse.

He watched as Peterson set out various pieces for the complete suit that would fit together as an airtight whole to protect the wearer from most hazards. It consisted of armor on legs, feet, torso, arms, hands, and helmet that fit tightly, but not too snug. At least theoretically. It appeared golden in color until the nanocamo was engaged.

After waiting ten minutes as Peterson pondered and rummaged through the various sizes, things actually got worse as he carefully and precisely began fitting Hugh with shin guards, vambraces for his arms, plus all the pieces for his torso and other body parts. It seemed to take forever before everything had been locked into place. Checking his timer, he saw that Peterson had, indeed, been milking the fitting for every moment he could. They'd been there half an hour before Peterson figured all the parts fit properly. As Hugh left, lugging the gear in two duffel bags, Peterson commented, "Petty Officer Karen Hall got the ensign in and out of here in five minutes so you wouldn't have to wait."

Hugh bit his tongue. Peterson's military specialties included armorer, so only he could do this job, but had he ever found a way to get even! He had to admit, it surprised him, given that he could have spaced him just days ago, but he'd rather have Prankster Pete than someone who was afraid of him. People who feared for their lives were prone to making bad decisions. If Pete had the confidence to play this prank on Hugh, it meant he had the confidence needed to help the team succeed.

Coming to that conclusion, he decided also that he would find a *non*-official way get even with Peterson. He and Sergeant Kevin Dunn had been pranking each other from the day Kevin reported aboard the estate, so he would just put all that experience to good use. A grin broke out in anticipation of seeing Peterson's face when that happened. Good things came to those who waited, after all. He even whistled as he approached the mess.

Entering, he found Ward and the others waiting with the simulator already set up, programmed, and ready. He dropped his gear and lay down on a mat beside Ensign Maeve uch Robert, looking briefly at her before placing the simulator hookup over his head. Making himself relax, he centered his focus entirely on what they were about to do. A map popped up in the simulator and the discussion began as to how to best reach and take the objective.

Next came a detailed review of the objective and how to hold and remove the food with the least breakage or possibility of getting killed. As he studied the objective, the simulator did the grunt work, calculating lines-of-sight, possible choke points for every approach by way of the streets around the complex, and likelihood for success from basic pre-programmed options. Hugh stared at the twenty warehouses within their wall for a minute as it did. How should they assault the area in order to take them all intact? The computer displayed less than a 10 percent chance for success from any direct attack. Hugh shook his head. Those warehouses covered almost three-tenths of a square mile. The Marines didn't have enough heavy weapons to secure even one of them without destroying it. Almost unbidden, the words came to his lips, "How many men would you estimate are in there, Top?"

Numbers and defensive densities began popping up over buildings, gun emplacements, and various locations Hugh identified as possible concentration areas. He realized that Ward must be subvocalizing as he evaluated the target area. The numbers began growing quickly as icons indicating unit sizes appeared on the map. It added up to over two battalions active on the perimeter wall; with a platoon per building that equated to another two battalions inside, not including rapid response forces. Figuring the normal one shift off, one in reserve in the warehouses, and one on the walls, there must be at least two regiments, maybe three, to meet Ward's professional estimate.

Ward spoke as the numbers totaled in a corner of the schematic, "I'd guess two regiments, max. They'll use the troops guarding the warehouses as their reserve since I'm sure they don't think anyone is getting over the wall. But if we figure three, we'll be on the safe side. Anyway, these companies are light, about 120 people each, three companies per battalion. Figure four hundred people, adding in the ash and trash per battalion, two battalions per regiment; that gets you to somewhere around three thousand men."

They certainly didn't have enough trained troops to do this directly, so sneaky would obviously have to do. Hugh grunted, "Two questions, Top. Can all of them fight? The tooth-to-tail ratio is usually ten to one, especially with people like these security types. Lots of cushy jobs pushing paper and little action required, so it ought to be about three hundred real fighters and thousands with guns they hardly know how to use. Second, why is the computer counting around ten thousand based on heat signatures?" Hugh asked, not as a gotcha but truly curious about the discrepancy.

"I agree with the theory as to how many are fighters, Your Highness, but if they're in there, they will likely all be armed. Even a pencil pusher with a gun can, theoretically, hurt somebody if he's very lucky. You have to count them as a threat for planning purposes. Remember the five P's."

Hugh and the others on the team chorused Hugh's earlier thought.

Ward smiled. "Exactly. As to the other question . . . magnify," Ward ordered. The figures on the map became clearer but still very small. "Again."

Now they could see men in uniform and lots of people out of uniform, some much smaller than the men on duty. "Children," whispered Petty Officer Pam West, after a moment. "Those are women and children we are putting in the line of fire."

Hugh felt numb as that hit him. Of course. Those women and children were in there because they had nowhere else to go. If they left the protection of their fathers and husbands, they'd all end up like the Enlightened here at the spaceport. "We can't ignore them and if we attack all-out, some of them are going to get killed. How do we convince their leaders to surrender without creating a massacre?" *This operation just became a whole lot dicier.*

Everyone began chipping in thoughts. Hugh could tell by their voices they all wanted to find a workable solution that didn't end up with a massacre they'd never be able to forget. Or live with.

He hoped the plan they were coming up with would work, otherwise he'd have blood on his hands that would never come off, unlike the gore he had picked up by shaking hands with Dr. Jacques to seal their alliance.

Halfway through the session, three of the warehouses on the map began flashing as food storage. Good news, because knowing where to go made planning easier. Fleisch and Dunn's recon through the tunnels had just made everyone's lives simpler. Reviewing the tunnel access points, a warehouse on the second row appeared to be the best target.

Hugh's mind flashed through options, clear, crisp, and controlled. At an almost subconscious level, Hugh felt grateful for all the hours of training Ward had put him through. In some ways, it made planning this assault a breeze. He shared his thoughts and then they made a concrete plan. Manipulating the schematic, they identified the best routes in and out: underground, in the open, through buildings, and by air. Phase lines for timing their approach and positions surrounding the complex were determined. Then they ran through some scenarios at high speed, not having time for more than that. They were committed and he prayed it would work. Sitting up, Hugh yawned. "Thanks for all the input. I think we can make this work."

As everyone broke into groups to assemble needed equipment and fine-tune the details of their parts of the plan, Hugh took a moment to look around the room at his team. *My team.*

Sergeant Major Ward had become so much more to him than a mentor. Gail Felt and Sally Carr were like the older sisters he'd never had. Tabi Fleisch, Abdul Jebet, Kevin Dunn, Vinnie Klostermann, and even Pete Peterson, as well as the other women of *Ambrose B*, Karen Hall, Pam West, and Sheila Kirk, were all extended family at this point. And Maeve uch Robert. What was she? How did he think of her? He didn't know how to answer that yet.

What he did know was that he wanted all of these people to come back to the ship safely. The memory of Tim Kennion lying dead on the floor came to mind. Leaders lose people, he knew, but he didn't think he'd ever be able to accept it without feeling an overwhelming sense of loss. He felt himself tearing up at the thought of the loyalty and steadfast belief in him the people in this room had demonstrated already, and the risks they would take tonight.

He turned to leave before anyone noticed, but caught Maeve's eye before he got out the door. He knew from the look on her face that she'd seen him becoming emotional. *Of all these people, she's really the only one who understands what it means to have others die for you.* He nodded at her and left.

Galactifacts for Kids 3500

Core Empire Imperial Elite Marines. For more than a thousand years, the Core Empire dominated the galaxy, driven by the high level of professionalism and training of their military, including army, navy, and Marines. One unit stands out as clearly superior even in this excellent group of men and women: the Elite Marine Commandos. The Elite, as they preferred to be called, were not chosen solely from the fleet Marine forces, but were drawn from all branches of service, as well as local planetary protection forces.

Prospective Elite Marine Commandos were taken to the planet Harwell for a rigorous two-year program of training. During the Core Civil War, Harwell itself suffered substantial devastation through kinetic bombardment. During that ten-year period, the remaining Elites suffered far higher-than-average losses, as they were often called upon for the most dangerous and difficult missions.

Following the war, it became a priority to restart the training program to replenish the Elites and maintain their capabilities as the premiere fighting force in the empire.

22

Movement to Contact

Spreitenbach, Alpine
1535 Local/1635 BBMT 8 November 3473

AFTER THE PLANNING SESSION BEGAN, it only took five minutes for Maeve to become completely confused about what they would be doing and how. Knowing her main responsibility, to take care of communications, she used the time to create a program to make that run more smoothly. But as for everything else? This planning session had been conducted so quickly, Hugh and Ward seeming to be so much in sync with each other, that it had almost been a blur. Luckily, she managed to download the entire plan onto her system for later review and reference.

Worse than her confusion, one significant question kept nagging at her: why did she need to go? If she only needed to watch a com screen and patch through calls, she could be a telephone operator back on the ship *without* having to wear armor. She had never worn it before and she hated it. It felt like being in a can, worse even than a vacuum suit, so confining she could hardly breathe.

Earlier, when she had returned to the ship from the hanger, gratitude had overwhelmed her. She never wanted to set foot on this planet again. Desperately wanting a shower to wipe away both the physical and mental filth, instead she had let Karen fit her with her prison of armor. The only thing that made that bearable had been the news that Hugh had to wear armor too. She understood that, as the heir, he needed maximum protection, but her?

As she picked up her stuff and stowed the headset away, she noticed Hugh over by the door to the mess, lost in thought.

His eyes moved from person to person, taking in the entire team. For a moment, he caught her eye and she saw such intense emotion on his face, she wondered what was wrong. And then she looked around, too, and it dawned on her. *Heavy is the head that wears the crown.* He might not have it yet, but already she could see how the responsibility of being just the heir apparent weighed on him. She could only imagine what he must be thinking and feeling right now, knowing that any one of these people might die in a few hours. She vowed to stop pouting over how he treated her. *Time to grow up for real, Maeve.* Time to be a team player and support Hugh so he could get through this test and pull the entire empire together. She didn't envy him the job. Not even a little bit.

FORTY-FIVE MINUTES LATER, SHE watched Hugh suiting up calmly, as if he had done this a thousand times. Karen came over and held up the first piece of armor for Maeve to put on. Resigned, she stood to have it fastened around her waist. Passing five minutes in a fog of meaningless small talk with Karen, amidst conflicting thoughts and emotions having nothing to do with the mission, she rose clumsily to her feet, everything strapped and ready to go with face shield up. Up, until she entered the combat zone, of course, after which she would be closed in like an oyster. But then Karen, signaling that she needed to test the system, closed the shield. Every time the face shield closed, Maeve felt a brief flare of panic, before forcing herself to concentrate on something else. And breathe. Relief flooded her as Karen flipped it back up.

"You can leave it that way until we get to the operational zone," Karen said, "By that, I mean after we get off the spaceport, anywhere a bad guy with a gun might be lurking."

Maeve nodded before clanking awkwardly toward the door. As she did, she enviously watched Hugh's almost effortless strides. *Show-off,* she thought sourly. How did he expect her to run the commo and battle screen with this on? Virtual keyboards, of course, but she could do without this steel straitjacket, a burden she didn't want or need.

Clomping onto the tarmac, she couldn't even feel the breeze whipping Sally's hair around. She felt miserably hot and immobile. In the last rays of sunset, she saw two sleds ready to go. Pam signaled her to step up. Karen carried the heavier load of Hugh and his armor which were already hooked on behind her. After Sally joined her on Pam's sled, they accelerated smoothly, arcing off after Karen's lead.

Maeve noticed a flashing red light on her heads-up. *Environmental*, it read when she focused on it. Hitting it with her chin, the suit became almost instantly cooler. *I wonder what else this thing can do?*

Another light strobed red as a little voice whispered, "Entering danger zone, enable all defense systems." Taking a deep breath, she flipped her visor closed. Then quickly she opened the operator's manual on the heads-up display with her face muscles and began reading feverishly. She had just gotten to leg power augmentation when their landing startled her, so engrossed in learning about the suit she had quite forgotten both her anxiety and her surroundings. She hit the switch for power to the legs and stepped off effortlessly.

Someone could have told me! she pouted to herself as she joined Hugh. No wonder Hugh moved around so easily; he had already known about the augments.

Moving off to follow Hugh, she saw Pam and Karen shoot back up in the air, quickly becoming invisible in the darkening sky. *Their stealth mode must be on*, she decided. Hugh, his eyes on her, stood beside a small, dark man she remembered seeing earlier. His steady gaze as she tromped toward him made her feel like a lumbering elephant.

Hugh formally introduced them, "Dr. Vintner Jacques, Ensign Maeve uch Robert." They greeted each other. As Maeve chatted with Dr. Jacques, she suddenly became aware of hundreds, maybe thousands, of people in the area around them, each showing up as individual icons on her display. Forgetting Dr. Jacques for a minute, she focused on clearing up the clutter. It took her two tries before she could create group icons instead of having a mass of individuals fill the screen. At that moment, she saw the doctor waiting for an answer to his last polite question, whatever it had been.

"I'm sorry, the suit distracted me for a moment."

"That happens a lot," Hugh said, with an amused smile.

She wished she could punch him for that.

Dr. Jacques stepped in to fill the awkward void. "You are doing very well for just getting started." She appreciated the compliment, regardless of the truth. "Shall we go?" he suggested.

Hugh remained still. Turning toward Maeve, chuckling, he said, "I agree about you're doing well. It took me a while to get the hang of these tin cans, too."

Maeve shrugged as Hugh asked Dr. Vintner, "Are your leaders here?"

Jacques nodded.

Hugh simply pointed to Maeve to start the next part of the plan. She projected both Hugh's image and a map of the area onto the side of a building for everyone to see. Above them, several drones hovered, prepared to amplify his voice as she broadcast it. "I'm Hugh Cascade. You are under my command tonight. If you don't want to follow me or my orders, leave. I expect to be obeyed and will enforce discipline on anyone who does not follow my orders, which may include shooting them. Do you understand?"

Maeve's eyes were firmly fixed on her control screen, but to her Hugh sounded like he meant business. Bluntness had its virtues. When he acted like this, she would willingly follow him through anything. *I hope these civilians get the message.* Even as she thought that, the sound of agreement came back from the crowd. *They've been taking orders from the Enlightened so long, it's become a part of their nature.*

Hugh sounded impatient as he spoke again, "When I ask for your agreement, I expect to hear *Aye, sir*, loud and clear. Do you understand?"

"Aye, sir!" came back louder this time.

"Do you understand I will kill you if you disobey my orders?"

"Aye, sir," rolled back over them much louder, like an ocean wave. Maeve, remembering her first days in the navy, smiled. It amused her to hear their disjointed enthusiasm, suddenly knowing she had crossed to the other side of the training divide. More, it fascinated her to see how Hugh got them to do what he wanted.

"You understand that we want to get as few of you killed as possible and that includes not killing the secret police if they surrender before we attack?"

This "Aye, sir!" did not come back as loud as the last time but still loud enough that the echoes off the buildings rumbled on for seconds after the masses had responded.

"The plan is for you to make noise, when I say so, not a heroic death charge into their machine guns. Do you understand?"

"Aye, sir." The crowd had gotten into the rhythm of it now, Maeve judged, because the volume grew ever louder with fewer straggling sounds afterward. *Pretty smart. Getting them to act in unison here makes it more likely they will follow his orders out there.*

Hugh continued, "This is how we are getting there."

On cue, Maeve brought up a map showing four columns and the streets they were to walk down to their positions. To keep things simple, there were four groups, one for each side of the warehouses, with a different color for each.

"These are the four leaders who will take you there." Maeve threw up the pictures of four men, Jacques, Hebert, the other man that stood with him from the beginning at the port, and two others with their colors. She attached one face to each of the four routes.

"Do you understand me?"

The crowd's "Aye, sir!" threatened to blast bricks off the buildings around them.

She saw a blinking signal on her heads-up display. Ward had arrived in position, just inside the target warehouse under a closed manhole cover. "Ward's ready to go," she told Hugh on a closed circuit. She didn't know what to call him out here. *Hugh* didn't seem formal enough in this setting and she felt odd calling him *sire*. She put the thought aside for the moment.

Anyway, she had prompted him as per procedure. He had the same heads-up display, but he'd been speaking to Jacques and a group of people around him, so he might not have noticed.

Hugh half-turned toward her. "Thank you, Ensign."

Maeve nodded to herself. Better to call him *sire* out here, then.

Returning his attention to the crowd, Hugh bellowed, "Good luck! Red group, follow Hebert down Dubois." A large mass went off with Hebert toward the spaceport's back fence.

Hebert followed a simple GPS/com that Klostermann had given him. Blue and green groups followed as soon as red cleared the area. Maeve also retasked several drones to gather intel, which kept her up on real-time events. Those columns straggling through the city were even worse than she had expected them to be. As soon as they left the rally area, they began to wriggle along like drunken worms toward their positions, with little groups getting lost at practically every intersection. During the simulations, neither Ward nor Hugh had been optimistic about everyone getting to where they needed to be because night moves were notoriously difficult, even for trained troops. With civilians, she doubted even a large percentage would make it. Just as she thought this, she saw a couple of hundred blues go wandering off into the night. She hoped they'd find their way back before the shooting started. Or ended, for that matter.

Hugh looked at Jacques with a smile. "Let's go. We don't want yellow group to be late for the party."

Jacques's "Aye, sir" indicated many things, but Maeve's concern about controlling her armor and not making a fool of herself in front of the locals, or Hugh, took most of her concentration, with the drones needing the rest of her attention. That left nothing for sorting out subtle meanings or subtexts. Maeve walked along almost like an automaton, paying more attention to her screens than where they actually were. Eventually, she figured out how to know when to turn by watching the icon for Hugh a little ahead of her on the street. Stopping one street over from the complex, Hugh and Jacques went off in opposite directions to place their portion of Jacques's civilians in the buildings facing the warehouse complex wall. Maeve watched the progress on her screen, waiting at the last intersection, until Hugh returned to show her where they would take up position.

THE SEWER TUNNEL MEASURED FOUR feet wide by five feet tall and smelled dreadful. Sergeant Major Sean Ward knew it smelled terrible, but he had been so many places, many of them worse than Alpine, that he simply ignored it. Directly behind him, Vinnie Klostermann and Kevin Dunn filled the tunnel because he didn't want some local, who barely knew which end of a gun to point, at his back. Being shot by friends made you just as dead. The twenty locals with them came next, followed by Abdul Jebet and Tabi Fleisch bringing up the rear. Unfortunately, those two and the people nearest them had drawn the short straw and stood in what Ward smelled. Having stood more than knee-deep in that kind of muck before, and probably would again, he felt for them. Regardless, he needed to be directly under the manhole cover, which gave him the added bonus of being relatively dry.

Ward smiled wryly to himself. *Wish Hugh could be standing back there in the muck with those boys . . . and girl. He definitely could benefit from the experience.* Every emperor needed to know what his orders might mean, and not just the death parts. There likely wouldn't be another opportunity like this for Hugh to get right down in the worst conditions in the name of duty on this trip, so he would just have to learn this lesson at another time and pla—

The thought ended as the stinking ooze triggered a memory. Could there be any worse conditions than those Hugh had already endured? Ward clenched his teeth. Deft. He smelled again the destruction after they had defeated that final charge, much worse than this place. All around him there had been nothing, only a moonscape of craters, bodies, and destroyed equipment, as dead as any orbiting rock in the heavens for hundreds of yards, no one left alive except him, Hugh, Doña Carlota, Carhart, and seven other Marines. He could see Carhart again, clear as day, smiling, offering him a deal if only Ward killed Doña Carlota and let Carhart take the boy. He often wished he'd killed Carhart back then. Fragging, the killing of bad or useless officers, held an old and honored place among the traditions of the Marines.

Of course, Carhart's prediction, that unless someone strong took control of the empire things would well and truly come unglued, had been proven true in spades. But that didn't matter. Ward had stayed loyal to his oath and, as a result, his soul remained intact, while keeping a fighting chance to fix things, an opportunity Carhart had thought impossible. Ward shuddered briefly. If he had given Hugh to Carhart, the lieutenant would have twisted this boy into something ugly. Hugh wouldn't have been someone Ward would be proud to call his emperor. Or his son.

He settled back. Having arrived with half an hour to spare, it gave him time to kill, to think. Though he knew being early easily beat the alternative, it still grated on the nerves. Every so often, as time crawled past, Ward checked on the progress of the columns on his com, relayed by drone, shaking his head at the mass of confusion.

Focusing in on Hugh and Maeve through his com, he nodded. Although a little more comfortable with each other, beginning to work together more easily and effectively, they still tried to maintain a proper military decorum and distance. Ward judged that Hugh, as a leader, had risen to the occasion, his almost subconscious calmness and command presence creating unity throughout the mob wherever he went.

He checked his timer before reviewing the plan. Again. Fifteen minutes, much too much time to keep his thoughts from wandering to Hugh, Maeve, Gail, and back again. Of course, if this little attack on the warehouses hadn't been essential for their survival, none of these things would be happening, regardless of Gail's desire to play matchmaker. Duty always came first. He checked the time and ran over what needed to happen. Again. Eight minutes until kickoff.

But, as he finished his review, Ward's earbud chirped. Time! From here the plan would change. *Focus on the goal and don't try to force the plan to work.* As his experience had taught him repeatedly, no plan, ever, survived contact with the enemy intact.

EVEN IN HER SUIT WITH all the technical aides and sensors active, Maeve found the night creepy, making her nervous.

Moving through an alleyway, Hugh and Maeve approached the rear of a building that faced nearly the exact center of the wall surrounding the warehouse complex. They took a position in an empty second-story office, about twenty feet by thirty feet, with good views of the gate and strongpoints on the wall. She zoomed in, enhancing her vision of the wall. Just as seen from the aerial survey, it consisted of concrete topped with barbed wire and broken glass, designed to keep out the rabble of this workers' paradise. The guns in the towers, spaced every fifty feet or so on the top of the wall, were more terrifying up close than they had been in the sim. Simulations couldn't kill you, however. If they had to assault that wall in reality, lots of people were going to die, easy pickings for those guns.

"I'll speak to the people across the street now," Hugh spoke formally, interrupting her thoughts.

"Roger," she replied, patching in the remote mic to the drones flying overhead.

"This is Hugh Cascade, heir to the Core Empire," Hugh spoke quietly into his mic. Hearing his voice rolling back at them from across the street, as he stood next to her, disoriented her a bit. The drones worked together, like a network of wireless speakers, ensuring Hugh's words could be heard from wide and far. Simultaneously, Maeve had hacked into the city's communications grid and Hugh's words were being broadcast from any audio, video, holo, or screen device already on.

Thankfully, *Ambrose B* came fully equipped to pull off lots of parlor tricks like this and Maeve had spent a considerable amount of free time going through the user's manual to see what other fun things she could do. She really enjoyed some of the more esoteric items on the list.

An older man in a black uniform dripping in silver piping stepped out of the protection of the guardhouse just to the left of the main gate, a gate not one hundred feet from Hugh's window. The street-side wall of the strongpoint had been heavily sandbagged and reinforced against rifle fire. Coming out into the relative openness of the front porch with no completely encircling cover showed him to be pretty brave, Maeve judged. The man reached the front half wall and shouted back. Maeve trained a parabolic mic on him when he did, so everyone in the command post heard what he said, "So what? We aren't in your lousy empire. Get out of here and go home!" He turned his back and began to leave.

Maeve heard Sally tut-tut behind her. Maeve agreed. In her short acquaintance with him, she knew that being rude to Hugh failed spectacularly as a good life choice in this sort of situation. With his face shield closed, Maeve could barely see the hard smile on the lower part of Hugh's face she knew meant things were getting real. When he looked like that, bad things were likely to happen, at least to whoever happened to be unfortunate enough to be the focal point of his attention.

Hugh's hard voice rolled over the street and warehouses like thunder, "Really, Commissioner Inoye, ignoring me is not a good career move."

The head of the man in silver and black snapped around at Hugh's use of his name. Maeve knew it hadn't been a tough trick, actually, to figure out the man's name. She had listened as Hugh had spent a good share of his time while coming over here discussing possibilities with Jacques's command group as to who might be in charge, and who might be sent out to talk to them. They had used every minute, actually, improving on the battle plan until they'd arrived, so Hugh had been ready to give the Association one last chance. As soon as Inoye stepped out, his features had been caught with sniper scopes, magnified, provided to people who knew the police personally, and independently confirmed by several of them. The information had then been given to Hugh. Inoye still looked shocked that an outsider knew his name.

Hugh continued, "I am here to negotiate a truce so you and the free city of Spreitenbach can mutually co-exist. If you don't agree, we will take over your compound and kill all of you."

"Tough words, off-worlder, but it has been tried, and those who did never even got over the wall. Most didn't get across the street. We will not negotiate." He disappeared into the safety of the fortified strongpoint. A moment later a spear of light from one of the air sleds blew up the strongpoint and everyone in it. The blaze from the explosion lit up the street for fifty feet in both directions, including the room Hugh and Maeve stood in, as well as the courtyard of the warehouses behind the wall. Groups of people could be seen huddled there, mostly armed, but they could also see masses of women and children. After a moment, the women and children could be seen fleeing for the doors of the warehouses.

Hugh broadcast again to the entire compound, "Last chance. I can negotiate or I can open you up like a tin can. You have five minutes. If the authorities do not agree to negotiate, anyone who doesn't want to be part of the massacre must leave or take over a warehouse and put out a white flag. Your five minutes start now."

Galactifacts for Kids 3500

Amazons. Matching the Imperial Elite Marines within the empire exists a unit of women that, until recently, remained virtually unknown outside military circles, Evie's Amazons. The name almost certainly refers to Evie Jackson, the co-founder with Constantine Jackson of Green Gardens, as well as the Core Empire.

The Amazons are specially recruited and trained as covert operatives and intelligence gatherers. Although most information regarding them remains classified, the little that is public knowledge indicates that they are tough and highly capable, an essential compliment to the Elites and integral to their success.

23

Plan Meets Reality

Spreitenbach, Alpine
1840 Local/1940 BBMT 8 November 3473

WITH HALF AN EAR, SERGEANT MAJOR SEAN WARD listened to the heir apparent, Hugh Cascade, trying to convince that horse's rear in charge of the Association to surrender peacefully. It had been the only potential plan they could come up with that avoided killing women and children by the starship load. Ward had laid a private bet with himself, nine-to-one against, since he didn't think these people had any sense. He knew Tabi Fleisch had fifty on the line with Pete Peterson, who took the same view of the situation Ward did, but only giving four-to-one odds to Fleisch.

The strongpoint exploding brought a hard, sure smile to Ward's face. He and Peterson had won their bets. Almost immediately, total confusion broke out above, the din, coming down to him through the manhole cover from the warehouse, truly amazing in volume. Ward heard women screaming and the sound of people above running aimlessly here and there, likely looking for somewhere safe. He could also hear the ter-rified voices of children. Sheer pandemonium reigned above. *Let's hope Plan B works as discussed.* He gave that seventy/thirty against, but that improved on Plan A's odds. If that didn't work, then they'd have to make do, whatever it took.

Nerves taut, Ward threaded a skinny eye—a very thin peri-scope—through the pick hole in the manhole cover. If someone spotted it, however, they were dead. Fitting the connector to his helmet that projected onto his visor so he could see, he turned the skinny eye around the interior of the warehouse. The manhole cover sat in the center of the building in an aisle or alleyway twenty feet wide that ran two hundred yards from the front of the building to the back, wide enough to allow forklifts room to maneuver. Stacks of boxes on pallets, some as much as twenty feet high, others as low as six, lined the aisle. Five fifteen-foot-wide truck doors spread at even intervals across the front of the building. *Ambrose B*'s survey on the way in had shown the standard interior layout to be a second floor supported by pillars spaced around the first floor. Several office windows on the second floor looked out front and back. Two regular man doors stood on the first floor along the back wall, equally spaced. Inside the building were four stairwells in the corners with four freight elevators spaced evenly, two on each sidewall. On the second floor, where he couldn't see them, doors opened onto the side walls from external stairs.

Carefully, he looked around. Women and children dashed randomly in every direction, and he feared some sharp-eyed youngster might kick things off early by spotting his skinny eye. Motion drew the human eye and he had to rotate the skinny eye to see.

Starting at the front doors, he examined the defenses. Five men stood near each door he could see, and he guessed that no more men had been assigned to guard each of the front doors, though to rely on an assumption, besides being embarrassing, could get you killed if you got it wrong. However, based on his experience, he estimated there were maybe thirty-five men on this floor, probably the same on the concrete floor above, with appropriate genuflection to Murphy and his law. After all, what could go wrong, would go wrong. Crossing his fingers, he had to hope Murphy would decide to visit someone else right now, because Ward had little margin for error on this operation. Put bluntly, he had twenty-five against at least sixty guns on the other side, which added to the pucker factor.

Searching for other potential problems, he examined the room a third time. The ceiling stood forty feet high with a crane system to aid in distribution, plus a fleet of forklifts. The attention of the men he could see appeared to be riveted on the festivities outside. About six or seven women and children, hard to tell how many as they shifted around in panic, seemed to be gathered in the alleyway near the back of the warehouse. Fortunately, that put them almost one hundred yards away, beyond any possibility of spotting nanocamo. Ward nodded. He could safely chance getting out early with all the noise and confusion.

Suddenly a couple of children, their mother trying unsuccessfully to catch them, dashed out of a side alley almost on top of the manhole. That woman and her children, as well as many more, would have died if Ward had popped out right then, so he eased back, letting a slow breath calm his heart. Killing civilians could rarely be justified. He didn't ever want to even be responsible for an unintended death, but would live with the nightmares, if necessary, to save the galaxy from total chaos.

Worse than the loss of life and the nightmares, though, would be Gail Felt's anger. She held a very high opinion of him he wanted to protect. Looking down, he whispered, "We'll wait for them to think about surrendering. His Highness gave them five minutes. Pass it on."

He heard Kevin Dunn whisper it down, followed by the next man. The words soon became unintelligible as they echoed and became lost in the darkness. He tensed once more. Sound could be a funny thing; an echo might bounce just right and be heard by the wrong person hundreds of feet away. Luck like that would not help him as he waited for the echoes to die away. Ward relaxed when Abdul Jebet spoke to him through the com, *"Easy for you to say, Top. You're not standing here with us in the muck."*

Ward smiled but didn't answer. The message had gotten to the other end. The humor lightened the building tension and he felt grateful for it. His nerves were still singing with tension, the way they always did on an op, but he appreciated any small relaxation.

* * *

MAEVE UCH ROBERT WATCHED INTENTLY, hoping these people would be reasonable while Hugh negotiated with them. What she had seen earlier today in the hangar left her no doubt as to how people on this planet treated their defeated enemies. She didn't know if she could take it again, especially if she caused it or participated in any way. Soundlessly, she began urging the security people, *Get out, get out, get out*, but no one did. Nobody left.

Suddenly on her screen, she saw a trickle of bodies, heat signatures fleeing into the night from the left wall of the compound toward the blue sector. She held her breath, but no one shot at them from the blue positions. They were going to make it! Hugh's optimistic scenario might work. Suddenly, her screen shifted as the images began falling, followed a second later by a sound coming from the compound, the rattle of Association machine guns opening up from that wall surrounding the warehouse complex. *No! They're killing their own people!* The images fell in grotesque rows, murdered by people who just minutes before had been their friends.

From the sky behind the blues' position, spears of light struck from Karen Hall and Pam West's sleds out at the strongpoints doing the shooting, hitting the men and women who had gunned down their own people. Those strongpoints blew up as beautifully as the first one just across the street from her and she couldn't find any regret within her.

Maeve's eyes stayed glued to the screen. Some of the bodies in the street were still moving. Heat signatures showed a few bodies coming out of the building nearest the refugees and dragging them inside. Some human kindness still existed in Spreitenbach, Maeve realized. The heat signatures quickly disappeared back into the building, but no one else tried to escape.

A gasp brought Maeve's head up from her screen. One of the spotters pointed to movement at a second-story window on a front row warehouse, not a food warehouse, to their right. A white flag! She heard Hugh say softly, "Mark that warehouse and make sure everyone knows." Runners sped off to alert the various groups and remind them that they must respect the flag.

The doctor leading the local forces, Jacques Vintner, spoke to the group leaders of the greens through a com, reminding them individually of the rules.

Maybe there didn't need to be any more death and destruction tonight? Maeve hoped that the still-smoldering wreckage of the strongpoints served as a sufficiently strong warning of what disregarding Hugh Cascade meant.

Maeve still feared—no, knew—that no matter how hard Hugh tried, there would be a battle tonight. The problem existed in the minds of those people over there. They probably thought Hugh acted like that Zilda Wilniak woman or their own commanders and would kill them whether they surrendered or not. She knew what desperation could make a person do. Shivering inside her tin can at the thought, she knew, or at least hoped, Hugh would never act like that.

How hard is it for him to order death like this? She had seen his face after he shot Paul Bhat, the executive officer on *Bring It*, a face tortured with what he had just done. But then, she had also seen him convince that sociopath Zane Weston that he could and would kill or torture him to death without a second thought. She thought the latter easier to fake than the former, but with every decision that led to death, did it become easier? What did that do to him deep inside?

Here, today, he appeared to be a good man, tough but fair. Why else would he give these secret police, men and women who had undoubtedly killed and tortured like those thugs, Weston and Gene Nantz, any opportunity to surrender? Why, except to save lives? By far the more difficult path, but he had picked it without hesitation. She thought of the Creed that he and everyone in the military took an oath to obey. For so many, that oath was just words they simply repeated. *But not for him.*

JUST IN CASE SOMEONE UP above had heard something and decided to investigate, Ward gave another quick peek around with the skinny eye. The coast appeared clear. Ward couldn't see Jebet but knew he would be smiling broadly. Anytime a soldier complained,

Ward knew it indicated things were normal. With his skinny eye, Ward saw people settling back down. In fact, the closest people to the manhole were a woman in a yellow dress and a child in blue denim crouched next to a pallet about seventy-five yards away and facing toward the truck doors in the front wall.

Time's running short. He'd kill those two when he popped out if he had to but didn't think it would be necessary. He sincerely hoped not, even though more lives than those two were hanging in the balance, at least hundreds of billions. Despite the increased chance of detection, Ward kept the skinny eye moving, verifying and re-verifying everything on his internal map. Nothing had changed.

Three minutes after Hugh gave his ultimatum, muted sounds of firing, followed by explosions, could be heard to the west. It couldn't be Hugh. Maybe some of the natives attacking early? Tapping his com link for a map, he got a bird's-eye view of the situation. *The secret police killed their own as they ran across the street!*

Concentrating on the situation map, he almost jumped as loudspeakers blared throughout the building, "All women and children to the second floor." Ward watched the woman in yellow grab her child, a little girl, he thought, and run to the side of the building, away from the explosions. *Good choice.* Quickly the four elevators rose up to the upper floor carrying full loads, while a steady stream of women and children climbed the stairs. He slid the manhole lid open under cover of the cacophony, voices echoing as they shouted to be heard, scuffling shoes rasping over concrete, elevators clanking upward and, behind it all, the sound of distant explosions.

He doubted the screeching of the manhole cover as he slid it open could be heard in the din. His chameleon skin blended into the background perfectly as he slowly slunk out. The one thing he couldn't hide, unfortunately: the black hole that hadn't been there a minute before. But no one seemed to notice it in the confusion. Ward had been fairly certain it wouldn't be, since the men at the ends stood facing out a hundred yards away. Right again. Sidling around so he could see clearly, he sent a silent com signal to Kevin Dunn and Vinnie Klostermann to follow and cover him, leaving the others below. His heads-up display showed they were out and in position, but even he couldn't see them unless within five feet. However, the smell of the sewer on their clothing would easily identify their location.

He began his recon, keeping it slow and easy. Chameleon skin, although amazing, couldn't perfectly hide him, and he had no intention of pushing the envelope unless he had to. Reaching the end of the aisle nearest the truck doors, he verified every-thing. Five men to each door, which meant twenty-five men, no reserves, at this end. Quick and silent as a shadow, he crept back to the manhole as the clock ticked down, hissing to the locals to get up.

He needed to move them quickly. Without chameleon skin, they could be seen, so speed would have to do instead. As they came on top, he pointed and assigned, nerves taut with ten-sion, ready to go into deadly action if—really when—they were discovered. If they weren't, which would take a miracle, he acknowledged to himself, they could take this place down nice and easy. Whatever happened, he breathed easier here in the open, his chances of survival having risen markedly since leaving the hole.

As Hugh's ultimatum expired, the building's internal lighting went out, surprising Ward. He smiled. The defenders were now silhouetted by the light streaming in through windows in the doors. Ward moved his men without waiting. As a defensive tactic, turning off the lights would give the advantage to the defenders over anyone attacking the warehouse through the glare of the fires and security lights outside the buildings. A smart move, but only if the attackers were all outside. With attackers inside and behind them, the defenders were worse than blind; they stood out as easy targets against the windows.

"Dunn and Klostermann, grab your teams of four men as planned. Prepare to take down the rear doors on my mark in two minutes." He watched them moving out on his visor.

As they left, Ward heard Klostermann hiss to his group, "Get lost and I'll kill you myself. Shoot before I tell you to, same thing. Hold hands and stay with me." Ward smiled thinly, Klostermann's order no less funny for being true. Both groups held hands to avoid getting lost in the dark.

He did worry a bit at the noise they were making. But, with everything going on outside, Ward doubted anything they did would alert the guards. Regardless, at this point Ward put a higher premium on these yokels he had brought not getting any of his Marines killed, so losing the element of surprise would be worth that price.

With the women and children out of the way, if he had to, he could turn this floor into a free fire zone with a clear conscience. If that happened, there could be only one way things could turn out: he would be in control of the warehouse at the end. Actually, having five Marines in chameleon skin took the sport out of it. If they had been forced to attack with all the lights on, they'd still have cleared the guards out in seconds from the time they started. The dark just made it more interesting, letting them attempt to disable guards instead of killing them.

He manhandled the other locals into three groups, pushing them away from the hole as quickly as possible so that Fleisch and Jebet could get out. He put four to one side of the hole and four to the other, keeping four standing behind him. "Stay put," he growled menacingly. They did.

As Jebet and Fleisch clambered out, Ward felt an overwhelming need to hold his breath. They reeked. The muck had soaked deep into their uniforms after standing in it so long. Unfortunately, he couldn't block out the smell with his suit rebreather since he needed to speak quietly with these people. Letting out his breath just a bit, he said, "Jebet, take four men and take the two front doors to the right, sixty seconds from mark. Fleisch, head to the left, go, same timing. I'll take the middle door straight ahead."

As they disappeared in the dark, Ward got ready to move out. "Hold hands," he growled to his men. Grabbing the free hand of the man at the near end of the chain, he placed it on his belt. "Don't let go." They began creeping forward as the time till action spun down. Moving up the aisle, his full attention became focused on his door. His visor had automatically shifted to night vision mode when the lights went off, so the scene remained clear as day for him. Behind him, his group shuffled and stumbled as loudly as a herd of elephants, but, apparently, the battle raging outside completely covered any noise made as they neared the front wall. Reaching the end of the alley, his night vision confirmed that the guards were watching the action outside. As the timer beeped, he couldn't hear any sounds of scuffling from the other teams. He prepared to surge into motion.

Turning to face the group so his voice could be heard as little as possible by the guards ahead, he growled, "Don't say anything, don't do anything, just stay put!" Having taken the hand of the nearest man off his belt, he moved stealthily forward toward a man standing five feet back from the door. He went down first, Ward cracking the back of his neck with the butt of his rifle. As he fell limply, Ward judged him probably to be dead. He felt sorry for the man but couldn't do anything to change that now. Approaching the remaining four, he waited for the all clear from the other teams, since he might have to take these men out by shooting them. Unluckily, they had huddled so closely together it would be impossible to take them individually, no matter what the entertainment holos might pretend. Over the next thirty seconds, he felt four buzzes against his skin. *Objectives secured.* Backing up a bit, he spoke to them in a conversational voice ten feet from his targets, far enough so they wouldn't be tempted to rush him, close enough to get them all easily with one burst. Ward said, "Drop your weapons or you're dead."

They jumped as if scalded, while immediately losing their weapons. Ward smiled mordantly. There were few things scarier than an unknown voice from the dark telling you you're dead. How do you fight in that situation? Calling out to the men behind him, he ordered, "Come forward and tie these four men up."

Each took a guard and fumbled through plasti-cuffing their wrists and ankles together. Ward checked the guard he had hit before rattling the doorknob. Definitely dead. Light streaming in from lamp posts outside showed people wandering around aimlessly in the street near him. Ward saw there were enough of them that if they rushed the doors, there could be a problem.

Grabbing his closest two men, he ordered, "Guard the doors and these men. Keep everyone out of the warehouse unless I tell you different. Shoot only if you have to." To the other two he said, "Follow me upstairs." On the com, he ordered, "Make sure the men downstairs know they are guarding the warehouse against intruders and let's go."

As they neared the stairs, Ward smiled evilly. "I can smell you, Vinnie. Better hope the men upstairs don't figure out where that odor is coming from." Klostermann's silence constituted the perfect response in Ward's mind.

Getting back on the com, he briskly directed, "Head up the stairs. Wait at the top for my word." Slinking forward up the right front stairwell, he followed Klostermann, barely able to breathe for the rankness spreading all around him. Ward commed the other three Marines, "We'll go in fifteen seconds and call on them to surrender. If they don't, Jebet's laser rifle should be able to cut through anything they hide behind." Speed now became paramount, stealth a distant second because surprise had helped them as much as it could. At any moment, someone upstairs might discover them and turn this into a real battle. They had too few protecting the doors downstairs to fight those outside and inside at the same time.

Reaching the second floor, Ward tapped his com, signaling Jebet to fire his laser rifle into the ceiling. A searing bolt, ter-rifying enough for trained soldiers on a battlefield, paralyzing when fired in the dark and by surprise, lit up the room and took a divot out of the cement roof.

Ward bellowed in his loudest parade ground voice to get their attention. "This is Sergeant Major Ward, Imperial Marines. We have control of the ground floor. Drop your weapons if you don't want your women and children killed in a crossfire. You will not be harmed if you comply immediately. This is your only warning." Even before he finished speaking, a clatter of weapons hitting the concrete floor could be heard. Using his night vision, he carefully scanned the large room, not finding anyone holding a weapon anywhere.

Comming the others, he asked, "You guys see anyone with a weapon?" Negatives answered him from all four. "Okay, lights on," he ordered. All around them, the prisoners as well as his locals shielded their eyes from the sudden glare. The Marine's night vision in the visor adjusted automatically, allowing Ward and the Marines to continue seeing normally. Speaking again in his parade ground voice, Ward directed the prisoners, "Everyone walk to the east side wall and sit down." Comming Dunn and Klostermann, he directed, "Send your men to collect the weapons and then have them cover the side doors. Don't worry about cuffs; we'll just have to keep an eye on them. Chameleon skin off so our people will know where you are." He left his on. It paid to have an ace in the hole. Last, he sent out the code for *objective secured*.

Comming Jebet, he said, "Head back to the ground floor. Get those forklifts moving downstairs and block the doors with pallets ASAP. I'll keep my guys with yours up here. Once you do that, you are responsible for the front doors."

"Aye, Top." The smell disappeared a minute after he did. As for Klostermann, his smell trailed behind him as he moved around this second floor. But by now Ward had zoned it out. It amused him to see that some of the prisoners began to look sick as he walked near them, though.

After the prisoners were secured, Ward commed Dunn, "Let your men know Klostermann is in charge of them now. Get back downstairs and take control of the back doors until they're blocked. When that's done, you'll be in charge of both ends so Jebet can work from up here. Use the men at both ends as a reaction force and let me know if there's a break-in you can't handle. We'll try to do most of the shooting from up here at the office windows."

"Aye, Top." His boots clattered down the stairs a minute later. "Fleisch, block the side doors up here."

"Aye, Top," she answered from the opposite side of the second floor.

The sounds of forklift motors starting up and the rumble of tires filled the cavernous building. Things seemed to be going well, but, after a bit, he began to get real itchy, that funny feeling he got with a planet about to fall on him. "How are you guys coming?" he commed.

"Just about there," Jebet's voice rumbled in response.

"Help is on the way, but His Highness says we may have company any minute. Jebet, Dunn is taking over when you're finished, so make sure your men know that. I want you up here as soon as you're done blocking the doors. Your lightning bolt thrower will do more damage from up high."

"Aye, Top." Jebet became laconic when in combat, saying only what he needed to.

Ward ticked off the tasks he had set in order to secure the building. They had taken control of all the people inside. The upstairs and downstairs man doors, which opened inward so as not to expose their hinges to potential break-ins, were almost all blocked with pallets of containers. The others would be soon. Lookouts posted at the office windows were watching for anything that might be an organized assault on the building.

One more thing occurred to him—something always did— "Dunn," he commed. "Make sure the sewer entrance is secure."

"Aye, Top."

ON THE DOT, AS THE five minutes expired, shots began to ring out from the buildings surrounding the warehouse compound. People chanted, yelled, sang. Two more strongpoints went up in flames. Maeve watched her screen as, inside the complex, forces rushed to the stretches of walls now undefended with their loss.

Five minutes into this noise and confusion, an icon flashed blue over the food warehouse.

"Objective secure," Maeve reported in a neutral voice, although she felt like singing and jumping for joy. The primary objective had fallen without any serious fighting. Even though her sensors couldn't see inside the building, she guessed there were probably bodies in that warehouse. Not as many as a pitched battle would have created, though, which made this much better.

Hugh's voice rolled over the area again, calm and triumphant, "We have one of the food warehouses. If you surrender immediately, you will not be harmed, although you will be exiled from the city. Throw down your arms now!" Guns began to drop out of some of the strongpoints and men came streaming down to the courtyard. Maeve's drone-eye view saw whole sections of wall empty, including a back corner. If they needed to breach, that would be the place. But many strongpoints were still defended, and from those streams of bullets began indiscriminately hosing down men, women, and children in the courtyard.

Speaking one last time to the compound, urgency filling his voice, Hugh directed, "All those surrendering, go to the corner warehouses. We'll try to protect you there."

Cutting off the amplifier, Hugh's voice lost all emotion as he gave his orders in a businesslike manner, "Pam, Karen, take out the strongpoints that are still firing, all of them. Ward, get ready for company."

Spears of light stabbed from the darkness, destroying the remaining towers along the walls. As if that had been the planned signal for a general assault, a wave of people rushed toward the broken walls, rifles sparking in the dark as they fired. On Maeve's screen, she saw them as heat signatures, the wave of bodies racing across the street from every side.

Interrogating the system, she realized her gut estimate to be right, there were many more people in that wave than had been with them at the assembly area. In the four hours since Hugh had agreed to work with Dr. Jacques to take these warehouses, word must have spread like wildfire about a chance for food, free of the tyranny of the People's Committee, as well as a chance for revenge on the hated secret police.

Maeve suddenly felt worried. None of these new people had been even spoken to by Jacques, much less had the fear of the Almighty drummed into them by Hugh or Klostermann. This could be a blood bath, and they would be partially responsible because Pam and Karen had blown up the wall based upon her target designation on Hugh's order. Thousands surged forward, tearing down the walls where Pam and Karen hadn't opened a way. In an instant, the wave crashed through, rolling forward. Maeve watched it all, frozen. One moment they had been facing a fortress, the next, they had taken it. White flags began sprouting all over the compound. They had won!

And then a fire sprang up in the warehouse on the left front corner. Random shots became ragged volleys. Another fire sprang up, this time in a warehouse on the front row. Focusing on the area, she magnified her view. Maeve gasped. A row of people kneeling on the ground fell over, shot as she watched. *Someone is shooting prisoners!* Beyond the windrow of corpses, a third warehouse burst into flames, white flags still hanging from the windows!

"*No!* Why are you doing this?" Maeve cried out, not even aware she had spoken aloud, hot, angry tears springing up, "We've won. Don't spoil it. There doesn't have to be more killing!" But the sound of shots firing rose to a roar. *Those people don't care.* Nobody cared. The killers, the people she and Hugh had let in by ordering Pam and Karen to destroy the defenses, were crazy with blood lust and the secret police were fighting back. But the people in those strongpoints had been killing the helpless, too. What choice did she have but to agree with Hugh in wiping them out? What could she do? Her heart bled as she watched.

Maeve's head snapped around as Hugh groaned, "Oh, no," and sped off. She heard his voice over the com, "Sergeant Major, there is a mob trying to burn people alive in some of those warehouses. I'm on my way to stop them if I can. I promised those people safe conduct."

She barely noted Ward's, *"Roger,"* as she watched Jacques and his command group follow Hugh, Jacques speaking into his com as he hurried after him.

At the door, Jacques paused, "I need someone to stay here and provide security. Cascade and I will be very unhappy if something happens to any of his team."

A snaggle-toothed man grabbed four others. "We'll make sure nothing happens to them," he stated boastfully. Jacques nodded before disappearing through the door. The five men settled down at the windows to watch the battle across the street.

"Hurry," she whispered to herself. "Save them, Hugh."

IMPERIAL MILITARY TRAINING STANDARDS

Army Cadet Training Course

Leadership is not management. It consists of personal qualities that inspire trust and confidence in others even in the face of certain death. Leadership cannot be taught but can be learned. This may sound paradoxical but is nevertheless true. The cadet will demonstrate leadership by example and understand what motivates those under his command.

24

Battle of the Warehouses

Spreitenbach, Alpine
1905 Local/ 2005 BBMT 8 November 3473

Sergeant Major Sean Ward kept fretting, something prodding him from the back of his mind. What had he missed? Minutes passed slowly until Abdul Jebet came back to the top of the stairs, puffing a bit as he lugged his laser rifle and its power pack. A sudden rattle of rifle fire and a hollow booming against the truck doors downstairs echoed up from below. Those truck doors would only go up if powered from inside, so they were safe for the moment. "Jebet, you've got the front up here, I'll take the back."

Jebet nodded before walking to a window to watch. Ward headed to the back, a very long way away when an attack could break out at any moment. Calling ahead to Vinnie Klostermann, he said, "When I get there, take two men as a reaction force. Rotate front to back and along the sides as you need to."

"Long walk between positions, Top," Klostermann observed.

"Use a forklift, find a scooter if you have to, but cover 'em both. We're spread too thin to do anything else."

Ward had been walking at a brisk pace, but still it took more than a minute and a half. Stopping to catch his breath a little, he realized he still had not fully recovered from being wounded on *Bring It*. He waved at Klostermann to go, but Klostermann didn't move until Ward deactivated his nanocamo, causing one of the men waiting to jump. Klostermann and the two men with him ran off at a sprint.

This is going to be a long night, Ward thought as his head ached.

Comming the team, he asked, "How many guards are tied up downstairs?"

Kevin Dunn responded, *"I got three."*

Klostermann answered a terse, *"Four."* Tabi Fleisch chipped in with six. Jebet added, *"Eight."* Ward chided them, "You guys are becoming softer the older you get."

Klostermann came back with, *"How many did you take, Top?"* Fleisch chimed in before he could even start to answer, *"Four?"*

"Four."

The other Marines whooped at him before he could defend himself, blocking the com circuit for a few seconds. "Okay, wise guys, knock it off. With the thirty or so up here, that gives us fifty-five prisoners." Killing solved some problems, but enough nightmares accumulated from the dead you had to leave behind that a normal person wouldn't kill if given a choice. He hoped he still qualified as normal. Unfortunately, a profession that killed for a living attracted a few warped souls who really liked it. Ward wouldn't tolerate having someone like that around, too unstable. Creepy, too.

Dunn added, *"Things are pretty quiet down here. I'm sending up two of the men."*

A clattering on the stairs announced their arrival before heads popped up from the rear, left stairwell. Ward eased the trigger finger that had subconsciously tightened before the first one appeared. The locals as a group, to Ward's practiced eye, looked like they might be okay. Now, if Jacques's outside people would get here quickly, they could load up and be gone in another twenty minutes to an hour, depending on how things were stacked.

An ocean of sound snapped Ward's head up, the level of firing rapidly increasing outside. Tapping the com unit for map function, he swore as it came up. Icons representing people not from any of Jacques's four groups were pouring into the area. He looked closer, trying to figure out the best route for getting his team, and the food, out of there.

The chatter of automatic weapons filled the air inside the building. Ward almost jumped. His concentration had been so complete a moment before that Fleisch firing on the ground floor of the building startled him. A loud crackling noise came from the other end of the building. That sounded like Jebet up front. The map clearly showed icons grouped around the man doors of his warehouse, in back also. He enabled his chameleon skin as things became hotter.

They're trying to get in, but those pallets make serious barriers. More firing, this time Fleisch and Jebet almost simultaneously. It seemed to be getting hotter. A little backup would be nice about now. "Pam, Karen, clear the perimeter."

Pam's voice came in clearly, *"We'll sweep past in ten seconds. Watch for anti-air missiles when we do, though. We've been picking up electronic signatures down there we don't like."*

After that wild assault wave washed over the walls, every anti-air weapon left in the compound had to be considered hostile. No matter who held those missiles, they posed a live danger to Pam and Karen. But the danger couldn't be helped, for the mission to succeed everyone had to take their chances.

"Roger." Ward headed for the windows overlooking the back. His night vision took over flawlessly as he looked out.

A minute later, a warning broadcast blasted the eardrums of anyone without protection in the area, Gail's voice filling the air, ordering the mob to back off Ward's warehouse. Ten seconds later, Pam and Karen strafed the mob outside his position. Many fled into the night, but some merely backed away, still circling the beleaguered building like wolves baying for blood. There were a good many that lay still or twitched slowly on the ground, though.

Involuntarily, he ducked as a river of rifle fire roared toward him. Glass rained down on him as bullets whizzed where his head had been seconds ago. "How stupid could I be!" he shouted aloud at himself. Luckily, with the torrent of sound caused by that swarm of deadly bees flying through the windows, no one but him could hear what he said. *What a green mistake!* He had almost been killed by forgetting that even chameleon skin couldn't completely match a high-light background to a dark outside. He had given everyone with a gun out there an easy target.

Ward took hold of himself. Interesting that, after all these years, a little thing like almost dying could still get him in a sweat. If he'd gotten himself killed, Gail would have been seriously angry with him. He smiled at the lame, but nevertheless true, joke. He'd have to be more careful.

He turned off his chameleon skin, both to remind himself and to give his people something they could hang onto in this mess. Picking up his head to look around the floor, he saw terrified civilians and former secret police alike groveling, including his four locals. Well, three locals, the fourth lay in a spreading puddle of red, killed by Ward's mistake. Shouting again, so he could be heard over the din of battle throughout the loft, he ordered, "All women and children to the middle of the floor." No one moved.

Standing, he strode forward, repeating himself as he walked. Bullets zipped through the air as he did, but, if he didn't show some courage, none of the civilians would even crawl away, and the blood of these kids and their mothers would be on his hands. "Crawl to the middle of the floor, now!" Pointing at the security men, he ordered, "Get pallets all around them for safety." At first, just a couple began to stir, then a few more, and finally a flood of people fleeing, some even standing to run to safety.

"You men," he shouted at the security people randomly pushing around pallets with forklifts, "build a fort of those boxes to protect the women and children."

Some of the men, though not all, began to work together, walling off both sides of one of the alleys with boxes of cans and sacks of flour and sugar. Flour and sugar would stop bullets as well as sandbags. At least some of them were thinking.

He faced the men who had been brave enough to protect their families as they finished. "Line up." Slowly he gave them a solid, silent inspection before speaking again, "If those people out there get in here, we're all dead, so we've got to fight together. Who will serve under me?"

Ward carefully measured the men who answered his call. The other eighteen hunched down, cringing as bullets ricocheted about. Of the twelve who said they'd fight, two gave him an itch between the shoulder blades when they agreed. "What are your names?" he asked those two.

"Fergus McAskill," responded a tall blond in a bland way.

"Report downstairs to Sergeant Fleisch. I'll let her know you're coming to help."

The man simply gave a quiet smile and turned to go. Ward watched him all the way to the stairs. Holding the com to his lips, he turned away from the others to speak, "Twelve of the remaining security police up here will fight with us. See if any of the ones downstairs want to fight for their lives, too. And be careful of the guy coming down the stairs. Code Pogue."

"Roger, Top. I've got just the place for him."

"Good. I'm sending the new men to cover the back and our locals to help Jebet cover the front. I think it's better to keep the two groups apart, so they don't accidentally shoot each other instead of the ones trying to break in. Jebet, you copy that?"

"Roger."

Ward looked at a little, ratty guy with bleached-looking hair, almost white. For some reason, he made Ward more nervous than the man he had sent downstairs. "Who are you?" he prompted.

"Shubert."

"That all?"

The little man sniggered before answering, "It's enough."

Something felt off about the man, something about his eyes, flat and greasy-looking, that rang warning bells even louder in Ward's head as he concentrated on him. Or maybe the way the other ten men inched away from him, trying to get as far from him as possible without giving offense, seemed odd. *Ferret in a hen house. This man kills for pleasure.* He had seen the type before.

"Okay, you men. Shubert will be with me and five men at the back windows. The rest of you, who is highest ranking?"

A medium-sized man, solid citizen written on him, raised his hand, "Armando Garza."

"Get arms and report to Sergeant Klostermann. I'm turning out the lights in twenty seconds, so hurry."

Comming Klostermann, he said, "Vinnie, send your four men forward to Jebet. I'm sending you six security guys to cover your doors, including a man named Garza who looks solid."

"I'll get them in place before I send the guys forward. We'll be okay."

Ward nodded to himself as the men he had picked headed out. *This might just work.* But, as he looked around, he felt prickles up and down his spine. Would these men with him kill him anyway, throwing away their only chance of survival to get him while he had no backup? *Well, as the man said, you pays your money and you takes your chance.*

He turned away from Shubert, daring him to shoot. Activating his rear helmet cam, he watched the little man pick up a rifle, caress it, then stare unblinking at Ward's back. Ward headed for the rear wall, the others moving with him. Shubert had a clean shot to kill them all and Ward saw him lick his lips.

I'm going to have to kill that one before the night's over. I probably ought to save some of these men's lives and take care of it right now, but these other men need to know why I did it when I do. Shubert followed without firing.

As Ward glanced around, he noted that Garza hadn't left to help Klostermann yet, but kept his rifle trained on Shubert. A shiver went down Ward's spine. That little man had seen Garza and decided to wait for later. Truly a dangerous man. As Ward's group approached the window, he ordered into the com again, "Lights out."

Screams of fear came from the women and children as the sudden dark descended. Darkness and screaming, when added to the smell of smoke entering through the broken windows, created a nightmare impression. Flames flickered outside, painting the loft with reds and oranges.

Ward bellowed, "Don't be afraid. We turned out the lights so those outside can't see in here to shoot. Men, stand beside the windows, not in front, otherwise you might be seen. Shoot anyone approaching the building unless I, or one of the other Marines, tell you otherwise. Or they have a white flag. Shoot to kill."

He watched as his six men got into place, Shubert at one end, as far as he could get from where Ward stood. *Going to go down the line using the dark to cover his killing, I bet. Wait until all eyes are busy, and then pick off these men one by one. Like a weasel, just can't get enough blood. I'm sure the Enlightened found him very useful before everything fell apart. Tonight, with everything in an uproar, he probably figures he can kill as much as he wants to, men first, then the women and children. I'll just wait for him by the next man and see what happens.*

Ward reactivated the chameleon skin and disappeared. Checking his map again before he headed to his overwatch position, he stared dumbfounded. Hugh refused to even try to stay safely out of the fray. Instead, he had charged through the gates to rescue the people in the warehouses, as if things weren't dicey enough.

Thinking back, he recalled making a perfunctory response to Hugh, but couldn't remember what Hugh had said. *He should know better.* Too late now to change things, though. He'd just have to hope Hugh survived the night. Then Ward would ream him out but good.

A FEW MOMENTS AFTER HE left, Maeve uch Robert heard Hugh's voice booming in the air once more over the compound, "Anyone setting fire to a warehouse or killing a prisoner will be immediately shot. If you have any desire to be free, free from overlords and free from guilt, put out those fires!"

It seemed that a few people were listening, but too few. Most were intent on vengeance or possibly just the chance to destroy. Looking out the window, she tried to find Hugh's armor in the chaos but couldn't. Bringing her heads-up display online, Maeve located him, followed by a comet's tail of yellow armbands. As for Pam and Karen, finding their grav sleds just required her to see where they were clearing a path at the moment. Maeve discovered she felt no sympathy at all now for the ones unlucky enough to have been strafed by Pam or Karen.

MANUAL FOR COURTS-MARTIAL (MCM)

Revised 3277 by Order of the Emperor, Charles Roland

War Crimes against Civilians

In a combat zone or during a time competent authority deems to be civil insurrection, a war crime is committed by the commission of these acts which would otherwise be under civil jurisdiction:

1. Intentional killing of non-combatants, especially women and children;
2. Hiding among the populous, thereby using them as human shields or hostages;
3. Rape;
4. Arson;
5. Looting;
6. Committing serious or grievous bodily harm while in the commission of felonious acts; or
7. Attempting to commit the foregoing or abetting the foregoing.

The precise legal basis for each of these crimes is set out in detail in the sections below.

The officer in charge must act to protect defenseless individuals and prisoners who have surrendered to his authority. Failure to attempt to so act constitutes intentional killing.

Competent authority must review all acts taken hereunder as soon as possible.

Trial: Full trial permissible but not required
Penalty: Summary execution

25

Hearts and Minds

Spreitenbach, Alpine
1920 Local/2020 BBMT 8 November 3473

GLIDING FORWARD TOWARD THE GATE in his armor, it seemed to Hugh Cascade as if he had entered a live simulation. He had purposefully not enabled the camouflage so his people could see him. He didn't care, or worry, about anyone else. So focused had he become on what lay ahead of him that he barely noticed the doctor, Vintner Jacques, and his men running full out just to keep up. Hugh lifted his suit's basic weapon, a multipurpose rifle with numerous modes that hooked up directly to the internal feed. He selected explosive rounds from the suit's inventory. Firing into the gate, it sagged inward, hinges twisting and broken, but remained partially attached to the walls. Surging ahead, he hit it full force like a battering ram. His armor looked impressive, and heavy, but the massive metal gate slowed him almost to a complete stop before it collapsed into a heap.

He really hoped Ward hadn't seen that little stunt. When he hit the gate, even with the padding in the helmet, his head had rattled around something fierce, ringing his gong. Guiltily, he admitted to himself that he'd done that successfully in simulation and really wanted to try it for real. He'd be smarter next time, he promised himself.

Intellectually, he knew new and dangerous tricks shouldn't be attempted in combat because, if they backfired, they could get you killed or leave you disoriented at the wrong moment. Well, he'd been lucky. Of course, he thought, shaking his head to clear it from the ringing, if he hadn't been in such a hurry, he wouldn't have tried it this time, either.

Probably, a little voice whispered at the back of his head as it disagreed with his rationalization.

Looking around as the dust that had been raised by the collapsing gates settled, he searched for threats. What he saw stunned him into immobility for several seconds. Only if he had been condemned to the deepest reaches of the infernal pit could he have imagined seeing anything like this, or so he would have believed before tonight. But here before him he saw arson, lynching, rape, murder, looting, all outlined in the lurid light flickering from burning buildings. As he stood there in the ruins of the gate, everyone began looking in his direction. *Either my impressive entrance or the suit is getting their attention.*

A hail of bullets began pinging off him as these crazed people reacted, waking him from his trance. Pushing the volume to max, he heard his voice boom from the drones still stationed overhead. "Lay down your weapons by order of Hugh Cascade, heir apparent to the Core Empire, and the free city of Spreitenbach. Anyone resisting or committing acts contrary to martial law will be summarily executed." His voice echoed as a thunder of doom around him. A few people, men and women, security forces and citizens, did stop, but most redoubled their efforts to kill someone, anyone, and destroy everything they could. A madness seemed to have seized them all, both sides.

Assessing what he saw inside the gates, Hugh felt torn. A warehouse to his right burned brightly, white flags still hanging from the upstairs windows. The roar of the flames made it hard to hear most of the battle around him. Sensors in his suit told him the fires were heating the air appreciably. A short way down a street leading toward Ward's position, Hugh spotted what might be a rape in progress. A group of men surrounded several figures struggling on the ground.

Ward waited, holding a warehouse with their ticket out of here. What to do? After a very long moment Hugh decided Ward could take care of himself. Hugh raised his rifle, firing a standard round as a warning over their heads. "Stop your activity now. Stand up and stay still," he boomed, hoping that discovery would be enough to stop it and somehow make them feel guilty. Unfortunately, under martial law, he'd still have to kill them if they were committing a rape.

Hugh shoved through the intervening crowds, plowing them over in some cases, to get to the scene between the warehouses. Arriving, he slid to a halt, valiantly attempting not to vomit in his suit. Lying in their tattered rags he saw three children and two women. All were bloodied, the children and one of the women moaning, curled into fetal positions. The other woman neither made a sound nor moved, staring blank-eyed into the night. Hugh could see from the blood and injuries she must have fought to the last to prevent this atrocity.

Men on the edges of the circle began slipping away, seeking the shelter of the shadows to escape, as he stood taking it in. But Hugh could see them, his suit automatically identifying each man who had participated in this atrocity. "Mark as targets, all men who were standing here when I came up," he commanded the suit.

"Marked," it confirmed. Flashing red carets strobed on each man. A red cloud descended on his vision as he began to fire target-specific rounds that essentially carried each man's name written on them. He wanted nothing more than to wipe these vermin from the face of the earth. Within seconds, not one of those men within the range of his sight remained standing, although many struggled on the sodden ground in agony from their wounds. As he ceased fire, he realized his throat felt raw from screaming as he killed them. He hoped that no one outside his suit had heard his rage, but really didn't care much. All but three down; those three having scooted around a corner before he began firing.

Hugh noticed Jacques standing behind him. *He must have seen the whole thing.* Hugh's thought came from a detached place deep inside, as he turned his helmet toward him. "Doctor, take care of these poor children and the woman," he asked gently.

His fury spent, but not quite, he added, "Kill any of these men who survived," the steel in his voice reflecting the coldness of his heart at this moment.

Ward's warehouse stood just about two hundred yards away. As he turned to take the quickest route toward it, Hugh noticed he seemed to have attracted a crowd of grim-faced men wearing the yellow armbands of the group that had marched with Dr. Jacques and set up positions across the street with him earlier. Silently, they stood in ones, twos, and clumps, all staring hard at him. No weapons were aimed at him. In fact, they were pointed away but all were standing, waiting.

Why are they doing this? Do they think I made a mistake? If they did, too bad!

Flicking open the PA circuit again, he spoke brusquely, "Under martial law, anyone caught committing murder, rape, arson, or looting is to be immediately tried and shot. If I catch them, I'll do it. If you catch them, ask me first, and then shoot them. If you can live with that, come with me. If not, go back across the street and let me do my job. Got it?"

"Aye, aye, sir," blasted back at him, stunning him with its ferocity, even in his suit. His first coherent thought credited Klostermann's training, only to be struck by an even more overwhelming one. They agreed with what he had done and *wanted* to follow him. He judged their numbers. They were by no means most of the members of the yellow group, much less a majority of those that had started with him tonight, but he figured they were enough to get the job done because they were committed.

"Before we go, ten men stay here with the doctor. Once he is through here, clear a path to Sergeant Major Ward's warehouse in the second row so we can get this woman and these children to safety." Pointing to his map as he projected it, he continued, "That one. Ensign uch Robert will guide you if you get lost or confused, so call her if there's a problem. I'll meet you there. The rest of you, let's go," he ordered and headed off, this time toward the nearest burning warehouse. Ward would just have to hold on a bit longer. So would his mission. Some things were more important than food. Fanned out around him on his heads-up display were icons representing the yellow group, each man willingly dedicated to try and create some order on this world. Following in his wake as Hugh clove through the sea of humanity between him and his objective, they charged forward with abandon.

Hugh had to go more than two hundred yards to the edge of the crowd at the burning warehouse but covered it in fifteen seconds with his augmented muscles, far outstripping his team and guard. Every second counted and he refused to wait. Terror that he would be too late almost strangled him as it rose into his throat, pushing him recklessly forward.

"Clear out, get out of my way," his voice blared from the drones overhead, following his path through the crowd. Some of the mob turned to stare, a few moved. As for those who remained in his path, he showed no compassion. He stepped on them, crunching and snapping bones with his steel feet, or when his steel arms connected to sweep them away. Keying the PA as he arrived, he announced, "I'm here to protect you. Open the door."

A massive truck door hesitantly began to creak upward, then froze four feet up, releasing a massive curtain of smoke. Reaching it, Hugh heaved upward, rending it off its track. Before him huddled about one hundred men, women, and children, cowering near the front to keep as far as possible from the fire devouring the building. Many had serious burns, all were coughing, almost overcome with smoke. He could see fire licking the ceiling and racing along the pallets, blocking any possible exit through the back, the closest way to Ward's warehouse. Now they would be exposed to the mobs longer as Hugh tried to get them to safety.

A tall, spare man in silver and black stepped up, straight and tall. "We tried to get out, but they shot at us and killed many of my men. They got Molotov cocktails in to start the fire while we had the doors open. We had clothing stored here and the fire took right off. Thanks for coming."

Hugh shook his head. "I pledged to keep you safe. I'm here." Looking around he saw a bigger crowd, mostly yellow arm bands, but more than when he started, with quite a few black and silver uniforms mixed in. Turning up the gain on his PA, he ordered, "You who are with me, I order you to shoot any arsonists you see. We are going to stop this riot. If you see a murder or rape, tell me. I will judge."

In the closeness of the suit, he discovered that his cheeks were wet but refused to think about it. All this death and destruction were his fault. He had tried to get the supplies they needed with the least bloodshed possible. Instead, he had unleashed an inferno of destruction. That made it his job to stop it if he could. He calmed his voice before saying anything else, "We're headed to the food warehouse held by my men. Some of you people help with the wounded and take them there."

Stooping, he picked up a horribly burned man with his left arm and headed toward a road leading to Ward's position only a short distance away. He didn't check his rear camera. If they weren't moving, he didn't have time to force them or explain why they should do the right thing. They'd just have to do as he commanded or he would do without their help.

Stepping outside, he heard a fusillade of shots coming from around a corner up ahead. Carefully looking around, he saw yellow armbands chasing the remains of the mob that had torched the warehouse. The man in his arms moaned, reminding him of his pressing need to get to Ward. Blood and pus were oozing down the man's side, white ribs stark against the black, charred skin of his chest. Gradually picking up speed, so as not to jar the man too much, Hugh soon caught up to the line of his men making its way forward as it pushed the crowd before it. *Almost like veterans*, Hugh thought, as they confidently fired, barely stopping for resistance. He wanted to run ahead with this nameless man he had rescued, but, unlike Hugh, no armor protected him. A stray bullet meant for Hugh would easily snuff out the man's tenuous hold on life.

Approaching the next street where he could turn toward Ward's warehouse, shots began again to ricochet off his armor. Shielding the man as best he could, he and those with him fired back. Hugh decided that he would allow the mob between here and there only three options, because he didn't have time to stop to reason with anyone: run, surrender, or die.

Walking out into the road between him and Ward's warehouse, he saw another warehouse blazing brightly to his left as men, and some women, danced in the light of destruction. Ahead, a ring of men and women ebbed and flowed like a storm surge crashing against a reef, trying to get into the warehouse Ward held. He kicked on the PA to full. "This is Hugh Cascade." He left out the part about the free city of Spreitenbach this time; he didn't have time. "Throw down your weapons and leave . . . or die." His voice echoed and rolled as the drones fought to maintain position as the heated air of the fires tried to force them higher.

Only a few listened, dropping their weapons to flee. Five seconds later, the rest died as Hugh attacked, the men with him spreading out in a line to either side of him, filling the street. Walking across the front of the warehouse, he opened fire. As if by command, those with him also fired a massive, scything volley sweeping the street of active resistance.

Stopping at the next corner, Hugh called five men to him. "Take this man to a door and get him inside." As they gently took the burn victim out of his left arm, Hugh saw a straggling line of wounded come out of the street he had just cleared, many burned. The people he had rescued were here.

The five he had detailed hadn't moved while he looked around, taking stock. "He's dead, Your Highness," one of his men, fear plain in his voice, said.

Hugh nodded numbly. "Take him and lay him inside anyway. Then go back to the other street we came down so we can get the rest of these people to safety. Watch our backs." Picking five more men, he faced them toward the uncleared portion of the street. "You keep this end of the street open. Shoot anyone who approaches. Give them one warning first, but shoot to kill if they ignore you. Keep this street open."

Opening his com link to Ward first, he spoke, "You all right, Top?"

Ward's grim voice answered, *"Just peachy, except for a certain cadet who didn't stay where I told him to and where he promised he'd be when this ended."*

Hugh grinned at the well-remembered tone. "I never promised, Top, I just said I'd be good. Without this food, we can't lift, plus you were in a little trouble. In addition, many of these security people surrendered, an action based upon my promise of safety. The townspeople were killing them, so what real choice did I have? By the way, heads up, you have refugees coming in at your twelve o'clock. Take care of them as well as you can. Dr. Jacques ought to be here shortly with some rape victims, also."

"Even so, Your Highness . . . ," Ward began.

Hugh cut him off, "Even so, my word is everything. It's in the Creed. It *is* the Creed. I swore to uphold my oath, to the death if need be. So, open the front and let these people in. I'm going down the west side now and then along the back. I have promises to keep. I'll tell you when I get there."

"Roger," came the clipped answer.

Hugh didn't wait for more. With the rest of his men—about twenty—he headed down the street along the right wall. Pockets of resistance fought and died or fled. With no cover in the street besides a few piles of debris and the outside stairwells to the second floors for the buildings on either side, nothing protected them or could withstand Hugh. Reaching the street along the back of Ward's warehouse, he wheeled his men before opening fire along the back of the warehouse. "We're at the rear, Top." A double com click acknowledged his transmission.

As he led his men across the back, he only counted sixteen men with yellow armbands still with him. He had no idea what had happened to the others, but a dozen men in black and silver had joined up along the way. Regardless, all of them, black and silver or yellow arm-banded, seemed to have caught Hugh's iron purpose and become extensions of his weapons systems. They began marching along the street between the back wall of Ward's warehouse and front of the warehouse to the south, leaving a clear path as they went. Clear, that is, of resistance, but littered with the dead and wounded who had refused to stand down or run.

Hugh's sensors caught an order from inside the warehouse that sounded like the sergeant major, but he didn't really pay attention to whatever he said. He had work to do, concentrating on the people he needed to subdue. As he walked, he felt relieved that there had been no firing from inside the warehouse. Sergeant Major must have ordered cease fire inside. No firing, at least, until they passed the last window. A bullet spanged and spun off his armor, doing no damage, followed by a second shot that took down a man to his left. Looking up, training his rifle on the window unconsciously as he did, the sight of a body with white hair flying through the air surprised him.

"Sergeant Major?" Hugh queried as they reached the far street, one now emptying rapidly as word spread of death incarnate coming to reap the wicked.

"A man just resigned. I assisted in his going away party. But it was time for him to fly."

Hugh laughed to himself. *Very punny.* Aloud, he said, "Thank you for making sure the empire gave him a proper send-off, Top. I'm sorry I couldn't attend." He heard Ward chuckle into his com in response.

Despite the humor, Ward sounded less than amused. It couldn't be that he regretted throwing the white-haired man from the window, could it? The man had taken a shot at the heir and the penalty mandated death, so there must have been another explanation. If he remembered later, he'd ask Ward about it. Now, many more warehouses needed to be secured before they burned down. Opening a channel to the commanders of the red, blue, and green groups, he kept it brief. "This is Cascade. Stop anyone else trying to get in. Shoot them if necessary, but only if necessary. Let anyone leave who wants to. Cascade, out."

* * *

Ambrose B
1945 Local/2045 BBMT 8 November 3473

Gail sat tensely watching the action from the cockpit. The sensors surrounding her brought her almost too much information. Ward's warehouse appeared to be relatively safe, but the rest of what had been the warehouse sector could only be described as chaotic.

Approvingly, she watched Hugh bring order to the area a piece at a time. As an experienced special operator, she knew better than to joggle his elbow while he worked. A distraction at the wrong time could get the wrong someone, him, for instance, killed.

Above her, she heard the dorsal gun mount whir.

"Whatcha got, Pete?" she asked.

"A bunch of people being clever, from what the sensors are telling me. Trying to sneak up in the dark."

To Gail, he sounded amused. She agreed, in space it was generally dark, which meant sensors didn't rely on visible light to do their jobs.

"Shall I light them up with a few rounds, cap?" he asked.

Gail smiled to herself. "No, we may need the ammunition later. I'll see if persuasion will work."

Activating the PA in a drone keeping track of the spaceport, she ordered, "This is a restricted area. Approaching within one mile is prohibited. All personnel within that perimeter will be shot without warning."

Watching the return from the drone, she saw that most of approaching mass immediately began to retreat toward the edges of the field. A few brave, and stupid, individuals had dropped to their stomachs and were crawling. They apparently thought this would allow them to get close enough to take the ship. And they were ignoring her sincere warning when she meant every word.

"Peterson, we have some people who aren't believers. We need to convert them. One short burst at the group of your choice."

She felt more than heard the dorsal gun rumble. Almost immediately, those who hadn't already run, that is those still alive, were running for the fence. *Smart. Won't have to do that again anytime soon.* She hated wasting ammo.

Her earbud chirped with an incoming com from Karen Hall. *"We're seeing lots of heat signatures converging on the warehouses. I don't think Hugh and Ward have enough bullets to kill them all. Neither do we; the energy pack on my sled is at 75 percent already."*

"Mine's 73 percent," Pam West added. *"Probably drawn by the fires."*

Karen chimed back in, *"Some people love disasters. They don't know they can end up in the meat grinder doing stuff like this."*

"I'll just have to persuade them to use better common sense," Gail responded. Positioning the drones took a few seconds in order to cover the largest masses.

"This is Captain Gail Felt, Imperial Navy. You are entering a restricted zone subject to martial law. Violators will be subject to summary execution. For your own safety, you are advised to not enter this area."

Going off the drone feed, she ordered Pam and Karen, "I'm giving you each four safe targets where I am not reading heat signatures. One short shot at each."

"Roger," came back from both. Thirty seconds later, most of the masses were going away, some very quickly. A few very brave, or foolhardy, souls were still approaching the warehouses.

"On your heads be it," Gail thought as she returned her attention to the battle.

Warehouses

2110 Local/2210 BBMT 8 November 3473

Time became a blur: knots of resistance, blood soaking the ground, scenes of horror he wished he could forget but knew he would always remember. Early on, someone tried to fry him with a rocket. If he had been closer when the missile fired, he wouldn't have had time or, more accurately, his suit's automatic reflexes couldn't have reacted quickly enough, to avoid it. The group around him, a group he began to think of as his bodyguards, shot the missileer and the people with her before he even had a chance to train his rifle on them.

As time passed, he realized that he no longer had a few dozen men and women surrounding him, but hundreds. Exhaustion began to overcome him, even with the muscle augmentation of the suit. With so many people helping him, he slowed down, sending out parties to clean up pockets of resistance. By the time he returned to the area near the gate, time had sped by. Bone weariness weighed him down as he stood vacantly searching for something to do next, his armor dented and sooty.

Suddenly an alarm went off in his ear, startling him, a schematic came up automatically, showing him the situation and routes to get there. He began running to help, a confused gaggle trying to follow him as he swiftly left them behind.

Commander's Belle
2230 BBMT 8 November 3473

Former Marine Lieutenant Austin Carhart stared at his screen, but things were just not coming together. Mostly he loved combat, but this coming situation could be a little exciting. A rap on the bulkhead brought his head up, interrupting his very unproductive line of thought.

The bosun, Mul Muktar, stood in the open hatch, his bulk almost hiding Captain Argus Steed standing beside him. Another headache, obviously, if both of them had appeared to add excitement to his day. "Come and sit, you two."

Steed and Muktar remained standing. That really brought up his antennae up. "What?" he demanded.

Muktar smiled thinly. "That cargo is still available at Francine and pays well," he stated straight out.

"We're not going to Francine, I have business on Keep Off the Grass."

Steed gave a look to Muktar. "Before going to the Shoal, you told me that you were headed there because it was less dangerous than one other place you knew of to get the information you need. Could that other place be Keep Off the Grass?"

Carhart stared at them, but neither one seemed to notice his irritation, which made him glare. And then he laughed. "It is. But I need that information, especially now that Dent is back."

Muktar nodded. "Dangerous game we're in, boss." Before Carhart could answer, Muktar went on. "In that case, we better plan a little better than we did for the Shoal."

Carhart felt a warmth toward these men who followed him but put on a frown. "You mean that I didn't plan and it almost got us killed?" Smiling a bit sourly at the thought, he added, "You're right. What do you suggest?"

Both sat. Steed asked, "Who are you going to see and what exactly do you want to get?"

"An information broker named Madam Aswini living on Keep Off the Grass is said to know just about every imperial secret. Unfortunately, upon occasion, people who go to see her don't come out." After he pause, he went on. "As I see it, we have two problems. I need to get Madama Aswini to tell me where Hugh Cascade, and bloody Imperial Sergeant Major Ward, are going. That means I need to figure out what we know that is valuable enough that she might be willing to trade for. I want Hugh Cascade and don't see any other way to find out where he might be."

After a long beat, Steed asked. "The second problem?"

"How to get out of her place with the information. Alive."

Mul gave him a hard smile.

The Core Empire

Chapter 13

This chapter examines how Emperor Allen, 2880 through 2928, almost single-handedly destroyed the empire by refusing to employ its strengths, which existed when he started but were undermined by his attempts to negotiate in good faith with all comers. By the end of his reign, the Dynastic Wars were in full swing and six sectors were essentially free of any imperial control.

26

Choice of Dooms

Spreitenbach City, Alpine
1950 Local/2050 BBMT 8 November 3473

MAEVE UCH ROBERT STARED INTO the night that had swallowed Hugh Cascade, the heir apparent, as he tried take control of the situation. Fear and also frustration filled her. She worried for his safety, but also desperately wanted to be outside, right there beside him, helping. But her orders were to stay here, in safety. *Safe!* There were more important things than safety. Hugh had known that and done something about it. She could see him saving people! What good could she do here? Routing calls like a mindless computer.

Sporadic reports came over the com as one or another of the Marines or Vintner Jacques's leaders reported in on their status or requested permission to execute judgment. She tried to shut the reports, the details of atrocities, out of her mind. She could barely cope as she considered that the killing and brutalization of those who had surrendered, even by their own people, became possible only after Pam West and Karen Hall, flying above in the air sleds, had destroyed the strongpoints at Hugh's orders. She tried to ignore Hugh as he issued quick approvals of punishment based upon terse explanations of what perpetrators had been caught doing. She listened as Hugh asked pointed questions, trying to ensure that no one was using summary justice as a means of settling scores. He always insisted on two witnesses. Though he could never be fully certain, they had no time for more complete trials or appeals, only justice, immediate, swift, final, to have any chance of ending this horror. If it could even be stopped.

Maeve kept a close eye on Hugh as he worked to take over one warehouse after another, trying to create islands of calm behind him. At the beginning, he had successfully cleared two of the warehouses on the far left side and their surrounding areas, including one of those that had surrendered initially. But he couldn't be everywhere.

The fury in his voice as he stormed from one emergency to another resonated with her own anger and despair. *Why don't these people take the opportunity we are giving them?* But she knew why: too many of these people hated each other more than they wanted to be free. With hate filling so many, Hugh and the others could do only so much.

Slowly, Hugh took additional warehouses under control, with the largest group being an irregular box of five. Two of the warehouses not under their control became entirely engulfed in flame while looters finished ransacking others. Yet slowly but surely, Hugh and his people asserted control, creating order from chaos.

Between the flickering firelight and the demonic cries and screams, Maeve feared she might go mad. Maeve turned off her external mic so she didn't hear anymore, but couldn't stop herself from staring off into the night as warehouses burned and weapons fired. Sally Carr tapped her shoulder. Maeve turned to look at her, turning her external mic back on. "Karen is on her way in to land on the roof, but I really need to find a ladies' room."

Maeve suddenly saw that much more than two hours had passed since the attack started. "Go ahead. I have these guys watching my back, plus the tin can." She left her external mic on with Sally gone.

The five men Jacques had left smiled a little uncertainly as she referred to them, but stayed out of the conversation. Maeve guessed that, after a lifetime of living in an authoritarian state, being mentioned by someone in charge probably made them nervous. Hopefully, things would change. But, for now, these people simply did not know how to make a choice and then take responsibility for the consequences, good or bad. Learning that provided the only way for things to get better.

Sally nodded her thanks and walked quite quickly out the door. Chuckling, Maeve hoped the facilities weren't too far away; she needed to go, too. She went back to watching the mayhem just beyond her window, trying to convince herself of it only being a video.

"Well, look what we have here," came a purring voice from behind her. Maeve spun, almost overbalancing herself with the suit's powered muscles. A figure from the spaceport stuffed into a red cocktail dress stood in the doorway. Behind her crowded some of the most vile-looking men and women Maeve had ever seen. Four of the bodyguards Dr. Jacques had left with her were kneeling with their hands behind their heads, their leader holding his rifle on them, smiling evilly.

The turncoat briefed Zilda Wilniak with evident pleasure, "Her guard is down the hall in the lav and another may be coming down from the roof. The off-worlder seemed especially concerned with keeping her safe."

"Great. Just what we need, a hostage to trade for what we want." Zilda looked pleased as she spoke with the traitor, "You take a few of my people with you. Kill the guard down the hall before she finds out what's happening. Some of these others will set a trap for the one coming down the stairs." She nodded at a group that quickly set off in the direction of the roof access.

Maeve triggered her alert signal while Zilda's attention centered on the others, warning Sally and Karen. Even so, she had known she had real trouble even before this evil toad had spoken. Keying her virtual board, she immediately started transmitting everything they were saying. She didn't speak, just dropped and locked her face shield and secured the suit's pistols into the pauldrons covering her hands.

"You just take your hands off those guns, missy," Zilda purred on. "If you're nice, maybe I won't turn you over to my men when we're done. I just want to see how much your boyfriend will pay to keep you in one piece."

A series of shots came from down the hall, causing Zilda to smile even larger. "You're all alone, now, so just take that suit off. I think it's just my size."

Zilda's people, the fifteen or so that remained, crowded into the room and began advancing toward Maeve.

Zilda smiled again. "I'll enjoy putting on that suit as much as I enjoyed it when I took this dress from the mayor's wife. Before she met People's justice." The men and women with her roared with laughter.

Maeve still didn't answer. Her display showed Sally's com live. She hoped the firing had been Sally taking care of the traitor and others sent to get her, and not the other way around. Bending her right arm up for a moment, Maeve fired into the ceiling, stopping the advance, before dropping it again to cover the mob. "You are all committing suicide by staying here. Hugh Cascade gave you a chance and you're throwing it away. Both of us look at situations like this the same way, which means I will kill whoever is still in this room in ten seconds. If I don't, His Highness is on his way here right now with a couple of hundred men from what I can tell, and he will finish off any of you I miss. People who ignore him don't get second chances."

Zilda threw back her head and laughed, just as gunfire came from the stairwell at the end of the hall. "You're all alone, girlie," she gloated, "and if you don't want it to go any harder with you than it already will, hand over the gun and get out of that suit!"

Maeve pointed her left-side pistol at Zilda. No one moved. It looked to Maeve like no one wanted to be the next martyr for the cause, but they still leered in anticipation, waiting for someone to be brave enough to take her bullets so the rest could drown her suit in bodies and drag her out of it. A countdown icon popped up on her heads-up display, causing her to jump slightly. *Lucky for me, the suit's enhanced muscles didn't let go of the guns.*

"You've had your chance," Maeve said, in steely tones.

"So have you, girlie," Zilda growled. "Take her, boys" The mass facing her surged forward a moment before the icon hit zero. As Maeve shot randomly into the mob, she watched Zilda go down. Then, from the hallway, a flurry of shots cut down the rear rank of the crowd facing her.

Between the surprise rear attack and Maeve's unyielding purpose, the eight to ten surviving members of the mob scattered. Some tried the door, despite the firing in the hallway, but most rushed for the windows to Maeve's left and right while desperately trying to avoid her guns. Although the windows stood twenty feet above the ground, most jumped anyway. Their landings sounded unpleasant to Maeve, but she refused to look, keeping her focus on Zilda instead.

A burst of firing from outside indicated that Hugh and his people had likely reached the front of the building before the jumpers could get away. She didn't exactly smile, but would still shed no tears for them, not after what they had planned for her.

From the corner of her eye, she saw Karen Hall, Pam West, and Sally Carr standing in the door, finishing off the last few trying to fight. Faces hard, her friends left no wounded. All but Zilda. Maeve had only nicked her in the leg so, after going to the floor, she had dragged herself out of the line of fire. Maeve walked over to her, gun rigidly held out in front of her. "I gave you a chance and you threatened to turn me over to your men, to have their way with me. Hugh told you the rules, but you wouldn't listen." Even now, Maeve's mind shied away from what this woman had threatened her with. She didn't even want to look at her. Nevertheless, she kept her gun trained between Zilda's eyes.

Zilda sneered up at her, pain evident in her voice. "You don't have the guts to shoot me. Neither did your so-called 'heir apparent.'"

Zilda started laughing, a high, crazy sound. "That's why I'll always win and people like you will always lose. You think laws matter, rules matter, honor means something. They're all empty words, only winning matters." Zilda's left hand pressed down on the wound in her leg, stopping the trickle of blood from the flesh wound. Then she laughed again, another long horse laugh.

Maeve's eyes focused on Zilda's laughing mouth as Sally screamed, "Gun!"

Before Maeve could look down, Zilda brought out a gun from under her leg near the wound and fired. Maeve's armor rang like a bell as a bullet hit her suit.

Maeve felt nothing but a tiny vibration, the little bullet not having enough penetrating power really to even dent the suit. Nevertheless, Maeve's hand tightened reflexively. With the augmented muscles in her hand and arm, the pistol in her arm and hand had not moved even an inch from where she had left it pointing at Zilda. When her finger tightened, Maeve shot Zilda right between the eyes. As she watched Zilda's head explode, Maeve began shaking as the realization of what she had done hit her. Somehow, she forced her hand to drop the gun. Sally put her arm around her, an arm Maeve couldn't feel inside her suit.

She hadn't meant to shoot that awful woman; that had been reflex, *an accident*. But another little voice whispered in relief, glad that she had done it. She knew Zilda had deserved it.

"You saved all of us," Sally whispered to her, "by sending out the alert before they could trap me in the lav and ambush Karen. I'm sorry we failed to protect you. We didn't even check to see if she had a hideout gun. Gail is going to have our hides for that. Let's get you back to the ship."

Maeve shook her head. "I'll stay until Hugh and the others get back. I'll go then. I have a job to do and I want to make sure they're all safe first." As she said that, it hit her: these were *her* people as well as Hugh's, and she would do anything to keep them safe. Checking her sensors, she saw things had begun to quiet down.

A short while later, Gail Felt's voice came over her com, "Sergeant Major says they're about ready to leave. They've gathered up some trucks and will be out the gate in ten. Before those trucks hit the road, I want Pam and Karen airborne, which means they barely have time to get you back here before the convoy is ready. It really is time to come home, Ensign."

Maeve gave another look around the room. The four guards who had been betrayed had left earlier, heading out to help Jacques, and would presumably tell him what had happened. That only left carrion in the room, the earthly remains of men and women who had proven they didn't deserve to live. Maeve walked stiffly out, barely trusting herself to remain on her feet. Karen stepped out ahead, leading the way to her sled. Maeve had thought earlier she hated this planet, but now she *really* never wanted to see it again.

A Primer in Core Empire Political Theory

Civil Government Organization of the Empire
Appendix B:74

Decree in Council—Admission of star systems to the Empire
April 12, 2532

In the last year since the death of Emperor Dave, a number of systems outside the galactic core petitioned for admission to the empire. Admission to the empire must follow an orderly process that will avoid ad hoc decisions that might create military and other obligations difficult or impossible for the empire to satisfy. The following criteria must be met for any system to be admitted as a member of the Core Empire. Nevertheless, the empire is not obligated to admit any system regardless of compliance with requirements. Admission is by grace, not law.

For admission, a system must be:

Located within the boundaries of any of the regularly constituted sectors of the empire;

OR

1. Have a self-sustaining population. Generally, this will require more than ten million adults residing on a planet inhabitable without artificial means.
2. Possess active gravitonic ships.
3. Be located within two days' travel of an imperial system.

By Order of the Emperor, Marvin

27

Protector's Oath

ARRIVING AT THE *AMBROSE B*, Karen Hall barely touched down long enough for Maeve uch Robert and Sally Carr to hop off before heading back. Maeve ran to the armory and tore her armor off before heading to the boarding ramp to watch for the convoy. It pulled in an eternity later—twenty minutes by the clock after Maeve had reached the ramp. Hugh Cascade rode the first truck, face shield up, armor sooty and scored from bullet scars and smoke.

From the size and number of dents she could see in his armor, he had been a popular target for people using firearms more powerful than the little gun Zilda Wilniak had tried to use on her. She guessed that many of the dents and scratches would have been serious or fatal without the armor. She silently blessed Sergeant Major Ward for insisting on both of them wearing it.

Gail Felt's voice came over the com, *"Maeve, help Sally store things on the inboard side. We're keeping Pam and Karen aloft until we're done here."*

"Aye, aye," Maeve responded.

But before she headed inside, Gail spoke again, this time with urgency, stopping her, *"There are a lot of vehicles coming, more than enough to just bring the food. Stand by action stations. We may have to pull the guys in from a mob."*

Maeve stepped out to the front of the entry port where she could see better and help if they needed her. Suddenly she felt naked without her armor. It had been comforting, knowing she could actually help if necessary.

Four trucks, all filled with boxes, stopped below her near the loading hatch. Across the spaceport tarmac came a hodgepodge of vehicles: trucks, cars, buses, even scooters. As they arrived, they pulled up more or less in rows facing the ship, their headlights bathing the tarmac and ship with a brilliant light.

Hugh Cascade had stepped onto the hood of the truck he had ridden back in, but now got down from his vantage point before walking out to face them. Hundreds of men and women spilled out of the assorted vehicles, surrounding him in a rough semicircle. Tearing her eyes away from Hugh standing at the focus of the crowd's attention, she began searching the crowd for threats. All the men and women out there were armed, but not one pointed a weapon at Hugh or the ship. Some of the crowd, not a large part of the whole group, wore yellow arm bands showing they had been some of the first to rally behind Hugh. More stood out in red, blue, or green armbands, lots wore silver and black uniforms. Many were bandaged or hurt. Regardless of their group, they were mingled together, centered on the figure in the dented suit.

A voice called out of the crowd, "Don't go! Stay and lead us." A chorus of voices, swelling to a roar, all demanded the same.

"Gail," Hugh said, "patch me into the PA, please."

Hugh's voice boomed out, broadcast by the drones overhead, "My friends, we have fought a battle together, one that will lead to reclaiming the city of Spreitenbach, and perhaps eventually the planet of Alpine, from those like Zilda, like the Enlightened, like the former leaders of the security forces. I wish I could stay, but I can't. I must complete my mission. There are so many others I have to help, also."

A man, in silver and black wearing the rank of a captain in the security forces, stepped forward, along with Vintner Jacques. Hugh removed his helmet and looked at them face-to-face.

Maeve could clearly hear what they were saying from where she stood.

"Don't go, Hugh," the doctor begged.

The captain nodded. "Only you can unite us. Stay and help us liberate this planet."

Hugh shook his head. She heard him speak to Gail on the internal com circuit, "Project the flag and Creed against the side of the ship, Captain." To the two men in front of him, he said, "I can't stay. I have a duty to more than just you. What I can leave is this."

He put his helmet back on, allowing him to use the mic. "I have been asked not to go."

A huge shout greeted this, affirming that they too wanted this. The sound grew until the ship seemed to be shaking. After a bit, it died down as Hugh just stood patiently, waiting. As he did, the empire's flag began to float over Hugh's head, as well as the Creed in letters of gold against the black night. As silence descended, Hugh spoke quietly, "I cannot do that. My duty calls me onward."

The response from the crowd came back immediately and overwhelming in its power, "No! Stay!" The call to remain rolled on for several minutes before dying down.

"But I must go," Hugh declared firmly, raising a hand to mute a renewed protest. "There is one thing I can leave you, however, something that makes me what I am. I welcome you to be my friends and protectors of right on this planet by pledging yourselves to the Creed you see behind me, the reasons I serve. If you do, what I am will be here through the long road to freedom and you will become liberators. Those who willingly wish to join me in that fight, repeat after me."

Hugh paused for a moment before beginning, "I swear protection for citizens and the weak."

The answering sound, although not as loud as before, came back clearly, distinctly, "I swear protection for citizens and the weak." Maeve found herself murmuring the familiar words that had a real meaning once again as Hugh spoke them, a thrill growing in her as she did.

"My word is unquestioned because integrity is the bedrock of my being."

The crowd's voice began to gain power, "My word is unquestioned because integrity is the bedrock of my being." Maeve spoke louder herself.

"I seek always to exercise true judgment in all of my acts."

Maeve almost shouted now to be heard along with them, "I seek always to exercise true judgment in all of my acts." She could feel her commitment to it growing as she confidently recited it with the crowd.

"I will exercise true and merciful justice in all circumstances."

The sound coming from the crowd began to hurt her ears, but she continued yelling along with them, "I will exercise true and merciful justice in all circumstances." Scenes flashing before her eyes of that justice dispensed tonight gave the words deeper meaning.

"I fear no sacrifice necessary to uphold my oath. I will carry every burden of my office, whatever the price."

"I fear no sacrifice necessary to uphold my oath. I will carry every burden of my office, whatever the price." The response from the crowd approached white noise, she couldn't even hear own her voice as separate from them.

"Perfect virtue is unattainable, but I will seek it as my goal in all I do."

"Perfect virtue is unattainable, but I will seek it as my goal in all I do." She felt herself transported, united with these men and women in their solemn covenant.

"I will fulfill my oath to the citizens of this planet, to the death. So help me God."

"I will fulfill my oath to the citizens of this planet, to the death. So help me God." The roar of the crowd rattled her teeth. She couldn't imagine what it must be like where Hugh stood.

"I now accept you as my friends and as the Liberators of Alpine. Reclaim and then protect this world well."

The mob surged forward, surrounding him, grasping his hand, pounding his back, trying to touch him or talk to him. These men and women loved him. Yesterday, they hadn't known he existed. Mere hours ago, they had either been opposed to him or followed him just to get food for their families but, in either case, hardly knew him. Less than an hour ago, they had stood together within the midst of carnage and gore, shoulder to shoulder with him, their rough justice stopping a massacre.

But now, this minute? These people knew what price he required of them and they actually were grateful that he would let them pay it. She could see it and hear it in their actions and voices. Tears filled Maeve's eyes. She wanted to go to him, too, but, unless she fought through the mob to get there, she would have to wait. Hugh truly amazed her. He had a desperate mission ahead of him still and needed to hurry, enemies could appear in the sky at any moment to stop him, and there he stood saving a world he would probably never see again.

Gail's voice came over her earbud, "Stand down, crew. Let's load up so we can get out of here." Tearing herself away from the scene after another minute, Maeve headed toward the mess and back into the kitchen area, before taking the internal stairs to the storage area where the conveyor belt entered. In a few moments, boxes began popping up. She stacked them on a hand truck as quickly as she could, before taking them to their designated areas. However, no matter how fast she moved, they began to pile up. Fortunately, Sally showed up just as she thought she'd be buried under the avalanche.

For a long time, they worked in silence, then Sally stopped and turned toward Maeve. "I need to say something . . ."

Maeve, a little apprehensively, wondered what she had done to upset Sally. The last twenty-four hours had been so filled with ups and downs, she didn't know if she could handle any more, but anguish etched Sally's face so deeply Maeve couldn't refuse her. "Go ahead. I'm listening."

"I am so sorry I left you alone with those men. If something had happened to you, I could never have forgiven myself."

"It's okay," Maeve answered. It really hadn't been Sally's fault. If Sally had been there when Zilda had come in, Sally would have become a hostage Zilda could have used to get Maeve to surrender before killing her. Maeve would never have been able to forgive herself if that had happened. "If you had been there with me, you'd be dead."

"But I should have been there to protect you," Sally said, eyes glistening with unshed tears, "I feel like you're my little sister.

You were all alone with those people and you never should have been."

Maeve stepped around the pile and put her arms around Sally, hugging her tight. "You're the big sister I should have had instead of the ones I do have," Maeve whispered to her. "I love you and know you'd do anything to keep bad things from happening to me." Sally threw her arms around Maeve, hugging Maeve tightly, too.

As Sally dried her eyes on her sleeve, she said, "We'd better get busy. I don't want Pam or Karen hearing about how we were acting all emotional."

Maeve gave a teary smile. "We'd never hear the end of it, would we?"

Grabbing boxes, they went back to work, chatting on about nothing in particular, just glad they were together. With everything stowed and all but Hugh and his small guard detail back on board, Maeve felt completely wrung out. Sweaty and tired, she headed to her room to grab her towel and things for a much-needed shower, when Gail announced over the com, *"Action stations. We'll take off in stealth. Hopefully, Ninth Fleet isn't anywhere around."*

Saying something very unladylike, Maeve quickly went back to Engineering. The shower would have to wait. *Again! How does a girl get a private shower on this ship?*

Pelting, Kari System
2005 Local 8 November/0005 BBMT 9 November 3473

A SWIRL OF COLOR MET Morgain uch Robert's eyes as she stepped onto the floor of the grand ballroom in the system's capital building. Men and women alike now queued to meet her and her friend. For tonight, he would be Don Giovanni, named after one of her favorite operas. It would not do for his real identity to get back to the empire. At least, not yet.

Next to her in the receiving line stood the system president and his wife and a number of other government officials. None of whose names she had bothered to remember. The experience could also be called intoxicating. "Thank you for visiting us, Your Majesty." "Will you be staying long, Your Majesty?" "Will you be basing a squadron here, Your Majesty?" "We would love to host you on our estate, Your Majesty." "You are so beautiful, Your Majesty. Our system now has a second sun."

Amusingly, Don Giovanni looked more and more disgruntled as the reception dragged on and a great many handsome men now clustered around her, shutting him out. It occasionally seemed appropriate that he be reminded as to who actually sat in the high chair. Of late he had begun to not treat her as the queen she would soon become.

ARCHIVED IMPERIAL CLASSIFIED DOCUMENTS

Declassified 24 September 3485
Test of Heirs Program
Proctor Course Revised 2612
Procedures for Transference of Proctor Responsibilities

The relationship between an heir and his, her, or their proctor is extraordinarily close for several reasons. After assumption of responsibility for an heir, proctors are the recipients of emotional feedback through the activated nanite loop that allows the proctor an understanding of the individual heir's motives. As judges holding life-and-death power over their charges, proctors must review each action of an heir under the individual proctor's care, which must of necessity include an understanding of the heir's emotions and motives for those actions.

Circumstances requiring transfer of proctor:

1. Death of proctor;
2. Proctor inability to remain objective or other incapacity;
3. Completion of five-year tour (if qualified replacement available); or
4. Determination by Proctor Board that such transfer is necessary for any other reason.

Procedure:

The newly appointed proctor opens a channel to Guardian through archeon. Any Class A, B, or C facility will connect. Guardian has a secure, separate channel that is capable of connection through all of these. Upon confirmation of channel, the newly appointed proctor enters his, her, or their code as well as the heir's code. A matching confirmation number must be received before the proctor is permitted to take over duties with regard to the heir. Following receipt, the nanites attached to the gems, as well as those already in the heir's system and the proctor's system, will be synchronized, and the test may proceed at any time thereafter at the proctor's discretion.

28

Report Card

Spreitenbach Spaceport, Alpine
0030 Local/0130 9 November 3473

As *Ambrose B* prepared to lift from Alpine, Sean Ward stepped onto the bridge, where Gail Felt sat alone. Hugh Cascade remained outside, talking to the liberators he had sworn in, with Abdul Jebet and Tabi Fleisch watching over him. Ward eased himself down gingerly onto the copilot's seat.

"Getting old?" Gail asked cattily. "I told you, before you went, if you recall, that you shouldn't go crawling around like a teenager through sewers and what not. You're just lucky you're still alive."

Ward wearily shook his head. "We'll see who's old. Your place or mine?"

Gail gave him a repressive look. "What would Sally think if she came in?" Wrinkling her nose, she observed, "And I have no intention of letting you near me in that state. You stink. We'll meet in the gym, after you shower. We've got things to discuss."

"It would be more comfortable in a room and more private."

Gail shook her head. "For someone in his fifties who should have grown up long ago, you're terrible. Also, in my opinion, if you go anywhere near a bed, you'll be asleep in minutes. You're falling asleep this second."

Ward's head had been drooping as she spoke and he didn't even try to deny her last point. Exhaustion almost consumed him and he ached all over. "Okay. Send the girls to shower first. Call us when you're done so we can get in there. Then, we'll all

357

go on watch, half on, half off, till we know the coast is clear from Ninth Fleet."

Gail shook her head again. "Sally and I need to get the ship to a safe hidey hole near a gas giant as soon as possible, so you boys can shower first. All but Pete and Hugh were swimming in the sewers, so it'll do a lot to make the air in here breathable again if you shower now."

Ward stood, swaying only a bit, and said, "Aye, Captain. Call Hugh in so we can go."

Gail stood abruptly and grabbed Ward's arm. "Sit back down before you fall down. We better talk now or we won't have an opportunity for a day or more. Hugh can have a little more time with his people out there, who obviously love him, while we hash things out.

"So, how do you think they did?" Gail asked.

Ward sank back with a grateful sigh. "I notice you said *his people*. Care to explain."

Gail gave him a deep look. "Hugh scared me to death out there tonight, but also made me so proud. You, too, I'm sure. My heart stuck in my throat from the moment he charged across the street to save you, leading from the front like a platoon leader. It's what lieutenants do, but he isn't as replaceable as if he were one of five lieutenants in a company or one of twenty odd in a battalion. He is the heir apparent. Without that suit, he'd be dead right now. If the defenses had been more organized with anti-armor missiles, he *would* be dead regardless."

"If we had been on a world facing an organized foe, we would have attacked them differently," Ward added sternly, followed by a softened expression, "but he did passably well out there tonight, and not only at the warehouses. He accurately assessed the situation and acted appropriately. And got lucky. But *how* he did it, keeping control, always seeking ways to get civilians out of danger as he fought furiously, that's what mattered the most." Ward's expression almost softened enough to show Gail his pride in Hugh, catching himself just in time to keep his face hard.

Gail shook her head, giving him a glare. "Stop trying to fool everyone. I know better. You care for that boy as if he were your son. *Our* son."

Ward shook his head, "And what would happen to the universe if people found out I have a heart? It is Holy Writ in the Imperial Marines that I face supernovas with a smile, a joke, and a combat knife. Besides, I may have to fail him yet, so I can't even let *myself* know I think of him as one of the sons I lost."

As Gail looked at him with tenderness, Ward basked in her love as a black hole absorbs light, wholly and completely. She said softly, "I swear, Sean, you're impossible." A tear dripped from the corner of her eye.

Ward just nodded. "Hugh really did surprise me by the way he gathered people to him, even in the midst of battle, and forged a unit. He has it, that spark he'll need to restore the empire. Did you see how he pulled people together by what he said and did, right from the start? This just might work."

"I saw it, too. And the drones recorded every minute of it. I wouldn't have believed it otherwise. Truly impressive, not least of all because it came from the heart. It is who he is. So how much progress toward passing the test did he make today?" Gail's question, asked mildly, caught him off guard. Ward figured his decision would also affect what she chose to do about Maeve.

Ward shook his head. "Not completely there yet. There are still some things he has to prove to himself, if not to me, as well as finishing the alternate test, so we'll let it ride a little longer. Besides, there's Maeve."

Gail nodded. "You mentioned before that, as proctor, you felt Hugh's feelings as if in a mirror. I experienced that tonight with Maeve. She felt scared, rightfully, as well as very angry, when that terrorist came out of nowhere, but, overwhelmingly, her feelings were concern for the others and the mission. She never lost her head. She impressed me, too. What did you think about her?"

"As you made perfectly clear the last time we discussed her, it's your choice. You're in charge," he added, a bit huffily, which made her smile tightly.

"Yes, I am, but don't act like a little boy with hurt feelings. What do you think?"

"Well played." Tipping his head to the side he gave her a long look before answering, "She has potential. Obviously, she would make a great empress by herself. However, as his wife, whether she should carry the Imperial Galactic Starburst along with him, only time will tell."

"So do you think I should give her the oath?" Gail asked carefully.

"As I said, it's your choice," he answered seriously. "You know the risks if she fails. Besides which, you don't need my agreement, remember?"

Gail shook her head, "You really are living dangerously. But you're right, I don't need your permission. However, I still value your opinion."

Ward thought, then sighed. "Do it," he said, pushing himself upright. "I'm heading for a shower and then bed, in that order. This old man has done enough for one day."

Gail stood with him and kissed him soundly. "I'll see you later, old man. About ten hours from now, I'll talk to Maeve and you can talk to Hugh. Then we'll need to get them together."

Ward grasped Gail's arms firmly, his strength belying his claim to exhaustion as he returned her kiss, leaving her breathless. "That's all the energy I have left for now. I'll see you after I speak with Hugh."

Gail laughed huskily, "It's a date."

THE CROWD AROUND HUGH HADN'T completely thinned out since he had sworn in his Liberators, as they had begun to call themselves. Holding his helmet in his hands, a golden glow of euphoria washed over him as his men, and a few women, crushed around him. He knew he had to leave soon but didn't want to lose this moment.

The former security captain cleared his throat once, and then louder. Hugh looked over at him,

"What is it, Captain Sephedra?"

"We need to have a chain of command after you leave so there isn't infighting. Who's in charge?"

Hugh felt himself fall to earth in an instant, right into a minefield. He had to choose, avoiding favorites or what might be considered doing that. "What do you and the doctor suggest?" Hugh asked to gain time.

Captain Sephedra, a whip-thin, short, swarthy man, smiled a hard, knowing smile. "I think I have much more experience leading men than the doctor and should be in charge. I also know the people won't follow a former security force captain for fear he'll be worse than the Enlightened. The Enlightened used us to terrify people and that reputation won't go away overnight."

Hugh found Jacques standing at his elbow. "Doctor?" he asked formally.

"Unfortunately, I agree with everything he said. If I lead, it is likely to become a real mess and we'll lose."

Hugh gave them both a hard look. *Thanks for nothing.* Taking a minute, he let his gaze sweep the field. The liberators, regardless of sex or former background, were mixing indiscriminately. Then it hit him, *That's it.*

Looking again at the two men facing him, while ignoring the large group surrounding them, people who were not bothering to disguise their interest in the conversation, he explained, "In the empire, the most worthy rule. I am here being tested to see if I can live up to the Creed you swore to uphold tonight. If I do, I'm emperor; if not, I'll be dead. I want you to find the most worthy men and women and make them your leaders. Get rid of the armbands, get rid of the silver and black, and find a uniform you can all wear. Dr. Jacques understands what you're fighting for, better than anyone I've ever listened to, so let him be your official leader. But you need to have a steady hand to organize the fight, so you do that, Captain, until you find someone better. Just remember that *principle* must always come before *expedience*."

Dr. Jacques grabbed Hugh's hand, smiling tightly, unable to speak for a minute, tears welling in the corner of his eyes. Sephedra seemed to have grown taller with the trust and direction Hugh had given him. Coming to attention, he said, "I'll do it or die, Your Highness."

Hugh patted his shoulder, careful not to do damage with his augmented muscles. "I'm sure you will. I'll be back as soon as I can to see what help you need. Now, I'd better get going. The sooner I go, the quicker I'm back."

Choruses of "No!" greeted his announcement, but no one physically tried to get in his way as he walked to the ship, shaking hands and waving. As the entry port clanged shut behind him, he watched on the screen as the crowd broke up to let them take off safely. He half raised a hand they couldn't see.

ARCHIVED IMPERIAL CLASSIFIED DOCUMENTS

Declassified 24 September 3485
Test of Heirs Program
Proctor Course revised 2612
Importance of Stressing Heirs

Reminder-Purpose of the Test: The Test is intended primarily to determine the underlying character of an heir and, secondarily, develop greater character in the focus areas. In order to accomplish both, stressing the heir is recommended.

Stressing can be psychological, intellectual, emotional, spiritual, or most effectively, a combination of the above. It is not just creating a situation in which the heir must rise to the occasion, but it includes how they react to the reduction of that pressure. Pushing an heir to his, her, or their limits and then letting off the pressure, especially after a major success, allows the proctor to more effectively evaluate the heir. When the pressure is most intense, an heir has the opportunity and incentive to shine because they know they are in the spotlight. Often an heir reveals who they really are after the applause dies, the adrenaline drains away, and they have to just go on living. The proctor must get to know what an heir is made of in order to determine whether, in fact, they are worthy to carry the Galactic Starburst.

29

Success Has Its Drawbacks

Ambrose B, Macanak 52 or Solidarity System
1225 BBMT 9 November 3473

HOURS AFTER LIFTING OFF FROM Alpine, Hugh Cascade slouched in the copilot's seat moodily staring at the gas giant majestically rotating below him. At the moment, *Ambrose B* hid behind an odd little potato-shaped moon, about two hundred miles long and seventy-five wide, swinging in orbit around the gas giant. Sensors strained to find anything that might indicate a hostile presence in the system.

Shortly after they had arrived at the moon, Gail Felt began rotating the women for showers, meals, and sleep, the men having taken care of that in transit. Four hours ago, the women had completed their rotation in the showers, and now both men and women were either sleeping or had already grabbed a few hours.

All but him. He had now been up more than twenty-four hours, but just couldn't sleep. The adrenaline draining away after the high from the battle had left him dead inside, but his mind refused to let him rest. Hugh stared into the screens whose blankness did nothing to occupy his mind. Instead, he brooded over every word, every scene from Alpine, replaying over and over what had happened, what he had said or done. *Or didn't do.* Before Alpine, he hadn't even known he could feel so strongly about people having the right to choose how they wanted to be governed. *Save me from self-regard as impervious to reality as the Enlightened or the People's Committee, because this is where it leads.* He pitied the poor people back there and hoped the hundreds who had taken the oath with him at the spaceport would be enough to start a change, but a world could be a big place when starting with so few.

To himself, he renewed his promise to Jacques that required him, except if he should die, to return. Period. At its most fundamental level, honor meant this to him and he would live it no matter what. Besides keeping his word, he really wanted to come back to see what happened, but he had no idea when or if he could. Not knowing if events would intervene made him irritable, on edge. Duty and honor shouldn't be a *maybe*. Alpine proved that to him.

Why did he feel that, to an extent, he had failed? Instead of an orderly and peaceful takeover of the warehouses, he'd gotten a nightmare. *I should have expected it and planned for something like that.* He feared he would be beating himself up over each unnecessary death, every atrocity he had come across, for a long time. Most of the people back there had only wanted vengeance and the bloodier the better. He had no qualms over the justice he had dispensed—those men wouldn't be repeat offenders— but why hadn't he been able to prevent it?

To him, it seemed plain that for Alpine to survive, the people would have to learn how to forgive and forget. Hugh shook his head. After last night, that appeared to be the least likely outcome. Jacques would try, as would the Liberators. One of the warehouses they had taken over had been full of guns and riot vehicles, so between the food and the guns, he figured the good doctor had a chance of staying alive.

Then his mind drifted to how close Maeve had come to dying. As he had listened to it all through the open com, he had been impressed with how calm she had been. His plans had taken into account the possibility of the area becoming a war zone, which meant anyone could have died by a chance ricochet or been accidentally shot by one's friends. He accepted that for himself. If he had died trying to keep his word, he willingly would have paid the price. But he hadn't even suspected the danger he'd placed Maeve in when they began. What had almost happened with Zilda scared him to death. He wanted to chew out Sally Carr but knew his feelings to be unfair, unreasonable. Why had he allowed Ward and Gail to send Maeve? He should have simply vetoed the idea.

Comparing how he felt about all the people in danger last night, Dunn, Ward, Pam, Karen, Klostermann and others, to Maeve's near-death experience, only Maeve's peril knotted him up. *She's so young. And already been through so much.*

He stood up, raising his arms toward the ceiling and stretching out the kinks. Despite having worn the armored suit, he felt battered and bruised. He couldn't imagine what the other members of his team felt like.

The suit had saved him and Maeve's had saved her . . . Again his mind had drifted to her. Unbidden, the thought of what might have happened to her filled his mind. He'd have never forgiven himself if she'd been hurt. *Or any of the team, really.* No, he couldn't say that. He accepted that the rest of the team were combat veterans. They knew the risks going in. Maeve had been forced into her role as a military officer. *She never actually volunteered for anything, really.* He felt a stab of empathy for her. He had volunteered to take the test, but had he volunteered to be an heir? No. The urge to go to her and speak with her about their shared experience pulled at him. He felt closer to her in many ways because of it. But he also knew going to her and discussing these innermost thoughts and feelings could be interpreted as something more, and he didn't want that.

He'd heard the whispers and giggles among the women. The Marines were less shy. They openly chided him about Maeve. Tabi Fleisch, the only female Marine, went so far as to refer to her as "the future empress," though never when Maeve was within earshot. The crew had paired them up, even though he and Maeve had never even shown any interest in each other. And he preferred it that way.

Do I? Yes. The test came first. Plus Doña Carlota had made it clear that most women would be poorly served by dating him. As emperor, the pressure for him to marry, not to mention how that would affect the woman he might consider as a future wife, would be immense. Destructive, even. *No, I'm better off alone right now. Absolutely.*

Carefully, he checked the scopes. Still nothing. Thoughts of Maeve kept intruding on his mind, and he banished them, each and every one that cropped up.

Gail came in a bit later looking rested, or at least not as worn out as the last time he had seen her. She hit the PA before announcing, "Stand down. Ninth Fleet doesn't seem to be around. Standard two-person shifts until further notice."

Sally Carr came in a moment later and waited in silence for him to get out of her chair. Stepping to the hatch, he noticed his personal com blinking. Keying it, he acknowledged the call from Ward.

"We need to talk about Alpine, Your Highness."

Hugh agreed, then asked, "Can't we do this later, Top? I've been up over twenty-four hours."

"You chose to skip your sleep, Your Highness," Ward responded formally. *"You and I need to go over Alpine while it's fresh. We'll meet Gail and Maeve in a bit for equally pressing business. I'll come to your quarters."*

"Understood. If you think it's that time sensitive, we'll do it now. See you in a minute." Hugh knew his clipped tone didn't sound particularly kind or warm as he answered. He had a few things to say, too.

Hugh wondered what Ward wanted to discuss. Ward would have several trenchant comments to share about Hugh's threats, his promises, and breaking his promise to stay away from danger. In Hugh's experience, Ward's biting observations and pithy sayings could flay the deck plating off a supernova. He involuntarily shivered in anticipation. Regardless, he also had a steely resolve to discuss the situation about what had almost happened to Maeve.

Ward waited for Hugh outside of his cabin, standing at parade rest, his face inscrutable.

"Sergeant Major," Hugh said, nodding.

"Sire." Ward reached for the door control and opened it for Hugh.

Ward followed him into the cabin. Hugh sat down at the small desk and turned to face Ward, who remained standing. "Let's start with the hangar. Did you think at all about what you were saying and doing back there, or just spouting off?" Ward asked without preamble.

Ouch! Hugh thought about this question. Leaning back in his chair, he said, "I didn't really think about it at the time, but it is what I really feel and believe. Actually, I would have preferred to add that smug guy's corpse to the pile in the middle of the floor. Zilda's too, for that matter, but I settled for the middle ground."

Ward's face remained impassive. "Do you really intend to check back on this planet, thousands of parsecs from the empire, just to see that these people are free to make more bad choices? How do you think they got into this mess in the first place?"

"I don't know how they got into this situation and I really don't care," Hugh retorted. "Regardless of whether these people themselves or their great-great-grandparents made the bad decisions that got them here, everyone should be able to make their own choices. No one is so smart that they can run anyone else's life. I lost my temper over the kinetic weapons stations and the coercion there. Ninth Fleet knocking out the controls made it the empire's problem and therefore my responsibility. I hope Jacques can pull something together, so seeing what he accomplishes would make a trip worthwhile. Since I promised everyone I'd come back, I have to. As long as I'm not dead, that is."

In an offhand, conversational tone, Ward responded, "I'd hoped you made the promises and threats for that kind of reason. A long time ago, I learned that evil has to be allowed to exist because, without it, there would be no real choice at all. We may not like it, but bad must exist for good to have any value."

Hugh agreed. "True, but more importantly, no one should have to be forced or bribed to do what's right."

Ward nodded, a contemplative look on his face, before he spoke, "Very few emperors ever really get to the point of feeling deep in their bones the importance of personal freedom, almost all having lived an elite life. You are a unique man, Hugh Cascade, but I am afraid the trials of your uniqueness are just beginning."

Hugh gave him an unhappy look before Ward went on, "Zilda committing suicide by stepping in front of a bullet made me happy. That tied up a loose end and gave Dr. Jacques a better chance to succeed. Zilda couldn't resist sticking her nose back into your business and, if she hadn't gone after Maeve, might have caused Dr. Jacques and the others real grief." Here Ward stared hard into Hugh's eyes until Hugh nodded slowly in agreement. "Regardless, I think you made a good decision, letting her choose her fate. And, based upon her choice, Alpine will be better off without her."

"Except that decision endangered other members of the team, especially Maeve," Hugh interjected, coldly angry.

Ward looked him directly in the eye. "You were busy taking care of critical tasks no one else could do, so we handled it. Maeve is extremely capable. She lived for years on Pogue's cruiser and didn't get caught. On Alpine she did everything she needed to do until help could arrive. She came out uninjured, the precise reason she wore armor." The *I told you so* that could have followed went unsaid.

This conversation's direction startled Hugh, but he couldn't deny the truth of it. Ward went on, "You accomplished important and necessary things last night, including saving thousands of lives without getting killed, because of the armor. Dying back there would have been a bad thing for the empire. I just want to remind you of a little talk we had before Nighthawk, about relying on others to help you get the job done. Do we need to have that talk again, Your Highness?"

Hugh sighed. "No, Top, we don't need to talk about it again. You and Gail did a great job of coordinating. So did Maeve. Without everyone's best, we wouldn't have succeeded." He meant that sincerely.

Ward nodded before continuing in a hard voice, "Then you need to tell them, each of them, personally. One more thing,

I have never seen anything like what you did last night with your so-called Liberators, pulling together men who had been at each other's throats just minutes before and, by the force of your doing what's right, creating a unit. Also, pure inspiration, administering the Creed before you left. It gives them something to fight for, together. I think they'll truly have a chance." Ward's critique had turned into praise, something Hugh had rarely heard, and it stunned him. Ward quickly went on, not giving Hugh a chance to answer or even enjoy the moment, "Please stand and put out your hand."

Hugh's anticipation abruptly spiked as Ward brought out the bag. Hugh had expected to be reamed out, and instead he stood one step closer to his goal. "The heir protects the weak with mercy and justice, taking no gift of any man, but treating all men alike."

As the purple amethyst rose through the bag, Hugh would have sworn it almost levitated into his hand. A great strength spread through him as he held it, until both arms felt capable of lifting any weight, carrying any burden.

"Protecting all men and women, treating all equally, is often hard to do but essential to the existence of the empire. Release the amethyst."

Hugh did and it sank back through the bag.

"Now, sit. We have one more thing to discuss, something that affects you but over which you have no say."

Alarm bells rang in Hugh's brain, but he had no idea what Ward thought so important. "Okay, Top. What's that?"

Ward sat down on the end of the bunk, leaned forward with his hands on his knees, and gave him a grin. "I can see I have you worried. Good." His expression became stonily serious. "Throughout the history of the empire, heirs have gone out, just like you are doing, to take the Test of Heirs. When things were calm, they could often go one at a time to keep the death toll low, thereby preventing more heirs from dying than necessary. However, of the forty or so times the test has needed to be administered, a good fifteen to twenty have been less than orderly."

To Hugh, the direction of this conversation felt decidedly ominous, but he remained completely in the dark as to exactly where it might be going.

Ward plowed on, "These other times saw multiple heirs all taking the Test of Heirs simultaneously. They all knew only one could rule at a time, and that once an heir completed the test and placed his nanogems into the starburst, any other heir who had begun the test would automatically die. It didn't matter to them at that time, because the great houses were all trying to control the empire and accepted the risk for that reason."

Ward took a breath. "That does not accurately describe the situation after the Qabal invasion . . . or now. During both periods, heirs disappeared without a trace during the test. The empire, then and now, faced desperate peril. So, as many heirs as possible have taken the test simultaneously for the good of the empire. Today, we desperately need someone to succeed as soon as possible and can't wait for heirs to try separately. That is why we asked you to risk your life before we knew exactly what the situation might be with the other heirs. Does that make sense?"

Hugh relaxed a little, still confused. "I guess so. We need an emperor yesterday, so we have to take the chance to maximize the odds of success. I've agreed to take my chances with that for the good of the empire. But I thought you said you had no one else."

Ward stared hard into Hugh's eyes. "We did say that, as we simply didn't know about the others who had gone out to take this test. We lost track of them. But now it's not just you in danger, Your Highness. We have found another heir."

At that moment, it suddenly began to make sense: Gail's refusal to let him or Maeve go out separately on Alpine; Maeve with him in the center of the protection detail, both of them in armor. Appalled, he whispered, "*Maeve's* an heir?"

Ward nodded. "Captain Felt is giving Maeve the choice to take the test right now."

Hugh exploded in a panic, "No, I won't allow it." If he became emperor, Maeve would die! *How can Ward do this? How can Gail do this to Maeve?*

Ward waited silently, examining Hugh before saying, "You don't have a choice. Gail decided, as Maeve's proctor, and not even I could stop her. It is likely at least one of you will die before the end, if not both of you. The odds are against you, which is why, if you recall, back on Jeffco, I didn't want you to take the test until you were older." Hugh definitely remembered Ward being *very* unhappy in that initial meeting with Admiral Hollister and Doña Carlota. Ward had known the low probability of Hugh passing the test and had wanted to avoid the downside. It hadn't been possible, and so here he sat. Alive, somehow.

Pausing once more for Hugh to grudgingly agree, he went on. "It doesn't seem right or fair but here you are. Both of you are risking your lives. There is one more thing you and Maeve need to know before we go on, but which we believe it is better to tell you together. You have at least a few minutes while Gail has her little chat with Maeve." Ward pushed on his knees, standing up, and walked out with only an enigmatic smile.

As Hugh sat pondering what he could do to protect Maeve against this new threat, a sudden unexplainable elation began to grow, starting in his hands, before it swept over him completely. What is this? Hugh wondered. It felt like nanites, but always before, the sensation had been associated with Ward giving him a crystal. He'd have to ask Ward later.

But then it hit him: *Maeve! Gail must be giving her the stones!*

A Primer in Core Empire Political Theory

Civil Government Organization of the Empire
Appendix K:308—Complete Speeches and Statements by
Imperial Leaders

Speech by Emperor Charles Roland to His Family, 4 August 3307,
during his final illness.

Persuasion is the art of encouraging another person to do what you want them to do when they did not initially agree. Some of you may think I never use persuasion. [Laughter] But I assure you that it is essential.

If I don't give people a good reason to follow me, whether in the military or civilian government, I would achieve nothing. During the reconquest, I would soon have been out there all alone and the Qabal would have won if the individual spacer had not agreed to the end being worth the price. Ultimately each man and woman had to decide. I spent most of my efforts not defeating the Qabal, but convincing my people. The same has been even more true since I came to the throne. People must *want* to do difficult things and my job is to find a way to convince them . . . with a minimum of arm twisting. [More laughter]

[Raul, the next emperor, attended this meeting.]

30

Equal Footing

Ambrose B, Macanak 53 or Sociality System
1300 BBMT 9 November 3473

MAEVE UCH ROBERT WALKED DOWN the passageway in response to Captain Gail Felt's summons with more than a little trepidation. As she entered the captain's cabin, Gail smiled, before waving Maeve to a chair. "Have a seat. We have a lot to talk about."

Maeve felt an odd tension in the air, something she hadn't sensed since she'd come aboard, which only increased her anxiety.

Gail's eyes focused on her like a laser. Maeve settled her thoughts to neutral, sitting with a natural grace. The silence stretched uncomfortably before Gail spoke, "I have been doing some homework on you." Maeve suddenly felt dread. *What now?* Gail gave a small smile before going on. "Nothing bad. We just need to discuss Alpine. Why did you kill Zilda?"

She had been expecting the question, fretting about it, to tell the truth. Why had she shot her? Taking a breath, she looked straight at Gail. "I could say that Hugh had decreed a death sentence on her if she ever showed up again, and that would justify my actions. But truthfully, that certainly doesn't really explain all of my feelings or even the main reason I did."

Gail just nodded. "Go on."

"I could say I shot her because she threatened to have me raped and joked about it." Maeve's hands began to move in her lap.

Gail nodded again. "Another excellent reason, which would be completely acceptable."

Maeve's hands twisted together, hard. "But really, it happened by accident. When she shot, it startled me and I fired back. Regardless, I should have shot her anyway. Everything we stand for, she is against. To her, laws are something to bind others and destroy them. If I had left her alive, she might have stopped Dr. Jacques from accomplishing anything at all because she would have used his decency against him. No law exists back there except what we brought with us." Maeve paused, suddenly unsure of her reasons, before asking, "Shouldn't I have shot her? Isn't that what the Imperial Creed means?"

Gail smiled. "You did the right thing, and you're correct as to what the Creed stands for. I am glad that you've thought it through. If you were again faced with the choice and chose to kill her, your motivations would still be in keeping with the Creed. Regardless, we wouldn't have left her behind. Alive. I am very proud of you, Maeve. You did everything you needed to do to keep yourself and others safe until help arrived. Your quick thinking with opening the com and sending the alert made all the difference." She smiled again. "So, let's talk about my research."

Maeve wondered why she suddenly felt so light. On Alpine, she had directly taken another human life for the second time in her life but, unlike killing the assassin who had shot her father, this time it had been tearing her up inside. Strangely, the fact that she had fired accidentally seemed to make it worse in her mind. Gail approving of her actions, as well as her motives, made all the difference. Her hands stilled and she sat forward to listen.

"I confirmed my suspicions as to why Admiral Davies assigned Priscilla Jenks to watch over you, or more accurately, why you were with her. I do have a question, however. Admiral Davies didn't assign you, Priscilla, and the others to *Bring It*, so how exactly did you end up there?"

Maeve hesitated, then answered, "We posed as a communications intelligence unit based at Camp Y, but attached to Home Fleet, not the base. That way no one ever bothered us. Captain Pogue needed a team that did what we were supposed to do, and I understand Camp Y didn't want to give up one of their own units, so they pointed Pogue at us. His XO, Paul Bhat, showed up in the middle of the night and told Priscilla that, whether we liked it or not, we were going with him immediately. He then dragged us off. The admiral couldn't be reached—he was off-planet—and using the archeon net to contact him might have blown our cover, so two hours later we were on *Bring It* headed toward Sector Thirteen."

Gail sighed. "I thought as much. Priscilla would never have blown her cover on a mission. With protecting you being her top priority, she probably didn't see any other alternative, so she went along with Bhat shanghaiing all of you rather than trying to find a creative way to avoid going. She remained your proctor until she died."

Maeve's brain became a jumble of conflicting emotions, memories, and thoughts. She struggled to keep all of that from her face.

Gail sat silently for a minute. Quietly, she started again, "As the only available female proctor, I have been assigned to you. Several years ago, I had an heir. Just like Priscilla with you, I protected her during the early days after the coup but, unlike your situation, my heir died. I'll tell you about her someday, perhaps. But now we have some critical business to take care of for the empire." Gail's eyes became bright, alive, as she sat up straighter. Maeve felt completely unsure of what might come next.

"Maeve, you have a critical decision to make. You *are* an heir, but one who has not yet begun the Test of Heirs. Hugh has begun the test, but what you do not know is that if Hugh fails, he must die."

The statement shocked her; she had never heard of anything so barbaric. Hugh had agreed to this? He must be dumber than he looked. And Gail seemed to be offering her the same thing.

"The reason it's an all-or-nothing proposition is that the empire can't afford to have competing emperors. Also, any heir who is taking the test when a new emperor completes all the steps necessary to rule, dies. Normally heirs proceed alone. However, as at the time of Charles Roland, any heir who is qualified must go forward in any manner available if the empire is to be saved. I would normally wait until Hugh succeeds, or fails, to ask you, because of that, but the empire is running out of time."

"Knowing that, Maeve uch Robert, are you willing take the Test of Heirs? If you decide to take the test, there is something Ward and I need to talk about with you and Hugh together. There is a way to go forward where neither of you dies, but for now, you need to know that death is a very real possibility. To pass the test, you will need to show good character in extreme circumstances, just like Hugh did aboard *Bring It* and on Alpine yesterday. To proceed is your choice, and yours alone. You can take as long as you like to decide; we can even continue this another time."

Maeve's brain froze. Why did everyone around her have to die for the empire? Strangely, that question relaxed her as she thought about her mother and father willingly serving the empire. They had believed it worth the price. So had Priscilla and Qi Mai Ling. The empire wasn't perfect, but it tried to stop animals in human form like Pogue and Wally Welks and Zilda Wilniak from running wild. That by itself might be enough to justify the sacrifice Gail was asking her to make. As for Hugh, he had agreed. How could she do less?

"I don't need any more time. Yes, I'll take the test," Maeve said quietly. A fiery resolve welled up in her, confirming her decision.

Not commenting on her declaration, Gail simply nodded and brought out a curiously made bag, just like the one Priscilla had shown her that last day. Maeve tried to focus on it but again couldn't tell what to make of it. Quietly, almost in a whisper, Maeve said in wonder, "That's exactly like the bag Priscilla showed me the day she died."

Gail's eyebrows raised. "What happened?"

Maeve teared up. "She pulled it out and had me repeat the Imperial Creed."

Gail appeared to hold her breath as she asked, "And then what happened?"

Maeve shrugged. "I felt something odd, but then she ordered the bag to self-destruct. I never saw her alive again."

Gail seemed to relax slightly and nodded, as if to herself, before focusing on Maeve again. Speaking formally to her, Gail began, "Maeve uch Robert, please stand." For the first time since she had come into Gail's quarters, Maeve noticed the imperial flag now hung on the wall behind Gail. It hadn't been up other times when Maeve had visited this cabin. Her apprehension increased. Coming to attention, she waited.

"Maeve uch Robert, being an heir in the line of succession to the Throne of Constantine, Core Empire, you are about to embark upon the Test of Heirs. The purpose of the test is to determine whether you are worthy to occupy the Throne of Constantine, to carry the Galactic Starburst, and to rule the Core Empire. Before I give you more information, I must insist that you promise to keep everything that is about to happen confidential."

Maeve wondered why Gail would even ask her, but she gave the obvious answer, "Yes, of course."

Gail flashed a brief smile of satisfaction. "Good. The Galactic Starburst is a representation of the galaxy seen from above and worn over the left breast. It will allow you to disable or destroy imperial ships and facilities that are in rebellion. If you choose to go forward, your options will be to succeed, be cleansed of the nanites, or die. As for cleansing the nanites, there is no way currently available in the empire to cleanse you, something you should know before proceeding. So, really, your options are succeed or die. Do you willingly agree to take the Test of Heirs?"

Maeve had no idea what the proper words were, so she simply said, "Yes?"

Gail nodded her acceptance. "To pass the test, you must prove your worthiness and understanding of what it means to rule. Recite the Imperial Creed."

Maeve momentarily froze. The Imperial Creed? She had joined in saying it just a few hours ago, searing its principles, if not its words, once more on her mind and soul. Even so, because reciting it had been bad for your health on *Bring It*, she didn't know if she had it perfectly memorized. How about the short version? Concentrating, she hesitantly answered, "Protection, Integrity, Judgment, Justice, Sacrifice, Virtue, To the Death?"

Gail imperceptibly shook her head before setting the bag on the desk. The sack spread itself open as Maeve watched, revealing fantastic beauty. Seven exquisite, breathtaking gems lay jumbled together. She couldn't tear her gaze away from them. She drank them in, marveling in the depth and richness of each one. Maeve finally felt Gail's eyes on her and realized that Gail had been waiting patiently while Maeve's emotions surged through her.

"Maeve uch Robert, the seven gems you see before you represent the test. The gems themselves have no real power but are impregnated with nanites that will become part of you until the day you die. As you pass each portion of the test, you will receive the gem it represents with its nanites. After today, only you and I may ever handle the gems again. Any other person will die. Do you understand this restriction?"

Maeve whispered, "Yes."

Gail went on, "These nanogems are integral to the functioning of the Imperial Galactic Starburst. Remember that the coup destroyed Emperor Cyrus' starburst, so a new one must be created for the gems and their nanites to plug into. The nanites on the gems of an emperor or empress activate the starburst and remain alive only until the moment of that individual's death, at which time they turn to slag. They are buried with the dead ruler and replaced on the starburst by the nanogems of the new monarch. However, the nanites cannot be fully awakened until after the gems are earned, so they can be placed in their proper places by you, and you alone. Once they are placed, the starburst will become deadly to any other person who attempts to wield it. Pick up the purple amethyst."

As if in a trance, she reached out with her left hand. She cradled the clear, light-purple stone in her palm, gazing at it before closing her hand upon it. A tingling warmth immediately enveloped her palm before running deep into her hand and arm. It seemed to project a shield of safety around her, repelling all ills.

Gail spoke firmly, a voice of deep understanding, "Now that you hold the amethyst, no one except you can handle it and live. The nanites will protect you and keep you safe, helping to heal you if you are injured or sick. Now, holding the gem in your left hand before you, repeat after me: I will provide protection to the weak as well as to every citizen."

Maeve stuttered as she started, helped by Gail, "I will provide protection to the weak as well as to every citizen."

"Replace the gem back on the cloth and take the topaz with your right hand."

Reluctantly, she let go of the purple gem, the shade of lilacs, one of her favorite flowers. Warmth filled her heart even as she did. Sighing, she forced her hand open, lovingly placing the amethyst back onto the table. Immediately, she picked up the topaz. The same amazing warmth filled her hands and arms.

"Holding the gem before you, repeat after me: My word is unquestioned because integrity is the bedrock of my being."

Confidently now, Maeve recited, "My word is unquestioned because integrity is the bedrock of my being." She saw a golden blaze erupt through her fingers, the topaz sealing her promise.

"Every citizen, every person in the galaxy must be able to believe that if you promise protection, you will protect. If you promise destruction, you will destroy. Every word you say must be true. Place the gem back on the cloth and take the sapphire with your other hand."

She now understood why Hugh said what he did back there. Eagerly, she replaced the golden stone and picked up the rich, royal blue sapphire. Disappointingly, she felt nothing special.

"Taking the stone, touch it between your eyes, repeating after me: I seek always to exercise true judgment in all of my acts."

Carefully placing the stone between her eyes, she felt sudden coolness spread through her forehead, behind her eyes, all the way to her ears. Her thoughts suddenly had a crystalline clarity she had never felt before. Clearly, she responded, "I seek always to exercise true judgment in all of my acts."

"Clearness of sight, depth of understanding, true hearing, all are required in order to act well. Wisdom is more important than learning. Place the gem back on the cloth and take the emerald with your right hand."

Slowly, she lowered her sapphire to the cloth, eyes lost in its brilliant, blue depths as she did. It belonged to her; she knew it. She placed the sapphire with the topaz and amethyst, taking the emerald with her empty hand.

"Taking the stone, touch it briefly to your lips, then repeat after me: I will administer justice that is stern, fair, and impartial, fearing no man's censure, taking no man's gift."

She rather feared justice. Pogue had made a point of calling all the punishments he had administered just. Slowly, she touched it to her lips for a moment. Again, nothing, but this time she felt relieved. "I will administer justice that is stern, fair, and impartial, fearing no man's censure, taking no man's gift."

"*Doing* what is right is more difficult than *knowing* what's right. You will often not know if you have acted correctly, possibly not until well after the fact. You must have a deep, securely anchored sense of right to judge in the face of dissent and criticism. Be firm, be fair, be consistent. Place the gem back on the cloth and take the ruby with your left hand."

Maeve traded the stones and looked up at Gail.

"Taking the stone, touch it to your heart, repeating after me: I fear no sacrifice necessary to uphold my oath. I will carry every burden of my office, whatever the price."

Suddenly, the stone seemed to burn her to the very core, searing her heart. Focusing on Gail as tears blurred her vision, she wondered if she had done something wrong. *Should it hurt this much?* Tears burned down her cheeks, but she forced herself to say, in spite of the pain, "I fear no-no," she stuttered, "sacrifice necessary to uphold my oath. I will carry every burden of my office, whatever the price." As she finished speaking, the stone ceased to burn, a strange sensation replacing the pain, one of being able to accomplish whatever she set out to do.

"All burdens exact a price. Know this as you take up this test. They also grant great strength. Place the gem back on the cloth and take the diamond with both of your hands."

Hastily, she put down the ruby and picked up the diamond, a glory of a stone filled with hints of the entire rainbow. Its faceted surface drew her in, filling her with wonder. She felt like singing or flying just holding it.

"Holding the stone, cup it out in front of you, repeating after me: Perfect virtue is unattainable, but I will seek it as my goal in all I do."

Maeve almost couldn't concentrate on the oath. Gail had called it a *stone*, but she didn't know! Holding it, warmth radiated through her. It was no simple, cold rock, but powerful, its strength filling the center of her being. It would never be just a *stone* to her. As she thought that, bottomless sorrow that she would never be perfectly worthy of this virtue gem, swept through her. *But I will try!* "Perfect virtue is unattainable, but I will seek it as my goal in all I do."

"Virtue brings both deep temporary sadness and overwhelming joy. Whether fearing the sadness or choosing wrongly, either will deny you the joy that knows no description. Place the gem back on the cloth and take the onyx with your right hand."

Maeve hesitantly reached out. Some stones had been friendly, others not so much. The onyx appeared forbidding and cold to her, but she forced herself to pick it up.

"Taking the stone, hold it in front of you as a sword haft, then repeat after me: I will fulfill my oath to the citizens of the empire to the death. So help me God."

"I will fulfill my oath to the citizens of the empire to the death. So help me God." Maeve felt nothing but certainty. She and the gems had promised each other and both would keep their promises. A vagrant thought intruded: Hugh must have made the same oath; no wonder he acted so seriously. A flicker of compassion for him overcame her.

"Place the gem back on the cloth."

Maeve released the onyx, following which, the cloth quickly folded itself back into a bag. Suddenly, for a moment, joy drowned her, a depth of feeling that had been gaining strength throughout the oath, an elation amplified and reflected from someone nearby. Gail, perhaps? She didn't think so. Maeve watched as Gail continued, untouched by the emotions swirling in the room. *Can't she feel what's going on?* She saw Gail smiling and happy, but that didn't reflect the way Maeve's heart pounded at this moment.

Gail put the bag away. "Do not seek the stones until and unless I release them back to you. They will kill you if you do. Do you understand?"

"I understand," Maeve answered softly. Hesitantly, she asked, "Is the men's oath the same?"

Gail smiled a little. "Similar. Very similar. But being men, it has to be different. After all, men are different, aren't they?"

Maeve smiled back, crookedly. "Aren't they just!" Gail chuckled, which made Maeve laugh, and then both were laughing.

Gail pointed to the chair. "Sit." Maeve did and Gail went on. "One more thing. We're going to tell Hugh you took the oath. If you both live to complete the test, you will have a choice to make at that point. We will discuss that choice when he and Ward arrive. So, if you understand what I have said to this point, please stand again."

Maeve wondered, a little resentfully, what kind of promise she now had to make. Must she agree to let Hugh win if they both passed the test? Gail brought out the bag again. This threw her off-balance. What now? "Hold out your hand. The heir sacrifices her all for others." The ruby rose through the bag. Maeve didn't want to take it. Sacrifice cost her too much!

"Take it," prompted Gail. Reluctantly, Maeve took it.

"Sacrifice is essential to success but is always worth it. Sacrifice is a choice of giving up something in service of something greater. Giving up the Academy could be a partial sacrifice because it served the empire's needs while you needed to hide for your own safety. That qualifier does not apply to your time on *Bring It*, where you chose to make several significant sacrifices: You gave up your true personality and identity to further the mission. You kept your head down when you desired to run to help your friends. You took a major chance by revealing yourself and then aiding people you didn't even know. The number one thing you did, however, you chose to do without any thought of reward or benefit to yourself: you blew your cover to help the heir. A truly major sacrifice."

That doing the right thing could be a sacrifice surprised her. What else could she have done under the circumstances? Was it likely that they would have found her if she had remained silent? Sure, ship's security found all of her friends, one by one, and killed them, but that hadn't mattered when it came time to open the way for Hugh to escape.

"Please let it go."

Just as reluctantly as she had taken it, she let it go.

"The heir demonstrates good judgment."

The sapphire melted through the side of the bag, rested a moment on Maeve's hand, then melted back through the side of the bag. As the stone touched her hand, the odd clarity she had felt before returned. This time it did not fade, however.

Gail smiled. "Being able to prioritize, determine what is important, then stick to those things is probably the easiest and most difficult thing you'll have to do. Successfully passing life's big trials depends upon what you decide beforehand. Good choices lead to good outcomes. You acted carefully on *Bring It* to carry out your mission to help the empire, always gathering as many facts as you could. Then you acted decisively, those two elements being the essence of judgment."

"The heir is true to the death."

The onyx rose to the surface. She took it. She knew what kind of price that stone really charged. Her mother, her father, Priscilla, and her team, even Tim Kennion, who she'd never met but watched die unexpectedly on *Bring It*, all knew the price. Yet, though the onyx appeared black as night, it seemed to ease her heart with light, disagreeing with her bleak assessment of the value of duty. Death did not end everything, it seemed to say, and doing right always exceeded the price extracted.

Gail smiled sadly. "Sometimes, most times, we don't see why we should make the ultimate sacrifice, yet back on *Bring It* you set those demolition charges that you believed would kill you, too, for your duty to the empire."

Suddenly it made perfect sense. If you didn't understand when you received that stone, you never would, Maeve supposed.

"The heir is virtuous."

Maeve couldn't believe her ears. Of all the gems, the diamond meant the most to her and seemed most likely to be the one she would never earn. To her, virtue symbolized her mother, perfect, sweet, loving, unstained by the world around her. She had never believed she could measure up to her ideal. *Gail thinks I'm virtuous!* As in a trance, Maeve held out her left hand. The diamond rose through the bag and she grasped it firmly, almost desperately. Her heart soared as she squeezed her hand around it. Her eyes shown with the joy she felt. She sensed light coming from every part of her, all powered by this diamond.

"Virtue," Gail began, "is not something you can buy or build. Virtue is something you are, in thought, deed, and heart. Never let it go, because if you do, it is extremely difficult, if not almost impossible, to reclaim. Even when given a chance to take the easy way out, you tried not to shoot Zilda and her people. You remained true on *Bring It* when it would have been so easy to fall to the level of those around you. You also were more worried about others on Alpine than for yourself. Let go of the diamond."

The diamond felt welded to her spirit, a part of her forever. She looked desperately at Gail, begging silently for her to let her keep the diamond.

"Maeve," Gail prompted, gently, "let go of the stone. It only *represents* virtue. Your virtue existed inside you already before you took it."

Maeve gradually opened her hand and let the diamond slide back onto, then through, the bag. She sighed her regret before realizing that the feelings within her hadn't changed. Gail had spoken the truth, you either lived it or lived without it. It would never, ever be a rock you could own.

Gail put the bag into her desk drawer before hitting the com. "Ward, you can come on down now."

ARCHIVED IMPERIAL CLASSIFIED DOCUMENTS

Declassified 24 September 3485
Test of Heirs Program
Proctor Course revised 2612
Failing Heirs

Unethical behavior by an heir violates the Emperor's Creed in a number of ways, including but not limited to Integrity, Judgment, Justice, Virtue, and Protection. Any of the foregoing should result in failing an heir.

Experience has shown that when heirs are in too close of proximity to each other during the test, the pressure of competition results in numerous violations of the oath. One problem is that heirs have been known to cheat for self-preservation. Another is the simple need to win at all costs. As a result of the potential for this increased pressure, it is strongly advised that heirs not share ships or otherwise be kept close together.

The third danger is from proctors becoming involved to the point of attempting to interfere, up to and including sabotaging, another heir competing with their heir. Actions of this nature will result in the failure of the proctor's heir and the removal of the proctor from the program by execution.

31

Another Way Forward

Ambrose B, Macanak 53 or Sociality System
1305 BBMT 9 November 3473

A RAP CAME AT THE hatch. Focused by the sound on who might be waiting outside, Maeve uch Robert suddenly knew Hugh Cascade stood there. Stunned, she realized she could feel him clearly.

"Come," Gail Felt called through the com.

Sean Ward and Hugh stepped in, making the cabin very cozy. Hugh gave Maeve a questioning look but, more surprising than the look, she seemed to be able to *feel* his confusion. *Can he sense my emotions, too?* Immediately, she felt deeply embarrassed at the very idea.

Gail glanced around before evidently coming to a decision. "Maeve, sit on the bed so Ward can take your chair. Hugh, sit next to Maeve."

Maeve noticed a look of apprehension on Hugh's face, while feeling his edginess. *Why is he so jumpy?* She watched Hugh move carefully around the chair to sit on the other end of the bed. *What's his problem? I showered.*

Ward examined them speculatively a moment before raising an eyebrow toward Gail, she simply bowed right back to him. "Thanks a lot, Captain," Ward said, not sounding at all grateful.

"Of course, Sergeant Major. You, after all, are the one who has been pointing out, continuously and loudly I might stress, your leadership role as the head of the Imperial Proctors, from day one of Hugh's test." Maeve could plainly see Gail's prim satisfaction as they bantered.

Ward shrugged. "Appropriately." He again faced Maeve and Hugh directly. "Couple of housekeeping things we need to discuss, as well as rules. Sire, I am officially notifying you that Maeve has taken the oath." Maeve realized that the emotions coming from him didn't include surprise or resentment, just anger. *Is he mad at me or them?* She didn't get a chance to think about it very long because the briefing continued immediately without either Gail or Ward asking for questions.

Impishly, seeming to relish the situation, Gail took over. "My turn. To this point, Maeve has received the ruby for sacrifice, the sapphire for judgment, the diamond for virtue, and the onyx for to the death." Maeve blushed a little as Hugh's admiration washed over her like a warm tide.

Ward broke in at that point. "As for Hugh, early on, he showed exceedingly good judgment and discernment, for which he received the sapphire of judgment. After *Bring It*, he received the topaz for integrity and emerald for justice."

He got the sapphire for judging me. Bitterness crept into her thoughts. As if she could read Maeve's mind, Gail's voice broke through her introspection. "Miss uch Robert," she began more formally, "I want you to know he did much more to earn judgment than just your interview. He has, in fact, earned the sapphire for numerous decisions he made before and after your interview, including the way he handled Peterson." Gail caught Maeve's eye until Maeve, somewhat unwillingly, nodded her understanding.

Ward continued, "Finally, Hugh earned the amethyst of protection, often one of the most difficult to demonstrate, on Alpine. You have both done well.

"The test parameters have been explained to both of you, including the fact that there are only a few ways out of the test. Pass it, submit to a nanite cleansing operation to remove all traces of them from your body—something not available at present—or die in failure. You have been told that if one of you places their gems in the starburst first, all other heirs die. Pass or die are the only options you know about."

Hugh's face became stoic, but his emotions roiled under the surface. Maeve felt anger, fear, and something else radiating from Hugh. *Protecting me again. That's getting to be a real habit with him. Haven't I proven I can take care of myself?*

Ward stopped for a moment, giving them a hard look. "What is up with you two? Before we go on, we need to clear the air." Hugh shrugged, but his apprehension added to her own. Inside she cringed; she didn't want anyone knowing exactly how she felt. Her emotions belonged to her! But what about Hugh? She could feel Hugh's eyes on her and the concern inside him. He *did* know how she felt. Internally, she writhed. Did she own nothing, have nothing by herself alone anymore?

She almost didn't hear Hugh begin to speak, "I, and I think *we*, have been feeling something weird. I know what Maeve is feeling, and I think she can do the same with me." Maeve turned to look at Hugh, surprised to see him looking searchingly at her. They *were* sensing each other's emotions. She blushed at the implications and quickly turned to face Ward.

Gail leaned forward intently. "That's not possible. Only nanites tuned to each other can let their hosts feel anything, and then only for a proctor who has been assigned that heir."

Awkwardly, Maeve said quietly, "I can feel him and I know his emotions exactly when we are this close." She gave Hugh a sidewise look to see him nod in agreement.

Gail sat back, a look of total disbelief on her face. "Ward? Have you ever heard of anything like this?"

Ward shook his head. "Never." He faced Hugh and Maeve. "The Gift, as it is called, is nothing more than a nano-transponder implanted in every proctor as well as every heir. If a proctor knows what to look for, he or she can feel the assigned heir. A proctor also receives a reflection of their heir's emotions so the test can be more accurate. I am not discounting anything you two have said, though."

Maeve hesitantly added, "My father mentioned something about gifts making it easier to get close to people. It didn't make sense, but this might explain some of it."

Ward looked pensive, apparently thinking. "Your father liked being known as an eccentric and could be very odd, but Robert and his ancestors were around the imperial family a lot over the last thousand years. They could know things about the Trace and Gift that proctors don't."

Maeve colored slightly. "Maybe the Gift let me know about Hugh, that he might be different, even from the moment he stepped onto *Bring It*. That may be why I decided to help him."

Turning toward Maeve, Hugh looked like he suddenly understood something that had been bothering him. "Ever since you arrived, I have usually known where you were *on the ship*, when I haven't been preoccupied, but I pushed it away as being some sort of emotional thing. Then, just now while I waited after talking with Ward, I felt a wave of joy that made no sense. Probably when you took the oath, our connection became stronger."

That could be nice, whispered a traitorous little voice. Aloud, she asked, "Can this be turned off?"

"No," Ward stated firmly, "you would have to be cleansed and that's not possible at this time." Facing them, he went on, "But we really came here to discuss something that affects the two of you together, and this nanite glitch, or whatever it is, could be useful. There is a fourth way for the two of you to complete the test. Emperor Dave set it up specifically for this situation, when two descendants of Constantine Jackson take the test at the same time. If both pass, and are not closely related, they can become co-rulers, just like Ira and Clara or Keiko and Christos. They both take a starburst, which controls, as you have been told, ships and facilities of the empire. I believe, from the historical records, that Dave added this because of what he saw in his parents Jack and Evie who ruled jointly. Apparently, Evie continued to act as queen of Green Gardens after Jack died, though she never formally took the crown of the empire. There is some question on that because Dave definitely set up the test with her. Regardless, to be more explicit, you would be emperor and empress together as husband and wife."

As Ward said this, Maeve felt from Hugh a sense of shock. As the meaning of Ward's words fully hit her, she and Hugh, at exactly the same moment, jumped up, exploding as one.

She heard Hugh's voice booming in the small cabin, "I've given up everything for the empire: my choice as to what I do, who I'll be, in order to try and save it! I won't let you take this last choice from me."

Maeve's voice joined Hugh's. "You're matching us up for the good of the empire? Where is love and happiness in all of this? I've given up my teenage years and what for? Why can't I have what my parents had?" she yelled as tears streamed down her cheeks.

How could Gail do this to her? She'd become Hugh's equal less than twenty minutes ago and now she *had* to agree to be his wife. Never!

Back stiff against the bulkhead, she continued her tirade. Hugh faced Ward and Gail from the middle of the room. Even through her maelstrom of emotions, she agreed with Hugh. They should have the freedom to make the most important decision in their lives. What freedom would she ever have, would *they* have, if they *had* to marry each other!? The empire asked too much!

After about thirty seconds of absolute bedlam, Ward boomed out, overpowering them both, *"At ease,* both of you." Hugh had taken a moment to catch his breath, preparing to continue, but Ward's roar stopped him cold. Even so, Hugh inflated his chest, ready to ignore the order, when Maeve saw Ward spear Hugh with a look and point to the bed. *"Sit!"* Ward ordered. Hugh shut up and sat. Gail gave Maeve a similar look and she shut up and sat without being told.

"That's better," Gail said. Her tone made Maeve feel as if she were a teenager being grounded. She could feel Hugh holding himself in, too. Such internal discipline impressed her.

Gail's voice became deadly serious. "You know what's at stake for both of you, personally, as well as for the empire, so grow up. You don't have to get married at the end of this test, but it is an option you need to keep in mind because if you both survive to that point, the *alternative* is that one of you dies. As for marriage, there are many independently good reasons for making that choice. However, if one of you dies beforehand, being co-rulers won't be an option or a problem anymore, so relax."

Maeve couldn't believe her ears. *Relax?* The ridiculous command made her want to jump back up and start yelling again. The second option of having her nanites cleansed didn't exist, and she doubted she would ever choose it anyway. That left marrying Hugh Cascade at the end of the test or one of them dying. What kind of choice would that be? She could tell Hugh didn't like the options any more than she did. *Of course, Hugh might be dead, so it wouldn't matter,* a little voice whispered. That thought brought no relief, sending shivers of apprehension up and down her spine instead. She caught Hugh looking at her, a questioning look on his face.

Ward stared solemnly at them, "There are worse things than marriage, believe me. Also, this is a very unusual situation. As proctors, we were trained *not* to put heirs taking the test together for several good reasons. A competition that is life or death can bring out the worst even in the best of people, including cheating, manipulating other heirs by creating false alliances, sabotage, and intentionally harming the other heir. However, we are proceeding with you together because we have no choice, which is why we explained the one positive exit strategy where both of you survive."

As she considered the thought, Ward continued, "Therefore, you will both be evaluated, from now on, as to how well you work *together*, as well as personally embodying the principals of the oath. And we *will* enforce all of the rules, no matter the cost."

Ward's face lost its hardness, in fact seeming to be a bit amused to Maeve. "And marriage is not as bad as death, but right now we need to discuss where *Ambrose B* goes next."

Gail gave Ward the evil eye and muttered to him, "Not as bad as death, huh. You better hope not." Ward just gave her a half smile with a twinkle in his eye but didn't respond. Maeve, despite herself, wondered what that meant for a moment.

Hugh noisily sucked in air, indicating he had been holding his breath, waiting for Ward to finish speaking. "Okay, so where are we going?" Hugh asked.

Gail suddenly looked much more serious. "Ward?"

"First, I want to ask Maeve some questions," Ward began as he focused solely on Maeve. "You said several false emperors had come through Nighthawk and been stopped by Pogue?"

"Two or three. He blew the first ship out of space. On the next one, he tortured the crew to death. I only heard about it," she shivered as she spoke, "and I don't want to talk about it. That made Priscilla decide to set up the scuttling charges, to allow real heirs to get through, I guess." Thinking for a moment, she continued, "I always wondered why we had come so far out. I guess Pogue got the first destination from a ship we captured early in the rebellion. I remember it seemed to be a ship like *Ambrose B. Fredrick the Great*, I think. But we also had orders from someone to go out there before Admiral Traynor found out about Pogue's treachery, so maybe someone like Morgain knew about Nighthawk and wanted us out here to catch an heir. And she apparently knew about Alpine, too."

Gail appeared stricken at the mention of the other stealth ship. "Marcus Jones," she whispered.

Ward's face went pale. "Pemberton Clark. Jones acted as his proctor," he explained to Hugh and Maeve. "A good friend of ours. The best imperial candidate, Clarence Martinez, went out first, following the standard path within the empire. He disappeared and I wondered why he didn't succeed. He seemed to me to be almost perfect. Clark appeared also to be really good. He went out about six months after Martinez. What you have explained tells me why he failed; he never got a chance. His proctor could only give the first leg until they completed it, so Pogue, or someone else, must have learned that Nighthawk was the first stop." Glancing at Maeve again, he stated flatly, "My guess is that Pogue didn't blow up the next ship, the first one he ran across in Nighthawk. They probably self-destructed to keep Pogue from getting the next leg from them. They must have somehow completed Nighthawk and were on the way out. The others Pogue captured didn't tell him anything, so they must have been on the way in. That might be why he could never go any farther."

He shook his head, before continuing, "There has always been a standard trail for the test that we used within the empire, in a much more controlled environment, perhaps even too easy. But with rebels all over, it is not available at this time. The alternate test outside the empire has been protected by memory blocks. Those dissolved completely after we left Nighthawk. Jeremy Dansforth, Charles Roland's proctor, took that path initially. At the time of the Qabal, he and many others attempted the alternate path: Nighthawk, Alpine, Deveroe, Pi Nu. Just like the standard path, each stop had a purpose, each subjected the heir to stress in very specific ways. The alternate route is not perfect but, now that we know rebels have found out about the first two stops, we can pretty much figure that all four are compromised, which is too much of a risk."

Ward thought for a moment. "Since the regular alternate route is no longer available, we'll never know how either of you would have done against the classic standards or the alternate route, but that might be for the best. Apparently, Dansforth and other proctors came to the same conclusion during the Qabal incursion. Charles Roland, as well as others, tried another way, the emergency route, which in some ways is the most dangerous path. When it became apparent rogue fleet units were interfering with even the alternate route, it lifted my last memory block. That means that, regardless of whether the emergency route might have been the best path to try you both on, there is no longer a choice. We have to go this way."

Tapping his fingers, he stared off into the distance. Sighing, he turned to Gail. "Do you have charts for Rhine River Cruises in your data banks?"

Gail's eyebrows both went up. "You're serious? You want to take a romantic cruise in the middle of this? And just why would I have something like that in the data banks?"

"You know very well why; your memory blocks have been removed as well. We can talk about romantic cruises later . . . if we survive. Right now, we need to know how to follow the emergency route. You'll have to access the charts with the special code, Emperor Constantine three seven two. If you make a mistake, the ship auto-destructs, so please put the code in carefully."

Gail gave him a half smile. "I know and I'll try to be careful." Pulling out her remote, she punched in the ID and password. A single name came up. *Lorelei.* Charts followed.

As the data downloaded, Ward just shook his head. "Things keep getting better and better. Okay, Captain. We need to cover our back trail a little better than we have. There is an itch between my shoulder blades I only get when I'm being scouted. I feel like someone, someone very clever, is tracking us. They could be using our preon drive trail. How do we lose them?"

"Black hole?" offered Maeve with a slight shudder. "I just remembered something else my dad said about the Gift and the Trace. He made it kind of a rhyme that made no sense at the time. It said something about, if you have the Gift and someone is on your trace, a black hole to hide is a lovely place, or something like that. Does that help?"

Gail gave her a sour smile. "It might, although I don't think anyone can find me when I want to hide with *Ambrose B.* I'll accept the *outside* possibility that it could happen, but a black hole's not a bad idea. One could hide a preon drive trail and, if Robert's little poem tells the whole story, archeon signals, too, if we got close enough. Either way, if we are being followed, we should be able to shake whoever it is."

"How close do we have to get to a black hole?" asked Ward.

With a shrug, Gail offered as a guess, "Just off the event horizon close."

Ward looked thoughtful. "Is there one on the way to Deveroe?" he asked her.

Gail nodded, without enthusiasm. "You really want to try this? Black holes can be very nasty." She examined the charts.

"There are three, and all are marked as major navigation hazards. We need to approach from the direction of spin, gun it, and hope we bounce off. It will take time to set up the approaches correctly."

"Let's get going," Hugh said, as he stood. "The sooner we get there, the quicker we're rid of our snoop. If they lose us at the black holes, they might just assume we are on our way to Deveroe and sneak ahead to try and ambush us. Let's do it."

As THEY LEFT, IT HIT Hugh, he hadn't thanked the Marines and Amazons for risking their lives out there tonight. Or Maeve for that matter.

"Top, I haven't told our people how much I appreciate the sacrifices they made today. Should we get them together or just call them on their coms?"

Ward looked at him deeply. "Good point. How would you take it if you were called in for a formal assembly to be appreciated or just a call?"

Hugh knew that the military loved ceremony, but somehow it didn't feel right. Ceremonies recognized, in front of an audience, outstanding individual or unit achievement with awards. He had neither an award to truly reflect the gratitude he felt nor an audience for the presentation. More, a ceremony felt somehow too impersonal.

Almost without thinking, he had taken the com off his belt as he thumbed the setting that called every com. "This is Hugh. If I could thank you individually for your heroism and sacrifice tonight, I would. Unfortunately, if I went down the list of your personal actions, we'd be here a long time, and I'm much too tired for that and I'm sure you are, too. However, without your efforts there would be many more dead back there, not to mention people hungry and without hope. You made a difference and should be proud of that. I want to make a special mention of the bravery and coolness of Ensign uch Robert in responding to an especially serious and unexpected threat. Personally removing a danger to those we left behind while protecting her teammates should not go unrecognized. Well done, Ensign. All of this means that the people of Alpine now have a chance because of you. Cascade, out."

Ward nodded, seemingly thoughtful. "Good job."

It surprised Hugh a little that Ward had just given him an atta boy. Was Ward getting soft in his old age? Something else to think about later. He wished he could have said more or expressed his feelings better, but his brain just wouldn't work any longer. At that moment he caught a reflection of Maeve's feelings, her pride and gratitude for what he had just said, plus a tinge of sadness he couldn't understand. Also something for later.

With that final responsibility of command completed, he had nothing more on his plate that he could do anything about at the moment. Exhaustion hit him as he headed for his cabin. The test and the competition with Maeve would have to wait for tomorrow.

www.ingramcontent.com/pod-product-compliance
Lightning Source LLC
Chambersburg PA
CBHW020637020726
47494CB00001B/230